STUMBLESTONE

CLIO GRAY

For my niece, Dr Olivia
Norfolk, who may not live long
enough to see the publication
of this book nor her own.
If in doubt read hers, not mine.

Praise for the author

Also by the author

1

The Border of Albania and Montenegro, Spring 1839

Down the wide street the company came, newly whitewashed walls a grimy pink from the ox-blood used to fix the paint. They passed between the fig trees growing on either side of the promenade, gnarled roots coiled about their bases like thick brown snakes, palmate leaves covered with fine red dust blown in from the south. A quiet buzzing of fig wasps crawling through tiny holes at each fruit's end to reach the recumbent flowers within, lines of ants running up and down garnering the sugary juice exuded from those tiny doors.

A peaceful scene, it might have seemed, unless you'd gone inside the cottages, found each one emptied of its inhabitants, signs of hurried departure that might have troubled you: saucepans of soup sitting untouched on home-hewn tables, slices of dark bread hardening in the noonday sun, cauldrons hissing and spitting as the last of the water inside them evaporates on feeble fires left to die.

Just gone twelve, according to the sundial you would have seen if you'd progressed further through the village, reached the patch of grass that once passed for a drying green, a sundial etched with Persian markings signalling the hours and minutes of the day.

You might have wondered how such an oddity had ended up in a backwater like this, a village on the edge of nowhere, tipping from the mountains into the sea somewhere between Albania and Montenegro; a village that had no name as far as any cartographer knew; a village that began and ended with its one wide street, and the green with the singular sundial at its centre.

You might have wondered about its history, only by the time you'd got to the green you'd have been so appalled by what you saw all thoughts of history and sundials would have gone out of your head, for you'd have seen the entire occupancy of the village scrummaged up as one—a heap of bodies piled ready for the burning; each one dispatched by a bullet to head or heart, or hacked by dagger and billhook. All thirty-seven of them, presumably all harvesters of figs or the fish they pulled from the waters of the sea lapping a few hundred yards away on the westerly side of the street. And only one of them alive.

The thirty-eighth.

A child of maybe five or six, who was crawling her way unseen out of the heap of her dead relatives.

'What the hell happened here?' Heraldo Pfiffmakler asked of no one, the entire clan coming to a halt beside him. Their garish clothes seeming completely out of place; the sugared violet-scented almonds they'd stuffed their pockets with, ready to throw out to smile-beaming children, remaining where they were. No amount of scent, violet or otherwise, able to stop the Pfiffmaklers gagging as the sea breeze brought the smell of blood wafting over them. Their approach sending up drifts of flies from the haphazard pile of bodies, buzzing briefly at the interruption before settling back to their feast, laying eggs by the hundreds of thousands, corpses soon to be rippling with their progeny.

Heraldo put his hand up to cover his nose then let it drop, the hairs on the back of his neck going up as he detected movement; a tale coming to the fore of revenants roaming the dark forests reeling up the mountains in this remote place. Tales his mother and father were so adept at concocting wherever they went, using details of the geography and topography surrounding them to spectacular and spine-chilling effect.

'Oh Lord,' he whispered, lunging forward, away from his extended family who remained still and standing as if grown from the soil like the fig trees back in the street. 'I think there's someone alive!'

Taking quick febrile steps about the horrid pile, unable to allow himself any nearer until he got to the other side where the girl was burrowing, clawing, her way out. Heraldo appalled at the blank whiteness of her face as it appeared, looking like a piece of vellum scrubbed clean, waiting for a life, a history, to be inscribed upon it. Her body spasming and then stilling as his shadow fell upon her, waiting for the end.

'It's all right, little one,' Heraldo encouraged, moving his body, shifting away its shadow, letting the sun fall upon the girl's face in the hope that she would see him for what he was—a travelling showman, come here to entertain, enliven this community with carnival songs, plays and puppetry.

Although plainly that time had come and gone.

'That's it,' he coaxed, the girl twitching but not moving until Heraldo's cousin Ludmilla materialised by his side.

'Let me,' she intervened, orange skirts so bright they might have melted snow.

'Come on, my love,' speaking with a gentleness Heraldo had only heard when Ludmilla cooed to infants in their basinets. Ludmilla moving closer to the carnage than he would have dared, taking hold of the young girl's bloodied, broken-nailed hands. Gently pulling her free.

Maybe you'd have done other than the Pfiffmaklers did, which was to go through the deserted village, tying anything of value to their already full carts, cosseting the single survivor. Wrapping the girl in shawls and blankets to stave the shivering she seemed unable to stop. The girl mute all this while, and no one seeing fit to interrogate her.

Maybe you'd have had *sang froid* enough to rootle through the charnel heap, dismantle it limb by limb, body by body, in hope of finding someone else alive or something of value you could later have pawned. Or maybe you'd have hightailed it out of the village to the nearest centre of authority and reported what you'd seen, handed the mute girl over to some uncertain future.

But that was not the Pfiffmakler way.

They'd been tinkers and entertainers for generations, always at the edges of society, always on the move. The girl adopted into their ranks without need for debate or discussion. Just another straggler with nowhere else to go who needed help and found it freely given, by most at least.

2

History Repeats Itself, as it Always Does

Croatia, Serbia, Albania.

A strange part of the world.

Complicated, harsh, and unforgiving.

Ancient countries coexisting side by side, constantly arguing about independence, self-determination, nationalism, religion, and the lines that need to be drawn between them all.

The massacre in the fig tree village merely the latest in a series of too many to count.

Another occurring not so far away, twenty-odd years previously.

Villagers set upon by others not their own. Pitched battles. Women and children sent running for the hills, scraggling together a few scabby goats and lame-legged sheep as they went. Women and children driven further up and away from easy pasture and escape.

Black mountains, dank caves, cold snow and ice.

Everyone getting skinnier, colder, icier.

Goats and sheep eaten and gone.

Everyone listless from lack of food, but no let up from their enemy who would not desist until the last of that unlucky village was destroyed. Not a hard task for men on the move against the stragglers who'd been fighting for their survival in those cold black hills.

Women of little use without their men or their men's weapons to protect them, of which there were none.

Women ravaged and dispatched.

Children dispersed, left to fend for themselves. A small mercy allowed by someone in command too squeamish to give the order to finish them off.

No fire by then.

No tinder, no flint, no fuel.

Nothing but cold frozen flesh, hacked and stored, that took all your strength to chew so you could swallow it; water gleaned by holding snow in your mouth until it melted enough to slip down your throat, mouth so cold the process sometimes took half an hour by which time your teeth were screaming, your gums retracting, your tongue unable to utter a single word. At which point you might take the option, as one brother instructed the other to do, to take up the snow you'd just peed on because, by Christ, at least it held a remembrance of warmth, a small tang of salt you'd forgotten you'd missed so much.

Stools squeezed out like cold hard stones.

No mother, no father, no guiding hand.

No tales, no bedtime stories.

No bedtime, no bed.

Nothing and no one at the end of that last long month in the mountains, excepting the two young boys who survived the snow until early spring when they managed to claw their way down the mountain chewing at the grass, the celandines, the unexpected primroses, as they descended beyond the snowline, desperate for anything green.

Teeth loose in their gums.

Souls far looser than their teeth.

And who could blame them for that?

Not the itinerant pedlar who'd stumbled over them as they'd crawled their way off their mountain. A man who'd picked them up, taken them in, much as the Pfiffmaklers had adopted their own survivor. Neither pedlar nor Pfiffmaklers having any notion their paths would one day cross because of their shared circumstance.

Only one man knowing it would be so, and with absolute certainty, because he had made it his mission to engineer it. A man who knew the verses of the Psalms, that *he who avenges blood is mindful of those who are lost, and does not forget the cries of the afflicted*. A man well aware that his tribe, his family, had been so afflicted there was barely a button, a boot, a sliver of flesh of any of them left. Generations of stories lost, names that would never be spoken of again except by him, who had started on his road to vengeance the exact same day he'd come down off the mountain, and would never stop until he reached its end.

3

Keys and Locks

The Pfiffmaklers were in dissent about what to do with the girl. She'd not spoken a word since they'd fetched her up, had not offered up her name, had said nothing at all. They assumed her to be Albanian from where they'd found her, and because of this a vague plan had been put forward. The second half of the Pfiffmakler clan, the Cordellinas, had some familiarity with the Albanian enclaves long settled in their part of Italy. Peppe and Rosa scouring their memories for any words of that language they might have tumbled over in their youth. Came up empty. The decision made to take the *Kunterbunt Trudelndschau*—the Higgledy Piggledy Travelling Show, which was their professional banner—over the Adriatic and into Italy to Cordellina strongholds. The initial idea for this course of action coming from Rosa, who'd been hankering for a visit to her homeland for years, her husband Wenzel swift to back her plea for there was nothing he wouldn't do for Rosa. Several times over the past few years she'd expressed that longing, indeed had mentioned it several weeks before.

Such a long time since we've been there, she'd said, *such a long time since I've seen my parents. I wonder if they've forgiven me and Peppe for leaving. I wonder if they're even still alive.*

Quite why she'd voiced that yearning there and then he didn't know, yet the yearning in those words he could not deny. Wenzel reddening beneath his beard, for it was unforgiveable she should have to wonder such things. Folding Rosa and her brother into the Pfiffmaklers was one thing, denying them a return to their past quite another. The Pfiffmaklers had their circuits, their routes and routines, and Old Grandmother at the helm refusing to divert from them. No one complaining about it until now. Not that Rosa had complained, merely that since she'd thought of the possibility of return to Italy she'd thought about it more and more, as had Wenzel. And when Hulde—as they'd chosen to call the foundling—had landed in their laps it seemed the perfect course of action. Heaven sent. The Pfiffmakler children quick to back the notion when Wenzel first brought it up.

New places we've never seen! New family we've never met!

Old Grandma not so easy to turn, arguing they should dump the girl first chance they got. Out-argued by Wenzel, who'd the backing of most of the family.

Quick thing, when we get there, Wenzel had said, *to give Hulde the choice of returning to her own people or staying with us.*

Ludmilla hoping for the latter although there were rumblings in the ranks, mostly from her sister Longhella who despised Hulde, hating how much time Ludmilla spent with her. Longhella and Ludmilla a couple of years apart, yet frequently mistaken for twins. Looking alike, dressing alike, doing their hair the same way, performing their turns in perfect unison, until it felt to Longhella like it was actually so. Ludmilla splitting a part of herself off to devote to the girl a betrayal cutting Longhella to the marrow.

'I don't see why she doesn't at least try to speak,' being Longhella's frequent grumble. 'And she could show some gratitude for being rescued. What does she do to help around the camp? Not a damn thing is what.'

'Oh leave her be,' her cousin Jericho more forgiving. 'Can't be easy, seeing what she's seen.'

'We don't know what she's seen,' his brother Lupercal pointed out, coming to Longhella's defence; in awe of her, admiring her long neck and the hair that hung down to her waist and shone like the sun on the sea when she brushed it free from plait and braid.

'Exactly!' exclaimed Longhella, gracing Lupercal with a smile revealing pretty, neatly spaced teeth. 'And everyone always say the young bounce back, so why doesn't she?'

Longhella not liking to say Hulde's name out loud in case its iteration implied her acceptance of the girl, which was absolutely not the case. Soonest they got to Italy and shot of her the better. Let everything get back to normal. Ludmilla's simpering around the child, as if she was made of snowflakes that might melt at any moment, really getting on her nerves. Not best pleased when Heraldo finally made some kind of breakthrough with the girl with his stupid little toys after they'd shifted up coast, approaching Zadar. Telling them all with tedious detail how it came about. How he'd been leaning over his makeshift workbench, a few sturdy planks of driftwood propped on several rocks, when the girl had approached. How quick he'd been to avert his eyes for she hated to be looked at straight on.

'Oh please,' Longhella had interrupted. 'As if you know what that little idiot is thinking.'

Heraldo ignoring her and going on. Telling the family how instead he'd fixed his gaze on the thin lines of the off-shore islands, which looked like half-spent pencils laid upon the surface of the sea.

'Oh my, how poetic!' Longhella interrupted again, shut down quickly by her sister.

'Tell us,' Ludmilla encouraged, and Heraldo did.

'Hello Hulde,' he'd said.

The girl immediately turning her head away, crumpling herself up into a small knot. Arms tightly wrapped about her body, legs rucked up beneath her, squatting indecisively on the edge of the dunes. A finicky thing, spooked by every shadow. At ease only when Ludmilla tucked her in at night, and each night taking Ludmilla's hand and kissing it gently before turning away and resting her head, open-eyed, on her pillow for an hour or so before falling into sleep, and all that hour clinging to Ludmilla's hand as Ludmilla recited tales of mountains, sea nymphs, anything that came to mind, anything that ended well and with good fortune. A nightly task Ludmilla had not once reneged on to Heraldo's astonishment, for Ludmilla had never been one to stick at tasks and see them though.

Until they'd found Hulde and carried her away.

'Come to see what I'm up to?' he'd asked, bending his body away from his work so she had full view.

'See this?' he'd gone on, pointing to a small wooden whittle of a sheep mounted on a tiny set of bellows. 'I'm making tinkle-boxes,' he'd explained, 'so every time I do this…' squeezing the small bellows, 'it does this.'

'Baaaa,' went the sheep, as the air moved through the tube Heraldo had fixed to a carefully tuned reed in the toy's throat.

'Baaaa!' he repeated, squeezing the bellows once more, holding the toy out to the girl. Hulde taking it, turning it this way and that before squeezing the bellows for herself.

Baaaa, went the sheep, and *Baaaaa* again a little longer as the girl got the hang of it and squeezed the harder.

'Baa, baa, baa!' Hulde exclaimed, as she figured out how it worked, held the little toy between her fingers. 'Baa, baa, baa!'

Her first words since they'd picked her up a couple of weeks previously, and she met Heraldo's eyes—if only briefly.

'That's right,' Heraldo had encouraged. 'So what do you call it?'

Hulde hesitating, examining the little figure, stroked her finger down its rough-hewn back.

'Dhen,' she said. 'Baa baa Dhen.'

Heraldo sweeping up the box lying by his work bench, tipping out its contents: more tinkle-boxes—cows, cockerels, horses, donkeys, snakes. Animals that made singular and easily manipulated sounds he could fix with his reeds and tubes.

'Mooo…'

He held up the cow and put it down again. Hulde uncurling herself, coming over to the bench and studying the small figurines, taking her time, selecting the one she wanted.

'Yaark!' screeched the cockerel. 'Yaark, yaark, yaark!'

'Chicken,' Heraldo informed.

'Pulë,' Hulde came back at him, enjoying the game. Heraldo storing up the word. The Pfiffmakler's having a fair scroll of language-litter beneath their belts from all their travellings, aided by a well-worn copy of Calepino's enlarged polyglot dictionary of eleven tongues. No Albanian in either, assuming that was Hulde's language given where they'd found her.

'And after the chicken,' he told the rest of the family, 'she went straight for the donkey.'

Hulde squeezing its miniature bellows.

'Braay!'

Sounding as grumpy as the real thing. Hulde actually letting out a small laugh and taking it from him.

'Gomar!' she announced happily, squeezing the toy again and again. 'Gomar Nikolla!'

Putting the toy down and quietly clapping her hands together, pointing to another.

'Gjarpër,' she said. *Sarper* to Heraldo's ears, Heraldo quick to recognise the cognate.

'Serpent,' he interpreted.

'Sssssss,' the tinkle-box agreed.

And then they were really moving, Heraldo shifting on from the tinkle-boxes and pointing to stone, wood, grass, before untying his boots (çizme) and taking his socks (çorape) off his feet (këmbët), heading off for a paddle in the sea (üje.), Hulde following suit, splashing about in the small breakers as if she'd not a care in the world.

'She's still a foreigner to us,' grumbled Old Grandmother Pfiffmakler, stern stiff matriarch of the clan, rankling from the decision to go to Italy which she absolutely didn't want to do. 'Gotta think she's one o' them Islamists,' she pontificated. 'Everyone knows there's hardly a Catholic or Orthodox left in them lands where we found her.'

'Will you never stop that rabid religiosity?' Wenzel chided. 'She's a child. She's hardly going to understand the finer points of theology.'

'But if she is an Islamist,' Longhella quick to form allegiance with her great-grandmother, 'then she should be with her own.'

Support coming from an entirely unexpected quarter.

'Longhella has a point,' Peppe said mildly, 'for if that's the case, the Italian enclaves of Albanians are hardly the place to take her.

The only reason they settled there was so they could carry on their Christian orthodoxy undisturbed.'

'Don't you want to go home?' Rosa asked, disturbed her brother appeared to be taking Grandmother's side. Peppe smiling his skew whiff smile at her.

'Of course I do. I'm just trying to think on the girl. We really don't know anything about her, nor what's best.'

'What's best is that she stays with us.' Ludmilla leaping to Hulde's defence, not willing to let the girl go without a fight.

'Says who? Says you and nobody!' Longhella staring her sister down, Wenzel about to intervene when Old Grandma came in instead, scratching the loose skin beneath her chin.

'Like I said before, we should ditch the girl. This Italy business is a load of crap.'

'You're forgetting,' Rosa put in, though couldn't meet Old Grandma's gaze, 'that we've already agreed to shift our route so we can take…'

Interrupted by Longhella flinging her wooden trencher down by her feet in disgust, eyes bright and angry, sparkling in the light of the fire.

'That's exactly what we've done. We've shifted everything! Great Grandmother so wanted to visit the Black Madonna of Montenegro before she died, and who knows when we'll…'

'That's enough, Longhella.'

Wenzel Pfiffmakler cutting off his niece, voice sharp as flint. Wenzel ordinarily a man as quiet and easygoing as the day was long except when riled or considered his principles under threat, as they were now. He'd promised Rosa they would return to Italy, to her home, and nothing would veer him from that course. Not Longhella, nor his grandmother.

'She's a child,' Wenzel repeated, 'one who's had to crawl herself out of a heap of bodies, for heaven's sake. So Longhella, you will stop your grumblings from here on in, and don't think I've not been hearing them.'

Longhella holding her uncle's stare for a second before dropping her eyes, kicking a petulant foot at her fallen trencher. Seeing it dangerously close to the fire's edge but making no move to retrieve it.

'And Grandmother,' Wenzel went on, 'with the greatest respect, you'll probably outlive the lot of us put together. The Black Madonna can wait. What can't wait is getting Hulde back with her own, whatever persuasion they might be. A child is a child. And while we're on the subject,' he stated, years of rebellion coming to the fore, 'I'd like to propose right now that this shift over to Italy be the start of a new order. That we keep the Kunterbunt exactly as it was before father retired.' Hard stare at his grandmother, who'd been pushing it in another direction ever since, her son Matthys finding fifty-odd years under his mother's thumb quite long enough, thank you very much.

'No more of the religious extremes. We keep our Advent and Easter mummeries,' Wenzel stated, 'but for the rest we are pure entertainment. Starting in Italy. Agreed?'

No argument there, except from Old Grandma who cast her grandson a vicious glare.

'Hear hear!' Peppe the first to second the motion, swiftly followed by Heraldo.

'I've some new thoughts on the Kaspar Larriscarri sections,' Heraldo added, flashing a smile at his great-grandmother who scowled back, put two fingers to her nose and rubbed it vigorously, about to argue, curses rising on her lips. Given no chance to intervene.

'And as for Hulde,' Wenzel stated loudly, 'I really don't care what some of you think of her being amongst our ranks,' sharp glance at Longhella. 'We've come upon her by happenchance, but we've a Christian duty to see her right.'

He looked over at his grandmother, daring her to disagree, but she merely averted her eyes from him and spat into the fire.

'Aye well. Christian duty,' she replied. 'Guess we can't deny her that.'

Scrunching up her nose exactly as Longhella had done, familial traits running deep. Everyone knowing her reign was over, that Wenzel was now head of the clan.

And thank God for it.

'And as I was about to say,' came the soft voice of Rosa, 'yes, we've shifted our route to accommodate Hulde, but it was never our normal way, to go to Montenegro. Instead we've been given the opportunity to head for home. Mine and Peppe's home. The first time we'll have returned since we left. Please don't refuse us that.'

Taking her husband's hand in her own, so proud of him.

Peppe's wife, Yssel, quick to agree.

'And an easy task to resume the other route to Montenegro later in the year,' Yssel enthusiastic, keen to smooth the waters. 'We could take a boat over direct from Abruzzo once we've visited the Cordellinas.'

'We should head there for Christmas,' Heraldo seeing the advantage. 'Bet folk in those parts haven't seen an Advent Play in years.'

''Cos they're all those damned Islamists,' Longhella muttered, 'just like Grandmother said.'

'Obviously not all,' Heraldo corrected, 'for wasn't that why we were heading there in the first place? So Grandmother could visit the shrine of the Black Madonna? Can't all have been converted, else the shrine would no longer exist.'

His logic impeccable, Wenzel casting a proud glance at his eldest son.

'Quite right, lad,' he said. 'So new plan is this. It's early doors far as the year's concerned. We'll take our time getting to Abruzzo. Plenty places we can set up on the way. Then, come late autumn, we take passage over the Adriatic into Montenegro, do our Advent pitches there. Visit the shrine as planned. Everyone agreed?'

All eyes swivelling towards Grandmother Pfiffmakler who'd been unnerved by the sudden unexpected shift in the power balance, which by God did not sit well, but she recognised the deed was done, and that at least Wenzel was giving her the grace to have the last say.

'It's a plan,' she agreed, voice gruff, pitch lowered by a lifetime of smoking bad tobacco about smoky fires, 'and don't sound completely idiotic.'

Later that night, as Hulde was lying open-eyed and Ludmilla was telling her stories, Ludmilla made use of all the words Heraldo had pulled out of her, put them into a context she hoped Hulde could make something of, conjure up her own tales:

There once was a girl called Hulde, who survived a very bad thing. She'd been feeding her chickens and cows, seeing to Mr Gomar Nikolla. She'd taken off her socks and boots and washed her feet in the sea, when up from the water came a great sea serpent roaring like an angry donkey. But Hulde was wise, and plucked up a chicken to feed the serpent and so was saved.

Hulde whispering the words she recognised as Ludmilla paused at each one, carefully referring to the list Heraldo had drafted, and only ten minutes into the telling Hulde closed her eyes.

Gomar Nikolla, Hulde repeated, before heaving a great sigh and turning onto her side, squeezing Ludmilla's hand. Ludmilla sniffing back incipient tears and carrying on her story.

So Gomar Nikolla, she began, for obviously it was an appellation of some meaning, *started off with Hulde the following morning. They went over the grass, and over the stones, heading for the trees that made up the deep dark forest...*

No need to for Ludmilla to go further into forest or tale, Hulde's hand relaxing, releasing her own. Ludmilla nevertheless sitting by

Hulde's side for the allotted hour, replacing the old candle with the new so the girl wouldn't wake into darkness after Ludmilla had departed. Ludmilla rejoining the family gathered around the fire of driftwood and dried seaweed.

A calm night, the sea shooshing quiet and regular over the shingle as if choosing not to disturb them. The islands' outlines smudged by the dusk and the low mist rolling and hanging about them, yet coming no further inland.

Heraldo withdrawing a pan of sizzling sausages from the embers at the fire's edge, another of charcoal-skinned potatoes, as Ludmilla approached.

'How is she?' he asked.

'Remarkably peaceful,' Ludmilla replied, folding her skirts beneath her knees, sitting on what had previously been Heraldo's workbench. 'I don't know how you did it. It's like you've unlocked her.'

Heraldo smiling as he divvied out sausages and potatoes amongst the family.

Would not have smiled so easily had he understood that yes, there was a key, and yes there was a lock, except that both lock and key—meaning Hulde and the Pfiffmaklers—had been carefully selected, placed into motion, cogs whirring. About to open a door entirely of someone else's choosing.

4

How to Listen to a Water Organ

The Pfiffmaklers were under way and on the road, bonfire kicked back into sand and shingle. Longhella's blackened trencher piled on top of their carts with the rest of their gear. Wenzel Pfiffmakler in the lead pulling the heaviest load, Heraldo shouldering the other half of the harness by his side. Threading their way up coast. The straits between mainland and islands resembling polished turquoise, sparkling and smooth, unruffled by wind or wave. Huge Dalmatian pelicans wheeling over the water, bellies pale and bright between dark outstretched wings; broad beaks held effortlessly aloft as they patrolled the space above their breeding grounds in estuary, island and lagoon.

Once at Zadar the Pfiffmaklers wound through its narrow medieval streets and leafy courtyards, Rosa and Peppe taking pleasure in the loud Italian dialects being shouted by the traders gathered in the flagstoned square about the broad tower that had once been St Donat's church, and now was an empty, circular high-ceilinged space into which folk retreated when rain and storm battered down on the stone.

The place a cacophony of karking Venetians. Zadar long a satellite of that city, until *La Serenissima* fell to the Austrians in1787. The native Croats bartering in their own language, others in German, each fully cognisant of their neighbours' tongues but sticking to their own or mixing them up willy nilly so outsiders were completely bewildered, feeling they'd stumbled into an ill-fitting jigsaw of local lingos.

'What a racket!' Heraldo happily observed, heading through the hugger mugger of crowds towards the majority of the town, which was squashed into a small isthmus jutting out into the Adriatic where the harbour lay. And good news when they got to the harbour and learned the patterns of the ships, that they could hole up on one of the islands before boarding the weekly trade ship going over to Ravenna from Zadar, thereby cutting off a huge part of their previously proposed journey into Italy.

'Which one's Ugljan?' Jericho asked, looking towards the islands not far abroad. Wenzel motioning with his thumb the hill-hummocked rise that was their destination, the family convening on the quayside, tired from their long days on the road. The men settling their backs against cart wheels, wafting hats in front of faces. The women gathering their water canisters, ready to refresh them at the *Trg pet bunara*—the five wells providing the town with its water.

'Can you spare me for an hour or so?' Heraldo asked his father, having picked out a single phrase from the many as they passed through the streets, eager to seek out its source. The enthusiasm as bright on his face as the sun was in the sky and not easy to ignore.

Wenzel smiled into his beard. Had never figured out how a boy like Heraldo could be his and Rosa's son, them both being so pedestrian in their outlook, so lacking in basic creativity. Fine when they were sticking to their well-worn scripts and able to add embellishments here and there; Heraldo's imagination fermenting through him like yeast through dough, firing off at every turn.

'Off you go, lad,' Wenzel said. 'We'll rest the family up while I arrange our passage. But not too long, mind. We'll need over before sundown.'

Heraldo tipping his hat in thanks.

'And take Hulde,' Wenzel added, 'considering your recent break-through.'

Heraldo eager to agree, skipping off down the line of their carts and approaching Ludmilla, to whose hand Hulde had been welded during the long walking.

'Want to come with?' he asked Hulde. 'Got something I want to see.'

Hulde looking questioningly at Ludmilla, who cast a quick glance at her mother, Yssel easy in her assent.

'Mind you get back soonest!' Yssel called after the swiftly dis-appearing trio, Heraldo clasping Hulde's other hand and setting off at too fast a pace, Hulde's short legs having to take small running jumps to keep up with him.

Yssel not at all sure what she thought about the girl. Certainly no animosity, as Grandmother Pfiffmakler and Longhella had made so evident, neither was she entirely comfortable with the family's swift adoption of the child. Wenzel's arguments as to what to do with her, where to take her, had been entirely reasonable, and she'd gladly endorsed them, especially once Rosa had had her say, for she held Rosa in the highest regard. Yet a rankling at the back of her mind about what might come of their taking Hulde away from that unnamed village with its twisted fig trees and blood-washed walls. She couldn't specify her trepidation, nor why she felt so uneasy at having Hulde in their midst. A girl who should have died, who maybe had died, if only briefly. Yssel a religious woman, of high emotion, feeling a shadow falling over them, the wheel of the world turning, bringing change. And not just Wenzel taking over the Kunterbunt, which was a blessing as far as she was concerned, but something other, she was sure of it. Something she'd seen back at that village, though couldn't for the life of her put her finger on it.

Something cold this way blows, and bitter bites the wind...

A line from one of their hundreds of street songs coming unbidden to her lips.

Yssel shrugging her shoulders, stiff from the harness. A shiver passing through her as she watched Hulde swinging like a tolling bell between Heraldo and Ludmilla, wondering what that bell might summon.

'It's called a Sea Organ,' Heraldo announced, as he led his charges on.

'Slow down, can't you,' Ludmilla demanded. 'You're dragging Hulde off her feet.'

Heraldo checking his pace, winking at Hulde who looked not a jot concerned. Her face flushed and eager, her small hand hot in Heraldo's own. He gave it a small squeeze.

'Sorry, ladies. Just real keen to see exactly what it is.'

And not disappointed.

After a few tangled questions he ascertained where the Sea Organ was, the three emerging onto a palm-lined boulevard merging into a hugely broad stone staircase descending right down into the sea.

'It's just a load of steps,' Ludmilla complained, wiping her free hand across her forehead. 'Can't see why—'

'Sssh!' Heraldo cut her off. 'Can't you hear that?'

He cocked his head. Ludmilla mighty amused when Hulde did the exact same, her eyes fixed on Heraldo's face.

'It's like,' Heraldo began, 'I don't exactly know what it's like.'

He went down a step and parked himself on it, Hulde an echo by his side. Hulde releasing Ludmilla's hand, leaving her behind. Ludmilla creasing her brows, tipping her head forward, eager to latch onto whatever it was the two of them found so fascinating.

'It's like the sea, and not the sea,' Heraldo whispered. 'It's like the sea is singing.'

He lifted his head and, as he did so, Hulde laid her own against his shoulder. The two sitting in such harmonious unison that Ludmilla, bereft, put a hand to her throat hating to see it, hating to be so excluded. She took a step towards them, squatted down at their backs, tilted her head as they had done. And then she heard it too: a soft, musical reedy sound seemingly rising from the steps themselves, arhythmical and yet mesmerising and unceasing.

'Hear it best when water's a bit choppy.'

A shadow falling over Ludmilla, Ludmilla quick to her feet, spinning herself around to face the interloper, hand at her girdle, fingers resting on the hilt of her knife. The female members of the Kunterbunt never slow when it came to matters of personal defence, a habit, Ludmilla reminded herself, she'd need to teach Hulde, if Hulde chose to remain with them.

'Hold up, young lady!' the interloper quick to ameliorate the evident agitation on Ludmilla's face. 'Was just going explain the workings to you. How they got the pipes fixed in beneath the steps…'

Heraldo on his feet, Hulde coming with him.

'There's niches in them?' Heraldo asked in the German spoken by his interlocutor. 'So what's the set up? My name's Heraldo Pfiffmakler, by the way. Very eager to make your acquaintance.'

He held out his hand to the newcomer, Ludmilla relaxing. Ludmilla once more taking hold of Hulde as the girl came up the steps. Ludmilla feeling secure as she grasped the girl's hand. Ludmilla suddenly wondering who was getting the most out of this relationship, her or Hulde.

'The Pfiffmaklers, is it. Well, kind of thought it might be,' casting a quick admiring glance at Ludmilla. 'Don't get many folk looking like a walking sunset around these parts.' He gave them a short crooked bow. 'Mighty proud to make your acquaintance,' he went on. 'Saw you all a few years back over in Klagenfurt when you had that tiger whatnot on a cart. Still laugh about that every now and then.'

Chuckling lightly as if to prove the point.

'Ah,' Heraldo nodded. 'Tipu's Tiger. Did go down rather well.'

Not the real thing, a copy made by Heraldo after seeing the life-sized original. The English Redcoat solider lying beneath the mauling tiger, representative of the Sultan Tipu's army's fight against the English during the Mysorean wars. An automata created by the Sultan himself, a crude organ hidden inside the body of the tiger so when the crank-handle turned the soldier screamed and the tiger growled. Or rather wheezed, in Heraldo's version, but had always amused. Pity it had gone down the side of a cliff one day when Lupercal and Jericho had been too busy admiring an eagle soaring over the Alps to pay the cart much mind.

'Thinking your steps here might function somewhat similarly,' Heraldo busily trying to work the puzzle out. 'Like a huge Aeolian harp, using water instead of air?'

The man didn't know what an Aeolian harp was, but that wasn't going to stop him. He'd been often abroad on the boulevard these past few weeks to explain to people how the Sea Organ worked, earn himself the odd coin here and there for his services.

'Kind of,' he said. 'Load of upright pipes set below the stones. Waves pushes air up through the pipes and reed valves, and out comes the noise of them through the holes. Not many people realise it.'

'It's pretty much what I do,' Heraldo admitted, smiling broadly, for he never tired of fixing up old instruments and finding out how they worked. 'And you, sir. Who are you who remembers us so fondly?'

Sounding like the showman he was.

'Aha,' said the man, clearing his throat, preparing to make his pitch, fortuitous indeed that he'd been walking along the boulevard when he'd seen the bright flash of Ludmilla's skirts and those long, luscious braids of hair swinging down her back. Knowing precisely where and when he'd seen them before, not to mention he'd been told to be on the look-out for them.

'My name is Andreas Zilboorg,' he enlightened them. 'Purveyor of All Things Echinos and Hedgehoggery. Igel, Iritch, Arichi, to give it several of its many names.'

Heraldo lifted his eyebrows.

'That's not something you hear every day,' he exclaimed.

'I'd be very glad to tell you all about my trade,' Andreas Zilboorg replied. 'But how about you introduce me to the rest of the family? Can't tell you what an honour it would be.'

Ludmilla restive. The Sea Organ one thing, the extended conversation between Heraldo and this Andreas Zilboorg tedious, and she didn't like the man. Had been on the carnival circuit her whole life, could spot a charlatan and a cheat at twenty paces, and Andreas Zilboorg was one of them top to bottom.

'It's about time we got back,' she put in. 'You know we've to be over to the island before nightfall.'

'To the island, is it?' the charlatan flashed her a smile filled with bad teeth and worse breath. 'Well there's a coincidence and a half! I'm heading there myself.'

Flinging an arm about Heraldo's shoulders, steering him back along the boulevard towards the harbour. Leaving Ludmilla and Hulde to trail along behind.

'I don't trust him,' Ludmilla whispered to Hulde. 'What do you think?'

As if the girl could understand.

'Iritch,' Hulde whispered back, repeating the Albanian word *Iriq* she'd picked out of Andreas's talking.

'Iritch indeed,' Ludmilla retorted, twitching up her orange skirts which blazed as the sun began to sink and then, without warning, the wind picked up and a thundercloud swept over them from west to east; no lightning apparent, only the low rumbling coming from its depths and the sudden torrential downpour released that had them soaked in a moment, the sky darkening from afternoon to vespertine in a second. Hulde squatting to the pavement, pushing her head between Ludmilla's sodden skirts, frantically trying to pull their folds over head and body.

'Jor, jor, jor!' Hulde's muffled voice was terrified, Ludmilla aghast.

'Heraldo!' she yelled, but the smacking down of the heavy-bellied rain onto the boulevard, the bouncing of it—going up four inches and then back again—and the rumbling of the thunder drowning out her call. Heraldo and Zilboorg merely quickening their pace, hands upon their caps to keep them in place as they ducked themselves down and began to run, the water splashing up about their feet. Ludmilla having no choice but to crouch down next to Hulde and hold the girl to her, pull her in. The rain tremendous, far louder than the Sea Organ had been. Ludmilla suddenly hoiked up by her elbow, the rain so constant down her face she'd no idea who was assailing her.

'This way!' she was commanded, and this way she went, lifting Hulde in her arms. The two of them hauled beneath a paltry tent keeping out of the worst of the rain. Another growl of thunder as the storm passed directly overhead, the rolling drumbeat of it so loud it seemed to shake the poles keeping up the canvas. Hulde holding her hands over her ears and moaning again and again: *jor, jor jor!*

Ludmilla blinking the rain from her eyes, wrapping her arms about the girl as she rocked back on her heels, removed one hand briefly to push away the tendrils of hair that had turned into rats' tails and whipped across her face. The storm abating quickly. The sounds of thunder moving on down the side of the Adriatic. Ludmilla seeing flashes from the thundercloud striking into the sea as the rain turned into hailstones and hit the water. All calming where she was, taking the time to see who had pulled them from the boulevard into his tent. A man, mid to late twenties, a ginger-haired poltroon who might have wandered in from one of the Kunterbunt's set pieces. Ludmilla proved correct when she read the sign-board leaning against the cart over which the canvas had been erected: *The Balatronic Ballet, a Marvel of Buffoonery and Japes.*

So, one of ours, she was thinking, about to speak when she heard an ominous creaking from one of the tent poles and looked up to see the swollen belly of canvas sagging right above her head where a great pool of rain had gathered and was about to collapse the lot.

'Oh no you don't!' exclaimed the man, leaping with easy grace from one foot to the other as he grasped the left hand pole and then the right, whipped them from their grounding plates so the canvas stretched down, released a great whoosh of water gushing into the street and away. For the few moments it took to dissipate they might have been crouched behind a waterfall, an illusion swiftly dispensed as the man deftly dismantled the rest of his tent, lining the poles up together, quickly rolling the canvas around them like a body in a rug.

'Looks like you've done that before,' Ludmilla commented, admiring the efficiency with which the task had been completed, lifting her head to the newly revealed sky that was as calm and oblivious as if the storm had never been.

'Don't suppose you're no stranger to it either,' the man replied mildly, catching Ludmilla off guard as he stowed his collapsed booth onto his cart. A few pitters of rain still falling in air clean and fresh, a warm scent coming up from the grass on which Ludmilla and Hulde were crouching.

'I don't know what you mean,' Ludmilla answered, perplexed. The man shrugging his shoulders, carrying on with his packing.

'No mystery there,' he answered easily. 'You're one of the Kunterbunt lot. But I'm guessing not that little sprite you've got bundled there on your knees.'

Ludmilla hugging Hulde closer to her breast. The girl had stilled, yet was shivering within the bounds of Ludmilla's arms.

'Who are you who knows so much about what absolutely isn't your business?'

Ludmilla wanting to sound sharp and bold, wanting to stand up and face this stranger, get her and Hulde away, but Hulde was still a shaking bundle of worry in her arms, unwilling to uncurl back into the world. And the girl was heavy. Ludmilla's calves beginning to cramp, so when the man held out a hand to her she took it, levered herself up on the strength of it, too slow to react when the man plucked up a blanket from his cart and placed it about Hulde's shoulders, rubbing at her gently.

'Gotta guess you picked her up in one of the border countries,' he said. 'We heard you was headed that way. Wanted to hook up, but no one was keen to get that far in, not with what's been going on down there.'

He twitched his lips, ran a hand through his sodden hair so it stood up in spikes.

Like a hedgehog, Ludmilla thought. Made the leap that this man was somehow connected to Andreas Zilboorg, one of the wandering fair acts who joined up every now and then with a well-established crew, eager to take advantage of all the town permits they'd garnered over the years. The Pfiffmaklers around a lot longer than most.

'So what's this Balatronic Ballet you're a part of?' Ludmilla asked, hoping to gain advantage, getting none. The man standing uncomfortably close, putting out a hand and brushing his fingers down Hulde's tear-stained cheek.

'So what have you seen, little one?' he asked, ignoring Ludmilla's question. 'And what is it so frightens you about the thunder?'

Ludmilla pushing his hand away.

'That's enough! Don't you go near her!'

The man holding up his hands in appeasement, shaking his handsome head. And it was handsome, Ludmilla blushing to realise she thought it so at such a time.

'Heard bad things happen there is all,' he replied, backing off.

'What do you mean?' Ludmilla persisted, looking up at him.

'*Jor*,' he said shortly. 'Albanian for *no*. Not that I'm well acquainted with the language, but you can't stop here for more than a couple of weeks without picking up the odd word or two.'

'But you know some of it?' Ludmilla leaning forward, despite her misgivings. Hulde unfolding herself, looking up at the stranger.

'Jor,' she whispered. 'Ju lutem nuk. No perseri.'

The poltroon hesitating, Ludmilla pushing.

'You understood that,' she stated. 'What did she say?'

Given an answer of sorts.

'*No perseri*. Not again,' the man explained. 'Think that's what she meant.'

Stopping himself from saying more. Already caught in a trap he'd no liking for. No great linguist, this man, but no great linguist needed to guess what the girl was saying, not when he'd an idea of what had happened to her.

Ludmilla's heart contracting like a purse-string tied and tightened, looking down at Hulde.

'*No perseri*,' Ludmilla reassured. 'Not while you're with us.'

Hugging Hulde to her, unaware of the stare Hulde gave over Ludmilla's shoulder towards the ginger-haired man.

'*No perseri*,' he was mouthing, though no sound came out, tapping a finger lightly against his lips. Hulde dropping her head back to Ludmilla's shoulder and closing her eyes.

5

Chess Games and Moral Quandaries

'Where's your cousin?' Wenzel demanded of Heraldo as his son approached, the Pfiffmaklers huddled beneath several lengths of waxed canvas hastily held above their heads as the storm swept in and overtook them. Heraldo laughing as he ran along the boulevard, Andreas Zilboorg desperately trying to keep up. Heraldo exhilarated by the thunder, the tremendous downpouring of rain, the sounds it made as it hit barrels, roofs, pavements. Heraldo amused by the gulls waddling dispiritedly along the edges of flagstones, beaks dripping, water sleeking off backs and wings.

Of Ludmilla and Hulde he'd given not a thought.

'Not far behind,' he stated, throwing an exuberant hand back along the way. 'Probably took shelter with one of the stall holders set up there.'

Heraldo taking off his cap as he nudged in beside his father, shrugging his shoulders like a duck that has just surfaced from the sea. Andreas panting as he made a move to join them.

'Come in, come in!' Heraldo beckoned eagerly. 'This here's Andreas Zilboorg,' he began his introductions, 'purveyor of all things hedgehoggery. And this is my father, leader of the Pfiffmakler clan.'

Wenzel angry at his son for abandoning Ludmilla and Hulde because of a little rain, but couldn't help smiling between his wilted moustaches at the nomenclature.

Leader of the Pfiffmakler clan.

A good ring to that.

The rain ceasing as the heavy-bellied clouds swept on down the coast, the sky a sudden bright blue above them as they removed the canvas from over their heads.

'Aye, well,' Wenzel subsided. 'Suppose they'll come to no harm and get here soonest. But it'll need to be soonest, mind, 'cos last boat's going over to the island in…' he flicked out his watch from his pocket, a rather grand affair Wenzel was proud of. 'Forty minutes,' he concluded, never mind that mariners as a rule were rarely shackled by pocket watches. Told six o'clock, and about time they started hauling their gear, casting a quick anxious eye down the boulevard. Heraldo catching the movement.

'I'll go fetch them,' he volunteered. 'Honestly, they were only yards behind.'

Wenzel acceding.

'Get you gone,' he told Heraldo, 'and make sure you're back…'

'I know, I know!' Heraldo wasn't daunted. 'Inside forty minutes. Back in a trice, family reunited.'

Family, Wenzel thought. And yes, he supposed Hulde was family, for the next few weeks at least. Turning his attention to the stranger Heraldo had brought with him.

'Andreas Zilboorg,' Andreas introduced himself again. 'Purveyor of all things...'

'Hedgehoggery,' Wenzel finished for him. 'I've not forgotten.'

Looking at the man with undisguised annoyance. Heraldo already away and no explanation why he'd brought this man to their doors, although Wenzel could guess. Andreas Zilboorg not the first person who'd tried to attach themselves to the Kunterbunt over the years, and no harm in that. The more turns they had with them the more money they were likely to make. But a purveyor of all things hedgehoggery? Unusual even to Wenzel, who'd seen his fair share.

'Precisely,' Andreas Zilboorg went on for him. 'Purveyor of All Things Echinos, Igel, Iritch, Arichi, to give it several of its many names,' Andreas repeating his well-worn script.

Wenzel shaking his head.

'I don't really care who you are or what you're a purveyor of,' Wenzel countered. 'All I know is that if we don't get our goods and gear over to the island on the last boat then we'll be stuck here for the night and...'

'Ah, but, and,' Andreas Zilboorg interrupted smoothly. 'I might be of some help there. I know the ferrymen well. Been about ships since I was a youngster so knows how to get in with them. And we've been rather in a hiatus since we got here, so first place I went. You know how it goes. Get to know the locals, get to know the ways out.'

Wenzel chewed his moustaches, looking properly at Andreas Zilboorg, seeing precisely the type of man he didn't want associated with the Kunterbunt: undoubtedly a slippery character, a dog who'd slip his collar for the smallest bone, to use one of Grandma's phrases. Then again, his previous enquiries about getting passage out to the islands had been met with less enthusiasm than he'd have liked.

'You can buy your passage,' the Italian *barcaiolo* had told him, 'but you've to wait your turn. It's been fierce full this week, what with all that's going on in Ravenna. You've a load of carts and I can't be certain of their weight. Gotta give the locals passage first, then I'll load your lot if I think us's room and space enough.'

So if this Andreas Zilboorg could help, that was fine by him.

Certainly they could wait until the morning, but Wenzel's thinking was to get over to the island. Settle for a few nights, wow the inhabitants the following days with a show or two, get the Kunterbunt enough money to see them safely over to Italy on the weekly trade ship to Ravenna. Hulde at the centre of his thoughts, to get her to her people quick as possible. Not immune to the fact that Hulde was the primary reason he'd been made king of the Pfiffmaklers, and to let her down, to abnegate his first promise as leader, could crack that authority from stem to stern. So he struck a bargain.

'Very well, Mr Hedgehoggery. You get us on that ferry tonight and you'll get a cut of whatever we earn tomorrow.'

Andreas held up his hands.

'Oh no, sir. I won't take your money. That's not what we want at all!'

Wenzel frowning, thinking of dogs and collars.

'What then?' Wenzel not missing the *we*. Andreas Zilboorg smiling, the stale smell of fish eaten for his dinner wafting over Wenzel.

'Why, I want my boys to see Italy!' Andreas announced. 'Such a grand place, so I've been told, and I gather from your son that's where you're headed.'

'That's correct,' Wenzel said shortly, cursing Heraldo for being so free with his words. Heraldo a blatherer of the first order since he'd been a child, a boy who'd no guile and therefore saw none in others.

'Just want to tag you, seeing as you're so expert,' Andreas flattered. 'Just want to follow in your footsteps, so's we don't go off track.'

'Very well then,' Wenzel nodded, it seeming a good bargain. Andreas away, the faint spraint of rain falling from the apparently cloudless sky making no mark on his already sodden shoulders. Wenzel looking after him, thinking *where's the harm?* They'd done the same a hundred times over with men more slippery than Andreas Zilboorg. So let him have his day, if he could deliver, and then let him have his bone.

'I'm assuming you have a name?' Ludmilla was asking, easing Hulde to her feet. Hulde immediately moving towards an open box of trinkets The Balatronic Ballet presumably sold at their performances, whatever they might be.

'Valter Poppelmann at your service,' came the reply, Valter giving a low bow, the hat grasped by his slim fingers scraping the ground in exaggerated courtesy. Ludmilla shaking her head, smiling all the same.

'You don't have to play the showman with me,' she said, sounding more haughty than she'd intended. 'We're all in the same game.'

Valter carrying on packing his wares, covering all with a waxed canvas exactly as the Pfiffmaklers did. Tying the edges down with ropes so the cart shouldering his livelihood and all he owned resembled a badly wrapped present, if one drably clad.

'Anything I can do to help?' Ludmilla asked, knowing there was not, feeling the urge to offer all the same.

'All done,' Valter said, as expected, 'except for that little box there.'

Nodding towards Hulde, who was hunkered down on her heels putting her fingers through the tiny models in the small box. Lifting one up and examining it before dropping it and selecting another.

'Let me fetch it for you,' Ludmilla said, making a move towards Hulde, until Valter put a hand on her shoulder and held her back. Put his finger to his lips as he'd done before.

'She can keep them. My gift from me to her. Guessing she's not been given much for a while, excepting you.'

Ludmilla about to question this enigmatic statement when Heraldo hove into view.

'There you are!' Heraldo's face shining, clothes steaming in the last of the afternoon sun that had a warmth to it as if denying the storm had ever darkened its doors. 'Father's getting anxious. Ooh,' he said, spying Hulde. 'What've you got there, my young sister?'

Straightaway to Hulde's side, down on his knees beside her as she held up an object from the box.

'Gaztor,' she volunteered, carrying on the game of the tinkle-boxes. Heraldo taking the figurine from her fingers: less than two inches tall, whittled from wood and painted with exquisite precision. Heraldo glancing up at Ludmilla, and from her to the man behind her who was busy checking the knots on the ropes securing his cart.

'Valter Poppelmann,' Ludmilla mouthed the name, Heraldo nodding his understanding.

'A clown, maybe?' Heraldo asked, placing the small figurine on grass so flattened by feet and rain the figurine's squared base had no difficulty staying upright. Dipping his fingers into the box and selecting another, painted a rich red, golden crown upon its head.

'King,' Heraldo prompted, Hulde shifting her attention, studying Heraldo's choice.

'Mbret,' Hulde answered, scrabbling through the heap, picking out another.

'Peshkop,' she announced, Heraldo's turn to do the looking and translating.

'Bishop,' he agreed. Another quick rummage.

'Soldier?' he asked.

'Ushtar,' Hulde appeared in no doubt. Heraldo looking at the box, seeing a small folded board tucked in at the side.

'This some kind of chess game?' he asked.

'We've adapted it,' Valter explained, turning from his cart, standing at Ludmilla's shoulder, red hair darkened by the soon-to-be-setting sun. 'One of our japes,' Valter went on. 'We sells 'em by the dozen after our shows. We adapt all the pieces to fit in with our buffoons. Gives folk something to remember us by.'

Heraldo getting up from his knees, tousling Hulde's wet hair as he went.

'Can we borrow this set?' he asked. 'It's just we don't...'

'It's already hers,' Valter interrupted. 'Just said so to your girl here.'

Ludmilla feeling a drop in temperature, not understanding it, nodding anyway.

'Got a load of 'em already piled and ready to go,' Valter added. 'Don't want to untie everything just to stick one more in.'

Heraldo looked from Valter to Ludmilla. He wasn't too good at reading people, not like Ludmilla was, but saw how stiff Ludmilla was standing, how she'd thrown back her shoulders like she was one of those granite stones you see on top of hills that had been there for centuries and would not be moved.

'That's real good of you,' Heraldo said, smiling briefly, replacing the figurines and lid, tucking the box in against his waist. 'Ready, Hulde?'

He held out his hand, Hulde taking it, although her eyes were fixed on the box as if she feared it was about to be taken from her.

'Well, thank you, Mr Poppelmann,' Ludmilla stook a stride towards Heraldo. 'You did us a real service back then, and I'll not forget it.'

'You'll not forget it?' Heraldo ribbed Ludmilla when they were a few yards away up the boulevard. *'I'll not forget it, Mr Poppelmann,'* Heraldo making a bad imitation of Ludmilla's voice, expecting a sharp jab in his side from Ludmilla's elbow, not that it came. Ludmilla merely marching silently by his side.

'Oh come on!' Heraldo jibed. 'What was all that about?'

Ludmilla twitched her nose in annoyance.

'Just being polite,' she said. 'And he did get us out of the rain after you and your blasted hedgehog man abandoned us.'

'Rain!' Heraldo laughed. 'You were afraid of a little rain! Come on. When have you ever been…'

Stopped by that jab in the side he'd earlier expected.

'It was…' Ludmilla didn't want to say the girl's name out loud in case it stopped what appeared a happy jaunt to Hulde's steps, her jumping up beside Heraldo, touching Valter's box every chance she got.

'It was Hulde,' she murmured to Heraldo. 'She went to bits when the thunder came. And I don't mean a little, I mean a lot.'

'Loads of children are afraid of thunderstorms,' Heraldo argued, wanting to get back to the main subject and how the Poppelmann fellow had looked so at ease and, more disconcertingly, proprietary standing at Ludmilla's shoulder. Ludmilla shook her head.

'It was more than that,' she said. 'I think she was remembering back to her village. Like maybe it reminded her of gunshots. *No, she kept saying, not again.*'

'And how would you know that?' Heraldo accused. 'Your Mr Poppelmann perhaps?'

Ludmilla's face flushed, next words coming out between clenched teeth, low but vicious.

'Think you're the only one can get a word out of her? Because you aren't, my boy. You really aren't. And what use is it to know what rabbit means? Or cow, or snake?'

'I never did a rabbit,' Heraldo retorted, wincing. Hated it when she called him *my boy.* Had done it since they were children, never mind she was barely six months his senior. 'And what happened to my breakthrough, as you called it?'

Ludmilla twitched her lips.

'Let's forget it,' she said, cupping her hand about Heraldo's elbow. 'Just meant this place is as chock full of different tongues as a puddle is with water, and mightn't hurt to ask around.'

Heraldo's good cheer back to the fore. Ludmilla quick to anger, quicker to forgive. A cloud passing over the moon having more malevolence than did she.

'Speaking of puddles,' he said, taking a quick step, jumping into one in their immediate path.

'Hey! Watch it you!' Ludmilla leaving him go, brushing the water droplets from her skirts, about to punch Heraldo hard in the arm when they both stopped short, Hulde letting out a gurgling laugh and jumping in and out of the puddle, splashing them both.

'Eh otchit oo!' she attempted to repeat, kicking the water up and up with her little boots.

'Eh otchit oo too,' Heraldo quick to respond, doing the same, Hulde's boots no match for his, the water catching her head to toe and right in the face.

'Ah ah…' Hulde bending down at the waist and cupping her hands, throwing the contents over Heraldo, Heraldo passing the chess box over to Ludmilla and doing the same so the two were like bairns in a sand pit, except that one of Heraldo's salvos caught a passer-by, and a very well dressed one at that.

'What the hell's bells do you think you're doing?' the man shouted angrily, looking from the pair in the puddle to Ludmilla. 'He some kind of imbecile?'

Ludmilla stifling her laughter.

'Some kind,' she replied, trying to sound stern, 'but not the worst. Never the worst.'

The man harrumphing, leaving them to it, a sermon already forming in his head to rebut the vile calumnies he'd not long read in Rosmini's *Trattato della Conscienza Morale* that had shaken the theological world in Italy to the core, attacking as it did the theory of Probabilism, the system of morals the Roman church held very dear. And here was an example he could use.

'It's perfect!' he whispered to himself, twirling his cane, going on his way, writing his speech in his head as he went: *Probabilism tells us that if the licitness or illicitness of an action is in doubt, then the lawful duty of the believer is to follow the option favouring liberty or forgiveness, even when the opposite seems —prima facie—to have been the more obvious option. Like a child and a man playing in a puddle...*

Oh, so much he could use here! So much to plough into his upcoming arguments in Ravenna where he was due to bolster Liguori's methodology of morals as being the logical way the Church should go. And now Liguori had been sainted they'd surely have to hear out his arguments.

And only two days to go.

Two days to hone his speech, his reasoning and his arguments.

So much resting on it for him and the Redemptorists as a whole.

And a canonised Redemptorist about to be laid to rest as a saint in Ravenna.

It was perfect.

'So I'm an imbecile?' Heraldo laughed, as the game came to an end, the puddle almost emptied, Hulde happy, Hulde tired, Hulde soaked. Heraldo picking her up, her legs wrapping around his waist, her arms about his neck, like dodder about an apple bough. Ludmilla chucking Hulde under her chin, making sure she was comfortable.

'Imbseel,' Hulde sighed, gliding into sleep as serenely as a swan moves over a lake.

'Imbseel indeed,' Ludmilla repeated softly, falling into step beside Heraldo. 'But of the best kind.'

Watching Hulde's head bobbing gently on Heraldo's shoulder as they returned to the quay.

'I didn't mean what I said earlier,' Ludmilla began. 'It was unkind and—'

'It was nothing,' Heraldo interrupted. 'Or rather no. It wasn't nothing. It was right.'

He would have shaken his head, but didn't want to disturb Hulde. Instead he slowly turned to face Ludmilla until he caught her eye.

'I think we've been going at this all wrong. We've been tinkering at the edges. We've been showing her cows and donkeys—no rabbits, mind...'

Ludmilla smiling, ashamed. She and Heraldo always so close, cousins maybe but more like brother and sister, brought up together, playing together. Ludmilla suddenly getting that temperature drop back in Valter's tent between the two of them. Heraldo always so protective of both her and Longhella and how it must have looked: that man Valter at her shoulder, his hand on her shoulder now that she came to think on it.

'Do rabbits make any noise?' she asked.

'Not unless you're wringing their necks,' Heraldo replied jovially.

'What do you mean about us coming at it the wrong way?' Ludmilla queried.

Almost back at the quay, could see the rest of the Pfiffmaklers putting on their harnesses, dragging away their carts, presumably about to board the ferry over to the island.

'I mean we've never actually asked Hulde what happened,' Heraldo said.

Ludmilla nodding agreement, her thoughts exactly.

'But maybe with this,' she shook Valter's box. 'We could try?'

'Draw a diagram of her village in the sand,' Heraldo went on for her, 'put the pieces in place, see what she does with them. Bit of a gamble. Might shut her right down again.'

Ludmilla chewing her lips, wondering if it was worth the risk.

'Let's talk it over with your father before we do anything,' she advised. 'She seems so happy now, so content.'

'It'll still be in her,' Heraldo said. 'You know as well as I that stuff like that doesn't just disappear, and the sooner she gets it out of her the better.'

6

On the Other Side

Andreas Zilboorg had been good as his word, pushing the Pfiffmaklers to the head of the queue waiting to board the single-masted felucca, much to the annoyance of some local island traders who'd been drenched through by the storm and wanted home.

'All in a good cause!' Zilboorg was shouting up and down the straggling line as the Pfiffmaklers were led to the fore and pulled their carts on board. 'For tomorrow they will perform the greatest show you'll ever see!'

Andreas proving a grand gonfalonier in advertising the Pfiffmaklers' wares.

'There'll be puppetry and acrobatics!' he shouted. 'Pyrotechnics, plays and pretty girls dancing! And there'll also be The Balatronic Ballet as you've never seen it before!'

Enough to calm the folk waiting in the queue, who were somewhat enthused. A visit from fairs folk promised to be a grand day out, and Lord knew the islanders could use one. The winter hard, spring late to start, and the markets in Zadar could do without them for a few hours on the morrow.

'Ever heard of these Pfiffmaklers before?' one man asked, puffing at his pipe, pipe tucked under his jacket for the ten minutes the rains had fallen, still burning when the worst had passed.

'Course I have!' his neighbour in the queue remonstrated, a man well known for being a braggart, making a wild deduction from the name. 'They're German, I think, but comes regularly over the border. Heard they're a hoot! And them girls are real pretty, anyone could see that.'

'I couldn't give a shit if they're pretty or not,' grumbled one old timer, who didn't find anything in life pretty any more, just one hard slog of a day following another, nothing to show for it but an aching back and feet being massacred by corns and tangled balls of nerves so he found it hard to stand for more than a few minutes. This queue a torture for him, as most of his life had been.

'But pyrotechnics!' his grandson laughed, and how easy that laugh. Made him want to knock every bone from every joint in his grandson's body.

'It'll be nowt but a damp squib, you'll see,' he grumbled, hating how brimming the lad was with a life not yet done, hating to be confronted by the fact his grandson might have a better, easier life than he'd had himself and how unfair it all was. Prejudice confirmed the moment the lad scampered across the gang plank, the queue abruptly halted, leaving himself behind.

'Full up,' the captain of the felucca announced. 'Gonna take this lot over and then do the unusual and come back for the rest of you, so kick your heels for the meantime.'

And kick his heels that grandfather did, kicked them right into the dust.

'Dunno why you've left us!' he shouted hoarsely. 'We's been over and over on that ferry for years and years and you're putting strangers in front of us?'

So angry he could've swallowed his hat, if it hadn't blown away in the storm. Another infelicity to grumble about, especially when he saw his grandson holding up his own cap in victory.

'Whole world's gone to hell,' the old timer muttered as he sat himself down on the wet quay, getting ready for the wait. 'Gone to absolute hell.'

The felucca was untied and soon under way, joined not far off shore by a school of porpoises dodging under its bows as they followed the underwater shiver of a shoal of sardines. Away in the distance the rolls of dark clouds moved on down the coast, lit up every few minutes by flashes of sheet lightning, the air smelling of rain freshly fallen, damp wood, tarred ropes, the scent of the open sea. The journey not long, but Heraldo taking the opportunity to reel in a few punters for the morrow, bringing out his lute, sitting on the side of the boat, playing a soft tune, singing a mournful song. Ludmilla chiming in with her lilting voice when it came to her verses:

Oh hark, the drums do beat, my love. No longer can I stay.
The bugle horn is sounding loud, and I must march away.
The government has ordered and I am given command
To join the fighting lads, my love, on the shores of a foreign land.

Ludmilla pleading with him not to go, or else to let her dress herself in uniform…

And I will be your serving man and together we shall stand
Beneath our country's banner in that foreign land.

Heraldo remonstrating:

Your waist it is too slender, love, your fingers are too small,
The sultry sun of Egypt, love, your rosy cheeks would spoil.
For the cannons they do rattle there and the bullets they do fly,
And silver trumpets sound to hide the dismal cries.

Ludmilla finishing up:

Oh cursed be those cruel wars, wherever they began,
They've stolen from our country many's the handsome man.
They've robbed us of our sweethearts, left to rot upon the sands
Of that dry and lonely bloody plain in that foreign land.

Their audience mesmerised, the grumbling man's grandson taking off his cap and holding it to his chest in memory of the brother he'd lost a few years back in one of those cruel wars, wherever they began; a few women shedding warm tears for their own bereavements.

'That was beautiful, my dears,' said Andreas Zilboorg, as if he was in charge of them, winking at Wenzel as he whisked off his hat, about to offer it around like a bottle-man, until Wenzel struck the hat from his hand.

'We'll have none of that, Mr Hedgehoggery,' Wenzel said, Zilboorg's face a mask of pleading though he meekly picked up his hat and put it back on his head.

'Money in their pockets seeing as how they're just back from market,' he offered in defence.

'You've done your bit,' Wenzel squaring up to Zilboorg, placing his stocky body between Zilboorg and the small crowd who'd gathered about Heraldo and Ludmilla as they struck up another tune, another song. 'You've got us on board and I'm thankful for it.

But don't think you're one of us, and don't you ever try to muscle in again on me and mine for if you do, our bargain is at an end.'

Zilboorg smiled, tapped his hat.

'Never knows until you tries. Not in our business.'

Walking away, Wenzel wincing, Wenzel looking over at Old Mother Pfiffmakler who was scrunched up in her usual black shawl watching the proceedings with interest.

'He's a snake,' she commented, as Wenzel approached, 'and ain't one what'll stay in the grass. Keep your eyes on him, Wenzel, else he'll be up your trousers and down your throat afore you can sound the alarm.'

Wenzel smiling, sitting down next to the old woman.

'Will always take your advice,' Wenzel said, hoping this was a rapprochement of sorts, hope quickly vetoed by his grandmother who merely spat out the side of her mouth.

'War might steal sweethearts,' she said, 'but war ain't no match for me, so watch your step, whippersnapper. I ain't consigned to the grave yet and I ain't finished. Not by a long chalk.'

Wenzel sighing, seeing his own battles stretching out before him, his own lonely plain, bloody or otherwise. Heading towards a foreign land, and whatever that might bring.

What it brought, when they drew up to the quayside on Ugljan, was a pleasant surprise; the small settlement of Preko quiet and pretty, backed by terraces of olive trees, grey trunks twisted with age, silvery underside of their leaves rippling in the breeze; the medieval fortress of St Michael a reassuring presence on the slopes to the west.

'Welcome to The Other Side,' the felucca's captain was jovial. 'That's what Preko means, by the way. Literally: The Other Side.'

'Fascinating,' Wenzel obliged, pulling on his harness.

'It is!' the captain enthused, happy to have ferried these Fairs people now he knew they weren't a mere group of scraggly pedlars come to fleece the population with substandard goods. 'And while you're here you must sample our olive oil,' he went on, 'the best this side of Italy—better even. And the sardines we soak in the stuff will melt in your mouth! Here,' he said, lifting a few jars from a crate. 'On the house. Enjoy our island, and if you'll take my advice you'll settle yourself along at the Bay of Jaz just up north and, by the by, I gather from Andreas you're wanting the Ravenna ship?'

Wenzel nodding curtly.

'You're in luck then. Weekly ship is going the day after tomorrow, and I'll see you booked for passage. Gonna be a full one, mind, so be at Preko quayside by noon and give them this chitty.'

Swiftly scribbling a pencil over a piece of paper, passing it to Wenzel.

'That's mighty good of you,' Wenzel said, slipping the man the last few coins he had in his pocket, the skipper taking them, turning away, rubbing his hands together in satisfaction. One good turn deserved another, and back he'd go to Zadar to pick up the rest of the waiting passengers and, while he was at it, get the message out that a performance was going on at Jaz tomorrow. Certain to have a few more trips than usual in the morning, and booking this lot onto the Ravenna ship a small price to pay.

Wenzel headed off in the given direction, the rest of the Kunterbunt trundling on behind him, everyone revived by the short sea trip, eager to plan out exactly what they would do the following day.

'Got to be one of the Plaff von Kahlenberg sketches,' Heraldo said, using the Austrian appellation of the witty personage who so often cropped up in plays across Europe.

Wenzel agreeing.

'And a Kaspar Larriscarri, and maybe a Harlequino for the Italian speakers.'

'Do we know anything Croatian?' Peppe asked, Wenzel scouring his memory, dredging up one such tale.

'There's that Stribor's Forest we came across years back. Can't quite...'

'That's right!' Rosa quick to put in. 'Wicked wife, saintly mother, naïve youth, helpful imps. We've all the makings.'

'A woman with a serpent's tongue. Now why does that strike a chord?' Wenzel looked fondly over at his wife, meaning a joke, not that it was taken so by Old Mother Pfiffmakler, a dark cloud at their backs who stabbed at Wenzel with her cane.

'Told you before, I ain't dead yet,' she muttered, Rosa rolling her eyes, Wenzel grimacing, Ludmilla coming to the rescue.

'It would be perfect for me and Heraldo.' she said. 'Our first solo outing.'

Longhella scowling.

'Isn't that the one where they put magpies into chickens' nests? Like a certain someone I could mention?' Longhella throwing a vicious glance at Hulde. 'And why does it have to be you and Heraldo? Why not me and Lupercal? We're just as worthy of an outing as you two gargoyles are.'

Longhella sniffing, Lupercal beaming over a smile she entirely missed.

'We can do it!' Lupercal said with enthusiasm. 'And we could use that backdrop we had for the last Kaspar Larriscarri sketch.'

Everyone looked towards Wenzel who took his time, this the first real decision he would make about the show's content and a lot riding on it, especially with that stab in the back from his grandmother.

'I think,' he said, 'Ludmilla and Heraldo would be better placed. They'll have to spend a few hours tonight going through their paces and I rather doubt Longhella and Lupercal would have the dedication...'

'That's just not fair!' Longhella protested, stamping a foot into the track they were travelling, Yssel putting out a hand to keep her daughter in check, knowing as well as Wenzel there was no way Longhella—never mind Lupercal—would have the concentration or inclination to perform the task on such a tight schedule. The two of them more likely to set off for a swim than get their heads down to a script and learn it as tightly as it would need to be learned.

'Wenzel's right, my dear,' she said, offering a placation. 'But you'd be perfect as a wood nymph, and Lupercal equally so as a helpful imp.'

Longhella grumbling, though not for long for they'd just rounded the headland and arrived at the perfect pitch at the head of the bay. Longhella doing exactly as her mother had predicted—as did Lupercal and Jericho—neglecting anything to do with the unloading of the carts, the erection of their tents, instead stripping down to their shifts and running headlong down the sands and chucking themselves into the warm water, laughing exuberantly, washing away the dirt and dust of the last few weeks' travelling.

The rest struck camp with practiced ease: bed tents up and furnished; fires lit; flour and water mixed into dough, put onto hot stones to cook; a cauldron hooked above a fire-pit, filled with the fresh ingredients Rosa and Yssel had purchased in the market on their way back from the springs, a fine stew soon on the boil. The olive oil and sardines the captain had given them decanted into communal bowls along with crumbled white cheese and walnuts already cracked from their shells.

Andreas Zilboorg setting up his own camp a small way distant, soon joined by his boys, or Valter at least. No mistaking that red hair. Ludmilla might have gone over to speak to him but, as soon as the bread was on and the stew cooking through, Rosa took Heraldo and Ludmilla to one side.

'We need to get you prepared,' she said, putting a finger to the side of her face where salt and sand had scratched out a rash, skin

51

usually plum-soft and smooth until it took umbrage with its environment. 'It's quite a long story, as I recall,' she went on. 'It'll need cutting down considerably. Think you two could manage a twenty-minute run?'

Heraldo and Ludmilla nodding, faces creased in concentration, neither wanting to let the side down.

'So, gist is,' Rosa giving them a potted version of the tale of the Enchanted Forest, 'handsome but gullible son...'

'That's Heraldo, all right!' Ludmilla put in, soon shushed by Rosa.

'...wanders into the enchanted forest, sees a serpent crawling from the trees, and next thing a beautiful woman appears whom he immediately falls in love with and takes away as his wife.'

'We can do all of that without dialogue,' Heraldo said. 'Just use drum rolls to build up the tension, and could be playing my lute.'

'Perfect,' Rosa agreed. 'I'll be the mother who knows straightaway the new wife is a wrong 'un and still has a serpent's tongue when she's angered, and nothing angers her more than her husband's mother.'

'How are we going to do the tongue?' Heraldo asked, Rosa and Ludmilla exchanging a glance, for so much so easy. Handsome but gullible indeed.

'Little piece of leather with a spring in it,' Ludmilla answered, Heraldo frowning.

'And you'll keep it in your mouth? Won't that make you gag? And how are you going to speak?'

'Sleight of hand,' Rosa chuckled, 'and no one better at that than our Ludmilla. Quick slip of it between her teeth, opens her lips and out it comes. And we'll only need to use it once or twice. I'm thinking the sleeve and the eggs. We can get rid of all the rest.'

'The sleeve and the eggs?' Ludmilla asked, this tale not well known by her, Rosa going on to explain, running through the tale in her head, tracing the paths and signposts needed to keep it right. Many of the shows they put on reflecting the makeup of the places they were in, utilising local folklore, adding flourishes that satirised or publicised the locale's politics. Other pieces mere entertainment, some ribald, some for children, some for children and yet still ribald—filled with nuances that had the children bemused and the adults guffawing with knowing laughter. No time for that with this tale. What was needed was a quick connect to the island population, cast them back to when they'd first heard it sitting on their grandparents' knees.

Rosa soon having her story straight, with a good bit part for Longhella and the younger boys, all rounded off with a rousing moral at the end.

'It's great!' Ludmilla said admiringly once Rosa had laid out the thread.

'Think we can pull it off?' Heraldo a little nervy, usually only supplying the music, never the main character on stage.

'My dears, we're Pfiffmaklers!' Rosa assured them. 'If anyone can pull it off then it's us.'

7

Into the Enchanted Forest

The morning broke clear and bright, filled with birdsong and bees and all that is glorious in spring-time, its lively intent contrasted by the soft mist breathing up from the calm waters between Zadar and the island archipelago upon which the Kunterbunt were encamped. Ludmilla and Heraldo up before the rest, going over their turns, checking their lines. Hulde staggering out a while later, yawning, stretching, looking for Ludmilla, finding her sitting with Heraldo on the sandy bay, the sea lapping gently at their unshod feet.

Folk on the road don't get much chance for cleanliness, going to sleep in the same clothes they'd woken in and staying in the same clothes for weeks on end if they didn't come across anywhere they could wash them out and get them, and themselves, cleansed and dried. Consequence being that many suffered scourges of lice and fleas until they hit a lick of water when—like Longhella, Lupercal and Jericho the night before—they took full advantage.

'Hulde,' Ludmilla said as the girl approached, holding out her hand, the girl taking it, but not with the fervent grasp she'd used before, a fact that should have pleased Ludmilla but did not, the girl having set off an aching in her body to have her own child, one who would adore her and whom she would adore in turn.

'Why not take her in?' Heraldo suggested. 'I'll go back up to camp, give you a bit of privacy.'

Heraldo getting to his feet. They might be Fairs folk who took advantage of water at every turn, but they were modest, no matter their age.

'Thank you,' Ludmilla said. 'She certainly enjoyed that puddle so let's see how she likes the sea. Come on, Hulde,' Ludmilla leading the girl across the sand towards a short bluff of rocks where she undid her dress, undid Hulde's, led the girl into the water. Only up to their knees at first, and then to their thighs, Hulde shrieking loudly as Ludmilla let go her hand and threw herself into the tiny tipple of waves so she was floating on her back.

'Come on, Hulde!' Ludmilla encouraged, Hulde's village being right on the shore so surely the girl had been in the sea before, Ludmilla splashing her arms, tasting salt, braids loosened by the slight current, flowing free on the equally slight tide. Soft touch of small jellyfish about her body, brought in by the moon to breed, would soon be lying dead and dying upon the beach.

Of a sudden Hulde joined in, chucking herself onto Ludmilla, laughing loudly, using Ludmilla as a raft, kicking her little legs up behind her, gagging and spitting as the saltwater went into her mouth and nose, obviously enjoying herself. Ludmilla turning stomach down in the water, Hulde on her back clutching her arms about Ludmilla's neck as Ludmilla swam out a little then back again to shore, the two sitting waist deep in the water, bobbing up and down, utterly at peace.

'Well there's a sight, and no mistake,' came a voice from nearby, Ludmilla looking up to see Valter Poppelmann standing boot-sure on the rocky bluff gazing down on them with undisguised admiration. 'You look like a couple of mermaids,' he added. 'Hope you're not trying to lure me in, because me and water don't exactly get along.'

Laughing softly at some private joke. Ludmilla embarrassed, outraged he thought he had the right to be watching them.

'What are you doing spying on us?' she demanded, aware he would also be able to see the little heap of their clothing and found yet more violation in that act of seeing.

'Just taking a walk,' he replied easily. 'Doing a bit of foraging: samphire, mussels, dead men's fingers—you know the kind of thing.'

Ludmilla did, early morning foraging a natural part of their day, but not hanging around watching other people bathe. And the mention of dead men's fingers—a type of seaweed—she found distasteful with Hulde being there, not that she'd told him how they'd found Hulde, although he'd seemed to have guessed some of it at least.

'Well hadn't you better be off about it?' she asked, Valter smiling nonchalantly down at her, before ostentatiously raising his head, sniffing at the air.

'But it's such a glorious morning! Where's the hurry?'

Squatting himself down on his heels.

Ludmilla frowning, Hulde studying a couple of empty snail shells she'd pulled from the seabed, shells abandoned when the moulted carapace of a crab floated by.

'Bosh,' Hulde observed as she held the empty crab case up to the light, apparently admiring its translucence.

'Bosh is exactly right,' Ludmilla said. 'Couldn't have put it better myself. You need to get out of here, Valter Poppelmann, and we need to get ourselves dressed.'

'Ah well,' he uncurled himself, stood up again. 'All good things come to an end. See you later, my little mermaids!'

He touched his hand to his temple in salute and was off, bounding over the rocks as if he'd known them all his days, no sign of any foraging pretended, merely a man who'd had his fun and was on his way.

'At last,' Ludmilla breathed, checking he was well out of sight before she got herself up from the water. 'Come on, Hulde. But my, that's pretty,' she said, taking the carapace from Hulde's fingers, leading her back to land, Hulde following like a puppy after a treat.

'All set, my lad?' Wenzel interrogated Heraldo the moment he'd had his first cup of bitter chicory coffee down his neck. Heraldo returned from the beach, unusually jumpy, squeezing one hand with the other as he checked once more over Rosa's scripted directions.

'I think so, Papa,' didn't sound too sure. 'Still have to brief the boys and Longhella about their parts.'

Wenzel smiling, Heraldo normally so certain about his music and the outlandish instruments he gathered and restored with the skill of a master. Throwing an encouraging arm about his son's shoulders.

'You'll be fine. Rosa has run everything by me and I've only made a few embellishments. Bit of potassium chlorate added to the saltpetre to aid the imps jumping from the fire, and a load of smoky fog for the forest scenes...'

Heraldo smiled weakly.

'I don't know...I'm not sure I'm up to this acting lark. I've only ever been in the wings before...'

'You wanted me to give the starring role to Lupercal?' Wenzel admonished his son. 'He'd have made the proverbial mud-mouthful of it, you know it as well as I do. And the secret to every successful show is to reel the audience in with something they're familiar with. I'd've adapted the marionettes if I could have, but...'

'Time's short. I know, I know,' Heraldo agreed. 'And what about the stage? And how are we going to work the backdrops?'

Wenzel squeezed his son to him.

'We weren't idle, last night, my lad, while Rosa was running you through your paces. Come and see.'

Heraldo went with his father, finding a square clearly demarcated in the grass, kindle in the fire-pits pits primed and ready. Peppe and Jericho practising flipping the backdrops: forest followed by homestead, then forest again, exactly as was needed.

'And the musical accompaniment?' Heraldo asked. 'I've not even spoken—'

'All taken care of,' Wenzel assured. 'No one's as proficient as you in that department but you've schooled us well. I've Peppe on drums, and you know how good he is at that. Yssel will be in control of the sound effects, so we've no worries about timing on that score. And then we've Jericho doing the luting. His first time out.'

'He is getting good,' Heraldo put in, 'and he's certainly ready for it. I've been thinking it for a while.'

'So nothing to worry about,' Wenzel assured his son. 'All will go smoothly, you'll see.'

Ludmilla brought Hulde back from the bay, discombobulated by the unexpected appearance of Valter Poppelmann, not that she mentioned it, and certainly not to Heraldo who eagerly informed her of the new aspects of their performance and what they should do, how they should stand, where they should move. Ludmilla ticking off each direction as Heraldo fired it at her, getting everything straight in her head, filing it away. Valter Poppelmann still troubling her. The more she thought about it the more incensed she became: how dare he stand there on that rock and look at her and Hulde in the water? It was against every code Fairs folk stuck to rigidly. They might be on the edges of society, they might be excluded from public bathing houses in most of the towns and cities they passed through, but for the Lord's sake, it was accepted that if one lot of people were washing themselves, particularly women and girls, everyone else steered clear. A courtesy Valter Poppelmann had chosen to flout, had seen her practically naked in the water.

But you look like mermaids.

Hope you're not trying to lure me in.

It was a terrible infringement and Ludmilla felt affronted, belittled, and yet—she hardly dared admit it to herself—flattered. That yearning for a child, come yawning out of her body like an unstoppable greed, finding in his actions something agreeable. Head a messy ball of tangled thoughts, ceasing as Peppe hurried up beside her.

'Folk are already gathering!' he whispered urgently. 'Island folk here, and a load over from Zadar who've just got off the ferry and are on their way.'

Ludmilla looking over to the stage, saw people spreading out cloaks and blankets, sitting themselves down; a couple of traders trundling in with their carts, opening up shop, selling lemonade, cold tea; a *pekara* setting out fresh cooked burek, flaky pastries filled with cheese, still warm from the oven; grilled rissoles and kebabs put to cook over charcoal burners along with paprika-spiced beans and sausages. Another armed with platters of vegetables drizzled with olive oil and slices of smoked ham the area was apparently famous for.

'It's become quite a happening,' Peppe said, rubbing his hands together. 'So quick back to camp. We've to run over everything one last time to get it straight.'

'Welcome to you all!' Wenzel shouted out in his best showman's voice. 'Welcome to our marvellous Higgledy Piggledy Travelling Show!'

Lupercal and Jericho somersaulting across the demarcated stage-ground, back-flipping over and over before leaping high into the air with ankles and knees supple and powerful as frogs' legs, twiddling their toes as they went, twisting their bodies, landing with grace and precision and back-flipping off again. Places taken by Longhella, orange skirts billowing out about her as she twirled balletically around the stage, throwing out handfuls of sugared almonds to her audience.

'Let the show begin!' Wenzel roars, Longhella making her graceful exit. 'Behold,' Wenzel's voice low, booming like a bittern through the reeds as drums began to softly roll. 'Let me take you to the Enchanted Forest of Stribor...'

The audience stirring at this reference they knew from childhood fairy tales. Drums getting louder as the boys dropped their first backdrop, revealing the Deep Dark Forest wispy with an ethereal fog appearing magically from the ground. 'And who do we see in the forest? It's Tomislav, son of his widowed mother, come in search of wood for the fire and mushrooms for the table...'

Enter Heraldo, accompanied by gentle lute music as he wandered slowly across the set.

'But wait!' Wenzel's voice is urgent. 'What do I see crawling over that fallen bough of wood?'

Ludmilla's scarf-wrapped rope quickly dragged into play, a handful of metallic dust thrown into one of the small fire-pits to distract as Ludmilla appeared with a quick flick of her serpent tongue.

'It's Josipa!' someone from the audience cries out for Wenzel.

'It is indeed, my fine young friend, but what will Tomislav do?'

Tomislav down on his knees in front of the serpent lady, kissing her hand, Ludmilla beautiful as Josipa ever was in these plays, bringing Tomislav up, the two entwining.

'He is so enthralled by her,' Wenzel supplies, 'that he takes her for his wife there and then...'

'Don't do it!' the audience shivering with dread and delight. They'd never expected one of their own folk tales to be brought to life, and so vividly, and threw themselves headlong into the action, exactly as Rosa had predicted: the children as enthralled as Tomislav, the adults reverting to childhood and joining in.

'Ah,' Wenzel shakes his head sadly, standing front right of the stage, milking his audience, playing it by ear. 'But we all know Tomislav is as gullible as he is handsome, and has no idea that the forest he's entered is Stribor's own.'

Quick flip of the backdrop, and Tomislav and Josipa are back at Tomislav's homestead.

'Who is this you've brought to our door?' Rosa, the hunchbacked mother asks, a mother as nameless in this play as in so many others.

'My wife!' Tomislav exclaims loudly. 'See how beautiful she is? How lithe and supple her body!'

A quick outing for Josipa's tongue as she regards the audience with haughty disdain.

'Because she's a snake, you idiot!' someone shouts, Rosa cupping her hand to her ear. So much of their performances guided by the reactions they provoke and Rosa quick to exploit it.

'She's a what? She's a snake?'

'She's an enchantress who's been turned into a serpent by Stribor!' an ancient grandmother tries to help her out.

'She's evil! Evil!' shouts a woman who is leaning so far forward she's practically squashing the child she's holding to her breast.

'Evil?' Rosa repeats, looking over at Josipa who merely gives her a spiteful smile as she is led off stage by her new husband, leaving Rosa to sit alone upon a rickety chair.

'Ah, but what am I to do?' She's distraught, distressed. 'My only son has married a serpent, but how will I make him see it?'

Taking from her sewing bag one of her son's shirts which has been torn at the sleeve, the sleeve snatched from her hand by the sudden reappearance of Josipa.

'You'll never make him see it,' Josipa spits, 'and the sooner you're gone from here the better.'

Josipa off as quickly as she came on, leaving the old mother broken and weeping piteously, the notes from the lute tugging everyone's heartstrings.

'What ails you, old mother?'

A new character enters the scene—Longhella in a pauper's dress, hair scraggled up in a wild heap about her head, a bundle of kindling beneath her arm.

'Oh but my dear!' Rosa is up with her needle. 'Your dress is all ripped. Do let me sew it for you,' and so she does, and in payment the pauper girl leaves the widow her grateful thanks and her armful of kindling.

'Throw it on the fire!' several members of the audience urge, Rosa looking up with puzzlement, but doing as asked and——the moment she does so——the fire-pits erupt with great whooshes of smoke and scatterings of golden sparkles, from which Lupercal and Jericho appear, rolling themselves onto the stage, cavorting like the fire-imps they are purporting to be.

'We can help you, mother,' they cry as they scamper about the stage, rolling over and over one another.

'But how?' Rosa asks, wringing her hands.

'Remember that serpents cannot resist the young of magpies, that magpies are to serpents as gold is to man. You'll see, mother, you'll see.'

Another huge billow of smoke and the lads are away, Josipa a horrible materialisation at the old mother's elbow.

'Go sweep the yard out, old woman,' she commands. 'And while you're there, don't forget to check the chickens for eggs.'

Josipa lifts up her arm in command, and out comes the serpent's tongue, clear for all to see, Rosa cowering, holding up her hands dramatically in front of her face.

'But my son!' she cries, accompanied by an ominously low roll of drums. 'What will become of my son?'

'Your son is lost to you,' Josipa is merciless, leaving the stage. The old woman on her own, until the young peasant girl appears again and flits across in front of her, nests appearing, black and white birds in each and every one.

'Bless you mother, for mending my skirts,' she announces, and Rosa begins to crawl on hands and knees towards the nests, staring at them with bewilderment and then joy.

'Tomislav!' she shouts. 'Tomislav! Come here, and bring Josipa with you!'

The entire audience lean forward at this invitation, knowing what will come, Jericho sending out an optimistic tune as in comes Tomislav, his hand cupped beneath the elbow of his beautiful serpent wife.

'Only see here!' his mother says, pointing at the nests. 'There's young magpies there instead of eggs! I don't know how it happened!'

Sprinkling of gold dust in the air as Jericho hurriedly leaves his lute and becomes a fire-imp again, he and Lupercal bowling themselves quickly across the stage from opposite directions.

'Show her, mother,' they get out before they're off again, and the lute is snatched up to build to a crescendo as Rosa points out the obvious. Josipa unable to resist, flicking out her tongue, going down on all fours and licking at each nest one by one.

'She's a serpent!' Tomislav's mother exclaims. 'Can't you see it, son? Can't you see her tongue?'

But Tomislav cannot. All he can see is her beauty and a chance he cannot miss, and the audience begin to hiss, get in their opinions.

'So like a man,' sighs one woman.

'Eyes in their bollocks but none in their heads!' shouts another.

'They puts rings through the noses of bulls,' adds a third, 'but gotta think there's better places.'

Heraldo uncomfortable, everything going off script, but sticks to his lines.

'I see nothing, mother,' he says, 'and I'll not stand for you to slander my wife. Be gone and away!'

Peppe to the fore with the drums. Yssel managing the smoke, wafting out a bit too much, several people in the front row beginning to cough.

Down comes the forest scene again, and old mother limping her way through it, and Wenzel's back on stage, covered head to foot in a cloak that's seems sewn over with lichen and leaves.

'So you've come to me at last,' he bellows, like the devil himself, 'to ask me for your bargain!'

And there's those drums again, loud and insistent and the audience are on edge for here's the nub of the entire tale, here the end of it, and they're not entirely sure which way the Pfiffmaklers will make it go. Stribor's Forest might be an old folk tale to outsiders, but to these Croatians it's an integral part of their history: visceral, reflective of their values as a nation long under the thumb of others. Here, in Stribor's Forest, holding their breaths.

'I can give you peace,' Stribor shouts, 'a land that has fences of silver, gates of gold. I can give you back your youth. All I ask in exchange is that I take away your memories and your pain, so it will be as if Tomislav never existed!'

Another backdrop replacing the last: an idyllic landscape, one hurriedly painted the previous night to depict olive groves by the sea, St Michael's fortress on its hill, a backdrop that is barely dry but does the trick, audience recognising their own idyllic island. Flattered, drawn in all the more.

'Don't, old mother!' the woman with the nursing baby shouts, aghast that anyone should even consider such a wager, her own child as glorious to her as the rising sun.

'Just get it done, woman,' an old man growls—same old man who'd been on the quayside cursing his grandson. 'He's offering you eternal youth and amnesia into the bargain, for God's sake! I'd rip my right arm off for such a chance.'

'He's right!' his neighbour joins in. 'You'd be young again! And who doesn't want that?'

Rosa holds out her arms, calls to Ugljan in supplication.

'Oh tell me trees, oh tell me stones, oh tell me sea! What should I do?'

The audience shouting out their answers, voices rising, arguing, prevaricating.

'I could never leave the island!'

'I'd rather cut my throat than lose my son!'

'I'd pay you a hundred gold guineas, if I had them, for a chance such as...'

'But think about Tomislav! Josipa will eat him alive!'

'And their children will be snakes! And if she doesn't eat him they surely will!'

'But old mother won't know it. She won't even remember him. She'll be too happy...'

'Enough!' Stribor's voice resounds above them all and the drums come on his heels, drowning everyone out, bringing them back to silence with their terrible noise, for it's like the air has turned to thunder and become heavy, and there's the sudden pervasive stench of brimstone in the air, thanks to Lupercal dousing some sulphur flowers with hydrochloric acid.

'Stribor needs your decision, old woman,' Stribor declares, the drums ceasing suddenly, everything still and quiet, everyone agog for the answer. For here is where the tale can diverge, where one reading of the story has old mother accepting the bargain, taking the easy way out, which means to the audience that Croatia too has taken the bargain, lowered all their necks beneath the yoke of foreign domination.

And then there's the other way, the hard way, the one where they fight on...

'I'll not do it!' Rosa declares, standing up, turning to face Stribor. 'I'll not do it!'

The audience clapping and hooting as a huge guff of smoke comes from the back of the stage and we see Josipa swaying and wilting, Tomislav behind her crying and calling her name, holding out his arms to her, the fire-imps rolling themselves like balls across the stage front, priming the fire-pits as they go, and up come coloured flames like miracles, great geysers of reds and yellows, blues and purple and, when the smoke finally clears, there in their homestead are Tomislav and his mother hugging, last glimpse of Josipa—serpent once more—slithering away into the gloom.

And so much clapping!

The folk of Ugljan on their feet, stall holders slapping rissoles and cuts of lamb onto their charcoal grills, checking their jugs of drink, making sure the pastries are warm and ready for the eating, anticipating the stampede that is bound to follow such an outstanding performance. One no one had anticipated, including them and theirs right at its core. Faces beaming, children screaming in delight, chomping on their sugared almonds. Lupercal, Jericho and Longhella taking hats amongst the crowd, collecting their well-earned coins along with back-slaps and handshakes. Congratulations due all round, the show only just begun and hours more to go.

8

The Balatronic Ballet

In the tent behind the backdrops, hidden from public view, the Pfiffmakler clan are gathered, some swiftly changing costumes, others checking instruments or their next lot of pyrotechnical aids.

'My God!' Wenzel said, as Rosa helped him from his Stribor gear, and he in turn removed the cushion she'd used as a hump. 'That went down better than expected. Well done Heraldo and Ludmilla, not forgetting of course our fire-imps, and our extremely pretty peasant girl!'

Longhella doing a quick curtsey to acknowledge the compliment.

'Still think I could've done the serpent woman,' she said, wrinkling her pretty nose. 'Not that many lines. Could've easily got them pat. Can pretty much recite them word for word...'

'And the tongue?' her mother reminder her. 'Reckon you'd have been up to scratch on that? Well done, by the way, my dear,' Yssel added, patting Ludmilla's arm. 'That was really well done.'

Ignoring the sour look Longhella gave her sister.

'You can do my turn next time,' Heraldo put in. 'I hated it! I mean, really hated it! Don't know how in hell you do it. All that stuff coming in from the audience? Gotta tell you, I near froze when they started yelling at me.'

Rosa smiled over at her son.

'It's part and parcel,' she said. 'Always got to tap into what's going on local, wherever you are. And my Wenzel certainly did that...'

About to say more, about to praise her husband to the heavens, when Grandmother Pfiffmakler made an entrance, tapping her cane with exaggerated care upon the ground.

'Oh but don't you think you're so clever, Wenzel,' Grandmother wheezed. 'Oh but don't you think you're so high and mighty. Getting yourself in with the natives is it? And oh, how clever you are.'

Stabbing her cane several times more, real vicious stabs that had the worms in the earth beneath squiggling and wriggling out of its way.

'Just had to put on a play that would put you up top, didn't you?' she went on, her voice an unpleasant screech, spit aggregating at the sides of her mouth in her anger so that even Longhella turned away, hanging her head as the rest were doing.

Except Wenzel and Rosa.

'It wasn't like that at all,' Wenzel began.

'It really wasn't,' Rosa agreed. 'It was the only tale that—'

'Talk about snakes!' Grandmother cut them both off. 'Just had to highlight the fact that the old woman would sacrifice everything for the love of her son, didn't you? Well, let me tell you this, mister. It cuts no ice with me. I don't love you no more than the oak loves the acorns it spills out across the land, and I don't no more care if you and yours rot like one of them acorns, or gets eaten by a pig, exact same pig as you are. And that goes for the changeling too.'

Pointing at Hulde with the end of her stick.

'She's the one what's split us down the middle, just like a serpent's tongue.'

'We're hardly split down the middle,' Peppe pointed out, 'unless by middle you mean you one side and everyone else the other.'

Grandmother Pfiffmakler narrowed her eyes, Yssel speaking up before she'd gathered her next mouthful of venom.

'It was just a play,' she said. 'The only one local to this region we knew. Maybe if you'd have…'

Grandmother wheeled about and would have stabbed her stick in Yssel's direction, but was feeling the need to lean.

'Maybe if I'd've what? Been invited into your little parlay about what to put on? I'd no say in any of this,' and now she did release her stick, waved it about her in a circle that included her entire family, 'because not a one of you ingrates had the grace to invite me in.'

And with that she stomped away, stabbing her cane into the soft earth like it was Judas himself, leaving all kinds of silence behind her.

'Gjyshe zemëruar,' Hulde was the first to speak, having no difficulty discerning what had been acting and what was not, and *angry grandmother* fit the bill precisely. Ludmilla had been concerned how Hulde might react when the drums began, if she might do as she'd done with the thunder, so had taken Hulde into the tent beforehand, let Hulde bang on the drum, asked Yssel to keep an eye on the girl throughout the performance. But Hulde had been fine. Hulde had been delighted, had clapped her hands harder than any of the Ugljan folk, put admiring fingers to Rosa's hump and Stribor's tactile costume, Yssel having to hold her back several times from joining in the action *ad lib*, particularly when the boys went rolling off like hedgehogs across the stage.

Changeling indeed.

But not the way Grandmother meant, Ludmilla more angry with the old woman than she'd ever been with anyone her whole life, feeling the rage of it, the injustice of her great-grandmother's words hot and hard in her chest like burning coals.

'If old ma wants a fight,' she announced, 'then I know whose side I'm on, and I'm taking as my battle cry what Hulde said. *Jeershay zemmerura!*' Ludmilla loudly repeating the words as she'd heard them, not that she'd understood them, holding a fist into the air.

'*Jeershay zemmerura!*' Lupercal and Jericho joined in, mainly because they liked the sounds of the foreign words, thrusting their own fists in the air like disgruntled workers on a striking line. Rebellion short lived. Wenzel quashing it with a single look at his sons and niece.

'I've no idea what that means,' he said mildly.

'Silly old goat would be my guess,' Rosa interrupted, hot under the collar from the old woman's challenge, hot in cheek, hot in vein.

'But she has a point,' Yssel the peacemaker put in. 'We did neglect to ask her opinion, and she's been over fifty years in the business. Has to be stuffed top to toe with tales, and it can't have been easy for her to have given up the helm overnight. And it was overnight. Let's not forget that.'

'And she's right about the girl,' Longhella getting some of her fire back. She wasn't about to step over that skewed middle line, but she'd always been a stirrer. 'Nothing would've changed if we'd not found her.'

Challenge coming from an entirely unexpected quarter, from Heraldo, who so rarely spoke up in family meetings, content to let other people's decisions wash over him so long as he was allowed to carry on mending and playing his instruments. He might have shrugged off his Tomislav persona along with his Tomislav clothes, and he might have hated the experience of being on stage, being put in the spotlight, expected to react as cleverly as the Pfiffmaklers handled all their various pyrotechnical accoutrements, but he'd not been immune to the appreciation with which their audience had greeted their little stage play, and particularly his father's master-stroke of knocking up some scenery that looked exactly like Ugljan itself. And no more was he ignorant of the fact that Old Mother Pfiffmakler had taken so vehemently against the girl, as she insisted on calling her, as Longhella also did.

Time to take a stand. Time to spell it out like he was seeing it.

'That's nonsense, Longhella,' Heraldo said, getting to his feet, taking a few short steps towards Ludmilla and Hulde, placing a protective hand on Hulde's head. 'What's happened has happened because it was needed. Change was needed, and I think we're all, even you deep down, glad for it.'

'Hear hear,' Peppe said, 'and the coins agree,' rattling the income they'd garnered from their Stribor play, which was more than expected.

'Quite right,' Rosa was emphatic. 'It's been needed ever since Lotte and Matthys retired.'

'Although we could have run the new act by Grandmother,' Yssel put in, oil on troubled waters, a little surprised when Wenzel took her side, rubbing at his thick beard.

'You're right, Yssel. I rode roughshod over her. Didn't for a minute consider she might take it as an attack. I'll go talk to her. No point her simmering until she bursts.'

'Let me go, Papa,' Heraldo stepped in. 'You need to get back to the show before it's stolen out from under us by that...'

His words bang on the mark for, from the other side of the backdrop, came Andreas Zilboorg's raucous voice, leaving them all to wonder how much of their family's business he'd overheard.

'Ladies and Gentlemen!' he was shouting. 'Grab your food and drink and bring it back with you to our stage, for you are about to see The Balatronic Ballet as you've never seen it before!'

The crowds not so eager, all well acquainted with Zilboorg and his crew who'd been regularly performing on the boulevard of Zadar for the past few weeks when the spring-markets were in full swing. Zilboorg immune to their apathy, merely shouting out his wares again.

'We've something new to entertain you with! Come on, boys, don't be shy!'

Lupercal and Jericho exchanging a furtive glance, Wenzel not missing it.

'What did you two do?' he asked, *sotto voce,* for he could hear the scuffling of moving feet and folk getting sat.

'Um, nothing much,' Lupercal whispered. 'It's just that Zilboorg fellow asked if we'd like to take a turn…'

'And you're always saying, Papa, that we should take a chance to learn…ouch!'

Wenzel's skelp caught him across the back of his head. Not a hard hit, Wenzel twitching a smile deep within his beard.

'Well, Grandmother was right about something,' he said softly. 'Warned me Zilboorg was a weasel in human skin. So get yourselves off. If nothing else it'll give us a bit of breathing space.'

Lupercal and Jericho doing as bid, skipping around the backdrop, entering the arena with their usual acrobatic flair.

'Quite keen to see what a Balatronic Ballet is when it's at home,' Wenzel added, as the applause began, with no great rapture. 'Come on, Pfiffmaklers,' he urged. 'Kaspar Larriscarri next, I think.'

The Balatronic Ballet was precisely what it claimed to be, namely two buffoons—introduced by Andreas Zilboorg—cavorting across the stage slathered in extensive facial makeup, outrageous costumes and wigs. Sometimes in slow motion, sometimes super quick, acting out a series of comic interludes. The audience a little bored, having seen it all before, until the act was immensely enlivened by the unexpected addition of Lupercal and Jericho become human projectiles, thrown with ease from one buffoon to another, sometimes expertly caught, other times not with apparently disastrous results until Lupercal or Jericho unrolled themselves, got up, did a few twirls and became juggling balls again.

Slapstick at its best.

'Have to admit they're not half bad,' Wenzel said to Rosa, as they got ready for their next set.

'Only because they've our lads with them,' Rosa admonished. 'Weasels in human skin,' she reminded him. 'Don't let them get under yours.'

The day was done, shows finished, money enough in the Kunterbunt's coffers to buy them passage to Ravenna where they would do it all over again, fill their pockets for the final leg of their journey. The crowds dispersed, the Kunterbunt pleased with the day, left with bottles and jars of the olive oil Ugljan counted as its best currency, oil the golden colour of fresh honey and all manner of produce preserved in it: herbs, cheese, even flowers of sage and chive.

The island breathing its content, folk returning to their homesteads replete and entertained. Pfiffmaklers relaxing, happy at a job well done, settling down for the night.

Only two jobs yet to be done, Heraldo involved in both.

He'd intended to go see Grandmother Pfiffmakler when he'd first proposed it, but with Lupercal and Jericho being involved in The Balatronic Ballet, Heraldo had to be the lutist for the Kaspar Larriscarri sketch, Jericho having no time to switch between the two roles. Coming off stage red as the peppers bobbing in their Preko oil.

Second was what he and Ludmilla had talked about earlier: confronting Hulde directly with what had gone on in her village. Heraldo unsure which task should take precedence; Heraldo sitting on the same bluff of rock Valter Poppelmann had stood on earlier that morning. Heraldo looking over the calm waters trying to strategize. Not getting very far with it. Prevaricating, if he was truthful. Watching the ease with which the sea birds spent their time, the precision of the terns speeding from air into the water as if there was no difference between the two. Red-rumped swallows skimming across the sands, picking off emerging flies and sandhoppers. Crowds of waders on the shoreline running quickly back and forth with the lapping breakers. It seemed impossible that over on the mainland, not far from his line of sight, there lay a village with its single wide street lined with fig trees ending in a pile of bodies that must be reeking and rotting in the spring-time sun. His eyes ran down the wriggle of coast seeking out notable landmarks like sailors did: looking for church spires, lighthouses, conglomerations of notable rock formations, sea arches, windmills, watchtowers, castles…anything that stood out and marked a place as being itself and nowhere else. If he'd had a strong enough eyeglass he was certain he'd be able to find Hulde's village, that street of newly lime-washed cottages leading to the green.

'I've spoken to your father,' Heraldo jumping as Ludmilla called at him from down below.

'And?' he asked, getting to his feet, watching Hulde who seemed so happy and carefree running along the sand with the small spade Peppe had whittled for her the previous night. Hulde digging it quickly into the sand, like those waders with their beaks, turning up an empty cockleshell here, a broken-off leg of starfish there. Each find apparently fascinating her, before she moved on to new and greater discoveries.

'He thinks we should give it a try,' Ludmilla answered, Heraldo leaping down beside her.

'I'm not so sure,' he said, brushing the stone grit from his trousers. 'Just look at her.'

Nodding in Hulde's direction, Ludmilla not needing to be directed, eyes already latched onto Hulde's every move.

'Don't you think it's odd?' Heraldo went on. 'I mean, it's like she's never played before. As if everything's brand new.'

Ludmilla sucked her bottom lip before replying.

'I don't see what's odd about it. She can't be more than, what, six?'

'Exactly my point,' Heraldo went on slowly, thinking out his words, thinking back to Longhella's statement that Hulde never helped out about the camp. 'By the time we were six,' he went on, 'we'd done all this. It was ancient history. We were more concerned with how we were helping with the next performance, how our fathers made the puppets, orchestrated the scripts. How our mothers made the sugared almonds.'

Ludmilla let out a short laugh.

'Not everyone is lucky enough to be brought up a Pfiffmakler,' she said. 'And how are we supposed to know what other folk do or don't do with their children, especially in Hulde's kind of village? She might have been sickly, kept indoors for all we know.'

'She looks robust enough to me,' Heraldo commented, as indeed Hulde did. Hulde, having located a small drift of seaweed, holding it up about her head, dancing in clumsy imitation of one of the Balatronic Balleteers she'd enjoyed well enough, as far as anyone knew. No one noticing how at one point, a slow part, she'd leaned forward, fixed her eyes on something, maybe in the act, maybe beyond it in the audience, that had significance, if only to her.

'And she hasn't given any indication of being simple,' Heraldo was saying.

'Anything but,' Ludmilla agreed. 'So what do you think?'

She brought the chess set out.

'Shall we do it?'

Heraldo kicking up the sand with the toes of his boot.

'I think we have to try.'

9

Clowns and Donkeys

'Quite a show you lot put in on,' Andreas was saying to Wenzel. Wenzel puffing on his pipe, watching the women getting supper ready, Jericho and Lupercal off with the bird-nets to see what they could add to the evening's repast. They'd sampled many varieties over the years, most they didn't know the names of. Hoiking shearwaters out of their burrows at night, snatching shorebirds from their nests and taking the eggs. A great delicacy in some breeds, disgusting in others, lessons soon learned. A favourite amongst the Pfiffmaklers being fig-birds, small warblers eaten fresh, dressed without being drawn, sprinkled with salt, brushed over with oil, wrapped in vine leaves and grilled. They'd spied a flock descending on the olive groves and hoped they might taste good, if only Lupercal and Jericho could catch some.

'And have to thank you for the loan of your boys,' Andreas added, Wenzel blinking away his pipe smoke, waving his hand at the small group of gnats gathering about his head.

'S'alright,' Wenzel said. 'Always happy to help folk out.'

'Loved your Kaspar Larriscarri sketch,' Andreas went on. 'Think we might pinch some of it. Not while we're travelling with you of course,' he added quickly. Wenzel taking no offence. Common practice for theatre troupes to pick up ideas one from another as they crossed trails, adapted them to their own needs and particular expertise.

'Enjoyed your act too,' Wenzel replied, somewhat abstracted. Seeing the small black-clad, bent-backed form of his grandmother wandering away towards Preko. Wenzel running his tongue over his teeth, for she was a matter unresolved.

Not worried by her heading off on her own. She often did the same, taking her evening constitutional as she called it, usually heading for a chapel or church of some description to make obeisance to the God she so fervently believed in. Maybe how she'd kept herself alive for so long, with all that praying; mind as sharp as her tongue when most of her contemporaries were buried six foot under.

What worried him was the way she seemed determined to prise open the rift between them until one or other were sure to fall in. Heraldo had promised to be the diplomatic bridge between the two. A mission so far unfulfilled, Heraldo having other fish to fry. Wenzel wondering how it was going. Had seemed a reasonable idea when Ludmilla had run it past him but, like Heraldo, he too was having doubts. While Hulde was under his care he was duty bound to see her right, ensure her well-being until he could pass her on to her own people. Assuming the people they were taking her to really were her own. Wenzel troubled by the incident with the spade, not that he'd witnessed it directly, only from Peppe telling him about it afterwards.

'It was real strange,' Peppe had said. 'She just couldn't make head nor tail of it. I might not be the best whittler in the world but honest to God, no one could've mistaken it for anything other than what it was.'

And how could that be?

Peppe was being modest. Wenzel had never met anyone so competent at carving wood. Their puppet shows immensely augmented since he and Rosa had joined the clan, Peppe with his carving, Rosa with her painting skills. Their stock characters brought to life, from the hook-nosed Kaspar and his wife to the babes in the crib to the mayor/devil/hangman figures Kaspar always got the better of, exactly as their audience knew he would.

But a child who didn't understand what a spade was?

It seemed beyond belief. Even if they'd been a peripatetic people always on the move they'd quite obviously been settled in that village over the water from Ugljan, and so must have cleared fields, created pastures, sown crops. It was only now he was thinking on it that he realised he hadn't actually seen any fields or pastures, sown or otherwise. And there'd been no livestock. No chickens pecking up and down the street, no lowing cattle, goats or sheep who'd gone unfed or milked since what had undoubtedly been a massacre. There hadn't even been any skinny dogs panting in the heat or nosing about the heap of corpses for scraps. The entire village had been completely silent, except for the noise the Pfiffmaklers made as they trod down the street, their carts left at the farthest end, and the birds twittering in the fig trees, and Heraldo saying *What the hell happened here*?

It was entirely possible the victors had taken all useful livestock captive and away, but what about the dogs? Endemic in every village Wenzel had ever trundled through. Usually old dogs, no longer capable of minding flocks or giving whelp, turfed out of their former homes, replaced by their progeny, tolerated unless they stepped out of line, started killing chickens or biting children or raiding tables when backs were turned, when they were summarily dispatched.

But there'd been none of that.

Nothing but the flies buzzing, the birds chittering, the cicadas zithering out their tunes.

And there'd been grass growing up through the cobbles in the street. Another of many facts he was bringing to mind, like how the cottages, despite being newly whitewashed, had the demeanour of dereliction. Ill-fitting doors halfway open, as if they'd been that way for years; thistles growing either side of the jambs, roofs covered with sprawled, thinning thatch; the water pump at the top end of the village rusted, its catchment area uncleared or cleaned, covered over with goose grass and fat hen. Wenzel uncomfortable he'd not registered any of this before. Wenzel beginning to form a theory no one was going to like.

Down on the bay Ludmilla and Heraldo were readying their plan, Ludmilla looking up the strandline, following Hulde's small dips into the sand as the slim tide slowly came in and flooded her excavations behind her. Ludmilla calling out Hulde's name, Hulde ignoring her, too intent on her task or possibly because Hulde was merely the appellation she'd been so recently assigned. Heraldo and Ludmilla agreeing their first aim must be to find out her actual name, and go from there to the rest.

Heraldo approached Hulde and studiously began to take off his boots and socks. Ludmilla smiling, following suit, placing hers neatly beside Heraldo's on the sand.

'Teez-meh,' Ludmilla said.

'Chor-aah-pe,' Heraldo said.

'Çizme,' Hulde said as she turned, catching wind of another game, pointing at their boots.

'Çorape,' pointing at the socks.

'Good girl!' Ludmilla clapped gently, before pointing at herself. 'Ludmilla,' she pronounced her name slowly, then pointed to Heraldo. 'Heraldo,' she said. 'Ludmilla and Heraldo.'

Obviously they'd been through this pantomime in the weeks since Hulde had been with them, but it was only recently Hulde had begun to speak, so no harm repeating the exercise and it paid off.

'Loodmilla,' Hulde repeated, not quite right, but not wrong either. 'Heraaaldo,' pointing at each in turn. Hulde putting her spade into her smock pocket and going to Ludmilla, hugging her arms about Ludmilla's waist.

'Loodmilla,' she whispered, before disentangling herself and, with the utmost seriousness, going to Heraldo and repeating the gesture, Heraldo giving her a small hug.

'And you,' he asked, pointing at Hulde. 'Who are you? Ludmilla, Heraldo, and…?'

'Hulde!' Hulde said. 'Unë jam Hulde.'

'Oonyearm Hulde?' Heraldo asked with surprise, the girl laughing at the joke, looking at Heraldo with amusement.

'Jo, jo, i trashë! Unë jam Hulde, ju jeni Heraaaldo.'

'So, *oonyearm* Heraldo,' Heraldo persisted, 'and *yoo jaynay* Hulde?'

'Po, po!' Hulde agreed enthusiastically. 'Unë jam Hulde, dhe ju jeni Heraldo.'

'Dhe unë jam Ludmilla,' Ludmilla joined in, 'dhe ju jeni Hulde,' pointing at Hulde, 'dhe ju jeni Heraldo,' moving her finger to her cousin.

'Po?' Heraldo ventured.

'Paw!' Hulde agreed.

Heraldo taking Hulde for a paddle, as they'd previously agreed.

Ludmilla couldn't fathom why Hulde had stuck to Hulde, despite it not being her name except by enormous and unlikely coincidence. She supposed the girl must have absorbed it. Ludmilla had used it often enough when she'd tucked her in, told her stories. Everyone using it at one time or another, except Grandmother and Longhella.

Possibly Hulde had been shocked out of her memory by what had happened to her. Ludmilla recalling a Romanian acrobat who'd misfooted, tumbled from his high wire, smashed up his legs and scrambled his head so he could no longer retain anything new that happened to him. Fine when he was talking of what had gone on before the accident, fine when he met people he'd known previous to that day. Absolutely not remembering anything that went on afterwards. Very disconcerting to say hello to him in the morning as he pushed himself along on his wheeled cart, legs now useless, and hello to him again a couple of hours later when he'd look at Ludmilla like he'd never seen her before.

'Well hello, my fine young miss,' he'd say on both occasions. 'And aren't you just the pretty one?'

The exact same words, the exact same leer. No notion he'd ever met her before. A deep lagoon into which nothing penetrated. Nothing there but the surface reflections, everything glancing off, dissipating from him the moment it was gone from his sight.

Ludmilla taking up her stick, sketching a crude facsimile of the mainland as seen from the bay, going from where they'd found Hulde up to Zadar and this island. Took from the box three figurines to represent herself, Heraldo and Hulde, waving a hand at Heraldo who brought Hulde in.

Herald throwing himself down beside Ludmilla, almost wiping Zadar off the map.

Hulde doing the exact same beside him.

'Oopmh!' she exclaimed, as Heraldo had done. Heraldo pretending surprise.

'What's all this?' he asked innocently.

'This is Ludmilla, Heraldo and Hulde,' Ludmilla explained, Hulde looking interested, blinking away the scratch of salt from her eyes. 'This is the island,' Ludmilla pointed with her stick, 'and the sea, and here's the boat we came over in, and the coast we travelled up.'

'Should we really do this?' Heraldo asked.

Ludmilla shrugged.

'I think we've got to try. I doubt she'll understand it anyway.'

'Well, not like you've drawn it,' Heraldo remonstrated, swiftly sweeping away the most part of her map and taking the stick from her. 'Honestly, Ludmilla, you're about as bad at drawing as you are good at everything else.'

Ludmilla annoyed he'd dismissed her careful handiwork, but having to admit his own quick rendition was magnitudes better. Watching his deft fingers conjuring up the scene with great accuracy: building Zadar out of a few straight lines and well-placed pebbles, marking the sea-line with some strands of weed, wiggling the stick over the surface of the sand to indicate water, drawing the path they'd taken. Marking Hulde's village with a few more pebbles down the side of the street, including a few lollipop outlines of trees. Stopping short of the pile of bodies at the farthest end.

'Ludmilla, Heraldo and Hulde,' he said, once finished, Hulde nodding her assent.

'And from across the sea we came,' Ludmilla joined in, as if she was telling one of her night-time stories. Heraldo helping out by swiftly grabbing a small piece of driftwood, placing the three chess pieces on it, moving it back towards Zadar.

'And from Zadar down the coast,' Heraldo continued, picking the figures up, mimicking them walking back down the track, falling silent, letting Ludmilla carry on.

'To where we found Hulde,' Ludmilla said, pausing. Watching Hulde. Waiting for a sign of understanding. Nothing. 'To Hulde's home,' Ludmilla prompted. 'So where is Gomar Nikolla?'

Heraldo completing the journey, bringing Valter's three painted pieces—clown, king and bishop, and absolutely no soldiers—to a halt in Hulde's village. Heraldo picking one up, dotting it in the sand as if it were walking up to one front door of each representative pebble house and then the next before leaving it alone in the street, taking a breath, keeping it in, hoping they'd not gone too far.

Hulde frowned.

'Gaztor?' she asked, obviously puzzled.

'Gaztor,' Heraldo agreed, saying the word as Hulde had, stress on the second part of the word.

'And Gomar Nikolla,' Ludmilla put in. 'Where are Hulde and Gomar Nikolla?'

'I think we've confused her,' Heraldo said. Ludmilla holding up a warning hand as Hulde slowly took out her spade, used its edge to draw her own additions to the picture. Large inverted Vs going up behind the village.

'Mountains?' Heraldo asked, looking at Ludmilla.

'Male,' said Hulde. 'Male shkon.'

'Maal-lay shkon?'

Heraldo beginning to habituate to the timbre of Hulde's language, how she emphasised the first or second syllables of her words so her voice went from loud to soft, from top to bottom. To him like hearing a musical instrument for the first time when he'd strummed it's restrung strings, or reconstructed its inner workings and took a guess at how it had been operated when originally played.

He picked up the clown, the figure Ludmilla had chosen to represent Hulde, toted it up and down the village, along the street and then up into the mountains, or what he assumed were mountains, as drawn by Hulde.

'Maal-lay shkon?' he asked. 'Gaztor Hulde?' he went on, pleased with how he thought he'd got the basics right, horrified when Hulde unexpectedly slapped his hand away and snatched the figurine from his fingers.

'Nuk Hulde,' she remonstrated, jamming the figure of the clown into the sand, her spade burying the chess piece without remorse. Heraldo putting his hands on hers after a few moments digging.

'So where is Hulde?' he asked softly. 'Where is Gomar Nikolla?'

Hulde looking up at him, eyes brimming with tears.

'I think we might've got this all wrong,' Ludmilla whispered. Heraldo trying one more time.

'Where did Hulde come from?' he asked gently, pointing with his stick not at the village but to her upturned Vs of mountains. 'Did Hulde come from here? With Gomar Nikolla?'

Hulde hesitant, Ludmilla having an idea, laying down the chess set, opening it up, picking out a figure, the most innocuous she

82

could find, one that looked like Pulcinella from the Commedia dell'Arte sketches. Hulde studying it, nodding with apparent satisfaction, taking it from Ludmilla's fingers.

'Hulde,' she announced, putting it right to the back of the mountains and walking it through them, up and down, in and around, until she reached the village when she exclaimed:

Said, *'Bam bam bam, bam bam bam, BAM BAM BAM!'* suddenly dropping Pulcinella and holding her hands over her ears, rocking back and forth, closing her eyes, whispering *bam bam bam* over and over, until Ludmilla knee-shuffled through the entire scene and put an arm about Hulde's shoulders.

'It's all right,' she spoke gently. 'It's alright, *jor pe-sair-re,'* using the phrase Valter had spoken over in Zadar. 'Not again, my dear. Never again.'

Looking over at Heraldo, who was disinterring the figure Hulde had buried, brought it out, brushed it off and slipped it into his pocket.

'I think we need to speak to Papa,' he said, Ludmilla nodding, looking back along the bay at the sanderlings and redshanks darting along the line of the sea as it crept its few tide-inches up the bay, a hint of white as it broke silently over the sand. Thinking of the Cordellinas and the Albanian enclaves with whom they lived cheek by jowl, like guillemots nest with gannets on differing sides of the same rock. Ludmilla feeling the hard pebbles of Heraldo's sketch digging into her knees, be it from Zadar or the village they'd presumed to be Hulde's own. A presumption now challenged.

She'd never been certain what they might discover when they got back to her mother's home where a common language might unlock Hulde's tongue, if she chose to have it unlocked. It occurring to Ludmilla, as she watched those stranger-sanderlings and redshanks, it might be better for them all, particularly for Hulde, if that unlocking was never done.

10

The Commonalities of History and Kippers

'So what's all this hedgehoggery merchandise you're apparently the sole world purveyor of?' Wenzel asked Andreas. Wenzel not really interested but feeling the need to say something to fill the gap, eyes glancing anxiously towards the bay from where he could see his son, Ludmilla and Hulde wending their way back to camp.

'Glad you asked!' Andreas full of it, always eager to tout his patter. 'Got skins stretched over wooden handles to card wool or use as curry combs; got single spines to take ink for those most intricate patterns the miniaturists are so fond of scribbling. Got any number of *Stachelkugeln* the Austrians and Hungarians like putting in their graves. Hold on, got one here,' he said, opening up his satchel, producing a spiked ball of red-painted wood. 'Hedgehogs the sign of hibernation and rebirth,' he pattered on. '*Igelkalb*, the locals call them there, hedgehog's calf, though don't know why.'

'Well actually,' Wenzel started, about to explain how the *Igelkalb* resembled a cow's uterus when it had just calved, cut off immediately by Zilboorg's next prop.

'And what have we here?' he asked, clumsy fingers holding up a vial of what looked to be full of cinders, quick with his own answer. 'An ancient Romany treatment used for all sorts. Burned hedgehog bristles. Very efficacious in the treatment of lung problems if thrown on a fire and the smoke breathed in; good for piles with direct application, and sprinkle it on an open wound and hey presto!' Andreas drew his hand through the air in an impressive arc. 'Heals like magic!'

Wenzel nodded, for he supposed that last could be so, ashes frequently used to dry cuts and abrasions, absorb pus and blood.

Though why burned hedgehogs might work better than anything else he chose not to pursue, not that Andreas gave him leave to.

'Believe it, my fine sir!' forgetting he was talking to an old Fairs' hand and not some gullible member of the public. 'Ancient Greeks have the hedgehog as the familiar of Artemis the huntress, so stands to reason it'll be the best animal to treat wounds.'

It didn't stand to Wenzel's reason, not that he bothered to argue, Heraldo a few hundred yards distant, and it didn't take an ancient Greek god to see that all might not be well.

'And then there's our hedgehog rattles!'

Wenzel sighed. This Zilboorg fellow was unstoppable.

'The Egyptians loved them!' Zilboorg went on. 'And everyone who is anyone knows how everything Egyptian is quite the fashion.'

Wenzel blinked away his irritation. Zilboorg having the right of it there. Egyptomania never waning since Napoleon invaded that country and plundered it for all it was worth, pedlars quick to take advantage, hawking mummified fingers, scarabs, amulets, and any number of other grave goods made from paste and cheap glass and about as far away from Egypt as you could get.

'But our greatest secret,' Andreas Zilboorg lowered his tone, as if there were spies behind every tree, 'is also our greatest seller.'

Another quick look about him, Wenzel puffing placidly on his pipe. Well acquainted with the hundreds of other vendors of hundreds of other animals and their afterlife parts.

'It's hedgehog oil,' Zilboorg whispered dramatically, producing a small ceramic pot in the shape of a rolled-up hedgehog that held the precious drops. 'Cures baldness, deafness and a vast number of other ailments,' Zilboorg made his pitch. Wenzel not listening. The mention of Egypt jogging out a memory. Long, long time since he'd thought of it, suddenly finding it relevant. Wenzel a mere nipper when a zebra had been brought over from Africa to Europe, off-loaded from one ship, stuck in a pen waiting to be manhandled onto another, bound for the English courts. And what a beast it had been! Its strangeness astounding. As peculiar to him as the hedgehog was familiar. He'd pushed himself into the crowds to study it up close, marvelling at the soft sheen of its pelt, its stripes, the black-and-white of it, how it had come to be that way. And the shine in the animal's eyes, the utter bewilderment, the obvious belligerence that hadn't been quelled by its capture one whit. About to hold out his hand, get a feel of its strange fur, when someone beat him to it. The man howling as his hand was bitten right down to the knucklebones, the zebra drawing back its lips, shaking that man's hand between its teeth until they were stained red. The zebra releasing its captive, sticking out its tongue, let fly a yipping kind of bray that out-muled a mule. Wenzel hearing a mad kind of laughter as it brayed and brayed within its confines and butted its head against the wooden fence, discouraging anyone else from going near.

You can take me from the veldt, it seemed to Wenzel to be saying, *but you will never ever tame me.*

And quite right too, had been his thinking then as now.

'Hedgehog oil,' Zilboorg was prompting, but Wenzel had had enough. An idea occurring why that particular memory had surfaced as Heraldo approached with Hulde by his side.

You can take the animal from the veldt, and you can take the girl from the village...

'Excuse me,' Wenzel said, standing abruptly, stopping short of saying he'd had quite enough of hedgehoggery in general and of Andreas Zilboorg in particular. 'Family business to attend to.'

Andreas holding up his hands, packing away his wares, getting to his feet.

'Don't mind me,' he replied, flinging his satchel over his shoulder. 'Guess you've a lot to deal with on that front,' he added with feigned nonchalance. 'Not that it's any of my business.'

Wenzel removing his pipe, about to retort that no, it bloody wasn't. Zilboorg swiftly away, leaving Wenzel vexed and angered that a comparative stranger should be so apprised of the Pfiffmakler troubles and how he might use it to his advantage.

For a man like Zilboorg would surely take advantage the moment he saw his chance.

'Can we speak, father?' Heraldo asked, had been slowing his steps until he'd seen Andreas leaving, Heraldo sending Ludmilla and Hulde off towards where the women were readying themselves for their last night on the island.

Wenzel's pipe had gone out during his tortuous conversation with Zilboorg, and he took his time getting it lit again, settling his haunches back upon the log thrown out of the sea in some long ago storm, motioning Heraldo to sit with him.

'I'm guessing this is about Hulde,' he said, puffing out thin plumes of grey-blue smoke now his pipe was back in action. 'Your little scenario not going quite as planned?'

Heraldo smiling grimly, shaking his head.

'Not exactly,' Heraldo admitted. 'You don't look too surprised.'

Wenzel removed his pipe, turned to face his son.

'You've always been a lad keen to get to the bottom of things,' he commented. 'Always quick to see the good, and nothing wrong in that. But I think with Hulde we might have been looking through the glass backwards.'

Heraldo blinked under his father's perspicacious gaze, cleared his throat.

'I agree,' he said. 'It seems, from what she's been trying to tell us, that the village we found her in wasn't exactly her own. That maybe they were only newly there, or maybe not there at all, not exactly.'

'Which means,' Wenzel went on for his son, switching his gaze, fixing his eyes on the bay and the conurbation of Zadar across the waters, 'we can't be certain if her folk were the victims of that terrible attack, or the perpetrators.'

Heraldo jiggled his knees.

'She seemed to be saying her folk came from the mountains. I don't think she'd any notion of that village at all...except for this.'

Taking out Valter's figurine from his pocket, laying it on the bole beside his father. 'She tried to bury it, and not just a bit but a lot.'

Unconsciously repeating Ludmilla's phrase about the thunder.

Wenzel picked the figure up, studied it.

'What's it supposed to be?' he asked, Heraldo explaining about Valter Poppelmann's chess sets, how Valter made them as trinkets to sell after their Balatronic Ballet shows, how the figures were carved and painted after the various stock characters seen in the plays the travelling theatres used.

'She absolutely rejected this one,' Heraldo added. 'Preferred a Pulcinella as her representative.'

'Well, that's natural,' Wenzel not put out. 'Young girl. Hardly going to see herself as whatever this is. Which is what?'

'A clown,' Heraldo said. 'Or might be just a man to her. But honestly, the viciousness with which she buried the thing had to be seen to believed.'

Wenzel puffed on his pipe.

'I just don't get it,' Heraldo said. 'And I've been thinking about it a lot. I mean obviously there's no doubt she was there, but there was something strange about that village...'

'Like how it was all broken down?' Wenzel prompted. Heraldo casting his mind back, seeing the place where they'd shrugged off their harnesses before heading down the street. Heraldo nodding.

'I couldn't put my finger on it before,' he said, 'but it was the pump...it was all grassed over. And now that I'm thinking on it...'

Heraldo paused, thinking on it.

'Those houses were on the verge of collapse,' his father said for him. 'And all that stuff we found in them?'

'Naught but removables,' Heraldo getting it at last, what had been bothering him about the place ever since they'd got there. 'Plates, cups and kettles. Nothing permanent. No saucepans hanging from the walls, no family bibles or books, no clothes lying about, no bunches of herbs, no bottles of pickles, no stooks of hay...'

'And no livestock,' Wenzel concluded the matter. 'Not even skinny-arsed dogs or threadbare moggies.'

'Nothing,' Heraldo murmured, 'but what folk like us might've brought with them for a casual stay.'

'Except they'd lime-washed the walls,' Wenzel reminded him. 'Which kinda says they might've wanted to stop on longer than they was allowed to.'

Heraldo taking a deep breath, recalling that heap of bodies and how bad they'd smelled, and yet how long had been the grass on the green where they'd been piled. How it had obviously not been scythed or tended for months, maybe years, allowed to sprout itself up with ragwort and all manner of weeds no true villager would tolerate. The ragwort in particular, being poisonous to all manner of stock.

'So whoever was trying to settle there hadn't been there long,' Heraldo got out, his father nodding his assent.

'So question is,' Wenzel put the point again, 'whether Hulde's people were trying to settle in the village, or another lot who objected to such settlement and chose to wipe them out before skedaddling.'

'Excepting Hulde,' Heraldo pointed out.

'Excepting Hulde,' Wenzel agreed. 'Another puzzle. Could have been on either side for all we know, caught in the crossfire and left for dead. Could have been a willing participant in the massacre. Girl might not know a spade when she sees it, but old enough to've been taught one end of a gun from the other, especially if she'd been sojourning in the mountains for any length of time.'

Heraldo bit his lip, not liking this possibility. The dead villagers left unburied due to callousness, expedience, or the simple lack of tools with which to break the ground.

'I just can't see it,' was all he could conjure in Hulde's folks defence.

Wenzel puffing at his pipe again.

'Like I said, son. Always seeing the good. But we're in a world where there's bad around every corner, boiling up at every turn. Politics,' he added, rubbing a finger hard against his eye, 'brings out the worst in people, especially when you chuck religion into the mix.'

Thinking on Grandmother.

Heraldo saying nothing, fixing his gaze on a violet carpenter bee emerging from its burrow in the dead tree-bole, shimmering out blue wings in the warm evening sun after a long winter's hibernation. It wasn't a bumbler, not particularly furry, looking more like a monstrous fly half the length of his little finger.

'Situation brings to mind stories your mama told me of her school learning,' Wenzel went on for them both, the smoke from his pipe making the violet bee twitch, flicker its antennae, shake its bright wings and take off. 'Near her part of Italy are lots of Albanians, brought in by their great hero Kastrioti who'd been fighting the Ottomans for a quarter century before teaming up with the Court in Naples.'

Heraldo watched the bee fly off towards the olive groves.

'Never heard of him,' he murmured, fascinated by the bee, by the beauty the world offered him every day, Heraldo seeing it anew with every dawn, every sunset, every shift of the seasons. Never one for school learning, which was mud and mire to him as his father well knew.

'No reason you should,' Wenzel replied mildly. 'But as your mama told it, he's the measuring stick for Albanians, at least those in Italy. Old Orthodox choosing exile over persecution at the hands of other types of Christians, the Turks going at them both. A fighting people of necessity. And that stuff don't neither lie nor sleep, goes on and on down every generation.'

Heraldo let out a despairing breath. All too complicated for him. He couldn't understand any of it. Couldn't understand why folk didn't just get on with their own lives in their own way and let others do the same. Insects and animals did it all the time. Always in conflict, always a battle about who ate who, what and where. No animus behind any of it. No belief systems at stake. No strategies of genocidal murder. All ultimately in harmony and balance. Thoughts flitting back to Hulde, to that emptied village, the stench that threatened to make him heave up his guts at the memory.

'Can put a zebra in a field of mules,' Wenzel commented, thinking out loud about how close knit were the Italian Albanians of the Cordellina strongholds. Friendly enough, though always sticking to their own. 'But that don't make the zebra a mule, no matter how long it lives in the same field.'

Heraldo not understanding, nevertheless reaching a similar conclusion by a different route. How some things, some people, just didn't mix. Recalling how he'd the runs one time, loosened his bowels behind a barn, only to see a dog come up a minute later eagerly lapping up his excreta, making Heraldo retch until his throat was raw, retching again every time he'd thought on it. Not that he'd wanted to, but it came just the same: an atavistic horror that had to be some kind of primitive survival mechanism.

Like a hedgehog rolling itself up into a ball at the first sign of danger.

There's badness about every corner, his father had said, but Heraldo couldn't figure what could possibly have been so bad that one lot of people had murdered another lot and left them like that pile of shite to be lapped at and pulled apart by crows and buzzards, foxes, rats and wolves.

'We should've buried them,' he murmured.

'I know, lad,' Wenzel replied after a few moments. 'Except we don't carry a load of spades and pickaxes with us any more than I suspect that lot did.'

Heraldo taking this in, seeing the right of it.

'Could've burned them,' he suggested. 'Given them some kind of end.'

Wenzel dottling his pipe, putting it out, stowing it in his jacket pocket.

'Which might've burned Hulde too, if she'd not got out,' the new leader of the Pfiffmaklers always a pragmatic man, 'even if we'd had the means to do it.'

'We should at least have told someone about it in Zadar,' Heraldo argued. 'Got them to go check it out.'

Wenzel putting an arm about his son's shoulders.

'What's done is done,' Wenzel tried to comfort. 'No one would've listened, not to travelling folk. And even if they did, they'd not've given a fig about what was happening over their borders, certainly not enough to ride off for days and days to find out.'

Heraldo supposed this was true. Couldn't shake his concern.

'What if we never find out?' he asked. 'I mean what really happened?'

Wenzel giving Heraldo's shoulder a quick squeeze before releasing him.

'World's a hard place,' Wenzel said. 'We pass here, we pass there, and ain't never going to understand what goes on everywhere. Might find out when we get Hulde back to her folk.'

'If they are her folk,' Heraldo unmollified. 'What if they're not?'

Wenzel sighed, stood up, nose catching the scents of stew in the making. Sage and basil in the mix, if he wasn't mistaken.

'Can't fix the world by wishing it,' he said. 'Just got to keep on ploughing on, hope we're lucky enough to stumble across the answers we're needing.'

Heraldo too getting to his feet, seeing the great roll of sky in the west turning from pale blue to vermillion to gold, layered plates of lenticular clouds rising from distant mountains, maybe Hulde's mountains, and had to be content with that.

'What were you saying earlier about zebras?' he asked, as the two headed for the main camp, the fire brighter than all the glow worms blinking up about their feet. Heraldo energised by the rhythm of life going on about them oblivious to their concerns. Wenzel recognising this easy change in his boy, a lad since early doors who could be moved from glum to gladness by the merest shift of a scratch of light across the sky or a burnet moth setting up from a thistle, a red anemone opening and closing in a rock pool as the tide came in.

'Weren't nothing, lad,' he said, cheered to have a happy Heraldo by his side, not wanting to darken the mood. 'Just meant that history's got a way of repeating itself, and nothing you nor I can do about it.'

'Like Lupercal and kippers,' Heraldo smiled broadly, his father joining in the joke.

'Exactly. Couldn't stop burping them up for two days straight.'

Heraldo laughing. Lupercal never eating kippers since.

A pity, Wenzel thought, history hadn't learned to do the same.

11

Quackery and Miracles, Side by Side

Wenzel got his troupe to Preko quay in good time, saw the trade ship rounding Ugljan in full sail, heading first to Zadar where stevedores were quick to offload the merchandise come over from

Italy. Bolts of cloth, metalwork, potash, soap, all piled up ready to be whisked off to market where they'd be swiftly bartered, bought and dispersed to the four corners of the town and beyond. Merchandise replaced by everything Zadar and its hinterland had to offer the other side of the Adriatic shores, loaded after were any passengers from Zadar and the islands, the Kunterbunt included. And there were a lot of passengers, crowded in side by side, elbows on the deck rails, chattering like a load of starlings settling on a favourite bush, eager and excited with their day.

Under way within the hour, ship's sails billowing and bellying as they caught the wind from the south, prow cutting quick and precise through gentle waves. A three-masted xebec, carrying four hundred passengers along with its cargo, skimming through smooth waters, the distance between Zadar and Ravenna to be covered within fifteen hours if the winds were favourable. Wenzel heart-jolted by the glory of the afternoon, the physical act of travelling bringing with it the implicit knowledge that tomorrow they'd be somewhere new, with new heart-jolting joys to be discovered.

Wenzel's peace and wonder shattered as someone nearby shouted out, loud and unmistakeably angry.

'Zilboorg!'

Wenzel shifting his attention to its source. None other than the captain, a broad-faced man with features as weathered and worn as the wood of his ship, the colour high in his cheeks as he marched swiftly by Wenzel and zeroed in on his quarry.

'Andreas Zilboorg!'

Zilboorg popping up from behind Wenzel's cart and attempting escape, but too slow, the captain grabbing at Zilboorg's collar, hauling him over the deck. Zilboorg's Adam's apple bobbing as he gasped for air, the captain unremorseful, unremitting, pulling Zilboorg up and shoving him against the guard rail and halfway over. Andreas teetering on his back between ship and sea, sweating as if the day was highest summer.

'You snivelling little thief!' the captain accused. 'Any reason I shouldn't just chuck you over?'

Several of his crew appearing at his side ready to do just that, bolted down and angry to their core.

Wenzel could have ignored it, could have let them throw Andreas Zilboorg overboard. Lord knew the man was as irritating as a pebble in a shoe and most probably deserved everything that was coming to him, but for the time being Zilboorg was ostensibly part of the Kunterbunt and therefore under his care. Sighed, stood up, intervened.

'Excuse me, captain,' Wenzel said, moving towards the miscreant and his all too willing executioners. 'Before you bung him in, can I ask what has been his crime?'

The captain narrowed his eyes, increased his pressure on Zilboorg's collar so Zilboorg couldn't get out a word, a whistling sort of objection coming from his mouth as his eyes bulged, flicking his gaze imploringly towards Wenzel who had been joined by several other members of the Kunterbunt along with a sizeable crowd of spectators.

'He cheated me and my crew with his hedgehoggery nonsense when we were holed up in Zadar two winters back,' the captain spat. 'Sold us his precious Oil of Iritch on the promise of it healing…'

He stopped short, suddenly aware of all the people gathering about them and was absolutely not going to admit to what Zilboorg's oil had been promised to heal, namely an outbreak of the sailors' curse. Or the clap, to give it its most common name. Common side-effect of being confined to port by bad weather.

'Suffice to say it made it worse, not better,' the captain amended, eyeing Wenzel, seeing in him a man of authority steady in his boots. A foreigner to these parts and perhaps not a man to stand for attempted murder without redress. Wenzel noted the hesitation and nodded calmly.

'Can see how that would rile a few a tempers,' he said, suspecting the captain wanted nothing more than to chuck Zilboorg in and fetch him out again after a few minutes of struggling and spluttering, hoping he'd learned his lesson. The sea calm enough, and plenty people on board to throw out a rope, but no guarantee of survival. Zilboorg might get trapped beneath the ship, or sink like a stone, air expelled from his lungs by the shock of hitting the water, or heart simply stopped by the fear of flight and fall, believing he was about to die. Wenzel having a small stab of pity for Zilboorg, as annoying as the man might be, for he was merely eking out a living on the edges, trying to make a way through life as were they all.

'Can I suggest an alternative?' Wenzel therefore asked, the captain loosening Zilboorg enough for Zilboorg to land his feet on deck. 'I happen to know,' Wenzel went on smoothly, 'that this Zilboorg fellow is as feared of heights as a mouse is of an owl. Might be more fitting to force him up a mast for the remainder of the journey. Get him out of all our hair.'

There was a collective and audible intake of breath as the crowd moved their heads forward an inch or two to see what would happen, the captain aware of the scrutiny, narrowing his eyes as he studied Wenzel. If he was a friend of Zilboorg's it certainly wasn't apparent, and he rather liked this plan, especially when Zilboorg got in enough air to squeeze it out again in a horrified extended *No!* that caught everyone's attention. Zilboorg smartly brought up to standing by the captain.

'Very well,' he announced. 'Up the mast it is. Men!'

His crew came forward and grabbed at Zilboorg's arms, Zilboorg fighting against them at every step, looking terrified as they dragged him to the main mast. Zilboorg's hands trembling as he laid them to the wood, missing his footing several times as the men shoved him on.

'It's up or in,' they growled and, for a moment, Zilboorg wavered, appeared to consider the option, then slowly began to climb. Several times he slipped, an arm or foot flailing wildly. The men and women down below oohing and aahing, judiciously stepping out of the way in case he fell, which seemed entirely plausible. Wenzel returned to his barrow and got out his pipe, allowing a small twitch of a smile beneath his beard.

Been around ships since I was knee-high to a grasshopper, Zilboorg had told him.

Wenzel looking up in alarm when the crowd suddenly shouted, women holding hands over their mouths as they all watched Zilboorg clinging by his fingertips to a rigging line, body flailing, looking like he really might drop at any moment. A heat coming up in Wenzel's face to realise he might have been utterly mistaken, that Zilboorg had merely been spinning tales to get him on side, that Zilboorg might really die up there, or rather down on the decking when he fell and hit, his heart proper thumping as Zilboorg finally caught his legs about the mast and got himself into a sitting position fifteen feet up, buttocks resting on a rope, arms clutched grimly about the wood. Precarious, but safe for the moment. Wenzel breathing a sigh of relief with all the rest.

'What the hell is Uncle Andreas doing up there?' Valter Poppelmann asked, materialising at Wenzel's elbow. Wenzel almost dropping his pipe in surprise, fingers nervously scratching through his beard.

'You must've missed the stramash,' Wenzel got out, blood pulsing in his throat. 'Captain was about to feed him to the fishes for some mis-selling a while back in Zadar. Thought this might be a better option.'

Valter laughing softly at his side.

'Well, you got that right, mister. Best performance he's given for years.'

Wenzel calming.

'Done it before then?' he asked. 'Going up, I mean?'

'Oh Crikey, yes,' Valter replied. 'Used to do quite the turn back in the day. Force a bet on someone, ending with uncle going up the rigging, almost dying…big pots of money when he came down again. Still,' Valter shrugged his shoulders, 'surprised he's got the agility for it these days. Can't hardly bend his fingers more'n he needs to get 'em about a spoon. Arthritis,' he added. 'Uncle's been bad with it a while.'

Wenzel looking back up the mast towards Andreas, wondering if his fear hadn't been real, if he might have preferred a ducking to such a painful climb. Recalling how clumsy had been Andreas's production of his products, how red and inflamed the joints of his fingers as he brought out the curry comb, the rattles; how hard for him to pick up one of those slim hedgehog quills for Wenzel's inspection. And how hard it was going to be for Valter, if such an affliction ran in the family, when his hands could no longer carve the little figurines for his chess sets, whittle or paint them with any accuracy. Quick vision of a man who'd had such extensive warts on his hands they appeared like the branches of a gnarled old tree, so cumbersome and heavy he needed help with the smallest of tasks.

And now here was Andreas Zilboorg, a man he'd disliked and dismissed, wanting to hang onto their coat tails and wring every last penny from anyone he came into contact with, the captain of this ship and his crew included. And yet why wouldn't he? How else was he supposed to get by?

He looked up towards Andreas in the rigging clinging on for dear life. The crowds had moved on now there was no apparent drama, no imminent threat that a man might spectacularly fall and die.

Andreas Zilboorg of no more worth.

Andreas forgotten.

All chattering about other things, about the latest news, the reason they were heading over to Ravenna which was the acceptance there of the relics of a newly canonised saint: an Italian, and a man a few of the oldest had known as a wandering preacher when they were young.

Andreas Zilboorg clinging to the rigging with his arthritic fingers passing from their minds as swift as a cloud blown across the sky by the wind.

Wenzel found it intolerable, called to Lupercal and Jericho.

'Get yourselves up there. Take him a bit of food and drink.'

His younger sons donning a couple of satchels loaded with tea, bread and cheese, scampering up to Andreas Zilboorg who, now that Wenzel was seeing the situation with new eyes, was looking distinctly uncomfortable, his grip upon the rigging not so fast as he'd previously assumed.

Odd how a mind-set can change in a second.

Tolerance Wenzel's new watchword. To find out all you could before you judge.

And back came Hulde to his mind, Zilboorg's situation honing his decision.

Time to confront the girl directly while they were on board ship and she had nowhere else to go, find out exactly how much she did or didn't know about spades and, possibly, guns. He'd allowed Heraldo and Ludmilla a run at it and they'd got somewhere, but not far enough. Language the main problem. Since on board Wenzel seeing see a solution, as many tongues uttered on board as there were people, and surely one of them had to have a minimal grasp of Albanian.

Grandmother Pfiffmakler viewed the Zilboorg commotion with a rare dollop of sceptical amusement, grudgingly admitting that Wenzel had handled the situation with admirable aplomb. Not that it would do to tell the upstart. She'd been thoroughly ousted from the limelight as far as the Kunterbunt was concerned, and was still spitting feathers—hell, could spit out a whole goose she was so angry. On the other hand, it had been kind of peaceful since the ousting: no decisions to make about how, where and when to go; no fittling about choosing one set piece over another, no head scratching as to how to make it fit to new circumstance, no head bashing of the younger members to keep them in line. Her old heart still a black knot of resentment against her grandson and the rest of the family for taking his side, but by God she couldn't quell the giddy giggling that grew up like a weed in her throat at the release. She'd been the *force majeure* behind her son Matthys all the years he'd been nominally in charge. Always a ditherer that boy, never mind he'd been in his early fifties when he'd bowed out, tired by all the tramping, preferring to grow oranges instead. And, stick in the craw as it might, perhaps he'd been right to do so.

Her perambulations over Ugljan had slotted certain parts of her life into order, starting when she'd seen a pair of magpies in their great black ball of a nest in the olive groves. Maybe primed to look for them by the Stribor play, the usual raucous chak chak chakking of their call subdued into a soft chuntering of courtship almost melodious. Back home in the Voralberg mountains some folk kept them in cages where they'd articulate rhymes just as softly, as if they were trying to speak, as if they were a different kind of bird entirely. Thoughts of home and childhood bolting through her like a kingfisher down a river at dusk: a bright startlement that's gone almost before you've noticed it, so unmistakeably blue and joyous you can't wait to see it again.

Same startlement in her when she heard mention of the name Alphonsus Liguori in that tiny Preko chapel: *her* Alphonsus Liguori. He'd been nearing ninety back then in 1786, and would be dead the following year; she just shy of twenty, her guts gnawed with recrimination to realise she'd married the wrong brother. Travelling down the heel of Italy, the Kunterbunt their own devisement and still finding its feet, her husband splitting off from the family fair following his refusal to take second string when his father kicked the bucket.

'You buggering well know I'm the best one for the job! Just because you're thirteen minutes older you think you deserve it? Think leadership yours by right?'

Old despisements and humiliations flooding inexorably over her, face flushed, skin prickling with sweat at how desperate she'd been back then. How hateful her life had become. Had dallied briefly with the idea of joining the Nuns of the Redemptorists she'd heard about in those parts. Was on the verge of absconding any way she could. Redemptorists or home, heading back to Voralbergs, joining another troupe on her way there, put her horse-riding skills to use. Could pull quite the acrobatic turn back then.

No wife of mine will shake her skirts about a bit of horse-flesh like a common whore.

No matter her prowess had been the first attraction. So vile that man.

You're like a quince that flowers but doesn't fruit.

I might as well have married a stick for all the use you are.

Even the ugliest pig can farrow, so why can't you?

Childless several years into their marriage. Both regretting the match. The glee he'd exhibited at stealing her from his brother blown away the moment he'd won his prize. No love there. Never had been, never would.

Strange opportunity arising when she'd learned the founder of the Redemptorists was still alive, eking out his years in Nocera at the foot of Monte Albino, a stone's throw from their camp, and she'd snuck away to see him. And oh, the knowledge that man had, the grace, the humility, the forgiveness. Him making time for her, blessing her, listening to her story, giving his advice.

'Let me tell you,' he'd said, 'what Moses told Korah: *Come the morrow the Lord will show who is his, and who is holy.* And this is what you must do, little sister. Be patient, have faith, never fear. For the Lord will know his own.'

Not at all what she'd wanted to hear, but he'd switched something on inside her head that never left, made her stick to the path she'd been given, bowing down to her husband's yoke. Being patient, having faith, pushing away the fear.

And the morrow had actually come: Matthys, like a miracle, born the following year.

Her one and only child.

Next her husband expiring from catastrophic blood poisoning after accidentally stabbing himself through the foot with a tent pole, leaving her in sole charge of the Kunterbunt and the macaronic crew making up their wandering few.

Miracles attributed to Alphonsus, her direct conduit to God. Her act of faith finally paying off, and about time too.

And now she had the proof, for Alphonsus, her Alphonsus, had just last week been canonised in Rome, admitted to the sainthood, being brought to Ravenna for his final resting place. God granting her the grace to learn of it when she was in precisely the right place, at precisely the right time. Which left her in a quandary about Hulde, who had inadvertently caused her to be in the right place at the right time; for if they'd not found Hulde they'd have carried on into Montenegro as planned and Grandmother Pfiffmakler might never have heard the astounding news about Alphonsus, let alone be witness to it. Might have died without receiving the vindication of his grace to her which had formed the framework of her faith throughout the rest of her life.

And Lord, how she was going to crow about that every chance she got! How God had favoured her, how she'd met a saint-in-the-making and been the recipient of not one miracle but two. Thought forming in her mind that when they got to Italy she would take the decision she'd abnegated fifty years previously and leave the lot of them to their own devices, renounce the entire family and join Liguori's Redemptorists.

Stick that in Wenzel's pipe and see how he smoked it, hoping it would choke him from the inside out. Forgiveness never a part of her religion, which had been the root of her grudge against Hulde in the first place. Nocera an Islamist hotspot, mosques growing up beside churches like noxious weeds. A besmirchment, she'd thought then, an affront to the Holy Redeemer. It not occurring to her it might have been the very reason Alphonsus had chosen Nocera to live out his days, spread his quiet message, scribe his many advocations of the need for the Church to reform, re-educate itself, become an instigator of social justice, of tolerance, giving help to those most in need no matter their religious affiliations.

Become an exemplar, like Christ Himself.

Grandmother Pfiffmakler ignorant of Liguori's teachings. He might still be the benchmark for theological moralism fifty years after he'd died, but outside Italy his writings were rarely read. And certainly not by Grandmother Pfiffmakler, who'd better things to do once she had the God-given gifts of Matthys and the Kunterbunt to take charge of.

She grimaced as she came out of the past and back to the present, having just spied the small form of Hulde at the base of the mast up which the snake Andreas Zilboorg had wound himself. The idea of having *that* with her on the holiest day of her life, when her own personal and newly canonised miracle-worker was to be laid to his final rest, was dreadful. The merest sight of the girl made her want to grate every bone in Hulde's young body and bake it into sacrificial bread to offer up to Alphonsus, seeing in Hulde the embodiment of everything that was wrong with the world: a heathen, a splitter-up of families and possibly a murderer, young as she was. Grandma no idiot when it came to logic. Figuring all the possible scenarios long before they'd crossed the minds of Wenzel and Heraldo. She'd no proof of it, needed none. Grandmother

Pfiffmakler, by God, by *her* God, absolutely knowing it, and that was enough for her. The child was poison. A boil growing on the side of the fair that needed lancing, cauterizing, getting rid of first chance she got.

12

Janus Woman, Janus Countries

'Hello Hulde,' Wenzel said, as he approached the girl. 'No need to worry about Andreas. He'll be fine.'

Watching Lupercal and Jericho skimming up the rigging with their fortifications as if they did it every day. Noting too that Ludmilla and Heraldo were some way off. Time to put his plan into action, taking the girl's hand in his, Hulde looking up at him with expectation.

'It's all right, my girl,' speaking in reassuring tones as he made his way towards the first bunch of people settling a short way down the deck.

'Anyone here speak Albanian?' he asked, most regarding him with disinterest, not wanting to get involved. A single woman holding up her hand.

'I do,' she called, sifting herself from the general mishmash of the fold. An odd looking woman. A weird disparity to her face. One half passably attractive, almost beautiful in certain lights; the other dragged down at eye, mouth and nose by a mass of urticarious scar tissue, blotched red and white, as if she slept on a bed of nettles every night.

'What are you needing?' she asked, Wenzel too concentrated on his task to notice her scars or the slight slurring they caused her speech. Wenzel giving formal introduction.

'My name is Wenzel Pfiffmakler,' he announced. 'Leader of the Kunterbunt Trudelndschau,' a slight thrill running through him to speak his new appellation out loud for the first time, and to a stranger. 'And I've a bit of a conundrum.'

'Haven't we all,' the woman replied briskly, raising her one functioning eyebrow. 'So how I can help?'

Moving her head to keep the good part in Wenzel's view, not missing the Kunterbunt Trudelndschau part of his introduction and seeing a chance.

'I'm in need of a translator,' he said, looking at Hulde. 'We picked this young scraplet up a while back, are having difficulty communicating. Managed a few words here and there, but that's about it.'

Livia Benedetta clicking her tongue, knowing how it was to be amongst strangers who didn't speak the same language, everyone hopping here and there trying find common root words until one or other side got gist enough to have a vague conversation.

'So what's your name then, my little pretty?' Livia said in her awful Albanian, chucking Hulde under the chin. Hulde didn't reply, looked confused, looked up at Wenzel for guidance, Wenzel squeezing the girl's hand.

'It's fine, Hulde.'

No notion that Livia's Albanian was so atrocious Hulde was having to pick through the words for meaning exactly as Livia had picked through the wastage at Zadar market to get her daily fill.

'Unë jam Hulde,' she said after a few moments, Livia knowing this much at least, and how to respond in kind.

'Dhe unë jam Livia,' she said. 'Very pleased to meet you.'

Holding out her hand, Hulde ignoring it. Putting two fingers below Livia's chin, as Livia had done to her.

'Tho themb?' *Does it hurt?* Livia feeling Hulde's fingers stroking down her scars, a touch so unexpected she lowered her head, moved the bad part of it towards Wenzel's scrutiny without conscious thought.

'Just a little,' she replied. 'When too dry is the weather or it's big damp.'

Searching for the words, finding them, putting them into bad syntax, but this scraplet understood.

'Like at sea?' Hulde asked. 'Like now?'

Wenzel bemused by the exchange of words he didn't understand, glad to see Hulde taking the lead and not the last. Seeing the woman Livia's face for what it was, wondering how it became that way. Boiling water tipped over her as a bairn in an Istrian village gone to ruin since the fall of Venice in 1797 when the Austrians cut off all trade routes to Italy. Nothing but subsistence living, scrape and starvation since. Decline steep and unerring during the following years. No room for a grotesquery like Livia in the family. An unmarriageable daughter. Plenty more to take her place.

'So, Livia, is it?' Wenzel asked, clearing his throat, Livia nodding. 'Very well then. Would you come along with us? We can provide refreshments while we talk.'

Livia happy to comply. Livia like a plant that had wound its tendrils about the nearest support once she'd left Istria, been happy there, earned her way. Until that support was ripped from her.

Livia Benedetta eager to find another, and here a chance. Ludmilla and Heraldo didn't see Wenzel leading Hulde away, but heard his loud shout asking if anyone spoke Albanian, both turning their heads as Wenzel returned with a woman who seemed to have half her face in permanent shadow. Neither perturbed. Oddity their daily fare. Piebald boys, Leopard Men, White Jesters, Bearded Women. All part and parcel. What perturbed them was that Wenzel had sought the woman out, plainly meaning to cajole the truth out of Hulde one way or another as they had failed to do. Ludmilla having a pulsing tic at the corner of her left eye and the heat rising in her throat at what might become of it. Heraldo hoping for the best, fearing the worst; fingering the little clown figure in his pocket as if it might bring them luck.

'Come and join us,' Wenzel brought the woman to his half of the Kunterbunt, Peppe and his family settling themselves at a small distance against the port side, eager for the first sight of the Italian shore. Grandmother Pfiffmakler nowhere to be seen, hardly able to look on Wenzel without spitting.

'This is my wife Rosa, my son Heraldo, and here too is my niece Ludmilla who's been taking special care of Hulde since we found her. And this is Livia, who speaks Hulde's language.'

Rosa quick with her welcome, plumping up a cushion placed on a box by her side, already partway through unpacking what they would need for the night: a few blankets, some food, the setting up of a small cooking barrel, packing its belly with wood and charcoal.

'Come sit, my dear,' Rosa said. 'I was just about to get the fire lit for supper and a brew.'

Livia sitting as bid, her belly audibly rumbling at the mention of food and drink after weeks of living on scraps and fountain water. She'd really landed on her feet here, and intended to make the most of it. No one batting an eye at her face, which had to be a good sign.

'What we need from you,' Wenzel took over, 'is to talk to the girl,' nodding towards Hulde, who'd settled on a blanket with Ludmilla, both sitting cross-legged beneath splayed skirts, Ludmilla brushing her fingers through Hulde's hair, Hulde smiling happily as she watched a couple of white cranes circling the tops of the masts.

'Find out where she's from and…well, after that it gets more complicated.'

Livia too looking up toward the cranes. A common enough sight, stopping here on their way to their northern breeding places, yet they transfixed her. On the ground, from a distance, a group of them could look like grazing sheep, but not up there in the air where they extended their necks and usually soared their way up into the thermals. Why this particular pair had chosen to follow the ship in the opposite direction, for a while at least, was a mystery. As was everything surrounding this Hulde child, as she was about to learn.

'Surely you know where she's from?' Livia queried. 'Unless you found her by the wayside.' Just as she'd been found and taken in. Some folk called it exploitation, if not she. 'You mentioned a conundrum?'

'Wenzel! So rude!' Rosa broke in. 'Let's first have something to eat and drink, and get Livia better acquainted with Hulde's story before we go barging in willy nilly.'

Ludmilla could have kissed her aunt. Always the rudder when Wenzel was at the oars, Rosa the one to look forward while he looked back. A grace in great need, now he was head of the Kunterbunt.

Rosa quick with the kettle, soon had cups of hot mint tea at the ready, putting a side of bacon in a pan and frying up Easter Puddings made from bistort, nettle tops and barley in its copious and tasty fat, a few fried eggs to top them off.

'This smells glorious!' Livia announced as she took her trencher, Rosa smiling indulgently as she saw the woman rubbing her lips together, obviously desperate to fall on the food as if she hadn't eaten in days.

'Tuck in, my dear,' Rosa encouraged, pouring out more tea laced with a little crab-apple verjuice to sharpen it up, cleanse the palate, cut through the grease. Livia not needing to be asked twice. Could have cleared the entire plate in a second. God! She'd not tasted anything so good in months! Tried to go at it slowly, though cleared her platter long before anyone else, to her great embarrassment. Rosa quick to intervene, placing another pudding on Livia's plate and the last of the bacon.

'Good to see someone enjoying my cooking,' she said. 'This lot,' pointing at husband and son with her knife, 'are as picky as children. Speaking of which,' she looked around abstractedly, 'where have Lupercal and Jericho got to? Not like them to miss a meal.'

'Still up top,' Heraldo said.

'Will they be safe up there?' Ludmilla asked, shading her eyes with her hand against the last of the afternoon sun, worrying for her nephews, not that they looked like they needed worrying about. Zilboorg, on the other hand, did not look comfortable, arms and legs crabbed about the mast as his bottom tottered on a rigging rope.

'Hope he don't tumble off during the night,' Wenzel said, following Ludmilla's gaze.

'Pfiffmaklers!'

A jovial shout from Valter Poppelmann, hair the colour of a vixen's back as it caught the dying sun.

'Just talking about your uncle,' Wenzel said. 'Think he can hang on overnight, or want me to go talk to the captain?'

'Pfft!' was Valter's reply. 'Let him stew. He deserves it. And he's a grip like a monkey. Gonna take more than a little sea voyage to dislodge him.'

Ludmilla irritated by this intrusion into their family circle, especially now Livia was with them and with what she had to do.

'Maybe you should go give him some support,' she said, next moment wishing she hadn't, feeling Valter's eyes running over her body, no doubt seeing it as he had when she'd been in the water practically undressed.

'Could do. Might do. Probably won't,' was Valter's reply. 'But who've you got here?'

Zeroing in on Livia.

'Well, if it ain't the Janus Woman! How's tricks? Begging must be going good.'

Valter taking out a toothpick and jamming it between his teeth, winkling out a bit of detritus that he examined before flicking it away with his thumb nail, going on before anyone else had the time to speak.

'So quite the troupe we've got going,' Valter said. 'Got your Kunterbunt, got The Balatronic Ballet and now the Janus Woman to boot. Gonna see good Fair's takings when us gets over the water.'

And off he sauntered, heading for Peppe's crew, no doubt to ingratiate himself there as he had so singularly failed to do here.

'Good riddance,' Ludmilla muttered, Heraldo batting at her arm.

'Thought you liked him, thought you…'

'Enough, Heraldo,' Ludmilla shutting him down. 'We should get rid of that Balatronic Ballet lot. They're no good.' Ludmilla's voice loud enough to carry over to the second lot of Pfiffmaklers. Heraldo twitching his jaw, embarrassed that Valter must have heard too, although Heraldo entirely agreed with the sentiment. He didn't know what had changed Ludmilla's view of the man but was glad of it. Switching his gaze to Livia, the Janus Woman as Valter had dubbed her, seeing how the good half of her face had coloured, the bad side more so, the red and white blotches intensifying so the scars looked newly cooked, like a side of salami hanging in the smoke.

'We can talk about that later,' Wenzel said softly, 'and yes, Ludmilla,' he held up a placating hand. 'I agree we've grounds to talk about their continuance with us after we reach Italy. But first, Miss Livia. Please excuse the interruption and the presumption you might want to join us.'

'But of course she'll join us,' Rosa put in, patting Livia's hand, seeing what her husband hadn't and that she was travelling alone with only the clothes on her back and a tattered bedroll that was thinner than the cape the woman had wrapped about her skinny shoulders. 'If you want to of course, my dear. You'd be very welcome.'

'Thank you so much,' Livia whispered, though kept her head bowed, unnerved by Valter Poppelmann's intrusion and the fact he might be travelling with them. A man she'd had dealings with before, if being forcibly pinned behind his Balatronic Ballet stall could be called dealings.

'All very pretty, aren't you, Miss beggar woman,' he'd said, 'when you're halfway south. Think on this as a favour.'

Pushing her head to one side to hide her scars. Not the first time she'd been offered such a favour. Livia not bothering to argue, not having the energy to fight. Just letting him get on with it as he fumbled to unbutton his trousers. A miracle she'd never become pregnant all the times men had chosen to help her out, her looking like she did. Saved that particular day by Andreas Zilboorg bustling around the front of the stall and calling Valter out. Valter sighing, slapping her lightly on her undamaged cheek.

'Come back whenever you like,' he'd whispered as he did up his trousers, walked away like a cockerel, as if he was the first and not merely the last in a long line.

Livia regarding Rosa Pfiffmakler with envy, a woman doling out tea and delicious meals to a family who obviously adored her. She'd have done anything to swap places with the woman. But at least she'd secured a place with the Kunterbunt for the while, just needed to steer clear of Valter which couldn't be that hard. Time to cough up her part of the bargain. She looked around for Hulde, who was nowhere to be seen, and breathed a small sigh of relief. She really needed to blow the cobwebs out of her Albanian conversational tools to make sure she was up to the task.

'Can I ask,' she spoke up, as Rosa cleaned out the pan with a handful of straw, 'what you're needing me to talk to the girl about? Is it her family? I'm assuming she's become parted from them some-how?'

Rosa carried on wiping at her pan, glancing over at her husband.

'Wenzel?' she prompted, Wenzel taking the hint.

'We're pretty sure she's orphaned,' he explained slowly. 'Found her in an abandoned village of sorts.'

Livia paused before asking where that village was.

'Border of Montenegro and Albania, far as we could tell,' Wenzel replied. 'Were about to head up into the Prokletije region to visit the shrine of the Black Madonna. Never been that way before,' Wenzel added, 'and not exactly dotted about with milestones, so couldn't tell you the name of the place.'

'How far from Zadar? On the coast, or in the hills?' Livia asked.

Wenzel filling his pipe, Rosa tutting, well versed in this particular stalling tactic, taking it upon herself to fill in the blanks.

'Took us just over two weeks to get up the coast to Zadar.'

Livia taking this in. No great thinker, Livia, but always a logical one.

'I don't understand why you wouldn't just go on. Villages might be a bit sporadic down there, but you'd soon have come across folk to talk to, take the girl in.'

'Sounds like you know the place,' Wenzel commented, Livia blinking three times in quick succession.

'Well, not really. But we passed through a few places—'

Interrupted by Rosa.

'Oh for Heaven's sake! Stop the shilly-shallying, Wenzel. Just get it said.'

Rosa shaking her head, putting another kettle on. Wenzel doing as bid.

'Like I said, we found her in an abandoned village...' quick glance about him for

Heraldo and Ludmilla, but they'd deserted. And so he told Livia about the village, how ruinous it had appeared and yet so newly inhabited.

'Thing was,' he ended, 'found a load of people there. Hulde the only one alive.'

'Where the hell has she got to?' Heraldo was asking, having left with Ludmilla the moment they realised Hulde was no longer with them. After they'd eaten they'd slung a bucket on a rope down to capture seawater with which to clean their platters and, in the several minutes it had taken them to complete the task, Hulde had disappeared from their midst.

They'd tried Peppe and Yssel first, who told them she'd wandered over and then gone off with Longhella to find Lupercal and Jericho.

So off they'd gone to the mainmast, finding Longhella there. No Hulde.

'Was here a minute ago,' Longhella said, looking about as if perplexed, the colour in her cheeks saying otherwise.

'She's lying,' Ludmilla stated as they moved away, Heraldo taking hold of Ludmilla's arm.

'Well, obviously,' he agreed, 'but your sister's as tight-lipped as a limpet. Let's just carry on looking.'

Going down one side of the ship and up the other, passing bustles of people settling down as the afternoon turned into evening gloom. No sign of Hulde. Back to the family, no sign there either and no hanging around, heading off to repeat their search.

'Where can she have got to?' Heraldo asked, looking about him, feeling the frantic tap of Ludmilla's fingers against his arm, their faces damp with worry and the fret of the sea as the wind rose and the sun sank, exiting with a last sharp glory of green that went unseen.

'I've an inkling what might've happened,' Livia was telling Wenzel and Rosa, settling down on the blanket Ludmilla and Hulde had vacated, glad for the warmth of the brazier now the afternoon had seeped into night. 'Not the specifics, of course, but we travelled a few years in those countries. In Albania, Serbia and Montenegro.'

'You keep saying we,' Rosa interrupted. 'So where are the rest of your troupe?'

Livia quiet for a moment, wondering how to get it said: how she'd been picked up from the roadside, taken in, looked after, getting on just fine for fifteen-odd years, until her own motley Fair of Wonders had been rounded up somewhere on the road between Sarajevo and Zagreb for disseminating unacceptably pro-nationalist views. Ringleaders arrested, publicly beaten and stuck in the stocks. Where they may still be, so far as she knew. The remainder of the crew skedaddling quick as they could; the draggles sticking together for a while, soon splitting off here and there at random forks in the road, herself meandering on until she'd the good fortune to reach Zadar where the begging was tolerably productive. The left-behind pickings at the market enough to keep her ticking over until she'd coins to get herself onto this ship to Italy. No clear plan in mind, until now, until Rosa. Immensely glad she'd held up her hand at Wenzel's call.

'We ran into some trouble,' she finally replied. 'People I was travelling with were mostly Croatians. Keen nationalists. That whole area is very troubled,' she went on, glossing over the particulars of her past. 'Greeks complaining Albania stole some of their land; Turks claiming the lot of it, sending out armed tax collectors folk can't afford to pay. Areas and tribes in the mountains they can't get at, fortified towns whose houses have real thick boltable doors, and no windows on the ground floor in case of siege.'

Remembering a visit to Gjirokastra, The City of a Thousand Steps. Tortuous stone stairways the only way to reach it, it was built so high in the hills. The entire place designed for easy barricade with five defensive towers, three guarded gates, a long aqueduct servicing the vast reservoirs contained within the city's substantial walls. Inhabitants wary, training weapons on them as they'd climbed the steps. Welcoming when they saw no threat, so long as you didn't want to stop too long.

'There's Christians who don't like each other, Orthodox and Roman,' she tried to explain, 'and the Islamists too. None rubbing along too well. Islamists, for the most part, heading for the hills, Christians congregating on the coast.'

Wenzel rubbed at his beard, Rosa speaking up.

'That seems widdershins,' she said. 'Wouldn't that make Christians easy pickings for the Turks?'

Livia rubbing at her damaged eye with a finger, weather too dry and too damp all at the same time, as she'd told Hulde.

'Not really,' she sighed. 'Turks don't mind the Christians for the most part, long as they pay their dues. Except the hardliners, who see it like they're being taken over. Christians settling in their old vacated villages, never mind they were practically invited, which they don't like at all.'

'And maybe the other type of Christians not liking them appearing to settle down under the yoke,' Wenzel observed. 'Thin edge of the wedge.'

'Maybe,' Livia agreed, wishing all the talking would stop, her belly aching with the unaccustomed amount of food; scars smarting and shrinking with the salt, the borderline between the good half of her face and the bad nipping and complaining like all those rival factions in the wild hills of Albania about which she cared not a whit. Too much conflict in her own world to worry about anyone else's.

Rosa seeing Livia's weariness, pouring out more tea. Yarrow and chamomile, with a pinch of the real stuff. Leaves from China kept for special occasions. Handing a cup to Livia.

'I think all this can wait,' Rosa said, 'especially as Hulde's not here—'

Livia interrupting, putting down her cup.

'You've got to understand how complicated those parts are,' needing to get it said, make her excuses in case whatever garbled conversation she managed with the girl didn't make sense to any of them. Couldn't bear the idea of being kicked out of the Kunterbunt before she'd properly got in. 'Like I said before, there's Christians hating other Christians, Islamists hating other Islamists. Christians and Islamists hating each other. Then there's all the tribes, and families within those tribes, having blood feuds going back centuries.'

God, she was tired. Had been tired most of her life. All that tramping from town to town, region to region, people gawking and prodding at her face. Wanting nothing more than to curl herself into sleep, hope everything would be better in the morning. Not that it usually was, yet with sleep came hope and the rejuvenation of her strength to carry on a little longer.

Wenzel puffing at his pipe, weighing all this up, taking a sip of his tea.

'Seems like a right old tangle,' he observed with heinous understatement, wondering if there was any point in Livia talking to Hulde at all, for how on earth was a girl as young as Hulde supposed to give it any meaning? Maybe there simply wasn't any to be found. Even if they understood who had massacred who, and whether Hulde had been an active part of it, which he doubted, what on earth would be the point in knowing? It would mean nothing to Hulde, nor them either, and would have no bearing on Hulde's future life once they got her to her people. Not her exact people, that went without saying, but near as dammit.

Rosa of the same opinion.

'Let's leave it for the night,' she decided for them all.

Looking up into the sky, seeing the first few stars winking in the welkin as it shifted from ochre to darkest velvet blue, covering them, swallowing them into its own. Rosa not worrying about Hulde, for wherever Ludmilla and Heraldo were there would she be, just as she'd been ever since they'd fetched her up from her godforsaken village, no matter which god it was who had forsaken her.

13

Heroes and Help-Meets

'Hoy!'

A shout went up to their left, Ludmilla and Heraldo turning their heads in unison. Hard to make out details in the gloom. Possibly a small black bundle going over the rails, or maybe a large black-backed gull taking off, or a pelican gliding by. Or maybe nothing at all. Either way Ludmilla pitched herself towards the sound with the force of her premonition, running to the scene of possible jettison. First to the rails, Heraldo on her heels.

'There!' someone yelled, small white flashes of skin breaking through a weird luminescence that covered the water's surface and broke against the sides of the ship, lighting up the shifts of its wake as a mass of phosphorescent jellyfish gathered, waiting for the moon to rise and brighten, trigger their once-in-a-life-time mating.

'It's her!' Ludmilla squeezed the words from her throat, though she couldn't possibly be sure.

'Man overboard!' Heraldo shouted, voice hoarse with horrid anticipation, skin jagging, shucking off his jacket, about to leap in when he was pushed to one side, beaten to the punch as someone climbed the rails and made an impressive arm-led dive that speared his body into the water like a lance. Quick to re-emerge, energetic in his swimming, legs kicking out kaleidoscopic patterns as he located the small bundle that was already sinking, a black void in all that light, dived down and brought it up, the bundle coughing and spluttering as it broke the surface and he held its head up and out.

'Ropes!' Heraldo barked, leaping off towards the bow, the ship having moved on regardless, thank God somebody already there launching one such out: a small empty barrel at its end as a flotation device and to ensure accurate direction as it was flung towards the two forms bobbing up and down in the waves, heads and shoulders barely visible as the jellyfish hordes were left behind, taking their pyrotechnics with them.

Forms dragged in nonetheless, one strong arm grabbing about the barrel, wrist twisting the rope about it to make sure it didn't slip, the other keeping the rescuee clear of the waves that were growing in height and depth as the wind rose and the clouds sped across the sky to hide the moon, the medusa sinking, lights extinguished one by one.

A body brought in. Hulde. Shivering, frightened, choking, alive. Swept up by Heraldo, soon joined by Ludmilla gasping with relief.

The other, hauled up in Hulde's wake, looking like he'd done nothing more than go for a quick dip. Red hair darkened by the sea into deepest chestnut, like when you break one open in the autumn and thread it onto a string to fire at one or other of your playmates, maybe soaking it in vinegar first to make it all the harder, more invincible. As Valter Poppelmann seemed now, hailed as a hero: back-slapped, back-lit by lanterns held high, skin shining, handed blankets. Valter refusing them, grabbing the neck of a bottle being thrust at him and glugging it down, standing magnificent within the applauding crowd like a warrior returned from victorious battle.

Not everyone so excited by this new drama, many staying in their bivouacs unconcerned. One not so unconcerned was Longhella, who'd rushed with the rest to see what was what, shrinking away when she saw who was being brought up from the water. A horrid itch to her skin and a tumble in her guts, for not long previously she'd delivered Hulde to Old Grandmother, who'd been sitting on an ancient fish crate near the bow. Longhella doing as bid, miming out the mechanics of Hide and Seek, a game universally understood by children the world over: *Rimpiattino, Werstedenspielen, Cache cache, Olla Piilosilla,* or any one of a hundred other names. Longhella running off a few yards, putting her hands ostentatiously in front of her eyes and counting loudly, peeking through her fingers as Old Grandmother lifted up her voluminous skirts and motioned Hulde under. Hulde smiling like an evil imp to be given such an unassailable hiding place. Hulde going into the dark folds and leaning her back against the crate, giggling quietly, content, stomach full, listening to the rhythm of the waves as the ship sailed on. Listening to the old woman humming some tune she vaguely recognised, joining in briefly below the old woman's skirts. Hulde soon nodding off, soon asleep, all notion of the game gone from her. Longhella apparently forgetting too for, after the counting was done, she'd sauntered off, leaving Hulde to Grandmother's devices, duty done.

All rushing back to Longhella now as she hung on the outskirts of Valter Poppelmann's victory march back to the Pfiffmakler clan with Ludmilla and Heraldo, the shivering Hulde bound in Heraldo's arms. The crowds sifting away, leaving them to it, eager to get back to their own and do a bit of gossiping about how a young child had slipped through the rails, plummeted into the sea, and how handsome and lithe had been her rescuer, how both would have been lost had it not been for the strange light that had cast itself through the waters. A sight they found stirring, joyous, God-given or mysterious, depending on their own particular world view.

'Pfiffmaklers!' Valter announced as he approached. Wenzel sat with Lupercal and Jericho who were tucking into bread, cheese and olives, having missed their evening meal. Rosa off to chat with Yssel and Peppe. Livia curled up in a blanket a few yards off, apparently asleep. All unaware of what had happened. The ship long and large, augmented by falling darkness, the increasingly volant wind and the concomitant actions of waves, the flapping of sails.

'I bring you gifts!' Valter shouted happily. 'Or rather, I bring you one. I bring you Hulde.'

Bowing low, waving out a magnanimous arm.

Wenzel couldn't comprehend why the man was acting like a prince in one of their plays, nor why he was dripping wet, nor why there were several young men keeping stride with him clutching bottles of strong drink in their hands, obviously eager to be in on some revelry Wenzel had no notion of. He stood up awkwardly, ankles and knees stiff with having been sat too long and, as he did so, saw Heraldo and Ludmilla approaching some yards behind. Each looking anxious and intent, and behind the two of them he caught a flash of orange skirts, another anxious face. Longhella. Had to be. No mistaking that profile. Though why she was tagging them and yet staying in the gloom, he couldn't fathom.

'I don't know what's been going on,' he admitted, as Valter Poppelmann intruded, a habit seeming to run in the family, casting a quick glance up towards where Andreas must still be. No sight of him. Night too hard down. Hoping Andreas would be able to see it through.

'Just gone and rescued your little Miss from the waves, is all,' Valter informed Wenzel nonchalantly. Heraldo appearing, producing the child, releasing her shivering form onto the blanket beside Wenzel's feet. Ludmilla wrapping her up in it, pushing Wenzel out of the way so she could complete her task.

'She's really cold,' Ludmilla worried, wishing Rosa was here with all her healing teas, rubbing at Hulde as she cosseted the girl, tried to get some warmth back into her limbs.

'I haven't got the faintest notion...' Wenzel started to say..

'Grandmother threw her overboard,' Ludmilla stated quietly, with absolute conviction. Heraldo quick to qualify.

'We don't know that,' he said. 'For why on earth would she do such a thing? It was really dark by then,' his words coming quick and fast. 'But it certainly looked like she was helped over and didn't just slip. Anyway, fact is Hulde wouldn't still be with us if Valter hadn't gone in and over and brought her out.'

Never any side to Heraldo, never one to say, or even think: *but actually, this should have been my victory hour. I was on my way over to fetch her when I was shoved aside by some freewheeler who knew he could capitalise on it, who knew this land, knew this sea, knew that with the jellyfish lighting up the water there was no chance they'd be lost.*

A rescue of economy then, a rescue with ends other than rescue in mind, a rescue bound to succeed if you knew the water and the medusa, like Valter Poppelmann did. A person who'd spent months free-diving down the lengths of rope strung from anchored rafts for the specific purpose of cultivating oyster beds; the same time Andreas had been perfecting his pretend falling-from-the-rigging trick. All tired of the road and the travelling, a winter really hard going. Andreas making the decision that for once they'd stop in one place for an entire spring and summer through. Valter fourteen, a living needing to be made. Oyster beds the obvious choice for strong young boys, not that Jodl had taken to it. Valter revelling in the fact he'd found something he could do better than his brother, discovering he'd talent for the task, nurturing the tricks needed to further it. The importance of a good clean entering dive, preferably from a high rock, that sent him down quick with its momentum without need for further effort. A strong swimming action to arms and legs. An ability to expel the air from his lungs the second before he went in instead of holding it, as instinct dictated, so that after several months of practice he could remain underwater for a full three minutes without need to draw breath. A record breaker back then amongst the oyster-gathering children. A talent once gained never lost.

The rescue of Hulde therefore, a cynical observer might have concluded, not quite so dangerous as it seemed, and very convenient for Valter Poppelmann, hero of the hour. Extremely unlikely now to be booted from the Kunterbunt, no matter the disgrace Andreas had indirectly brought on them, not to mention Ludmilla's loud aversion to The Balatronic Ballet.

As Wenzel's next words appeared to confirm.

'Well, Valter. If that's the case, then I can't thank you enough.'

The several young men who'd accompanied Valter whooping, shouting out their laudations.

'Never seen anything like it!' the first acclaimed. 'Went in after the girl like a pike after a minnow! Didn't hesitate. Heard that man's *hoy* and went straight to it! Straight up and over the side.'

Wishing he could've been that man, that he was braver, made of the same stuff.

'That's right!' agreed the second, not a jot of altruism in his body, and no way he'd have done what Valter had, more than happy to be a stalwart witness. 'And didn't hesitate! Didn't even stop to take off his boots!'

'And they's what'll sink you,' a third averred, shaking his head like a wise old man. 'Know it meself. Almost drowned coupla winters back when I got lobbed into the water on a fierce bad wind and all the fishing nets got tangled up beneath the boat. Had to kick the bastards off my feet just to get back to the surface.'

Wenzel not paying much attention to these plaudits, studiously ignoring the bottle the men were passing around, wondering how to get rid of them. Concentrating instead on Ludmilla binding Hulde up in blankets to keep her warm. Their last comments filtering through only because he'd right then cast an eye at the preening Valter Poppelmann who was standing in the Pfiffmakler circle like he belonged, which he did not—Ludmilla right on that count. Andreas's public condemnation had seen to that. If the captain wasn't aware of their association others certainly were. Much to talk about. Though Valter obviously didn't see it that way, was evidently presuming his rescue of Hulde had secured his and his family's place with the Kunterbunt.

Wenzel hadn't liked Andreas Zilboorg. A slime of a man who'd offer you one thing and give you another, yet Zilboorg old school. A conman trying to get on, keep body and soul together. Coughed up when challenged, went up the mast, for heaven's sake. This Valter Poppelmann, Wenzel was coming to consider, was something else.

For Valter Poppelmann was standing in his stockinged feet.

Valter Poppelmann had no boots on.

And when, given what Valter's young admirers had just said, did he have the time to take them off? He supposed Valter could have kicked them free while in the water, yet according to Valter's gawking coterie he'd not stopped swimming since diving in, fetching Hulde up and coming back out.

Wenzel feeling an itching in his beard and not from lice. Wenzel very particular about that, keeping his beard combed, washed and oiled on a regular basis. Finding a wrongness to this whole situation, beginning with Heraldo telling him how Hulde had battered that figurine into the sand, followed by Ludmilla's absurd accusation of Grandmother Pfiffmakler that was nevertheless bolstered by Longhella's shiftiness. The two always tight, particularly in regard to Hulde.

Also to be considered was Valter's very opportune rescuing of Hulde so soon after Ludmilla had mooted the kicking out of his act from the Kunterbunt. Add to that Heraldo's conviction the girl hadn't just slipped as children do, especially when they've never been on board a ship before and have no idea how fleet the change can be from calm to lurch and dip when night brings with it wind and wave.

He juggled the possibilities.

Grandmother Pfiffmakler's aversion to the girl so all-consuming she'd inveigled Hulde to her with Longhella's connivance for the express intent of throwing her overboard. It didn't seem credible. She might blame Hulde for shifting the power balance from herself to Wenzel, but must have known it would have happened anyway.

Had been on the cards for months. Hulde merely the catalyst setting it in motion.

On the other hand was Valter Poppelmann, and about him Wenzel couldn't decide. His rescue had, by all accounts, been heroic, foolhardy, spontaneous. Although not so spontaneous he mightn't have prepared for such an event by taking off his boots, which implied he might have actually precipitated it.

Or maybe the girl had simply fallen in.

Except she hadn't, if Heraldo could be believed, Heraldo who'd seen a bundle going over the rails and not through. And Heraldo he believed above all others. His firstborn son, who'd never lied in his entire life so far as Wenzel knew. Heraldo simply not made that way.

Wenzel torn down the middle.

Only one person he could think of who might be able to shed light on Hulde's near drowning, and him a man he wouldn't trust further than he could spit.

14

Meeting the Numinous

The stars moved around the bowl of the sky, wind settling, clouds clearing, moon fulsome and bright. All not lost for the jellyfish, a few more nights yet before the moon turned its face from the sun and began to darken. Wenzel gazing up at it, thinking of Livia, how she resembled it at quarter, half in light, half in shade. Caught a short flash of red in one of its craters. A gloriously rare sight that made him blink and catch his breath. A meteorite strike he knew, pluffing up dust as it hit. Told so by an astronomer with whom he'd been lucky enough to witness it once before. A man who spent his days pontificating to the public: *plant this food crop when the moon is new, harvest this one when full*. Presenting charts and mathematical equations to bolster his predictions. All nonsense, of course, but he had to earn a coin. Spent his nights otherwise: staring into the heavens with his homemade telescope, jotting down notes on this ascendant planet or that, plotting their transitions and the courses of the various comets periodically burning their way through the sky. A man who'd travelled hundreds of miles to witness eclipses when the sun was blotted out by the moon and the world shifted into evening in the middle of the day, when the birds ceased to sing and the wind changed direction until the moon moved away, the broody dark become light again.

Three times I've seen it, and I'm only sixty-one, he'd told Wenzel, *so time yet for another.*

A fascinating man, who Wenzel hadn't thought about in years. Staying with the Kunterbunt a few months before moving on. Wenzel sitting by him on a hillside on the outskirts of the Alps, Heraldo at his side. Lupercal and Jericho toddlers who couldn't keep still longer than a bee stays on a sage flower.

'Just you wait,' he'd said, 'we might be lucky.'

And wait he and Heraldo had, and lucky they were: rewarded by the stupendous sight of that red flash up there in a dark crater of the moon.

'It's a miracle of the universe, a mere few granted witness,' the astronomer had sighed, despite him having predicted the event to within a matter of hours. Wenzel forgetting the man's name. Not forgotten was the utter joy on Heraldo's face as they'd sat there, freezing their bottoms off, Heraldo's small warm hand clasped in his own as the world shifted a notch in the universe. Heraldo afterwards asking all sorts of awkward questions: *How do meteorites work? And how are they different from comets? And why was the light up there red?*

The start of Heraldo's investigations into everything Kunterbunt, the start of him taking stuff apart and putting it back together, usually better than it had been before.

Oh, you moon, Wenzel thought, tiptoeing away from his sleeping family, making his way down the deck, treading light and careful so as not to wake the huddles of people all pressed into sleep against the ship's sides. Sounds of gentle snoring and the lapping of the waves against the boards an arrhythmic, faintly musical companion as he reached the mainmast. Found a crewman slumped a little way off leaning against a winch, too tired to keep watch, shove Andreas Zilboorg back up if he tried to get down under cover of night.

'Andreas!' Wenzel gave a loud whisper. 'It's me, Wenzel Pfiffmakler. How're you doing up there?'

His salutation met with a short series of soft groans, and then Andreas's croaky reply.

'Not too bad. Kinda seized a up a bit, which makes the clinging easier.'

A short laugh followed, evoking Wenzel's admiration at Andreas's fortitude.

'Thanks for sending your boys up,' Andreas croaked on, clearing his throat, a slight creaking as he shifted his body into better balance. 'Real boost, that was. Especially the tea.'

Wenzel glancing at the crewman, whose head lolled up briefly at the interruption though didn't wake, or possibly chose not to. Guard duties clearly not his strongest suit.

Wenzel's turn to clear his throat.

'Can I ask you something?'

That weary laugh again from Andreas.

'Ask away, friend. I'm not going anywhere.'

'Did you see anything of the stramash that went on earlier? When the child fell into the sea?'

Short silence then, Andreas sniffing loudly, wiping his nose against his sleeve before answering.

'Bird's eye view,' he got out with difficulty, a cramp starting in his calf muscles. Nothing he could do about it, scrunching his face up against the pain. Wenzel hearing the exhalation of Andreas's breath in the still, dark night.

'Could you see how she went over?' he asked, not wanting to be too obvious, not wanting to lead or implicate, clutching his hands together as he waited for the answer, which seemed to take an age. No notion that tears were leaking from the corners of Andreas Zilboorg's eyes as the cramp worsened and then suddenly ceased, leaving him able to breathe again, think again, cast his mind back.

'Didn't realise it at the time,' Andreas spoke softly, trying not to move, not wanting to provoke that cramp again, not at any cost. 'Thought someone was chucking a load of rubbish overboard, like they do. But then someone yelled...'

Letting out a long sigh as he trailed off.

'The things people do,' he finished. Perhaps thinking on his own situation.

'I'm sorry I got you up there,' Wenzel apologised. 'Thought I was doing you a favour. Thought they might have lobbed you in otherwise. If I did wrong, I'll gladly make it up to you.'

That unnerving soft laugh again. Wenzel looking up, could just make out Andreas tilting his head.

'Some favour!' Andreas replied, Wenzel's heart sinking until Andreas qualified his answer. 'But rest easy, friend. You made the right call. Can't stand the water. Can't swim, unlike my Balatronic nephews.

Wenzel halting then, wondering what to say next, it coming to him that although he'd met Valter Poppelmann several times, which was several times more than he'd wanted, he'd never clapped eyes on his brother, except during their show on Ugljan when he'd been unrecognisable in his theatrical makeup and costume. It occurring to him how odd that was. He had to be here on the boat for, according to Zilboorg's own statement, he'd only hooked up with the Kunterbunt so his boys could see Italy. He'd assumed sons at the time, should have realised not, given the discrepancy between their names: Zilboorg and Poppelmann. But never any sightings or interactions with the second Poppelmann brother. An issue he would need to pursue. One last question to ask. No point shilly-shallying, as Rosa would have said.

'Could you see who lobbed Hulde over?' he asked Andreas. 'Man or woman? When and where?'

He didn't expect Andreas to throw Valter into the grinder, but fervently hoped he could clear his grandmother from the mix. No immediate answer, the guardsman suddenly grunting awake, taking umbrage to find Wenzel there.

'What the hell d'you think you're doing?'

On his feet, looking angry, leery, casting his eyes about him and up the mast. Wenzel taking a few steps backwards.

'Just checking on your prisoner,' Wenzel quick to respond. 'Making sure he's safe and secure up there.'

The crewman subsiding.

'Aye well,' he said, bleary with sleep. 'Nowt to be looking at, so get you gone.'

Wenzel away, but hearing Zilboorg's last words to him.

'T'were real dark,' Zilboorg said. 'But can tell you it weren't no woman. Shape all wrong.'

Andreas sighing, Wenzel's heart leaping. He hadn't really thought it, not of Grandma Pfiffmakler. Relieved all the same.

Thank you, Andreas, he murmured under his breath as he returned to the fold of his family, finding them as he'd left them. With one addition. Old Grandma herself, who'd steered clear of them the whole journey. Licking her wounds, Wenzel had supposed.

She was a bit way off from the others, had dragged a crate with her and was kneeling on it, arms resting on the boat-side, looking out to sea. A sight so odd Wenzel stopped short, took in a couple of sharp breaths as he approached.

'Thought I did it, didn't you,' she said softly, without turning her head. Reminding Wenzel of insects Heraldo had once told him about who had hearing organs located on wings, legs or abdomens. And maybe had eyes there too, for all he knew. He shivered to think on it, how alien it had seemed then, and more so now. Grandma Pfiffmakler apparently having similar abilities, knowing who was approaching. He came up beside her and leaned his arms next to hers, took in what she was seeing: another load of moon jellies glowing green out there in the sea a few hundred yards off, maybe having more luck than the last.

'Didn't really believe it,' he spoke softly. 'But you know how it goes, Grandmother. Got to check everything out, and Longhella was—'

'Now that you're leader, you mean,' she cut him off, Wenzel surprised at her placidity. No bitterness, no rancour. Just a statement spoken, and not even to him but to the sea, to the darkness, to whatever lay beyond them on the other side. His grandmother uncommonly still. Usually jittering and busy as a jay on a scatter of nuts. Her calmness, her kneeling on the crate unnerving. Like she was young again, Wenzel thought, or as young as he'd ever known her. Maybe late thirties when he'd been born, and late forties when he'd been growing up, when he'd already viewed her as old and decrepit. Same age he was now. His marriage coming later than expected, and his children too.

'Didn't mean it to go like it did,' he said, fixing his eyes on the heavens where he knew she believed her God resided, glad she had some comfort in that at least.

Oh, you moon.

'Had to happen,' was her unexpected reply. 'And you done me a favour, Wenzel.'

Wenzel so shocked he couldn't get out a word.

'Gonna leave you when we get over,' she went on. 'Gonna do what I meant to do fifty years back.'

Wenzel mystified.

'How'd you mean?' he strangled out the words, wrong-footed, not knowing where she was going, what she was telling him. A life without Grandmother Pfiffmakler in it seemed unimaginable. This woman a forceful presence during every day he'd taken breath, and all those days assuming he'd known her through and through: a bitter old bird, if a strong one. A woman who saw the world in black and white: Kunterbunt one side, religion the other. Her trying to meld the two together over the years, increasing their church cycles, decreasing those secular. And now here was something else.

She lifted a hand from the boat-side, brushed it through the grey hair on her temple.

'Lots of things you don't know about me,' she said quietly. 'Like how bad it was early on, before I had your father. And how hard it were after your granddaddy died. Left me to my own. Me and the straggles of the Kunterbunt we'd managed to amass.'

Wenzel seeing what he'd never done before: the younger Grandmother Pfiffmakler out there on the road with a young child, trying to keep it all together, and her a woman. How bad that road must have been, how difficult menfolk from the fair circuit might have made her life until his father had grown enough to take over the reins, although Grandmother still pulling the strings. But all those years before, keeping it all together, establishing routes, making contacts, securing acts enough to make the Kunterbunt viable. Visibly in charge again when Wenzel's father had bowed out. Until Wenzel himself had snatched it all away in a moment, after all she'd done. How shabby that must have seemed to her, and how disrespectful.

'I'm sorry, Grandmother,' he whispered. 'Forgive me.'

Nothing then but the sounds of the ship ploughing ever on through the water.

He supposed there must be crewmen out there, more awake than Andreas's guard, to keep them going straight and true, just like Old Grandmother Pfiffmakler had kept the Kunterbunt going through thick and thin, and himself and his family in occupation and funds. He felt wretched. Hung his head. And then, the softest touch on his hand as Grandmother laid her old claws upon it and Wenzel shivered, realising she'd not touched him for years, indeed hardly touched anyone. Not a hugging woman, Old Grandmother. Never had been.

'She hummed to me,' she said, looking straight over the water. 'I hummed a hymn, and she joined in. Only for a few minutes, but she joined in. And then all was clear. It was Alphonsus showing me the way, just like before.'

Grandmother quiet. Wenzel not understanding. Alphonsus a name he'd heard several times on the voyage. Never the context.

'Stayed my hand,' Grandmother Pfiffmakler murmured, 'for before that I might have… God forgive me…for I believed her a…' She stopped, searching for the word, Wenzel holding his breath, utterly perplexed. Grandmother finally shaking her head.

'I believed her a besmirchment I couldn't tolerate, not at the greatest moment of my life. But you were right, Wenzel. She's just a child in need of a protector, and thank the Good Lord she's found one in you.'

Wenzel realising he was being graced with some great secret, that Grandmother Pfiffmakler was laying down the crown, giving him the reason why, even if he was too dense to fathom it out.

'What do you mean, the greatest moment of your life?'

Wenzel feeling stupid with his question, his inability to grasp what was really going on.

A scratchy squeeze of his hand from his Grandmother.

'Only wait, lad, and you shall see.'

'But see what?' Wenzel frustrated, pulling his hand away, rubbing roughly at the sides of his beard. 'Why won't you just tell me?'

The sound of a rusty violin being scraped by a rustier bow. Wenzel blinking, throat slowly tightening as he realised its source.

Grandmother Pfiffmakler doing what he'd never heard her do. Grandmother Pfiffmakler laughing, Grandmother Pfiffmakler kneeling on her crate, looking out to sea and laughing.

'Always so impatient, Wenzel,' she admonished, turning towards him, cupping her hand about his chin, tapping his cheek lightly with her fingers. 'I'm afraid you get that from me.'

Wenzel hardly able to bear it, taking her hand in his, looking at her—properly looking at her—searching every crevasse on her worn face, every crinkle, every shadow. Seeing her not as the construct of Grandmother Pfiffmakler, who'd been cruel and kind in arbitrary measure, who'd ruled the Kunterbunt with an iron rod for fifty years. Seeing her instead as an individual, a woman who'd carried his father in her belly. An old woman now, and yet such joy in those dark eyes, and how they sparkled! Twin moons reflected in their corners like maybe Saul's had done on the Road to Damascus. He'd never seen her like this, was coming to realise he'd never fully seen her before, not like she really was, with all the baggage of her past piling up on her shoulders year on year, carrying them all up there with it. Bent by those years, by that weight and responsibility. By him.

'I just want to know what's happening, Grandma,' he whispered, needing absolution, needing answers, needing to know how and why she'd turned from the person he knew into someone else, or perhaps had reverted into the person she'd always been if he'd ever tried to find out who that was, which he had not.

'Come the morrow,' this new incarnation of Grandmother Pfiffmakler comforted, 'the Lord will show us who is his, and who is holy. Someone very wise once told me that, Wenzel, and come the morrow all will be clear.'

'All well?' Rosa murmured, as Wenzel tucked himself in beside her, curving his body about hers, pulling the blanket back over the two of them, shutting them off from the world.

'All well,' Wenzel whispered back. 'Go back to sleep, my dear.'

Rosa not hearing, Rosa already sinking into dreams filled as always with good things, as good people's dreams are apt to be. Not so Wenzel, who found he couldn't sleep at all, kept his eye on his grandmother as she knelt on her crate the whole night through, keeping vigil with her, though for what and why he had no idea.

Oh you moon…

Wenzel finally falling into uneven sleep, seeing himself walking down the wide street of the village where they'd found Hulde in her huddle of corpses, the newly whitewashed walls still a grimy pink from the ox-blood that had not yet faded. Passing between the sporadic scatter of fig trees that grew either side of the promenade, the gnarled roots escaping above ground to coil about their bases like thick brown snakes, the fine red dust covering every surface.

Waking in a sudden sweat.

Questions popping into his mind like those autumn mushrooms that grow up overnight after rain.

Where had the ox-blood come from?

Why has he never met the second Poppelmann brother?

How long had that red dust been lying?

What was the hymn Hulde had joined in with?

Why was Grandmother Pfiffmakler acting like it was the Second Coming?

His head buzzing so loudly he wasn't sure if he had a god-almighty headache or was being given some kind of revelation. Hulde the source of it. Hulde a spring bubbling up from hard ground and washing over them, and over Grandmother Pfiffmakler most of all.

Verse from Revelations popping onto his lips:

Brought out of tribulation, washed white by the blood of the lamb.

Not all of Grandmother's teachings lost on him. The irony tickling in his throat so he couldn't stop himself, had to lever himself up on one elbow as he began to laugh. Softly at first, but gaining a momentum all its own until he was crying with it. Rosa's strong fist punching him in the ribs the only way to stop it.

'God's sake, man,' she chided, sitting up, rubbing at her eyes. 'You'd better be choking to death on a fishbone to be waking me so early.'

Wenzel shaking his head, rubbing away the tears, more happy to be alive than he'd ever been, never minding that the rest of the Pfiffmaklers were grumbling all around him at the interruption to their sleep.

'What's going on?' Heraldo first to speak.

'It's still dark. Why's it still dark?' Jericho asked, a pantomime of sleepiness as he sat up, yawning wide and loud as he stretched his arms and brought them in again, inadvertently catching his brother on the side of his head with his elbow.

'Ouch!' Lupercal mumbled, swatting ineffectively at his attacker.

'Oh but look!' Heraldo exclaimed, always a lad bright as a pin the second his eyes were open, on his feet a moment later. Wenzel catching the excitement, standing too, seeing what Heraldo was seeing, grabbing Rosa's hand and dragging her up with him until both were leaning their waists against the boards, the sun a mere shimmer on the eastern horizon, a mother-of-pearl pink heralding its way. Oh but not so glorious a sight as the huge school of dolphin that were arcing through the waters to left and right of them: sleek-backed, sheen-bright, small and large, all eager to get to where they were going. Some throwing themselves up and out of the water on their tail fins, white bellies shining in the first shafts of dawn, flinging themselves backwards with abandon into the salty sea only to launch themselves up again and again, as if this was the finest of days, as if they'd never seen the like.

As if they'd never get to do it again.

'Oh my,' Rosa breathed out the words for them all. 'That's really something.'

Giving her husband's hand a quick squeeze as they watched and watched and watched, until the dolphins were too far away to be seen.

'Forget what I said about fish bones,' Rosa murmured, nuzzling into Wenzel's neck. 'That was worth waking anyone up for.'

'Brand new day,' Wenzel murmured. 'Brand new day.'

And by God it was, all of them breathing in the freshness of it, seeing the sun slide up as if someone was changing the backdrop, dressing the stage for a play whose contents they weren't yet privy to, the narrator beginning the story for them:

Night turns to day for our weary travellers, and they are greeted by a most glorious sight as the sun rises, lighting up the sky in the east, lifting the darkness from their eyes...

'I can see the coast!' Lupercal shouted. 'And look, there's a sail boat!'

'And another!' Jericho quick to join in. 'Looks like there's a whole load of them!'

A flotilla of fishing boats returning to port after a long night's work: holds, decks, nets and barrels filled to bursting with the slapping bodies of tuna, swordfish, anchovy and albacore...

And behind them the sleeping ship awakes, friends and enemies alike. A tide of people arising from pallet and mattress, packing away their goods and gear, goaded into action by our heroic Kunterbunt who are to the fore.

'All right, Grandmother?' Wenzel asks, all heads turning in surprise to see her small black form kneeling on its crate, unaware she'd joined them.

'Never better, son,' Grandmother replied, the cast shocked not only by her presence but by her words, and the expression on her face: the serene smile that looked so out of place and yet like it belonged.

'Look at all that sand!' Ludmilla taking to the stage, seeing how different the two sides of the Adriatic were: Croatia rocky, filled with inlets, islets, pebbly beaches, mountains stern and steep above the towns and villages that hemmed its waters, shading them when the sun has moved towards the west. But here, on the Italian side, all is open, wide and expansive, Ravenna a soft pink rise of towers and turrets, churches and spires, houses painted every colour imaginable. A gingerbread city, inviting the travellers in.

And so, Ladies and Gentlemen, our stage is set, our players in the wings ready to entertain you.

Another quick switch of backdrop as the ship hove in. All about them hustle and bustle, brio at its best as fishermen unload their catches, set up their stalls, a gaggle of women descending, taking over, flashing their gutting knives, setting to with alarming speed as they divide one set of fish from another, get them sorted, get them skinned and split, dressed and filleted. Put them into barrels of oil or brine or hooked onto lines to dry in the sun. Hawkers shouting out prices as the folk of Ravenna poured in to fetch up what they needed for the day's cooking, get the best prices. Bakers and vegetable growers soon on the scene spilling out their wares, displaying them on carts, swiftly erected trestle tables or merely the sacks they'd been transported in. All shouting at the tops of their voices for someone to buy this or that and how fresh it was, how green and delicious.

The Kunterbunt starting off aimlessly down a street until Grandmother Pfiffmakler tugged at Wenzel's sleeve, urging him in the opposite direction.

'So this is it,' he said, not demurring. 'Your great day?'

'My great day,' she agreed.

'To do with this Alphonsus?' Wenzel took a stab in the dark. Grandmother Pfiffmakler having nothing more to say.

The crowds dense, hard to navigate. Every street filled wall to wall with people on the move, all apparently in joyous mood, flags waving from every house they passed. Grandmother leading the way, Wenzel following; the rest of the Kunterbunt hauling their carts behind them as Grandmother Pfiffmakler set a fast pace. Grandmother Pfiffmakler pausing only once, stopping briefly in her tracks, retracing them, returning to where Ludmilla was marching along with Hulde clinging to her hand.

'Do you mind, my dear?'

Taking Hulde's hand in her own.

Ludmilla acceding as she always did to Grandmother Pfiffmakler. Grandmother humming softly as she set off again, feet sure on the cobbles, Hulde easy by her side, Ludmilla anxious at her back. Grandmother leading them from the backstreets onto the main thoroughfare, the Via di Roma, following the directions she'd gleaned from someone on the ship, not hard when it was all most of them could talk about, taking them to the Basilica di Sant'Apollinare. First sight of it a glimpse of the top few courses of the circular brick-built bell tower nine storeys high, if you counted the windows set into its walls, as Heraldo did. The streets quieter now, though not for lack of people but because the people themselves were quieter, heads bowed, reverent. Heraldo catching the sound of someone singing. A chant obviously liturgical but melancholic, elliptical, intonated like an Arab or Hebrew song. A type of singing Heraldo had heard only once before, part of the Offertorium of the Ambrosian Rite. Heraldo knew it straightaway, had stored it up in his head because it had been so beautiful, so moving. Heraldo eager to find its source. Soon located, as Grandmother drew them into the courtyard of the basilica that was packed from gate to grass with a silent congregation on their knees, heads bowed. Grandmother joining them, Hulde with her. A single monk standing on the top step of the entrance to the church giving sad and subtle voice to the *Ecce apertum est Templum tabernaculi.*

Eyes closed, face and hands held up to the rising sun and the coming day.

'Oh my,' Heraldo whispered, transfixed, transported. Wenzel uncomfortable beside his son in their shared harness, not so imbued by the communal belief of the congregation who understood they were about to partake in the numinous. Wenzel scratching the side of his mouth, uncertain what to do next. Wenzel seeing his grandmother on her knees with the rest, and Hulde too. Feeling like the script had been rewritten and he'd been shoved on stage without knowing any of the words.

And so, my friends, the scene has changed.

Our heroes have been led into parts unknown, and the next chapter of our tale must begin.

15

Andreas and the Pope Decide

Andreas had spent the night in hard concentration. Several things to mull over, firstly to keep clinging grimly to his perch, another how he was going to fleece the crowds when they reached Ravenna. He would have rubbed his hands together if he could, except they were as knotted up as the ropes that served the sails. Coming down in the morning excruciating, even with the help of Wenzel's boys. No way he could walk, joints swollen and inflamed. The Pfiffmaklers solicitous, Rosa pressing liniments on him, Peppe whipping up several leather supports to wrap about arms and knees, holes cut for patellae and elbow knuckles to facilitate flexibility. But hard enough to get off board, and futile to imagine he could keep up with a Kunterbunt being led a furious pace by Old Grandmother Pfiffmakler.

'We can't just leave you,' Wenzel stated, his sense of honour denying him that possibility, despite it being precisely what he'd rather do.

'No choice,' Andreas taking the blow with good grace. 'Feeling as wooden as one of your puppets. Gonna take a bit of time to get everything working again.'

Wenzel concerned, wondering if he could get Andreas on one of their carts. Not a chance, fully loaded as was Andreas's own. Andreas reading his mind, saying the words he'd already rehearsed.

'You've done enough. You've been real kind. And you've no need to worry on my part. Boys'll look after me.'

'Maybe we could meet up later on,' Wenzel suggested, Andreas letting out a creaking chuckle that brought Wenzel's guilt to the fore.

'No need, man. Honest. And where would that be? Guessing both of us know Ravenna about as much as we know the moon.'

Oh you moon. The thought in Wenzel's head like a drift of gossamer clinging to a tip of gorse.

'It don't seem right,' Wenzel persisted, seeing no solution. Not so Andreas.

'Tell you what,' Andreas volunteered, as if the idea had just popped into his head and not put there by someone else who'd foreseen the problem, knowing how stiff and sore Andreas would be come the morning. 'Tell us where you're heading and we'll catch you up, once I'm mobile.'

Wenzel ran his fingers through his beard. He'd hoped that after Ravenna the Kunterbunt's debt to Andreas would be fulfilled, no matter Valter's rescue of Hulde about which he was undecided. But seeing Andreas as he was now, hardly able to move or walk, let alone perform, his conscience got the better of him. A Fair's person in distress was a Fair's person who couldn't be ignored.

'Well that's a plan, I suppose. Though don't know the exact route we'll be taking, only that we're heading south to the Abruzzo region.'

Not wanting to give too much away, not wanting The Balatronic Ballet to haunt them the whole way down.

'Might need to be a tad…more specific,' Andreas said, letting out a short groan as he pulled up a trouser leg, began to rub Rosa's liniment into a knee that looked like a deformed potato the colour of dark beet. Wenzel wincing as Andreas took up one of Peppe's leather struts and, with obvious pain, with crabbed fingers and swollen knuckles, began to tie it into place.

'We'll be sticking to the coast,' Wenzel admitted. 'Stopping in towns and villages a few days before moving on. Aiming to take our time, get there, and then back over the water to Montenegro.'

Only realising now that maybe that's not what they'd be doing at all.

Gonna leave you when we get over, Grandmother had said. And thinking of Grandmother he took a quick look around him, saw her staring at him, saw those black eyes alive, intent, eager to be gone, fingers twitching on her cane. Wenzel wanting to please her in this last hour of care. Putting out his hand to seal the bargain.

'So that's settled then,' he decided. 'We'll linger a little longer in the nearer places than we might have, hope you can catch us up.'

Andreas taking Wenzel's hand awkwardly, with rucked fingers, dipping his head.

'Mighty good of you,' he said. 'Other folk would have just dumped us, but not you, sir. Not you. And can't tell you how glad I am for it.'

Wenzel's cheeks colouring, eager to be gone, eager to be shot of this hanger-on for the time being at least. Eager to see what constituted Grandmother's Great Day and why it had turned her from Hulde-hater into Hulde-who-has-changed-my-life.

So away Wenzel went, Grandmother Pfiffmakler in the lead, Kunterbunt soon lost in the crowds dispersing from the pier in droves.

Valter Poppelmann appearing at Andreas's side.

'Go well?' he asked, levering his uncle up. Andreas slapping away Valter's helping hands.

'Jeez, boy!' Andreas exclaimed, pain raddling through his body like he'd been set on fire. 'Weren't all an act. Still gotta get meself fixed up. Reckon these supports are gonna do me good.'

Valter left off, looked away into the crowds, caught the highlights of Ludmilla's and Longhella's fiery orange skirts flashing through the dreary blacks and browns. Picked at a melon seed caught between his teeth.

'Hope you got what was needed, for gotta say it. Them Pfiffmakler girls is mighty handsome. And now they've got the Janus Woman with them, what's not to like?'

Andreas frowned, hating the way the lads sometimes talked about women, about girls. An idea why they did it, hating it all the same. He might be a charlatan, a con man, a man who spieled words faster than a stream in spate. Still had his values. Not as binding or high-sounding as men like Wenzel Pfiffmakler, but had them all the same.

'You shush your mouth on that,' Andreas said. 'If I ever catch you doing what you tried to do to that poor woman …'

'And what are you ever going to do about it, old man?'

Valter unconcerned, Valter laughing in his face. Andreas grinding his teeth, more angry than he'd been in years, and not just about the Janus Woman although he remembered the incident right enough. Valter having pushed her up against the back of their shack, the sight of that woman's face. Not the burned part, lost to emotion by her scars. As unable to move as he was now. Recalling instead the labile half of it, the part that said *I don't want to do this, but what choice do I have?*

The snake in human skin not so inhuman. Andreas touched by the Janus Woman's fate as he'd been by the concern the Pfiffmaklers had showered on him, as few others had done during his long life trawling around the circuits.

Looking hard at Valter, staring him down.

'I'll tell you this for the first and last time,' Andreas ground out. 'Yes, we'll trail the Kunterbunt, for they're our best ticket out, like Jodl wanted. But neither you, nor your brother, will act on any of the baser sentiments you might have. Am I clear?'

Valter Poppelmann flicked away his toothpick.

'Clear,' he agreed. 'Though can't speak for brother Jodl. You know what he's like when he's the bee under the bonnet.'

As Andreas did. Jodl never a lad who took commands lightly. Who'd always forged his own way, formed his own views. Who could be as vile a boy as Andreas had ever known. Who'd stamped with wholehearted enthusiasm on the young toads that came out in spring-time on the edges of tracks and byways. Jodl unrelenting, squishing them beneath his boot until all that was left were a few greenish smears in the dust. Such needless acts of cruelty oft repeated in a variety of ways, Jodl nothing if not inventive. His answer always the same when asked why.

But why not? What have they ever done for me?

And just when you thought Jodl had to be black through and through he would surprise with some gesture of largesse: give you his supper portion when there was hardly a scraping in the pot; or climb to the top of a tree and bring back a sackful of apples, carefully rummaging through his find, handing the best to whoever was nearest, keeping the worst for himself.

Jodl a true Janus, not one forged by circumstance like Livia had been.

Or no, Andreas corrected himself, that was too glib. Both brothers suffering circumstances making them what they were. They might be as dissimilar in nature as they were in looks. Valter with hair the colour of an over-ripe pomegranate, Jodl's dark and thick. Valter indolent, self-involved, unable to plan more than a few days ahead. Jodl focused, forward thinking, always hatching plans and schemes.

'Should have been a bloody philosopher!' was Valter's not infrequent comment when Jodl laid his latest plan before his brother, the two raising their lips in identical half smiles, sly and secretive, cutting Andreas out.

Or a general, Andreas thought at such times. Jodl a man for whom wars might have to be invented, if they didn't already exist. Which was maybe why he was so good at chess. And not just good. Could play five or six games all at the same time, the boards set up on one long table or on the ground, Jodl flitting from one to the other, moving this piece or that with no apparent thought. Andreas able to count on his fingers the few times Jodl had got into stalemate, the fewer times Jodl had definitively lost.

He'd made them a lot of money when they were in towns and cities where chess was all the rage in the coffee shops. Could have kept them all in coin if more places had people who played the game seriously enough to bet money on the outcome. How Jodl did it was unfathomable to Andreas, who'd barely mastered the basics, found the intricacies of strategy completely beyond him and therefore gained no joy or satisfaction from the challenge.

Valter, true to character, had never even tried.

'No need for the two of us to be geniuses,' Valter had said, contradicting himself by inventing The Balatronic Ballet Souvenir Chess Sets, deftly carving and painting pieces in the guises of common characters from street theatre and Commedia Del'Arte. Pulcinellas and Pantaloons, Pierrots and Pagliaccios, Scapinos and Scaramouches, Kaspar Larriscarri and his usual combatants. They'd almost been arrested once when Valter made the likenesses of the opposing kings and queens of a set far too well, their profiles clearly identifiable as real people, warring factions of a city state they'd had to leg it out of pronto.

A conundrum, those two boys. So alike in some ways, so disparate in others.

Formed by their shared circumstance.

Andreas couldn't shake the thought as he watched the Kunterbunt disappear into the crowded streets. Same thought he'd had when he'd picked the boys up as war scraps, the two squatted by the side of the road in their rags, stinking like bad barley that's been left to rot in a field after a storm has done with it. A rare moment of compassion when he'd stopped, allowed them to show him their trick acrobatics, which had been appalling—but not them. Not the boys themselves. Aged eight and ten he'd later discovered, though they'd looked younger. One red-headed, one dark. One expansive and ingratiating, which had been Valter. *A true showman,* Andreas had known it straightaway. Could see it all in his head: *Orphans! Ladies and Gentlemen. Snatched up from these troubled times in which we live!*

And then the dark haired boy had spoken up.

'Take us with you, mister. You'll not regret it.'

So certain those words, and so sure those dark eyes when Andreas had looked into them, seeing a lake whose depths had never been plumbed, challenging you to do it, see what was there, take its riches for your own. Had taken up the gauntlet, taken the two raggedy boys with him, declared them nephews if anyone asked too closely. Knew what went on in those wild hills they said they'd come from, gleaned a little more when they'd trusted him enough to squeeze out their story drib by drib, drab by drab. Dropped an unguarded comment about this or that. A terrible story. A jigsaw of blood, bone and hatred, red and raw as a slab of newly butchered meat in these boys if you scratched below the surface.

So no wonder they were as they were.

A miracle both were halfway normal.

Might have been an interesting conversation he would have had with Old Grandma on that score, had that situation ever arisen.

'How long are we going to stop here?' Ludmilla was asking, disliking that Grandmother Pfiffmakler had commandeered Hulde, was making the girl kneel with her in the courtyard of the basilica. The monk had finished his singing, the congregation beginning to stir. Scratching here at a tick bite, rubbing there at an itchy nose, coughing loudly into a handkerchief. Not a one of them making any move to go. All settling on their haunches, chatting amongst themselves, eagerly anticipating what would come next.

Wenzel as eager as Ludmilla to be gone, not that Grandmother looked like she was going to shift soon. They needed a meeting place. He'd shrugged off Andreas and his boys for the while but wasn't going to leave Grandmother in the lurch, and certainly not when she had Hulde with her. He needed a plan and had none, was starting to sweat under the pressure, until Peppe gifted him his out.

'I've just found out what's going on!' Peppe said. 'A real pleasure to hear the old language of my youth,' quick sigh, quickly going on. 'Gist is that today, right here, right now, they're bringing the relics of a new saint here. An Italian, the first for ages!'

Wenzel looking at Grandmother Pfiffmakler. So this was it.

'Bigger news for us,' Peppe went on undeterred, 'is that it's coinciding with the Sausage Festival. Time of year when folk from all over the region bring out all they've been curing and smoking the whole winter through. And that's right up our street!'

Wenzel could have kissed Peppe. At last something he could work with.

'And where is that street? Where's it being held?'

Peppe laughing.

'It's a real stroke of luck! They've got a fairs ground already set up in the hippodrome just down the way. Entry a bit strict, by all accounts, because of the saint thing. Everyone's to register, get proper passes. Should be easy enough for us, with all our documentation. Perfect place to go!'

Perfect place to go, except that Grandmother held all those precious passes, letters of passage and recommendation gleaned and bargained for during the long years she'd been in charge of the Kunterbunt.

And Grandmother Pfiffmakler apparently having other things on her mind.

'I need to speak to Grandma,' Wenzel said.

He didn't believe she'd withhold them, although one last act of spite was not beyond her.

'Peppe, get everyone to the fairs ground, wait for me there. Heraldo, get one of the boys to help you with the cart.'

Taking off his harness, rolling his shoulders at the release.

'What about Hulde?' Ludmilla anxious by his side.

'I'll bring her back with me,' Wenzel announced, decisive, in charge, seeing what had to be done and getting on with it. Everyone quick to obey, the Kunterbunt soon away.

Straight line from the back of the basilica, first turn left, next turn right and they were there, joining the long line of traders and entertainers eager to be in on the Sausage Fair that was going to be so much busier now Pope Gregory XVI had brought a saint to their doors.

What a gift!

Not that Gregory had thought to check out sausage fairs when he'd considered Alphonsus for canonisation. His reasoning entirely other. He'd negotiated his way through numerous political and religious revolutions since his election in 1831, with this faction or that challenging the power of Rome, having to send out papal troops to quell uprisings all over Italy. Not to mention the outrage of the French army barging their way into Ancona and seizing it for their own, their concomitant acts of cruelty forcing him to call in the Austrians for aid, God help him. He'd managed to get shot of both French and Austrians the previous year, but trouble by then brewing all over Europe. Spanish bishops being driven out in droves by Jansenist reformers; Prussian clergy threatening to refuse to put into action papal dictates; hundreds of faithful clerics in Russia being deported to Siberia, the nuns of Minsk massacred; France and Poland equally unstable and unreliable.

Time to put his foot down.

Time to reunite the vast majority of the Catholic Congregation who'd no knowledge of all this manoeuvring and manipulation going on behind the scenes.

Time to demonstrate to all these dissenters that Italy, and he— Bartolomeo Alberto Cappellari—held the keys of St Peter and was not to be trifled with.

Time to pick a new saint out of the line-up, whip up popular support, get the masses to realise that an Italy united was a stronger Italy, and a Church united was a stronger Church. One name springing immediately to mind. A man who'd died as recently as 1787, so within living memory, who'd founded a movement dedicated to the teaching and education of clerics who would take that teaching and education out to their communities; a man to whom miracles had already been attributed with good provenance, and many more witnesses coming forward as soon as his name had been publicly announced. A man who'd laid the foundations of the moral theology he hoped would soon be central to the Faith, Liguori's theory of Equiprobabilism a middle way between the preceding strictures of the Probabilism of the Jesuits and the Probabiliorism adopted with such enthusiasm by Innocent XI. Such hair-splitting didn't matter to the man in the street, but in the higher echelons of the Church it was absolutely crucial.

His preferred candidate already beautified, named a Doctor of the Church a mere twenty-three years previously. A blink of the eye, as far as church history went, and by none other than Gregory's three times predecessor Pius VII, about whom no one had a wrong word to say. Quite a rarity amongst popes, as Gregory well knew. The history of papal indiscretions, nepotism and manipulation of power enough to fill volumes.

Alphonsus Liguori it had to be.

Canonised in Rome, as was usual, and a more popular candidate would have been hard to find. The attending populace so great that one Franciscan had been crushed to death by the crowds, another escaping by the skin of his teeth.

Next task to decide where his body would finally be laid to rest.

Ravenna the obvious choice, its Archbishop being Gregory's friend.

Chiarissimo Falconieri Mellini to whom Gregory had given the influential post of Cardinal Priest of San Marcello, the consistory of the College of Cardinals, the preceding year, certain to take the line Gregory chose. And no political upheavals tied to the town, no arguments with the papal states. Ravenna an anachronism, converting to Christianity in the second century a mere one hundred and fifty years after Christ had died. A town that could not only claim authentic Christian lineage but prove it, having churches built by Theodoric himself, mosaics going back to the fifth century extant for all to see. Ravenna midway between top and bottom of Italy, with some of its churches still clinging to the ancient Ambrosian rites normally associated with Milan, which would please the northern half of the country no end, and the southerners ecstatic this new saint had been born a Neapolitan. Just as important, as far as the proselytising went, was that never once had Alphonsus left Italy. A man true to his roots for the entire stretch of his ninety-one years of life.

If Gregory had made a list of all the attributes he could have wished for he could have come up with no one better. Alphonsus Liguori the perfect candidate to reunite the warring factions of Catholicism that were splitting the Church apart.

16

Saints, Popes, and Sinners

The crowd in the courtyard of the basilica was on the move, rising like a swarm of sand-flies as several grand carriages drew up to the gates, Archbishop Mellini stepping out with his retinue, his Cardinal's cassock the bright colour of a rosehip after rain, cap hemmed with a twisted string of red and gold, as was the cord holding the heavy gold pectoral cross to his chest. He'd agonised briefly about whether to stick with the lesser dress of Archbishop, Gregory instructing otherwise.

'A Cardinal must show himself, my friend. Shine your elevation amongst the crowds. Be like a rising sun to them. It's not every day you're going to lay to rest a saint, and a brother at that.'

And by brother, Gregory meant Italian, one of their own. All three of noble birth and attaining the highest ranks possible in the Catholic hierarchy: one an Archbishop and Cardinal Priest of the consistory; another a Pope; the third having just been sainted. Three points of a blessed triangle holding this propitious day between their outstretched arms, declaring their shared intent to defend the true church against its enemies, bolster the growing nationalism that would one day make Italy a single entity instead of a collection of warring states.

Despite his rank, Mellini was nervous at the duty Gregory had laid on him. He'd always known he'd do well in his profession, his family's connections would have seen to that. Surprised all the same by how swift had been his rise. Ordained six days before his twenty-fourth birthday in September 1818, appointed Archbishop of Ravenna eight years later, and only twelve years after that—at the age of forty-three, far younger than was usual—Gregory seeing fit to ordain Mellini a Cardinal, and not only a Cardinal but the Cardinal Priest of San Marcello. He knew his path had been smoothed, his future moulded towards some end he couldn't see, and what struck him now, as he stepped out of his grand carriage in his even grander garb, was the gift a fellow bishop had sent him on his electorate to the Conclave of Cardinals. A biography of Alphonsus Liguori. It couldn't have been more propitious, like Isaiah prefiguring the birth and death of Christ.

Mellini's face calm and statesmanlike as he made his slow, straight-backed way towards the basilica, the crowds parting, bowing, praying, strewing spring flowers beneath his feet. Not a one of them aware of the turmoil going on inside their newly cardinalised Archbishop, that his stomach was churning with trepidation, skin sweating beneath his habit with the fear of being put to the test, prove himself worthy of all he'd been given, that he, God forbid, might fail. Might trip up on his habit or his words, forget the lines and religious theatre it had taken him weeks to learn.

He took a few deep breaths, tried to calm his heart that was nevertheless singing like the first song thrush in spring, about to accept a saint into his See.

The excitement about him was palpable, sweetened with the scent of the petals he was crushing beneath his feet. His chosen attendants at his back. His fellow celebrants, his deacon priests, his two good lords and true, the young acolytes bearing the gifts about to be offered in reflection of the Rite of Canonisation. Candles, bread, wine, turtle doves and singing birds.

The choir of the Monastery of the Blessed Virgin Mary of Mount Carmel already in situ, singing those beautiful chants unique to the Ambrosian Rite. Mournful, exquisite, preserving their eastern intonations. Mellini feeling like he might be climbing the slopes of Mount Carmel as he took his way up the wide stone steps of the basilica, gaining confidence with every rise, shedding doubt and strife.

About to enter into the greatest honour of his life.

'Grandmother,' Wenzel whispered. 'Could I have a word?'

Grandmother Pfiffmakler crossed herself, rose on creaking knees, looking up with irritation. Wenzel oddly reassured to be dealing with the old grandmother and not the new.

'It's about to begin,' she hissed, as she levered herself up on her cane. Wenzel about to help, stopped by the flash in her eyes he knew so well that said *Don't you dare! I might be old, young whippersnapper, but I can manage perfectly well on my own.*

And she was right, he supposed. She'd managed fine enough all these years with the Kunterbunt, and would manage fine enough without them. A relief to understand the truth of it, if it really came about. Wenzel smarting as she whacked her cane about his calves as she'd done when he was eight years old.

'Heaven's sake, boy. Just spit it out! You've always been a ditherer, just like your father. We've no time for any of that now.'

Looking angrily towards the throng bottlenecked at the steps as they gawked for a sight of the approaching Archbishop Cardinal. Her wanting to be in there, banging her cane left and right to get a better view.

'There's a fairs ground setting up a few streets away at the hippodrome,' Wenzel said quickly, Grandmother tutting loudly.

'Trust that lot to take advantage of what's supposed to be a Holy Day,' she said completely without irony, as if the Kunterbunt hadn't done the same on a hundred occasions. Wenzel briefly distracted by her *that lot,* as if she was no longer a part. Grandmother putting a hand into a pocket.

'Suppose you're wanting these,' shoving a tattered shagreen wallet at his chest.

Wenzel hesitating, had expected a fight, a show of resistance, a bargaining of power. Grandmother banging her cane on the ground with impatience.

'Just take them,' Grandmother sighing, voice softening. 'You're gonna need 'em every step of the way.'

'Thank you, Grandmother,' Wenzel said, placing his hand briefly on her shoulder. 'Come and find us after all this is done.'

'For our last hurrahs, you mean?' she laughed scornfully, shook her head. 'No, lad. This is it. This is my time.'

Wenzel aghast.

'You can't just leave! What are you going to do for money? How are you…'

The question dead on his lips as she took his hand in hers.

'Don't need much where I'm going. I've enough, Wenzel. And I've had enough.'

Dropping his hand, cocking her head as the bells in the tower began to ring out joyous arpeggios as Archbishop Mellini hove into view and began to climb up the steps.

'But Grandma!'

Hot tears in Wenzel's eyes, looking around as if there was something he could do to stop her. This wasn't how it was supposed to be. She couldn't just disappear out of their lives. Grandmother Pfiffmakler apparently having other ideas.

'Look after them,' she said. 'God knows, it will give you a headache every day for the rest of your life. But you chose it, Wenzel. Time to suffer the consequences.'

She started forwards. Wenzel unable to leave it, not like this.

'Grandma, wait!'

Tears running down his face, shimmering on the edges of his beard.

She turned her head back, look on her face like an angry wasp, eyes blinking spasmodically as she met Wenzel's own. And then did something she'd never done, not even to her own son for fear of softening him; put out a hand and caught the tears on Wenzel's cheek, rubbed a thumb gently at his skin.

'You'll be fine, Wenzel. You'll do just dandy. Anyone had to do it? Glad it was you.'

And that was it.

Grandmother Pfiffmakler off, throwing her cane about, creating her way.

'I'm an old woman! What d'you think you're doing pushing me? Have you no respect for your elders?'

Wenzel smiling despite his sorrow. Same Old Grandmother, right to the end. Wenzel following her progress as she moved through the crowds. Heard her voice gossipy in tone as an old man took her elbow and, astonishingly, she allowed him to do it.

'I knew him, you know, Alphonsus Liguori,' Wenzel leaning forward to catch her words, for this was news. 'Met him when I was a young woman in distress, met a saint in the making...'

Grandmother's voice drowned out by another pealing of the bells, not that Wenzel needed to hear more. All puzzles solved, and no wonder she considered it a miracle, their happening to be here on this very day, at this very time, and all because of Hulde...

'Hulde!' Wenzel called. Sniffed, blinked, wiped his tears on his sleeve. Rewarded by a small tug at the back of his jacket and there she was, standing behind him all this time.

'Hulde,' he breathed out his relief, went down on one knee and took the small hand she was holding out to him. 'You're all right! Thank the Lord, you're all right.'

And thank the Lord he did, not a usual occurrence.

This no ordinary day.

'Come on, you,' Wenzel said, giving Hulde's hand a squeeze. 'Let's get you home.'

Or as close to home as she'd known these past few weeks.

Hopefully not as close to home as she'd ever get.

'Well, what a relief!' Andreas exclaimed, Valter having just imparted the news about the Sausage Fair. 'And it's not that far. Pretty certain I can make it on my own two pins.'

Adjusting Peppe's leather supports that were doing him remarkably well, casting a look at Valter who was frowning. Not a good look on his normally handsome face, throwing his features into imbalance, accentuating the sharp square of his chin, the thinness of his lips as he sucked them in.

'Got to tell you something, Uncle.'

Andreas skewing his mouth at the appellation. Fine when other people were around, disliking it when it was just him and Valter, or him and Jodl come to that. Not that Jodl was often that familiar.

'What's the problem?' Andreas demanded. 'Means we can hook back up with the Kunterbunt straightaway instead of trailing them down country. They're sure to find out about the Sausage Fair sooner or later.'

Valter didn't answer immediately.

It had taken an age to get Andreas up and mobile after they'd disembarked from the ship. Valter, at Jodl's instruction, quick to use the time to find out what was going on with the crowds descending on Ravenna. Precisely what Jodl had been doing Valter didn't know. Rarely did. Jodl a closed book to him, as he was to everyone. They'd travelled with Andreas for years, told him something of their past but never all. The All a stumbling block for Valter, who preferred not to think about it.

Who blocked it off at every turn.

Who, in consequence, rarely suffered it to flit across his mind. *Take what you can get and run,* being Valter's only philosophy.

No idea how hard and disagreeable he could appear to other people, nor would have cared if he did. Caring very little about anything, liking the liberation it gave him. Despising close-knit groups like the Kunterbunt, how they fluttered and protected, fought for their own. He'd stuck with Andreas out of habit and because he provided a safety net, regular food and direction. If he'd ever found a better option he'd have been off like the wind.

'Jodl's gone,' Valter said. 'Thinks he's better off on his own for the now. Means there's no Balatronic Ballet for the moment.'

Valter regarding Andreas's puzzlement with amusement.

'And where exactly has he gone?' Andreas asked, as if Valter would ever know the answer. Andreas shaking his head in irritation at the futility of the question, letting out a sigh. Always trouble, these boys. Still thinking of them as boys, though they were long past being so. He'd never anticipated, when he'd gathered them up, they'd be with him for so long. Expected them to move on first chance they'd got, though they never had. Or rather, he qualified, had never had the chance, not being the most likeable of children, possessing a triad of traits that were never admired singularly and certainly not together. The two of them selfish, callous and singularly averse to friendships of any kind. Andreas never pushing them to go and, even as men, they'd not left him. Maybe because they'd grown used to him and he to them. A family, if an odd one, although the brothers would never admit it.

At least Andreas hoped it was so. Tried another tack.

'Don't suppose he's told you why he wanted us over to Italy.'

Not bothering to make it a question, Valter not bothering to reply.

'Well, all right then,' Andreas ploughed on. 'So what? We stop here until Jodl joins us?'

'S'pose,' Valter replied, maddeningly vague. Andreas used to it. Andreas not up to arguing or trying to make Valter spit out details he most probably didn't know. Jodl always the leader as far as these two went.

But the why of this journey was troubling him. Never once had Jodl or Valter tried to influence where he was taking them, Andreas sticking to routes he'd utilised for the past three decades. Until they'd arrived in Zadar on their regular circuit, Andreas ready to shift as usual after a week. Not so Jodl and Valter, who were adamant they wanted to stay put for a while. He'd no idea why, for it made pickings slim, no one wanting to see The Balatronic Ballet more than a few times, given their limited repertoire. And there was only so much hedgehoggery any man could sell. Then, out of the blue, Jodl suddenly announced they needed over to Italy. Andreas arguing against it.

'I've never been,' he'd said. 'We won't know any routes, where the fairs are. And the Italian they speak mightn't be the same as here. And what about money? How are we to pay for passage?'

'No need to worry about that,' Jodl confidant, cocky, commanding. 'We'll find a way.'

And so they had. The Kunterbunt rolling into Zadar a week or so later, heading straight for the harbour. Valter doing his usual, listening in, finding out where they were going. Jodl quick with his plan.

'Get yourself in with them any way you can. Play the fairs' card,' Jodl ordered. And it had been an order, Andreas under no illusion on that score. Reins whipped away from his hands with such speed his palms itched with the offence. Not the first time Jodl's quick transitions had made Andreas's blood pulse in his throat with annoyance, nor, as now, without growing trepidation. Andreas wondering if Jodl hadn't known the Kunterbunt were on their way before they'd known it themselves, so fortuitous was their coming.

Jodl having some goal Andreas didn't know about, and didn't like it.

Andreas wondering if Jodl and Valter had engineered the plan of chucking the girl overboard precisely so Valter could rescue her, seal their pact with the Kunterbunt. Andreas couldn't prove it. Like he'd said to Wenzel, it had been dark, his body tortured in the rigging as he'd tried to keep himself stable and safe. Had told Wenzel it had definitely not been a woman who'd thrown the girl overboard. Hadn't told Wenzel that when her attacker had snatched her up and bunged her over Andreas had been about to cry out in protest when the figure had turned very swiftly and looked right up into the rigging, drawing a thumb across his throat. Andreas getting the message loud and clear: *make a squeak and you're done for.* Features hidden by a scarf about his face, but that quick slice of his thumbnail eerily familiar. Suspicions bolstered when Valter—Valter, of all people!—dived in after the girl. Valter, who'd never done anything kind or unsolicited for anyone in all the time Andreas had known him.

Andreas worrying about it, wondering if the brothers were capable of such a dangerous stunt. Andreas worrying more to realise that yes, they absolutely were. They were reckless, could be cruel, and he was angry at them all over again. Even more so when it had been Wenzel's boys, not Andreas's own, who came up to help him.

And, now he was no longer focused entirely on getting his arms and legs to work again, he was furious with the two of them, looking on Valter as he might have looked at an ant he'd inadvertently stepped on in the street. No regret, only mild disgust.

No idea what Jodl had in mind since Andreas had engineered him into Italy as asked, but Andreas, cowardly and sly as he was, made a decision he would have deemed brave had he understood its consequences. Nineteen years he'd looked after Valter and Jodl, carried them, cared for them, but he was not an idiot. Knew something had changed with the brothers or, more particularly, with Jodl. As if they'd broken back into the razor sharp pieces they'd been when he'd first found them. Valter's treatment of the Janus Woman proof of that. And no way he was going to spend his latter years putting them back together yet again. His joints getting stiffer with each successive season. A few more bad winters out in the open and he'd be needing crutches, shoulders to lean on.

And neither Valter nor Jodl would provide for him as he'd provided for them.

Enough was enough.

Decision made.

He'd hook back up with the Kunterbunt soon as he could, no matter what Jodl or Valter had to say about it. Spill out his misgivings to Wenzel Pfiffmakler, put the two brothers on a plate and hand them over. Let Wenzel Pfiffmakler, with all his high and mighty principles, divvy them up as Andreas had never been able to do. Throw himself on Wenzel's mercy in the faint hope that his last years weren't going to be as miserable and difficult to cope with as he feared.

Life never just sun and roses.

Real life was biting insects, scratchy thorns, bad water and never enough food.

Kipping in tents and moving carts from place to place to scrape a living.

Take what you can get and run.

Except Andreas could no longer run.

Andreas hardly able to walk.

'Tell your brother I'm off to the fairs ground,' he informed Valter, securing his hedgehoggery backpack on his shoulders, securing the straps. 'If you want to join me then so be it. If not, I'll understand.'

Andreas Zilboorg hobbling off down the street. Valter making no move to join him. Andreas ten yards distant when Valter shouted out.

'See you soon, old man!'

Andreas closing his eyes to the taunt, Valter as casually cavalier as his brother had always been. Only thought in Andreas's mind being how quickly and far he could get from the two of them, and how much he wanted to meet the Kunterbunt again, be a part of their normality.

God help me, he muttered, without turning, never wanting to see either Valter or Jodl again.

Two decades of caring gone down the pan in an instant.

Had always known that family was a bad idea, and yet burning to get to the one that was the Kunterbunt, get to them without dragging his own false family behind him. Crabbing his way up the street towards the hippodrome where the fairs folk were gathering.

God help me, he muttered again, hoping that would be the case, that he'd find the Kunterbunt before Valter and Jodl found him.

17

Into the Fair

Town clerk Panizzi was getting bored sitting at his makeshift desk at the entrance to the hippodrome, nevertheless was meticulous and officious, inspecting every document thrust his way, writing down the names of the folk he chose to let in, handing them their passes. Dismissing those he deemed unworthy with a quick decisive shake of his head.

'Not good enough,' he'd say; or, 'These papers are surely forged!'

Most of those turned away of dubious character: purveyors of alcohol, children who could only be pickpockets without a jot of paper between them; men and women he suspected to be tricksters, practitioners of various gambling games. The Sausage Fair might be going ahead as usual yet, in concession to the Holy Day going on at the basilica, he'd been instructed to debar anyone of such ilk.

In entire agreement. If he'd had his way the Sausage Fair would have been cancelled, but no. It brought in too much trade, people travelling for weeks, sometimes months, specifically for it.

Those refused entry grumbled, if not for long. Two armed guards seeing to that. Highly likely they'd mill away around the other end of the hippodrome, burrow themselves into the legitimate attendees already setting up their booths and stalls. Wouldn't know he'd seen a way around this, had everyone officially let in given a red ribbon to tie about their sleeves and, soon as the grounds were officially open to the public, he and his guards would be working up and down, quarter by quarter, snatching up anyone who didn't have one. It wasn't foolproof by any means. Probably already a ribbon seller set up making a fortune, but Panizzi had a good eye, would be able to spot the real thing at a glance for he'd had his wife and daughters sew small white crosses on each official ribbon in remembrance of the saint about to be laid to rest here. His small contribution to the honour being bestowed upon Ravenna. And what an honour! His stomach skittering when he recalled the large creamy white vellum letter arriving on his desk. His task to sort the mayor's correspondence into what was important and what was not. Turning it over to find the impress of the Archbishop stamped into its purple wax, the message from Cardinal Mellini—yes, cardinal!—that Ravenna was to host a ceremony of the highest importance, namely the acceptance of a saint. And then, oh the glory! Included was the original missive to Mellini written in Pope Gregory's own hand confirming the same.

The greatest day in Panizzi's mundane life. He'd read both missives several times until their contents truly sank in, checking and rechecking the seals to make sure one of his sons wasn't playing him the most tasteless of jokes, for they were fond of that. As irreverent towards the Church as so many of their generation were.

Not him.

Town clerk Panizzi loving the Church and Ravenna in equal measure, and this day marking a glorious future. Folk flocking in from all over Italy, and would soon arrive in droves from the rest of Europe once they learned the embalmed remains of Saint Alphonsus Liguori were being preserved in the basilica of Sant'Apollinare. Not just a dubious finger or arm-bone but his body entire, exhumed whole in his coffin and so well embalmed forty-odd years previously—God-blessed, as Panizzi chose to believe—that he might have been laid in his sarcophagus the previous week. Sanctified in death as in life, transported from Rome to Ravenna; passing through Nocera, where Alphonsus had died, along the ancient Via Flaminia, the artery by which the lifeblood of early Christianity had permeated Italy with such speed, and so fitting that Ravenna's saint had made such a journey.

He shook his head, wiped his glasses, his internal monologue disrupted by the next set of applicants. Panizzi looking up, dismayed by the long line still waiting to be admitted to the hippodrome. This day of all days he'd wanted to be finished early, get to the basilica, be part of the momentous.

Instead he was stuck here behind his desk.

'Name,' he barked.

'Wenzel Pfiffmakler.'

'Purveyor of?'

'Entertainment. The Kunterbunt Trudelndschau.'

Panizzi looked up sharply, narrowing his eyes.

'Type of entertainment?'

'We perform theatre and puppetry,' Wenzel said smoothly, 'mostly of a religious nature.'

Wenzel no fool, noticing the types of people being turned away, their carts loaded with barrels of wine or beer, haversacks rattling with dice and counters, rolled-up betting games sticking out from their tops.

'Examples?' Panizzi no fool either, glancing down the line of the Pfiffmakler family, catching the bright orange of the girls' skirts.

'We do a great many Advent and Easter Cycles,' Wenzel went on. 'Deluge, Creation of the World, Martyrdom of the Saints. That sort of thing.'

This last was not strictly in their repertoire, figured it couldn't hurt, and he was right.

'And you've passes from other places?'

Wenzel producing Grandmother's shagreen pouch, Panizzi impressed by its authoritative contents.

'Very well,' he said, writing down Wenzel's name, handing him their pass.

'How many of you?' he asked.

'Ten,' Wenzel's reply automatic, blinking suddenly to realise he'd forgotten to include Hulde. Then relaxed. He'd forgotten Hulde, but Grandmother Pfiffmakler was not with them so the numbers were right. Panizzi carefully counting out ten red ribbons, handing them to Wenzel.

'Tie these about your right sleeve. Keep them on at all times. And keep your pass handy. There will be checks.'

And checks there would be. Panizzi adamant that this great day, this great week, not be sullied by drinking and gambling. Curious too to see what this lot would produce, if they'd put on something in honour of Ravenna's newly acquired saint.

'Next!' he shouted, taking a quick look at his pocket watch, desperate to be away. But duty came first: to his superiors, his Church, and Ravenna, in that order.

Wenzel left him to it, leading his family on towards the green, twitching his lips as he wondered if Andreas and his Balatronic Ballet would pass muster. He couldn't see a reason why they would. Maybe he'd never have to clap eyes on any of them again. Thought soon gone as he negotiated his way through the throngs setting up their stalls, surprised by how ordered they were. Surprise soon explained by a soldier stopping him in his tracks.

'Show your pass,' the man demanded, Wenzel quick to produce it. 'Entertainers, eh. Why aren't you wearing your ribbons?'

Wenzel flummoxed. Had never been to such a supervised fair. Usually everyone just poured in, set up where they could, a flock of redwings settling on a field.

'Was waiting until we were allotted our plot,' he explained, the guard mollified, waving his hand.

'Entertainments at the back. Food sellers, tradesmen, then entertainment. But says on your pass you're doing religious theatre?'

Wenzel nodding. All to do with Grandmother Pfiffmakler's big day. Sausage Fair not to be allowed to interfere, and no wonder the clerk at the entrance had been so assiduous in turning the drinking and gambling fraternity away.

Not at all the impression the town wanted to give its many religious visitors.

Getting one of those headaches Grandmother Pfiffmakler had warned him about.

'Exactly,' he got out. 'We'd like to put on something that celebrates Ravenna, given what's going on at the basilica. Although I'm afraid we're new here, had no idea...'

Unexpectedly interrupted by the guard, who handed back Wenzel's pass.

'With me, then,' he commanded. 'I think we can make an exception in your case, and I've just the person you need to speak to.'

Wenzel quick on the man's heels, motioning the rest of the family to follow.

'Set yourselves up over by the hedge, and get yourself speaking to Helmut Knibb there.'

Pointing at a stall toting books and mechanicals, trestle tables covered with them; crates underneath left, right and centre filled to bursting with more.

'Want to know about Ravenna,' the guard said, 'then Helmut's your man. And get your blasted ribbons on.'

He brought his boots quickly together with a sharp snap and moved on.

'Show your pass,' Wenzel heard, as the guard moved off. 'And what's that ribbon? That's no ribbon, not an official one. So get you gone.'

The guard giving a boy a vicious whack about his shoulders with his truncheon before hauling the lad off. 'And tell the rest of your little *ragazzo* friends they're not welcome here. We'll have no thieving, no sleight of hand, no...'

The guard's voice lost to the general hubbub, Wenzel feeling the stab of that headache again for this was shaping up to be no ordinary fair. Theme not so much sausage, general debauchery and delight. More like Grandma Pfiffmakler's old fare. Religious, upright and pedagogic. No tried and tested ribald Kaspar Larriscarri sketches to entertain the crowds. No lovelorn star-crossed lovers, no whimsical folktales espousing magic and ungodly enchantment. What was needed was the uplifting, the highbrow, links to church, cardinals and popes, to Ravenna's sacred past.

If they were to make any money the Kunterbunt, namely Wenzel, was going to have to come up with something relevant, and come up with it fast.

18

Saints and Tigers

Grandmother Pfiffmakler got to the top of the steps by aid of her new helper, who was agog at the news she'd actually met St Alphonsus in the flesh.

'There's a book inside the basilica,' he confided, 'in which folk can add their memories of him.'

'And their miracles?' Grandmother asked quickly.

The man nodding energetically.

'Them too. Did you…? Did he…?'

'He did,' Grandmother could not have been prouder, felt ten years younger, indeed felt like that young wifey again, in mind if not in body, come newly from Nocera with a saint's blessing on her head. The man beside her appreciative.

'Then we've to get you to the front. Get you grand-side. There's going to be a bit after the ceremony when… Hey, Ettori!'

He pulled his charge to one side, held up his hand, raised his voice.

'Ettori! Get yourself here!'

Grandmother dizzy as folk pushed past her, all eager to get in; saw with dismay the vast atrium of the basilica filled wall to wall. And the walls magnificent, covered top to bottom, clerestory to nave, with glittering mosaics; twenty-four pillars of Constantinople marble marching down towards the altar area where a platform had been raised, Mellini already atop being led to his throne beneath the rich baldacchino rippling gently overhead. No pews, just the press and heat of bodies cramming themselves into every available space. It was stifling, and she was overwhelmed, wishing she'd thought to bring Wenzel with her, brought him into her secrets so he could at least find her a place she could rest, prop her up long enough for her take part in the celebratory mass.

'Ettori!'

Her companion's voice so loud in her ear she almost wrenched her arm from his, was about to do exactly that, find her own way, beat a path open before her with her cane, when the Ettori fellow appeared. A young monk, face visibly perspiring, beaded on face and clean shaven cheeks.

'It's madness, Susinno!' Ettori spoke quickly, breathlessly. 'I know I was supposed to keep everyone in rhyme and rank, but honestly! These people! We'd need an army to keep them in order.'

He swept an arm about him to indicate how hard he'd tried, how spectacularly he'd failed. Grandmother's aide shaking his head, unsurprised.

'Good news travels fast, my friend. But we've a more urgent matter to attend to.'

Tugging at Grandmother Pfiffmakler's arm.

'She's a witness, Ettori. This lady here's a real live witness.'

Ettori blinked, looked from Susinno to grandmother, stumbling forward as more eager congregants shoved him in the back and barged their way in.

'A real live witness?' he repeated Susinno's words. 'Are you sure?'

As if Grandmother Pfiffmakler wasn't there, as if Grandmother Pfiffmakler hadn't been a fairs person for over half a century, able to pick out weighted coins the second she saw them. Put her knowledge into use.

'Knew him, met him, had miracles done by him,' she stated. 'That enough?'

Ettori hesitated. People had being trying to trick him all morning to get themselves better places for the ceremony, but Susinno was to be trusted—an elder of the church—and this woman old enough to have met the saint himself.

'This way,' he said, leading the two off, taking them though the crowds with his cry of *We've a witness! Make way! We've a witness!*

Grandmother beaming inwardly, though no one would know it: face sharp and hard as an almond baked in the hot Italian sun. Ettori's words working nonetheless, people making way for her, hands reaching out to touch her clothes as if she could confer a blessing on them. Ettori taking her right down to the altar area before which two lines of seats had been erected, filled with men and women Grandmother Pfiffmakler's age: old folk who claimed to have met St Alphonsus earlier in their lives. Two seats left, Grandmother Pfiffmakler taking one, Susinno squatting down on the cold flags in front of her, leaning his back against her shins, claiming his place. Susinno sighing. Susinno, elder of the church and one of the council who'd made the rules about who was allowed to sit where and who was not, taking advantage of his position as he'd never done before. Susinno feeling the small kickings of Grandmother Pfiffmakler's feet against his back. Susinno not to be moved. Front seat granted him by serendipity, by a small act of kindness helping an old woman up the steps, and was not going to be budged.

Last seat taken a few moments later by an elderly man all of a jitter, who stumbled over Susinno and would have fallen into Grandmother's lap had Ettori not quickly righted him and set him down in his seat. Grandmother didn't complain, hardly noticed, stupefied to have been granted a such a grand view, heart on fire with anticipation, this the apex of her life. The Black Madonna of Montenegro nothing by comparison, ashes to this rich wine whose headiness was flooding through her. An Archbishop Cardinal a mere few yards away from her, and the coffin that contained the remains of the man who'd changed her life right in front of her, resting at an upward angle upon a bier so covered over with garlands of flowers none of the intricate carvings in its black oak could be glimpsed. So close that when two white-cassocked acolytes came forward and reverentially removed the lid to reveal Alphonsus to public view Grandmother's lips parted, let out a breath she felt she'd been holding in for years.

'It's really him,' she whispered involuntarily, moving her upper body forward, hands trembling on her cane, tears flooding her eyes. It seemed impossible that the face whose every line, every crease, she'd remembered vividly for half a century, right down to the comb lines in hair and beard, the faint tracery of broken blood vessels on nose and cheeks, could have been so perfectly preserved.

Truly he looked exactly as she remembered him.

Another miracle, she thought.

'It's uncanny,' murmured the old woman sitting to her left.

'It's incorruptibility,' said the man to her right, who was still jittering, suffering a palsy that made his muscles spasm of their own accord, hoping this new rub with the numinous might cure him.

'It's the mark of a saint!' another man said at Grandmother's back. 'And it's going to turn Probabilism on is head! You won't know this,' he dropped his voice as he spoke to his neighbour, 'but it was only a few days ago I got my finest example to state my case. A man and a child jumping about in a puddle. In a puddle!'

He would have gone on, as he often did and at great length, had not the opening of the coffin signalled the start of the ceremony, the choristers placed to left and right of these ancient witnesses getting to their feet as the acolytes took up hand-bells and tolled them one after another until the sound was continuous and the crowd in the atrium stilled, Ettori and several of his brethren finally managing what they'd been unable to do on their own: clearing a path from the outer steps right through the basilica down to altar and stage.

All is ready, Ladies and Gentlemen.

You might have seen theatres and puppet shows.

You might even have seen the spectacular pyrotechnics of the Kunterbunt's Creation of the World.

You might have walked down the wide streets of an abandoned village and discovered a girl, blood-boltered, emerging from a pile of corrupting corpses.

But let me tell you this, Ladies and Gentleman.

Let me tell you this, Grandmother Pfiffmakler.

Open your eyes.

Open your ears.

Open your heart.

Open your soul.

For you'll never see the like again.

168

'Helmut Knibb?' Wenzel asked, as the rest of the family settled, eased harnesses from aching shoulders, figured out where to place their makeshift stage and the pits for their lights. A good spot they'd been given by the guard, very good. Right behind the food sellers and some way from the other entertainers, so folk traipsing from the front of the fair would be sure to see them first.

Helmut Knibb an old man, grey hair sparse about his head, beard going almost to his waist.

'That's me,' he said amicably, as Wenzel approached, Heraldo quicker, Heraldo tearing off his harness soon as he saw what Helmut Knibb had laid out on his stall between his many books.

'Oh my!' Heraldo dancing on his feet, fingers touching first one mechanical device and then another. 'How many types of cranks have you got here? And all these pumps! And look at that jack! Is it hydrostatic?'

'Why yes it is, young man,' Helmut replied, ignoring Wenzel, picking the object up. 'The pump has a hollow base, takes water through a pipe into the ram to raise the cylinder. And I've added a valve operated by a thumb-screw that lets the water back in incremental—'

'To lower the load?' Heraldo interrupted.

'Precisely,' Helmut agreed. 'You're very perspicacious.'

Wenzel frowning, not that anyone noticed.

'And this?' Heraldo asked, picking up another object from between the towers of books.

'That,' Helmut said, adjusting his spectacles, taking a closer look at this lad who was so taken by his work. 'That's a modification I've made to an ellipsograph so the attached pencil makes its movement according to the rectilinear shifting of the studs in their grooves.'

'That's genius!' Heraldo quick with his appreciation. Wenzel having no idea what they were talking about, but Heraldo getting in with this man fine with him. Letting them go on for five, ten minutes more, talking cams and gears, wings and cross-heads, piston rods and cog-wheels, before he called a stop.

'Apologies for interrupting,' he said, though neither Heraldo nor Helmut paid him any mind.

Wenzel cleared his throat.

'Excuse me,' he said loudly. 'I understand that my son's interest in your work is…'

'You must be very proud of him,' Helmut Knibb turned his face to Wenzel, beard quivering as if there was a dormouse in there trying to fight its way out.

'Indeed I am,' Wenzel averred. 'But we're here to ask your help not in the mechanicals, although I'd be delighted if you'd lend your time to—'

'It's not often I meet someone with such avid interest,' Helmut interrupted, looking over at Heraldo who'd moved onto something new, was already dissecting the object in his head, would happily have set to with screwdriver and spanner if he'd been allowed. 'So how may I help you?'

'It's like this,' Wenzel began, having finally caught the old man's attention, although Helmut's eyes had already drifted back to Heraldo.

'Careful with that,' he admonished. 'That there's a Jacquet-Droz original.'

'No need to worry, sir,' Wenzel said, a trifle impatiently. 'Heraldo reconstructed a Tipu's Tiger from scratch when he was…'

The old man swivelled his eyes back to Wenzel, Wenzel blinking under the intensity of his gaze.

'Did he now? Well, how interesting. And where did you come by such a thing?'

Wenzel waved his hand dismissively.

'We didn't. We saw one on show somewhere and Heraldo, well, he figured it out. Made his own. Took him months.'

Helmut Knibb played his fingers through his beard, dark eyes glittering, fixed on Heraldo.

Like an owl on a vole, Wenzel thought.

'If we could get back to the business in hand,' Wenzel tried again, 'I'm sure Heraldo would be glad to…'

'Of course!' the old man giving a quick shake of his head, turning it fully towards Wenzel, Wenzel finding the mobility of that neck, and the immobility of the man's body, peculiar and disturbing.

'You need my help, I think you said?' Helmut added, suddenly effusive, attentive. 'So what can I do you for?'

The choir was singing. Lilting, melodious, lachrymy given substance and voice as down the cleared walkway, between crowds and marble columns, came Mellini's fellow celebrants: the Abbott leading with the Processional Cross of his monastery affixed to a tall staff, keeping it perfectly straight without sway or dip, a feat of balance any fairs' man would have been proud of. Immediately behind came the two good lords holding aloft vast candles, made from the finest beeswax, on which were painted on the one a clear portrait of St Alphonsus and on the other the Ravenna coat of arms. Next came the deacon priests and four monks holding the four poles of the umbraculum, woven from white cloth and gold thread, that protected and announced their sacred gifts. With slow and solemn step the celebrants neared their destination, passing the rows of witnesses, the choir ceasing and stilling, their collective voice overtaken by a single monk chanting the opening of the Offertorium as he'd done on the steps outside.

Ecce apertum est Templum tabernaculi
Behold the Temple of the Tabernacle

Grandmother Pfiffmakler shivering in her seat, eyes fixed on the men who were placing their candles, the height and breadth of new-born children, into holders either side of the bier. Wicks set alight, candles to be kept burning the entire week the incorruptible body of St Alphonsus was to be kept on open view.

And up the steps to the altar platform went the deacon priests, bowing to their cardinal on his throne, holding out pyx and barrel for his blessing. Mellini doing as Gregory had advised, rising like the sun from his throne in his bright tunic, taking a few steps forward, regarding the gathered populace before him, as awed as they by the moment, by the solemnity, the sanctity they were being granted which would be as near as any of them would get to attending an actual canonisation in Rome.

The monk came to the end of his chant, and now Mellini was properly on stage, nervous as any Pfiffmakler despite his previously learned script.

'We receive your gifts, Ravenna,' he intoned. 'We receive the candles, whose wax symbolizes Christ's humanity and whose light represents the splendour of the life of our new saint. We accept the flame that tells us of the love of the faithful for God and the fire of Charity.'

Took another step forward, taking the pyx from his deacon priest.

'And today we celebrate the ancient sacrifices that brought us to the true path, to the living Body of Christ.'

Placing the pyx on the altar, opening its lid, spilling the hosts onto to a silver platter. Taking the barrel of wine, now unstoppered, pouring its contents into the waiting chalice, a simple wooden cup Mellini favoured for higher masses.

'And we thank God for the fruit of His vine,' Mellini went on, 'and all it represents, namely charity, devotion and compunction.'

Debatable whether any of his audience exhibited such noble emotions on a daily basis, certainly not Grandmother Pfiffmakler.

'And now the two turtle doves,' Mellini went on smoothly, getting into his part, the priest bringing them forward, 'who remind us of the power of the Holy Spirit and the peace that came after the Deluge which swept all wickedness away.'

Turtle doves shuffling and cooing within their bars as Mellini kissed the hand that offered them and the priest went down on his knees and kissed Mellini's sandaled feet. The second priest arriving on cue with his own offering of seven songbirds.

'And here are the Souls of the Just, the representation of the seven-fold blessing bestowed on every saint...'

Mellini pausing as he placed the cages on the altar, one at either end for, as he did so, one of the small songbirds, a blackcap, usually so elusive, released a rippling melancholic tune. A startling sound in the vast atrium of the basilica, Mellini so close he could see the bird's throat quivering with the effort, wing feathers riffling. And, seized by the moment, he leaned forward, released the catches and out went the blackcap, followed by linnet, throstle, robin, blackbird, warbler and woodlark. All fluttering away into the eaves, the audience holding up their heads to see them, trying to divine some significance in their going. Mellini hearing a small tutting at his back from the priest who'd employed several small boys for several long days to ensnare them, him worrying every night he'd not got the right ones, had paid good money to a bird seller to have them identified as the right kind for the job.

Mellini smiling broadly, pulled back his shoulders, nodding his head at the choir who began their next chant *sotte voce* so as to emphasise and not drown out Mellini's next words, which told the congregation of the life of Alphonsus, followed by the prayer of sainthood.

In honour of the Blessed Trinity, for the exaltation of the Catholic Church and the growth of Christian Life, with the authority of our Lord Jesus Christ...

And then the mass proper, with all its bells, incense and genuflections, a mass going by the book until it was halted every now and then by the singing of a blackbird or a robin when everyone stilled, waited, uplifted by this unexpected addition to the glory of the day. Mellini at those times holding up his hands, stopping his voice, letting the birdsong flow and go before carrying on as if it had been planned this way, as if the birds were part of the service which, in a way, they were. And so perfect, so apt. The Souls of the Just joining in.

No thoughts at all that the birds might be singing out in desperation, believing themselves lost in a crepuscular forest they did not recognise, calling for kin to show them the way out.

'My advice is to stick close to home,' Helmut Knibb was saying. 'The early history of Ravenna is provocative, to say the least. Capital of the Western Roman Empire in 402, Theodoric defeating Odacer whom he supposedly murdered with his own hands at a peace conference; recovered by the Eastern Roman Empire for Justinian; became an Exarchate, second only to Rome in power. And then you've the murder of Eutychius, the last Exarch, when Ravenna became the seed for the notion of papal states...'

Wenzel held up his hands.

'That's all very helpful,' thinking it anything but. 'And if we had a week to plan then we could certainly put it to use in every detail. But we've to get something going for tonight. You see my problem?'

Helmut wound his fingers through the end of his long beard, thumbs hooked into his belt.

'I do,' he said slowly. 'Do you know anything of Ravenna at all?'

Wenzel shook his head.

'You've never been here before?'

The muscles at the sides of Wenzel's mouth stiffening, perceiving insult. Helmut raising his eyebrows, apparently much amused, at least to Wenzel's interpretation. Wenzel letting out an irritated sigh.

'Tall order,' Helmut said quickly. 'But don't despair. I might have the very thing. Ever heard of St Peter of Verona? Well no, probably not,' he added, as he saw Wenzel's eyes narrowing. 'And no reason, of course, that you should. But his life and death were made for the stage: childhood cruelty, burning globes, heroic death at the hands of heretics. Sound good?'

Wenzel sniffed, mollified.

'Well yes,' he admitted, conjuring up a scenario in his head to fit these random pieces of information together, how they could be used, who should take what parts, what effects could be used to emphasise the dramatic. 'Sounds exactly right. And sounds to me,' he added, the thought only just occurring, 'that you know a bit about theatre.'

Helmut Knibb cocked his head to one side, unhooked his thumbs from his belt.

'Did a bit when I was younger,' he said, 'until this.'

Rapping the knuckles of his right hand against his upper right thigh, a dull sound Wenzel knew well. Fingers on cloth on wood. Which explained the immobility of the man's body, the way he'd skewed his neck around from Heraldo to Wenzel that Wenzel had found so unnerving, and why Helmut had not moved a jot since the start of their conversation. Wenzel scratched at his neck.

'No need to look discomfited,' Helmut said. 'Lost it in a good cause. Was in Genoa in 1800 when Masséna and his Frenchies marched into the city and the Austrians put us under siege. Almost two months we was all trapped in there.'

He tapped his leg again, unexpectedly laughed.

'Oh but we didn't give 'em an easy time of it! Kept going at them, us few partisans, us few true, every chance we got. Got this,' he indicated his leg, 'chopped off after it got infected. Only a shot to the foot, if you can believe it, but blood went bad.'

Wenzel could believe it. His opinion of Helmut Knibb shifting from suspicion to admiration. He'd not much grasp of history, though knew from Peppe and Rosa their childhood had not been quiet, that turbulence in Italy had abounded.

'And honest,' Helmut went on, 'we thought we was going to win, that the Austrians would break the siege, and then the bloody plague broke out and them Frenchies couldn't wait to sign a waiver and run for the hills, or rather for the coast. Ran back to their mammies, like the rats they were.'

No jubilance to Helmut's words, only the deepest bitterness that his victory had been no victory at all, merely a consequence of unforseen circumstance. Italy under Napoleon's rule a few years later, despite his sacrifice to the cause.

'Hey, Mr Knibb!' Heraldo broke onto the scene, eyes bright as those of the dolphins they'd seen on the way over, and almost as big. 'Know anything about this?'

He held up a book, opened it to the frontispiece, tapping at it with a finger.

'*On the Compensation of Physical Forces in the Human Voice Box,* by Johannes Peter Müller,' Helmut read out loud. 'Hmm. Only published earlier this year; got it…let me see, ah yes. In a crate sent me from Berlin. Always keep a stash of scholarly books for the academics. Got a little book shop over on…'

Heraldo's fingers twitching, too polite to interrupt but finally finding it too much.

'He did this experiment,' he broke in. 'Used a severed head and his wife's piano to figure out how the human voice produces so many tones.'

He looked from Helmut to Wenzel, patently expecting the penny to drop, which it did not.

'Don't you see?' he explained, throwing up a hand in exasperation. 'Think what we could do with the marionettes! And the tinkle-boxes! We could use all different types of membranes at different tensions over different shapes to alter pitches and reverberations, just like he explains right here in this book. We could make them so much more realistic!'

Helmut nodding, understanding.

'You mean you could make a Tipu Tiger that really roars?'

Heraldo blinking at the reference.

'Well yes, that too. Although I was thinking more of the Kaspar Larriscarri sketches. How we could get them more in character, more distinctive than just, well, don't take this the wrong way, father,' glancing at Wenzel, who tipped his head to tell his son to go on. 'Well that falsetto you use for the wife?' Heraldo blushed. 'It's not exactly…um…well, it's kind of obviously you…'

Wenzel had been keeping himself in a tightly lidded box all day, wrestling with the problems of Andreas, of Grandmother Pfiffmakler's sudden and dramatic leave-taking, getting the Kunterbunt into the fair and what they were going to put before the paying public in less than eight hours. Now, seeing his son here before him, as bubbled over with new ideas as a burst pipe, everything seemed to fall into its right place, the trajectory of events that had brought them here to Ravenna seeming no longer a problem but exactly as it should be.

He raised his head a fraction and, in the same action, breathed deeply, rolled his shoulders, felt the knot at the base of his neck loosening.

'You're right. My Mrs Kaspar Larriscarri has always been atrocious,' he confessed, smiling at Heraldo, 'so how's about we buy that book? And how's about you, Helmut, give us a bit of expert advice on our evening's entertainment?'

'We've got something fixed?' Heraldo's attention immediately switching to the task in hand. 'What are we using?'

'St Peter of…' Wenzel wavered, Helmut supplying the particulars.

'Of Verona. And now you've brought the subject up, there's some very interesting effects we could put to use. I'm sure too we could do as your son suggests. I've a bag somewhere of leather scraps and vellum we could scrape down and stretch...'

And so the three went on, getting the story straight, planning the narrative they would use, how they could emphasise the salient parts of the story.

The owl, the vole and Wenzel committed to putting on the best kind of show.

Countdown beginning, the rest of the family brought in for consultation; scripts, props and theatricals argued over and then agreed upon; parts divvied out.

The only one not happy being Longhella, who came up to Wenzel after all had been decided, though not to her delight.

'Why am I being given such a sordid part?' she demanded of Wenzel. 'Why am I the one who has to put the final blow to Peter? Couldn't you have invented some kind of romantic part I could really get my teeth into?'

Wenzel patient, but no longer willing to put up with his niece's constant desire to be centre stage.

'There is no romantic part, Longhella,' he explained. 'This is religious theatre. It's all about the life and validation of a saint. We can't just make up a part to suit you. But,' he added, seeing Longhella's face shifting into an ugly frown, 'when we're out of Ravenna we'll find you a leading role, don't you worry.'

Longhella did not look happy, cast around for her usual sparring partner, who was nowhere to be seen.

'Grandmother would have given me a better part,' she argued. 'And where is she anyway? Why is it that suddenly you're having all the big ideas? You might've taken over but she should get the last say, no matter how grand you think you are. And all because of that shitty little girl!'

Wenzel blanching at the venom and lack of respect, grinding his teeth, spitting out in the moment what he hadn't meant to say until later that night, when their performance was done, when he'd spoken first to Rosa, Yssel and Peppe. Longhella so exasperating the words were out before he'd thought them through.

'Because she's left us. Grandmother Pfiffmakler has left us, Longhella. And she's not coming back.'

Brief gratification for Wenzel as Longhella took in this statement, her face shifting from puzzlement to disbelief to downright slit-eyed anger.

'What do you mean?' she demanded. 'Grandmother would never just leave us. She'd never do that. You must have done something to make her—'

'I did no such thing,' Wenzel stopped her short. 'She's always been her own woman. She's made her choice, and it's a choice that doesn't include any of us. Even you.'

Longhella looking like a branch torn from its tree.

Wenzel wishing back his words.

'She's gone, Longhella,' he said, soft as he could. 'She told me herself at the basilica. Gave me all the letters of introduction, all the passes. She wants a different end to her life than staying with us.'

'She wouldn't do that!' Longhella shouted, stamping a foot, drawing stares not just from their own company but from a couple of nearby store holders.

'She wouldn't do that,' Longhella repeated.

'She did,' Wenzel tried again. 'She's found her own way…'

'She's found blasted nothing!' Longhella exploded, 'and I'll not leave it like this! I'll not!'

And thank God Wenzel had only cast her as the hand to slay St Peter of Verona because Longhella was off through the fair and back down the streets towards the basilica, pushing everyone out of her way as she did so, desperate to find her great-grandmother with whom she'd always had a bond no one else in the family ever understood. Except Longhella and Grandmother Pfiffmakler themselves, who recognised in each other like for like, hard bitter fruits from the same vine who despised the roles women were forced to lead, kicking against the trend every day of their lives.

Not that they would have been able to articulate it.

'Maybe she should join the convent too, save us all a lot of trouble,' Wenzel muttered under his breath as Rosa approached.

'What's going on?' she asked, placing a hand on her husband's arm. 'Something wrong?'

Wenzel sighed.

'Something wrong and something right,' was his ambiguous reply, rolling his shoulders again, feeling that knot reforming, that headache coming back. 'Get the family together. Something I've got to tell you all.'

19

Dramas of Differing Stripes

Longhella got to Sant'Apollinare as the crowds were spilling out, all glad for the fresh air after spending so many hours in church. Everyone feeling blessed, feeling holy, and mighty annoyed by the girl who was pushing against the tide. Longhella ignoring all the tutting, the *what the beggeration do you think you're doing?*'s lobbed at her from every side.

Barging her way up the steps, having failed to find her great-grandmother outside. Went through the emptying basilica like a fury, orange skirts in a whirl, eyes scanning the thinning congregation. No care for the grandness of the marble columns, the beauty of the ancient mosaics, the obvious pomp and circumstance indicated by the raised stage at its end with its altar, throne and baldechino, not even noticing the incorruptible corpse of St Alphonsus. Pausing only when a blackbird sang out in the graduated gloom of the church, a sound so incongruous Longhella checked her stride and, as she did so, made out Grandmother Pfiffmakler's unmistakeable outline at the bottom of the church on her knees, some religious personage in bright red plumage apparently giving her his blessing.

'And so you are accepted as witness, your miracles recorded in our book of legend,' the man announced as Grandmother Pfiffmakler raised her head.

'And so is given to you the Body of Christ,' Grandmother Pfiffmakler taking the host on her tongue. 'And His Blood.'

Grandmother Pfiffmakler taking a sip from the wooden chalice. Grandmother Pfiffmakler looking like nothing Longhella had ever seen before: a humble old woman in a line of other humble old men and women on their knees. The celebrant moving on to her neighbour, starting his routine all over again.

'And so you are accepted as witness…'

'Grandmother!' Longhella shouted. 'Grandmother!'

Grandmother Pfiffmakler's bowed head hearing nothing but Mellini's words, too consumed by the honour being given her. The Eucharist being administered to the *bona fide* witnesses, as deemed by the deacon priests, who'd interviewed each one, by the Archbishop Cardinal himself. A small flourish Mellini had found appealing and apt for, after all, these people had met a saint. Kissed his hand, been given his blessings, his advice.

It was the least he could do for them, at the tail-end of their lives.

'Your miracles recorded…'

'Grandmother!' Longhella wailed.

Mellini looking up, stopping mid-sentence, scanning the few congregants who'd stayed for the last of the ceremony, seeing a young woman in obvious distress. Ettori bearing down on her, grabbing at her elbow, trying to haul her away. Ettori's face flushed, wanting to do the right thing. Had been wanting to do the right thing all day, finding out in the worst way that crowd control was not his natural bent, didn't want to fall at the last hurdle, and a wailing girl was not what anyone needed when the final procedure of the most important day in Ravenna's recent history was being enacted.

'Come on, miss,' he tried. But Longhella was strong and resisted. Had always been strong and resisted.

A skill Livia Benedetta would have respected, had she been here.

'Get your hands off me!' Longhella shouted, batting Ettori away. 'I have to see my great-grandmother!'

Archbishop Mellini straightened up, oddly enlivened by the interruption.

All had gone well. He'd remembered his words, hadn't tripped up, hadn't deviated from the script Gregory had given him, apart from releasing the song birds and this private giving of the Eucharist.

'Wait,' he ordered, Ettori turning fully towards him, looking impossibly young, indecisive and incapable. Why he'd been given the task he had was a mystery. Not so the girl, whose face depicted a tragedy unspoken, a star of the stage at the apogee of the drama, waiting for the rest to unfold.

'Bring her forward,' Mellini commanded, Ettori obeying, Longhella already on the move, bright skirts swishing. Grandmother Pfiffmakler, finally registering the sound and the cause of the interruption, turning her head.

'Oh my child,' she said. 'What are you doing here? Didn't your uncle explain?'

'You know her?' Mellini asked unnecessarily, as Grandmother Pfiffmakler forced her way up from her knees to standing, her cane buckling with the effort, Mellini sending out a hand, helping Grandmother Pfiffmakler onto one of the seats set out for the witnesses.

'Of course I do,' Grandmother Pfiffmakler said. 'She's my great-grandchild. I'm so sorry she's causing a ruction.'

Longhella staring with disbelief at Grandmother Pfiffmakler apologising.

'Is this to do with your new calling?' Mellini enquired softly, having learned of it from the deacon priest who'd taken her statement.

'Can't think what else it would be,' Grandmother grumbled, looking sharply at Longhella, and yet a tug at her heart to see the girl so obviously upset, wondering if, of them all, the girl would miss her most. Not that she'd expected this.

Mellini rather touched by the small domestic scene unfolding. Had taken a bit of an interest in Grandmother Pfiffmakler when the deacon priests had been filling him in on the witness's lives, hers by far the most interesting. A woman who'd travelled further abroad than the rest put together, and Lord only knew what she'd experienced during a lifetime of travelling from village to village, town to town, city to city, country to country, fair's ground to fair's ground, from Italy to the Alps, from the Alps to Germany, from there to the Pyrenees, Croatia, Hungary...

The startlement afforded by her decision to join a convent of the Redemptorists, at the grand old age of seventy-two, the moment she'd heard the news about Alphonsus was throat-grabbing stuff.

Far and away the best witness of the lot.

He placed his hand lightly on her shoulder.

'Don't worry about the interruption, Grandmother,' he said, unconsciously using the soubriquet Longhella had conferred on her. 'Let's see if we can't find you some place private to talk. Ettori!'

He waved his hand at the young monk who was trailing the girl, now only a yard or two away.

'Please take Signora Pfiffmakler into the sacristy with her great-granddaughter.'

Lowering his voice as he removed his hand from Grandmother's shoulder, speaking to her with a confidentiality that had her shivering internally from stem to stern. An Archbishop, a Cardinal Priest, whispering in her ear. Her Holy Day getting holier by the moment.

'Wait for me there, Signora. I'll come find you. I'd like to smooth your passage to the Redemptorists, if you will allow me the honour.'

If you will allow me the honour!

Other old folks' hearts might have stopped from the sheer shock of this statement, but Grandmother Pfiffmakler was made of sterner stuff. Grandmother Pfiffmakler creaked to her feet.

'Thank you,' she got out, had been about to add *Your Lordship, Your Grace,* but couldn't for the life of her remember the correct nomenclature, settled on nothing at all. 'You've been most kind. I don't think anyone could have been kinder.'

Ettori flurrying to her, taking her elbow, leading her on; Longhella silent and pale on the other side, as out of place as the songbirds still darting about from eave to eave seeking escape, the only one gone from them being the linnet, less feared of people than the others, following the departing crowds, soaring up into the open sky and then down again, zeroing in on the marram dunes where the sea hemmed the shores, finding the right stretch of beach, the right bush, the right nest it had laboured so hard to construct from grass and moss, and lined with sheep's wool.

Finding it deserted.

Its hen gone.

The five blue-white speckled eggs rotting in the late spring sun.

20

Martyrs Old and New

It took Andreas Zilboorg a long time to get to the hippodrome under his own steam, pushing one foot after another, backpack getting heavier with every step, ankles complaining, knees swelling, despite Peppe's leather constraints, fingers getting stiffer by the hour. Fairs' ground almost full by the time he got there, the queue of people applying to get in querulous and impatient, town clerk Panizzi hot and annoyed at his table. Despite all the onerous hours he'd spent here he'd still not been able to get away and now it was clear he'd completely missed the ceremony at the basilica, despite the fact that it had gone on for hours; his temper was short and sharp as a nit comb, letting hardly anyone else in.

'Name!' he demanded, as the man before Andreas approached his table.

'Peterle Bolasco, purveyor of ...'

'Don't care what you're a purveyor of,' Panizzi scowled. 'Is it anything to do with sausages or religion?'

Might have laughed out loud at another time to be asking for such precise qualifications. Not today.

Peterle Bolasco hesitating, and hesitation enough for Panizzi.

'Denied,' he announced. 'Get on your way. Next!'

Andreas shuffling forward, his legs killing him, shuffling too through the options he'd got. Hedgehoggery clearly not going to make the cut, and still no sign of Jodl and Valter, so Balatronic Ballet off the market. Time to take a gamble.

'Name,' Panizzi demanded.

'Andreas Zilboorg,' he supplied. 'Latter addition to the Kunterbunt, whom I believe are already here.'

Panizzi looked at Andreas, went to his book, checked his entries. Flicked through several pages, looked back up.

'Anyone to vouch for you?'

'Not until I'm in there,' Andreas said. 'Got problems with my legs. Takes me a long time to get anywhere. Got left behind.'

Panizzi doubtful, though remembered the Kunterbunt crew from earlier in the day, had thought at the time he might want to look them up later, see what they had to offer. He was tired and fractious, but this old fogey really did look like he was on his last legs and on this day of all days he allowed himself to be lenient. Just the once.

'Here's your pass, then,' he said, scribbling one out. 'And here's your armband. Make sure to keep your armband on at all times, for there will be checks.'

Handing over pass and ribbon, Andreas taking them gratefully, hobbling off on his way.

'Next!' Panizzi shouted, not that Andreas cared.

He was in, and Jodl and Valter—unless they'd been very lucky—had to be out.

Sighs of relief for Andreas.

All he needed now was to find the Pfiffmaklers.

'Everyone ready?' Wenzel asked, getting nods from all round.

Seven o'clock at night and the crowds buzzing, eager for a show. Sausages bought, basilica emptied, Lupercal and Jericho hoop-lah-ing through the fairs' ground doing their usual eye-catching backflips as they called out their wares.

'The Life of St Peter of Verona about to be given dramatic form!'

Such was their shout.

'Come see your nearby saint presented as never before!'

Acrobatics abounding, people drawn in by their antics, sausage merchants and food sellers rubbing their hands together, knowing the first tranche of evening entertainments were about to begin and thereafter would heighten their profits. This no usual fair, this a fair celebrating Ravenna as the town welcoming into its own the relics of a saint.

Big news for them all.

Folk gathering in droves around the square of stage demarcated by various small holes dug in the ground, the charcoal in them beginning to glow, two carts shoved together in the middle to form a stage, backdrops in place to shield the actors from their audience. Wenzel regarding the mass of people settling on the grass with relief and mild alarm. The show needed to be good to set these folks' tongues tattling, spread the news, make the next performance even better attended than their opener, if that was possible.

Longhella not yet returned. Yssel had fretted, had wanted to go find her.

'Relax,' Wenzel assured. 'She'll either be with Grandmother or else sulking somewhere nearby. You know how she can be.'

Yssel supposed he was right. Longhella could be stubbornly sullen for an entire week if it suited her. Nevertheless had told the boys to look out for her while they were doing their tumbling invitations to attend the performance. No sign yet, and no time either to worry about it. Their play about to begin.

'What did you find out?' Jodl's dark hair shining like a starling's back as he shook his head, having just shoved it under the piazza's fountain to clear away the dust. Valter taking a step backwards as several shaken droplets caught him in the face, swiping viciously at them with his fingers for they were warm as blood and he didn't like that, not one bit.

'Kunterbunt got into the fair as expected,' he reported. 'Uncle too.'

'Uncle!' Jodl snorted. 'Don't know why you still call him that.'

Valter shrugged.

'Got to call him something, and always irritates the hell out of him.'

Jodl gave a brief taut smile.

'Suppose there's that. But times are a-changing, brother. Time to cut the strings.'

Valter rolled his head on his shoulders. He wasn't at all sure he wanted to go on with Jodl's plan. Happy enough with how things were: simple, uncomplicated. Trundling along with Andreas from one place to the next. Nothing to worry about, food in his belly, could have gone on like that for the rest of his life. Never one to concern himself with goals and targets, not like Jodl who'd had his goals and targets fixed in him for years, like nails hammered into wood. Jodl the hardest type of wood cleaving to the hardest type of nails. He blew a breath out between his lips.

'Can't see why you're bothering with any of it,' Valter said. 'It's all so long gone. Why can't we just go on like...'

Jodl flinging out a hand, gripping his brother hard by the shoulder. Valter flinching, trying to shove Jodl's hand away but Jodl, as always, was the stronger and would not let go. Squeezing harder as he spat out his reply.

'It'll never be gone until that man's done for. And we've never been so close as this.'

Valter cleared his throat, trying to stand tall and strong, put over his point of view.

'It's been twenty years, Jodl. I just don't get the point of...'

Jodl squeezed harder, digging in his nails. Valter squirming. Jodl growling between bared teeth.

'Twenty years is nothing! This is to do with honour, our honour, our family's honour. And I'll pursue it until the end of my days if I have to, as should you.'

Valter sighed, submitted.

'And what about Andreas?' he asked, aware he was appearing weak, but his earlier confrontation with Andreas had come back to him like an unpleasant taste in his mouth. How he'd threatened Andreas, called him an old man, asked him what the hell was he going to do about anything. He'd meant it at the time, having Jodl's words fresh in his mind. Had since been having doubts. Valter like a drum that always played Jodl's tune whenever he was near. Tune fading the moment he was out of ken.

'What about him?' Jodl dismissive. 'He's weak and he's sick. He'll expect us pretty soon to carry him. And we don't need extra baggage now we're on our way.'

In Valter's mind to say *but he's carried us for years,* not that the words came out.

Jodl giving one last hard squeeze to Valter's shoulder before releasing him.

'We're on our way, brother. And no one, especially not dear Uncle Andreas, is going to stand in our way. Come on,' he added, cuffing Valter about the neck. 'I've a coupla folks I want you to meet.'

'Everyone ready?' Wenzel whispered, rubbing his hands together in excited trepidation.

'Ready,' everyone agreed, including Livia who'd been surprisingly enthusiastic when approached to take on Longhella's part in the proceedings.

'Very well then. Let's begin.'

Lupercal carefully lifting the contraption Heraldo had knocked up a few hours earlier—a hollow cylinder sealed at one end by a thin velum membrane from which a long spring protruded—and began to shake it slowly from side to side, producing a long low rumble as of rolling thunder. Jericho adding to the effect, setting a spill to a fuse that threw up a flash of light, a huge guff of smoke. Wenzel nipping in front of the back drop and up the steps onto the carts, materialising in front of his audience as if from thin air.

'Welcome! Welcome, Ladies and Gents,' raising his arms like a prophet. 'Welcome to our humble show.'

A grand entrance, and one he capitalised on.

'It is our great pleasure to be in Ravenna on this wondrous day and, in celebration, we present to you the Life of St Peter of Verona!'

From behind the backdrop rose a glowing paper globe filled with cotton shreds soaked in oil and set alight, words on the paper clearly visible against the soft glow of its inner flame.

'Behold the *faro* of the martyr, and the words he wrote in his own blood as he lay dying,' Wenzel announced loudly, '*Credo in Deum.* Three short words that he lived by, as should we.'

He paused, his audience enthralled as they watched the paper globe gaining height like a second moon, the first one fortuitously etched behind it in the evening sky; gasping with awe as the *faro* suddenly exploded with the loud crack of a lightning bolt, releasing a shower of silvery vermillion sparkles cascading down behind Wenzel, lending the illusion that he was glittering as if in soft rain.

'And so begins the life of St Peter,' Wenzel began his narrative, Ludmilla appearing, cooing at a baby cocooned in her arms, singing a soft lullaby accompanied by Heraldo's lute.

Lah-lay my delight, my desire, my sweeting,
Lah-lay my little child, my one and only darling.

Soul-softening stuff, Ludmilla doing another couple of verses as she swayed her baby, getting everyone on side before Wenzel skewered the scene through its heart.

'But they are Cathari, Ladies and Gentlemen,' calls Wenzel. 'They call themselves The Truth, believe they have the true way of it, but they are heretics! An abomination to the church!'

Another loud peal of thunder, another crack of lightning. Ludmilla's face distraught and confused, holding her hands over her baby to shield him.

'They believe the world to be ruled by Satan! By Beelzebub himself! That God has no hand in it!'

The audience open their mouths in horror as horns appear to extrude from Ludmilla's head, from the child's head. An addition to the act proposed by Helmut, using one of his water pumps operated by a quick press of Ludmilla's fingers to release the reservoir held in the *faux* baby's body.

'You know how it goes!' Wenzel pontificated. 'How the Cathari were deluded by the devil; how a group of them saw an apparition of the Madonna and the Christ Child sprouting horns, and how our saint quashed that illusion by offering up a consecrated host to the supposed virgin!'

Heraldo coming on scene as St Peter, holding out a consecrated wafer. Heraldo shouting out his words, still not liking being on stage but this a mere one liner.

'If you truly are the Mother of God, then kneel before your Son and worship Him!'

Horns disappearing as quickly as they'd come, and Heraldo too. Wenzel continuing the narrative.

'The man our boy became knowing only too well the way of the faithful, despite his family's heretical ways.'

Ludmilla swiftly off scene, replaced by Jericho and Peppe as Peter and his wicked uncle.

'And look now how he fights for the true belief!'

Peter squaring up to his uncle.

'I believe in the creed! The only true creed! The creed of our Lord Jesus Christ!'

Peppe taking hold of a broom handle and viciously swiping at his nephew, apparently beating him to a pulp. Peter down on the ground. So young, so small in the face of this fury. Peter rolling himself into a ball, stream of bright red blood apparently flowing all around him.

'Seven years old,' Wenzel intoned, 'and our saint has already gone against his father, his family, his uncle. Only seven years old, and able to see through their lies, their misguided misinterpretation of the scriptures. Seven years old, and wiser than any of us.'

Sighs from the crowds as Peter crawls from the scene, a more pathetic and proud a figure they'd never seen.

'And so he grows, my audience, my congregation,' Wenzel goes on, 'and our saint in the making becomes a man, becomes a preacher, becomes a great preacher.'

Peppe back in different guise. Peppe now the older Peter reciting the all-important Credo, knowing it word for word from his childhood, had meant to give a potted version, a little discombobulated when the crowd joins in the chant as if he were a real priest, letting it flow. Letting them have their moment.

I believe in God, the Father Almighty,
Creator of Heaven and earth.
I believe in Jesus Christ, His only Son, our Lord
who was conceived by the Holy Spirit,
born of the Virgin Mary,
suffered under Pontius Pilate,
was crucified, died and was buried,
descended to the dead
and on the third day, rose again.
He ascended to Heaven and is seated at the right hand of the
Father.
He will come again to judge the living and the dead.
I believe in the Holy Spirit, the Holy Catholic Church, the communion of

saints,the forgiveness of sins,the resurrection of the body,and life everlasting.

Amen.

Peppe apparently a priest—who'd have thought it?

Wenzel astonished by this reaction from the audience, although many were fresh from the basilica so perhaps in the mood. Time to inject some drama into the set, which had been quite difficult given how dull Peter's life was as martyrs' went. Heraldo coming up with the answer, setting his life to song, Peppe and the cast acting out the gist. Lupercal tumbling along at the front, back and forth, forth and back, throwing a handful of this and that onto the fire-pits' charcoal to emphasise one event or another with an up-burst of coloured flames and sparkles and his own acrobatic leaps.

Our hero leaves his family and the Cathari, sings Heraldo accompanied by his lute.

Derided by curses and charivari,

Yssel and Rosa pelting Peter's back with rotten fruit.

But he takes no mind,

Leaves all behind.

Flash of bright green from the fire-pits, Peppe treading slow but youthful across the stage.

He takes his way out of Verona,

Tramps through Padua, Mantua and Cremona,

By Parma, Reggio and Modena,

Ending his travels at Bologna.

Flames go up in yellow glory, Lupercal throwing himself into the air. Doing a perfect somersault before landing.

His journey is difficult and dangerous

Joyous and momentous;

Surviving bandits and marauders

Peppe set upon by Jericho, fending him off.

To knock at the doors of the Dominican Order.

Bright white flash, Wenzel now the gatekeeper.

What brings you to our doors? Heraldo sings, words repeated loudly by Wenzel as he interrogates the newcomer.

To enter into the true cause, Heraldo prompts in song.

To enter into the true cause, Peppe speaks earnestly and humbly.

From where have you come? Wenzel loud, Peppe leaping onto the stage to declaim his origins and embrace the true church.

I've come to escape the dumb…

Flash of orange, shower of sparks behind Peppe who is speaking as Heraldo is singing:

Obedience to kith and kin,
And all their heretical beliefs therein.
I've come to present myself before my Lord,
To take His Credo as my sword.

Sword magically appearing in Peppe's hand, snatched up from behind the stage and brandished large. *Credo in Deum* painted on its broad wooden blade.

And with this sword out our hero goes, Heraldo sings,
To vanquish the heretical views of his foes.

Ludmilla and Yssel on now, bowing down at Peter's feet, pleading loudly for forgiveness as Peppe pins his Sword of Truth to their necks.

And many Cathari does he bring into the fold, Heraldo sings on;
Reconciling them with the true beliefs of old.

Two huge flames firing up from the pits, exuding too a barrage of green-tinted smoke, and now Peppe/Peter is on his knees on the stage, and Wenzel is conferring on him his greatest role.

St Dominic himself gives Peter honour,
St Dominic himself makes Peter Prior
Of several houses, for he is a regenerator,
A true venerator, and next an Inquisitor.

Lupercal again, quick leap across the stage from left to right that has every fire-pit going up in red, blue and silver sparks, and the audience ooh and ah, aware the finale is just around the corner, amazed when the smoke clears and there is Wenzel alone upon the stage, Peppe/Peter gone from them; Peppe/Peter dipped down behind the stage donning grey beard, and the black mantle on top the white habit that marks his calling.

Heraldo, behind the scenes, swiftly swapping lute for mandolin, fingers for a plectrum, the sustained notes he can thereby produce being exactly as envisaged, the audience holding up their faces in rapt expectation as he thrums its limited strings, a melancholic sound, Wenzel taking the cue.

'The end is near, my friends,' Wenzel announces sombrely. 'The end is almost due for behold, our great man, our St Peter of Verona, as he takes his last journey.'

St Peter duly appearing from behind the stage, accompanied by Jericho.

'Only one year after he has been made Inquisitor, and after all the great deeds he has done, he and his companion,' Wenzel intones, 'take their way from Como to Milan...'

Peppe and Jericho, in their white and black habits, move slowly across the grass that makes their stage.

'To continue their preaching, to continue their turning of the Cathari heretics back to the true cause.'

No mention of how many supposed heretics Peter had exiled, excommunicated or condemned to death. Not at all within their remit.

'And now it comes...'

Loud rolling of the drums, Livia in men's clothing stealthily appearing from the right, Rosa similarly attired approaching from the left. Heraldo keeping the melancholy of the mandolin going as, behind the scenes, Yssel keeps the drums rolling and Ludmilla sings out in sad and tremulous voice.

From Como to Milan they went on God's duty, Heaven sent,
But assassins are on their trail. Their intent
To curtail their Holy Mission with terrible decision,

And from behind the rocks they leap...

Livia and Rosa with awful masks upon their faces doing exactly that, the drums increasing their intensity, the audience leaning forward, open-mouthed in horrified anticipation, Ludmilla lifting her voice to minor key.

With weapons sharp and cudgels stout,
And with no warning
They tear the veil of morning
And they strike!
They strike!

Ludmilla's voice at fever pitch as the assassins hurl themselves towards their victims, shrieking like the devils they are, taking over the lyrics though it could no longer be called a song.

And into the heart...of the companion... they send the knife, snarls Rosa, puncturing her words with the effort of doing just that: thrusting in the dagger once, twice, thrice.

And take away his life! she shouts in triumph.

The companion falls.

The companion screams, sighs and bleeds. Peter leaning down to aid him, the audience taking an audible gasp as they understand what must happen next, that by this action of helping his friend he is laying himself wide open.

Livia's turn and she's right in the moment, turning towards the audience, raising her glinting weapon high, a guff of red smoke coming up to left and right of her.

And I, she screams like a banshee, Peppe/Peter looking up in some alarm, holding up an unscheduled arm, for that axe might only be silver-painted wood but it could still do some serious harm...

And I, she screams again, *with my axe will cleave you,*
With my axe will leave you...

Down comes her axe, a whisper away from Peppe's ear, Peppe flinching and sweating, flinging himself to the ground exactly as the real Peter might have done…

With your skull split from stem to stern…

Livia is almost breathless as her axe strikes the ground next to Peppe's head and Peppe's hand, with a visible shake, releases the fake blood that flows about his head…

To show you what you earn

Livia's voice shrill and loud, Livia taking aim again, which was not in the script…

When you turn…

Another blow, another strike, wooden blade hitting the grass, catching the tip of Peppe's nose…

Against your family!

Livia standing tall, Livia throwing her blood-dripping axe upon her shoulder and taking a step backwards to view her handiwork, unaware the drumming has ceased, that everyone is staring at her, and not only the audience but the entire cast of the Kunterbunt. First to recover being Rosa who rushes to her fellow assassin, takes her firmly by the elbow, forgetting her last words as she leads Livia away. Wenzel getting himself swiftly together, adapting the script, ditching the last part of the homily, sticking to the drama of the moment as created by Livia's performance.

'And so ends the earthly life of St Peter, Ladies and Gentlemen!' he shouted. 'Writing out *Credo in Deum* in his own blood!'

Peppe's arm moving feebly as Wenzel leaps onto the stage.

'Commending his soul and that of his wicked murderer to God!'

Heraldo also quick to react to changed circumstances, taking up the thunder-box and sending out a loud grumbling roll that flows over stage, slaughter and audience.

'And on this day of all days, on this night of all nights,' Wenzel shouts into the storm, 'think on our martyrs and saints, think on their sufferings, how great were their deeds, how generous their souls right down to their very last breaths! And with that sentiment, Ladies and Gentlemen, our humble show is at its end.'

He closes his eyes, bows his head.

Peter and his companion remaining dead on their field of glory.

Lupercal flinging handfuls of dust into the dying fire-pits to send up a last cascade of sparkles.

The audience shake themselves, let out a collective breath, take out their coins ready for the buckets Ludmilla, Yssel and Lupercal have at the ready.

And then a low growl of real thunder rolls in from the Adriatic and the sky skitters with a single flash of sheet lightning, a splash of rain down and gone before it's hardly come. And everyone blinks, and everyone thinks it has to be St Peter himself rolling out his applause and everyone, after a brief moment of Holy silence, begins to talk and chatter excitedly and thank the Lord they've been here as witnesses to this most blessed of days.

Only one person missing from the multitudinous awe, who'd sat down with the rest but couldn't take what she saw. Not with those masks, that axe, that terrible outflowing of gore.

Hulde burning from the inside out, like St Peter's *faro*.

Her two short years of memories flooding through her like a bore.

Green mountains. Hot sunshine. White flowers. The smell of goats. Grumpy old donkey called Gomar Nikolla.

Black mountains. Damp caves. The cold and snow. Gomar Nikolla gone for food.

Huge sweating bulk of their last white ox pulling a creaking cart.

Dark scary forests. Crawks of black-winged birds. Sharp thorns.

The walking, stones hard and uncomfortable beneath thinly soled boots.

Her father's strong hands sweeping her up onto his shoulders.

The village. The gnarled trees.

Days of sweeping and cleaning.

Buzz of flies when they cut the ox's throat, blood used to thicken the paint for the cottages. About to eat their first meat in months.

Calling themselves at home.

Safe for the moment.

And then the wolves coming down on them, her mother scooping Hulde up.

Running along the wide street towards their menfolk.

The stamping of feet behind them.

Snarls of the pack on their heels.

Men with scarves about their faces herding them together on the green.

The swords, the billhooks, the daggers, the guns, glinting in the moonlight.

The hacking, the shots, the blood, the sighs, the screams.

The wet warmth of her mother falling over her, curling about her, closing her off.

Boxing her in.

Keeping her safe.

Warm body-box.

Sounds of shouting, whooping, clinking metal.

Voices, commands, shoving, stink of meat.

Running boots.

Fear. Dark. Aloneness.

Weight of silence whumping in her ears like swans flying low.

Body-box getting cold and stiff, trapping Hulde in, keeping her safe.

Locking all those bad images up inside her.

Mother taking them for her own.

Taking them with her when Hulde left her behind.

Hulde feeling safe even when she'd been hurled into the sea.

Thinking herself back within that box. Mother all about her. Nothing to hurt her.

And she'd been right. All well.

Until right now, when that person in the mask had lifted up his axe and smashed right through the lid.

21

The Granite of Hills and Men

'What the beggeration happened out there?' Wenzel demanded, wiping a hand across his forehead, Peppe shaking his head in complete agreement as he stripped off his robes.

'Thought that blasted woman was really going to do me in!' He blinked at the memory, rubbing his injured nose. 'Thought you said she'd never been on stage before.'

Wenzel pulled at his beard.

'That's what she told me. Guess you never really know folk.'

Rosa handed her husband a wet cloth to wipe his face and another to Peppe to staunch the mix of fake and real blood dripping from his chin.

'You men can be rather dense at times,' she said lightly. 'I'll bet that's the first opportunity she's ever had to strike back at life and what it's done to her.'

'Never done a damn thing to the woman,' Peppe muttered.

'Not you personally,' Rosa explained, 'although I don't doubt there's other men who've—'

'Where is she anyway?' Wenzel interrupted. 'She did rather a good job, Peppe's nose notwithstanding.'

'Sent her off with Yssel to prepare some food for the interval,' Rosa answered. 'And we're going to have a feast. Got a load of free food from the stall holders, stuff that couldn't last out the night, as well as some great sausages.'

'Did someone mention sausages?' Heraldo quick on the scene at the mention of food. He was absolutely ravenous.

'I did,' Rosa was indulgent. 'You did a magnificent job today, my boy. Can't think of many folk who could have come up with song and verse quick as you did.'

'Your mother's right,' Wenzel agreed. 'First-class work. That St Peter's got a lot to answer for. Duller life I've hardly ever come across.'

'Apart from his heroic assassination,' Peppe put in, fingers once more palping his bruised and bleeding nose. 'And Jericho needs a pat on the back on that score. Great piece of dying, that was, for a first timer.'

'Either way,' Wenzel announced, 'we've work to do for the next show in what? An hour? And we've to keep Livia in whether Long-hella turns up or no. And is she back yet, by the way. Does anyone know?'

No one did, neither was anyone particularly worried, including her father. Peppe sighing and sucking in his breath.

'That girl. More trouble than a bucketful of wasps. I'll organise search parties,' he said. 'Can you spare a couple of bodies before we do the second show?'

Wenzel nodding, everyone knowing how Longhella could be, and only a ten-minute walk from here to the basilica. Even so. Girl alone in an unknown town. You had to look after your own, even if your own was being deliberately annoying and had tried to sabotage your show right at the last minute.

'Whoever you need,' Wenzel agreed. 'But got to get everyone back soon as.'

Glancing up at the sky, first performance done in twilight for maximum effect. Night soon down, second performance not far off.

Grandmother in the sacristy.

Grandmother waiting for a personal conversation with the Archbishop of Ravenna himself.

Grandmother accepted into the Book of Witnesses to the canonisation of a saint.

Grandmother feeling like the most important person on the earth, apart from Alphonsus himself.

Grandmother's special day interrupted by Longhella's histrionics. So much for slipping quietly away and leaving the Kunterbunt to their own.

'You're not really leaving us, are you?' Longhella asked, the moment she was brought into the sacristy and Ettori had softly shut the door, Longhella's lips trembling, eyes bright with tears. Grandmother knowing Longhella could manufacture this particular expression on demand, a natural actress, great for the stage. Didn't believe Longhella was acting now.

'I am, my dear,' Grandmother said. 'Come. Sit for a minute.'

Longhella did as bid, taking the time to fold her skirts carefully, prettily arranging her ankles the one over the other. Grandmother smiling at the affectation. Yssel was going to have to watch this one, or she'd be belly out before she hit sixteen.

'You probably can't understand this,' Grandmother began, Longhella cutting in.

'That's just it! I can't! And you weren't even going to say good bye!'

'Longhella,' Grandmother warned. 'Don't you ever interrupt me. You know perfectly well what I think of that.'

'I do, but Grandmother...'

Grandmother rapping her cane sharply across Longhella's ankles.

'Hush, child. Close your mouth and open your ears.'

Longhella hung her head but was not going to apologise. Grandmother sighed.

'As I was about to say,' she paused, in case Longhella was fool enough to interrupt again, which she was not. 'Very well then. I'm old, my dear, and you don't know what that's like. I've bunions and corns on my feet. I've a heart sometimes beats too fast or goes so slow I get dizzy.'

She shook her head. First time she'd admitted weakness to anyone.

'I'm tired, Longhella,' she sighed. 'That's the simple truth of it. I'm tired of all the walking and talking. Of keeping everyone in order.'

Longhella breaking in, too impassioned to stop herself.

'But now Wenzel's taken over that's not a problem! And we could make you a travelling cart, get a donkey to pull you.'

Grandmother feeling irritation and affection in equal measure.

'You know what happens to every donkey we've ever had,' she chided, Longhella hanging her head.

'We eat them,' she whispered. 'When we're hungry in winter, we eat them.'

'And where would I be then?' Grandmother asked. 'Sitting pretty on a cart that no one can pull is what. And the next day back to tramping. Wait till you get bunions and corns, see how you like it then.'

Longhella sniffing quietly, putting out a hand, placing it on Grandmother's skirts.

'I don't want you to go,' she said, quiet and earnest, tears dropping from the long lashes Lupercal so admired. 'Do you really have to?'

Grandmother's old peach-pit of a heart cracking slightly at this declaration.

'I do, my dear. If I don't go now then I never will. Do you really want me to see out my last days dragging my old bones about with my feet screaming bloody murder and my head having to listen to your blasted uncle giving out orders left, right and centre?'

Longhella raised a small smile. Always her old grandmother, pointing out the worst.

'S'pose not,' she agreed.

'S'pose not is right,' Grandmother said decisively. 'This is my one chance, Longhella, to get out. Only other option is to go live with Matthys and his beggaring oranges, get bossed about by that simpering wife of his. And I'll tell you now, I'd rather chuck myself off a cliff than put up with that.'

Longhella smiling properly now.

'They weren't that bad,' she said, looking up, seeing Grandmother's cross face creased with lines. No smile there, not yet, just that small twitch in her cheek that said it wasn't far off. Longhella probably the only one of the Kunterbunt to see it often enough to know what it presaged.

'Oh my Lord, child! But how that Lotte would love to have me in her kitchen! *Don't do this, don't do that, do it this way. Get out of my cupboards, give me that spoon!* No,' Grandmother said. 'I'll not have it.'

Longhella quiet for a moment, before speaking again.

'But who'll look out for me when you're gone?' she asked.

Grandmother taken aback by the simplicity of the question and the truth of it, for she'd always favoured the girl over the others, always seen an echo of herself in Longhella, taken her side in any argument, Longhella returning the favour. She put her hand on Longhella's own and patted it softly.

'You'll be fine, my girl,' she said. 'Reason I know is because you're just like me, and that means you can get through near about anything. Let me give you two pieces of advice: don't throw yourself at the first fancy man who takes your sway, and don't never ever, and this includes the upstart Wenzel Pfiffmakler himself, let anyone tell you what you thinks is wrong.'

Too much for Longhella, who flung herself sideways and clutched at Grandmother Pfiffmakler's waist, tears abounding, Grandmother touched but finding the situation slightly distasteful, grateful for the soft knock on the door and it opening a few moments later, a red-faced Ettori butting in.

'So sorry to intrude, but the Archbishop's getting ready to leave. He'd like a word if…'

'I'm ready,' Grandmother reverted to terse, levering Longhella up. 'It's time,' she said. 'My great-granddaughter is just leaving. Longhella,' she commanded, Longhella obeying, lifting a tear-stained face that made Ettori's heart skip a beat, young as the girl was.

'I'd be happy to escort her back to—'

'You'll escort me nowhere!' Longhella cried out, taking her great-grandmother's advice to heart, wiping at her face with her hands. 'But you'll tell us where you're going?'

'Your uncle already knows,' Grandmother said. 'Now be off with you. I'm not missing a private audience with an Archbishop for anyone. Not even you.'

Longhella casting one last look at her Grandmother Pfiffmakler, and there was the smile she'd been waiting for.

'Be good, my dear. You're the one I shall miss the most.'

'And I you,' Longhella said formally as she delivered the last line of this particular play. Longhella turning, orange skirts flashing past Ettori as she strode up the nave.

'A bit of a firebrand,' Ettori observed, as he watched her go.

'My flesh and blood,' Grandmother Pfiffmakler stated with menace. 'And the best of them, and God curse any man gets in her way.'

Except it wasn't a man who got in Longhella's way.

It was Hulde, short legs on the run, head bursting with bad memories, Longhella zeroing in on the girl as she ran towards the basilica and Longhella simultaneously leapt down the steps in sad fury and grabbed at the girl's arm.

'So it's you, you little viper!' Longhella's distress dissipated the second she clapped eyes on the girl, her understanding of Grandmother Pfiffmakler's leaving done and dusted, accepted, but her anger bitter and boiling now she was presented with the primary cause. And someone visceral on whom she could vent her anger, someone less powerful, someone who could take the rap.

Valter's throat was tight with resentment. He didn't want to meet any of Jodl's blasted friends. Found it hard enough to put the two words *Jodl* and *friends* into the same sentence, for he'd never had any as far as Valter knew, apart from Valter himself. And that hardly counted, and probably didn't even apply, not in the strictest sense. Not that he knew much about the existential nature of friendship, having no direct experience of it. He knew Jodl had hooked up with some coves in Zadar, the reason they'd stayed there as long as they had and the reason, he assumed, Jodl had wanted over to Italy. Had hardly clapped eyes on Jodl these past few weeks, not even on the boat. Jodl steering clear of him and especially of the Kunterbunt. He wasn't exactly sure why. Had an inkling he'd been trying hard to ignore.

Something similar happening before a couple of years back, the last time they'd visited Zadar on Zilboorg's usual route. Jodl sneaking off to some tavern or another every night, coming back reeking of drink and dark ideas. Not that Jodl ever got drunk. Not Jodl, who always needed to be in control, unlike Valter whose faults in that direction Jodl frequently lambasted.

'Take a look at yourself!' he'd shout, when Valter had had one too many, when Valter had slumped to the ground after botching his last few chess pieces and spilled the last of his wine. Valter never drinking in taverns, disliking crowds, preferring to stick to his own.

'You're pathetic, Valter,' Jodl would declaim with contempt. 'Absolutely pathetic. You need to find a focus, hitch yourself to a cause. And God knows, you've got one big as an elephant right in front of your nose.'

Valter didn't know what an elephant was, but understood insult and insinuation. Occasionally tried to fight back.

'Don't want nothing to do with your buggering elephant!' he'd argue in his drunkenness. 'Just wanna be left alone. Get on with…'

'Get on with what? Living your life as if nothing ever happened?'

Which was exactly what Valter wanted.

'God's sake man,' Jodl would say, or variations on the theme. 'When are you ever going to get that it doesn't go away? That all this,' sweeping his hand about the tent, 'all your stupid little chess pieces is just you doing it all over again in miniature, waiting for someone else to get the hell on with what it's really all about and what's needed doing.'

Valter usually giving up at that moment, giving in.

Telling Jodl he was right.

Not telling Jodl that his carving and painting of the chess pieces was the only thing keeping him sane. That by watching people play out the battles of his youth on his little chess sets, with all their different outcomes and possible scenarios, Valter was free to believe it could have happened differently, had maybe never happened at all.

None of that an option now, being dragged off by Jodl to meet his blasted friends. They'd all be nationalists of one stripe or another: Croatians or Albanians, gassing on about Serbia getting some independence a few years back. And had, back in December, created a proper constitution. And if the Serbs could do it, why couldn't they? Croats freeing themselves from Italians and Hungarians, Albanians from the Turks. All up for grabs.

Time to rise up and fight, like Serbia had done.

Zadar a melting pot catching itself alight with nationalism.

It made no difference to Valter.

Bloody Serbians uprising being what had caused all his and Jodl's problems in the first place. And now Jodl finally had a name he would never ever give up tracking.

Valter didn't care.

Valter didn't want to be here.

Didn't want to be associated with any of it.

He wanted to be back at the fair's ground eating all the different types of sausages on offer. He wanted, an astonishing thought, to be with Andreas. Andreas, always calm and even, taking the two brothers at face value. Never judged.

And there was that stricture in his throat again to realise that not only did he dislike his brother. He actively despised him.

'I'll not go,' Valter said, coming to a stop in the middle of the road. Jodl turning to him, eyes bright, black as his hair wetted by the brief fall of rain brought on by that thunder roll coming in from the Adriatic.

'You'll not what?' Jodl demanded. Valter always weak as a stem of grass when it came to Jodl's say so. Not today. Valter shaking his head, feeling the bruises rising up on neck and shoulder from Jodl's previous insistent hold on him.

'I don't want to meet any of your buggering friends,' Valter stated. 'I don't want to know what any of you have done or what you're going to do. I just want to go back to—'

'Go back to what?' Jodl hissed. 'To dear old uncle? To normality? After all I've been telling you?'

'Especially after all you've been telling me!' Valter able to whip up a rage as easily as his brother, and who wouldn't? Given their circumstances. 'I don't want it!' Valter shouted. 'This ain't my road and I want you to leave me be!'

Jodl paused. Jodl calculated the odds. Jodl nodded.

Jodl, astoundingly to Valter, acquiesced.

'Then so be it, brother,' Jodl said. 'But be advised: this is it. You make this choice and it's the parting of our ways. It means you will become my enemy. And you know what I do to my enemies.'

Valter swallowed.

Valter faltered, thought on Andreas Zilboorg and the Kunterbunt and all the joys of all the fair's grounds they'd ever visited: the braziers firing up, the various cuts of meat being griddled and rizzled, their fats spitting and crackling, the bay leaves floating on vats of butterbean soup, the chicken joints marinated in herbs and garlic, those olives he'd had on Preko, the rank aroma of sweating donkeys and horses and that tar sometimes put on their hooves to stop infection, the slight permeation of urine that caught at the back of your throat a constant from every piss-pit dug at the back of every fair.

Valter trying to sort through the implications of the situation, the stark choice Jodl was giving him.

Valter coming to a decision.

One that had him flat on his back in the wet dust once he'd voiced it, head-butted by Jodl, a stream of blood pouring from Valter's nose and a pounding in head and eyes.

'Just a taste of things to come,' Jodl said matter-of-factly, as if he did this every day, which maybe he did, this last while at least.

'Jodl,' Valter whispered, blood hot and salty in his throat from partially biting through his tongue.

'Don't you Jodl me,' Jodl stated quietly. 'You and me, brother? We're done.'

Jodl spitting in his brother's face where Valter lay scrabbling in the dirt, tears leaking from his eyes to realise the enormity of his brief rebellion.

And no way Jodl would ever take him back, not even if Valter begged.

Jodl as hard and unforgiving as the granite of the mountains that had withstood ice-ages and glaciers.

And easily as cold.

22

A Bad End to a Long Day

Brother Ettori was overwhelmed by the day. It had been long and holy, living up to all expectations and surpassing them. Not the best shepherd in the world as far as crowd control went, yet so much to boast about when he got back to the monastery. Not that boasting was encouraged. Had to be said, though, the brothers not admitted to attend the service would ask questions and he would answer: tell them how he'd had personal interaction not only with the Archbishop but also with the witness Mellini had taken such an interest in. How the girl in the orange skirts had intervened so dramatically. How he'd been the one to take them to the sacristy, earwigged a large part of their conversation, which had been incredibly touching. How he'd been charged with tucking the old woman into a carriage, organised by the Archbishop himself, that would take her to Nocera and her new calling.

All in all, a grand day.

Probably the grandest day he would ever live through.

Obviously he'd never mention the thrill he'd had at seeing Longhella striding into the basilica, the embarrassment he'd experienced when he'd opened the door to interrupt them and seen her long lashes dripping with tears as she clutched her arms so fervently about her great-grandmother's waist, or how magnificent he'd thought the girl as she'd pushed right past him, told him she didn't need any help, thank you very much.

He'd never had any doubts about his calling. His attraction to this random girl on this most unusual of days no great mystery, a little troubling, enough so that after he'd seen the Archbishop and his retinue away he went to sit on the steps of the basilica, take in the emptiness of it now all was done. Listening to the birds, wondering if the robin he was hearing was the same one Mellini had released in the basilica. About to go on his way when he heard something else, something other. Moving slow and soft towards its source, which lay some way over behind the privet bushes demarcating the basilica's courtyard. Pushing away the leaves, the flowers that were loaded over with mining bees, seeing a small girl there, curled in on herself and, looking briefly up, seeing a flash of firebrand orange skirts moving briskly down the street leading to the hippodrome. His heart sinking in his chest as he looked at the child, no blood but plenty pummelled, knowing who must have done this.

The great-granddaughter.

The girl who'd inflamed his latent desires, if only for the briefest moment.

Help me, Jesus. Crossing himself quickly as he went down on one knee and scooped the girl up, held her in his arms like he would have an ailing lamb back at the monastery farm. Her eyelids flickering, which he took as good; her mouth slightly open, breathing softly but not quite regularly, which he took as bad. Ettori wondering what to do. The basilica and its courtyard deserted, as was the street beyond. He supposed he could have knocked on a couple of doors, though most folk would be at the fair. And surely this girl must have come from there too, maybe following Longhella. Possibly a younger sister going one step too far. He'd had younger sisters back in the day, knew how irritating they could be. Not that he could contemplate doing anything as vicious as this to either of them. This smacked of the personal, and had been cruel. The girl in his arms couldn't be more than five or six, and she was light as a bird's nest. It would take a special kind of person to slap her about, and he flushed to admit he was thinking on Longhella as special in any way.

The girl's lips were moving, Ettori bending down towards her.

'Nurna,' he thought he heard her say. 'Nurna. Baba, Baba.'

Words he recognised. Albanian. Mama and Papa.

'Don't you worry, my little one,' he said, getting to his feet, bringing the girl with him. 'I'll take you to your baba. Just you hold on, my young one.'

He was going to get into trouble by not returning directly to the monastery, but couldn't just leave the girl in the bushes whimpering for her father who probably had no idea where she was or where to look for her and would be worried sick, and whether Longhella would tell him was moot. Had a name at least, earwigged from the conversation in the sacristy. Wenzel Pfiffmakler. And how many people in the world, let alone the fair, could go by that name?

Ettori's eyes bright as he made his way down the darkening street carrying his small bundle. He'd thought, on exiting the basilica, his day could in no way have got better, and yet it had, for here he was bringing home a lost child, setting his feet for a fairs' ground, a place forbidden him yet having legitimate reason to visit. No trouble finding it, there by nightfall, funnelled off to the spectators' entrance, excess trades folk still being barred entrance by an irate Panizzi twelve straight hours on post, never having anticipated that this late on in the evening they would still be trying to inveigle their way in. No notion how stubborn or desperate such folk could be. Panizzi seriously considering allowing one of the guards to let off a shot to keep them all at bay.

Awful thought to know he was going having to do it all again the following day.

Ettori going in as an obvious spectator, the child hoisted to his shoulder, her head nestling against his neck in a manner he found indescribably comforting, reminding him of carrying his sisters just so when they were young. The hippodrome a dizzying maze of traders, Ettori unsure where to go, knocked into every now and then by folk hurrying on their way from one place to another; Ettori surrounded by a turbulent mass of humanity far busier and determined than those in the basilica; going up to the end of it where he'd been told the entertainers were, before coming right back to the start and asking all over again. Getting a bit desperate.

'Excuse me! Excuse me!' he tried to ask, ignored, time and time again.

'I'm looking for Wenzel Pfiffmakler. Does anyone know Wenzel Pfiffmakler?'

He addressed his words to no one in particular, eyes wide open for those bright orange skirts he was ashamed to admit he wanted to see again. But did not. Saw only folk hassling and bargaining at stalls, a brief flash of something like a firework some way off, the sounds of the crowds in his ears, the smell of sausages and cooking in his nose. He tripped, didn't know how, and fell to the ground, the girl going with him, spilling from his arms.

'Need a hand, monk boy?'

Ettori getting himself on his haunches, legs ungainly splayed.

'No, no thank you.'

'Too polite for his boots,' said the man, who thrust a hard hand beneath Ettori's armpit, hauled him along the ground into a dark ginnel between two lines of stalls. Ettori blinking, wanting to go for the girl who was already being bundled up by another apparent helper.

Menace here, he knew, if no idea why.

'Think we's gonna take your burden offa you,' said a second man.

'Stroke of luck, this is!' Ettori heard in the background, as a boot came down on his chest. No idea that his shouting out the name Wenzel Pfiffmakler had been caught and heard by men eager to catch and hear precisely that name. Men here to stock up on food before setting off into the fair proper to find out which route they were going so he could snatch the girl later on. First idea being to have them take the girl down Italy, save him the trouble. Jodl making a rare miscalculation in thinking he could count on Valter, his spy in the camp. Valter no longer to be relied on. Valter and Andreas would undoubtedly return to Zadar now the Balatronic Ballet was at its end. Jodl not displeased with the way it had turned out, felt an itch of excitement to be re-adapting, re-planning, especially since the girl had literally been thrown in his path by a helpful boot.

'Will leave you go if you don't squeal,' he told Ettori.

Ettori couldn't have squealed if he'd tried, all the breath knocked out of him.

'Good boy,' said the man, as if Ettori was a performing animal. But Jesus Christ, the girl! An innocent being carried off by thugs, on this day of all days. Ettori was not to going to stand for it. He struggled, got himself over on his side and shot out an arm, grabbed at the ankle of the man who'd stamped on him, enough to make him stumble though not topple, but gave Ettori a quick window.

'Help! Help! Kidnappers!' Ettori yelled, loud as he could.

'Fuck's sake,' the stumbler growled. 'Think you're real clever, don't you?'

Ettori seeing a large boot raised above his head, heart hammering so hard he could hear it, closing his eyes, believing he was about to die.

'Leave it, Javarek,' one of his accomplices commanded. 'Stroke of luck's one thing, killing monks is another.'

The boot hovered, got itself back on the ground. Ettori sensing the whoosh of air, the stink of trodden horse shit, as it passed him by.

'Don't see what's so special about them,' the boot man grumbled. 'Just as bloody Christian as that lot in the village.'

Ettori hardly able to breathe.

'Because they aren't any part of it, you fucking idiot!' Rescuer and kidnapper all the same man. 'Want to get the entire buggering Italian religious up against us?'

Ettori wincing at the crudity, yet joyous release he wasn't about to die in the dust.

'Bargaining chip's been shoved in our laps,' the same man went on, 'so let's get gone. And you,' switching his attention back to Ettori. 'You find them and tell them we're not done, not by a long chalk. Tell the Pfiffmaklers that if they follow the girl they'll have us to reckon with. And next time around, monk boy, we won't be anywhere near so generous. Tell them that, and see how they like it.'

Jodl straightening his back, smiling as they strode away with their prize, savouring the upcoming suffering and grief the Pfiffmaklers would undergo when they discovered their precious little rescuee gone. For of course they would follow. Folk like that always did. Would track him, chase him down until they thought they had him. Be there at the end of the game when he would reveal his final card, push his last pieces across the board. Already anticipating the jagged high of victory, the surge of adrenalin he always got from the win: the only intense emotion he ever experienced, apart from anger. A sad state to be in, many would have thought. Not so Jodl, who wouldn't have had it any other way. This the truest way to live: one goal, no distractions, one last throw of the die and all would be done.

Ettori sweating badly, still trembling when one of the stall holders came over and levered him up.

'You all right?' the man asked, helping Ettori to his feet. Looking a little sheepish. 'Heard it all going on,' he apologised, 'but seen the likes of them fellows before over the water, and not right prudent to interfere.'

'Who are they?' Ettori got out on the first breath he could muster, ignoring the mud and detritus on his habit.

'Independents. Separatists. Illyrians. Don't rightly know. Not men to mess with, either way.'

'But they've taken the child!' Ettori shouted. 'They've taken the child!'

Starting off on his heels, held back by the stall holder's firm grip.

'Kinda figured that. But ain't no use you going after them cack-handed. Not on your own.'

Ettori stilled, for the man was right.

'Do you know where I can find the Pfiffmaklers?' he asked, the store holder rubbing his grizzled chin, another appearing at his shoulder.

'Ken what line they're in?' the second man asked, wanting to help. Kidnapping of children top of his list of things he never wanted to see, had nevertheless seen and been too cowardly, or sensible, to intervene. Ettori drew in a deep breath, ordered his mind.

'Entertainment,' he got out. 'Theatre, I think. Call themselves the Kunterbunt.'

His helper, a real helper this time, quick to see the light.

'The Kunterbunt, is it? Well yes. Heard on them right enough. Doing their second show right this minute. Heard the first one went down a storm.'

As did the second.

Livia as magnificent in this performance as she'd been in the last. Livia become a star of the stage, although instructed quite specifically not to hit Peppe's nose on her third strike, which she did not.

'It's so liberating!' Livia exclaimed, as she came off stage. 'I don't know when I've ever felt the same!'

Rosa patted the woman's hand.

'You're a natural,' she said. 'And thank the Lord you've joined us. Means I can stay off, that you can take my parts.'

'But don't you love it? Won't you miss it?'

Rosa made a face.

'Never liked it, never wanted it. My calling's always been to do with painting puppets and backdrops, preparing food.'

'But it's so exhilarating!' Livia couldn't get enough of it. 'It's like you're yourself and someone else all at the same time!'

Rosa smiled, until she saw Longhella sneaking into their perimeter looking sly as always. Gone for the entire shift of two performances, no thought in her head how they might have filled her part. A selfish child, no matter Yssel might think otherwise. Rosa always critical of how the girls had been brought up, as if they were precious jewels and not simply working parts of what had made the Kunterbunt so successful for so long. Ludmilla understood, but not Longhella who seemed to think the entire world had been made just for her.

'That girl,' she muttered under her breath. 'Would you mind tending the stew while I nip off for a while?' she asked Livia, knowing full well the answer, Livia ecstatic to be given the task. Livia so happy to have found some kind of belonging she'd have swallowed broken glass to stay with them. The diametric opposite to Longhella, who was looking so extraordinarily smug Rosa could have slapped her.

''Where've you been, young lady?' Rosa asked the girl. 'You know you missed both your curtain calls?'

No concern from Longhella, who shrugged off her aunt's accusations.

'Went to see Old Grandmother,' she explained, 'when no one else could be bothered.'

Making Rosa roiling mad.

'That's no excuse, young missy. You could have wrecked the performance, and you knew how much was riding on it.'

Longhella, infuriatingly, merely flicking at her skirts.

'So how did it go? Did you miss me?'

As if the theatres of the world rested on Longhella. As if the entire Kunterbunt began and ended with her.

Rosa quick to disabuse her of that notion.

'Actually no. We found a very convincing surrogate, and from henceforth she will be taking your place in this particular performance. I don't know what you've been doing all this time, but while we're in Ravenna you're back to being the nonentity you are.'

Harsh words. The nonentity scowling, beginning to think through what she'd done. If Rosa was angry now, which plainly she was, she was going to explode when Hulde came crawling back on the scene pointing out Longhella as her punisher. But it had felt so good, giving that girl a taste of the world. It never occurring to Longhella that Hulde had experienced far worse. And she'd done no real damage, just a couple of slaps here and there before the girl had folded up like a marked card and kind of gasped. And there was always the possibility she wouldn't come back at all. And Longhella all for that.

Bad luck for Longhella then when Ettori, dishevelled and mud-spattered, came bursting into their ranks.

'Where's Wenzel Pfiffmakler? I need to speak to Wenzel Pfiffmakler!'

Longhella frowning as she saw him bashing into part of the backdrop in his haste. It took her a couple of seconds to recognise him, wasn't worried. Most likely here to talk about Old Grandmother and her brushes with the good and great.

Nothing to do with her.

'Can I go now?' she asked her Aunt Rosa, with a defiance Old Grandmother would have admired, which Rosa merely despised. Rosa tutting and shaking her head.

'Get you gone, girl. But take heed. This isn't done with.'

Longhella raising a beatific smile.

'Still gonna need me,' she said. 'Nothing much doing with striking down an axe a coupla times and hollering out a few words, but I still knows all my other parts and no one else's gonna pick them up overnight. Or however long we're stopping in this shit-hole.'

Rosa angered all over again by Longhella's attitude and choice of words, had an opinion about how she could use them against her niece and so let Longhella go. Time needing to be spent with Livia. Longhella not the only one who knew every act, every script. Rosa far longer at it than Longhella had ever been and willing to bet her last coin that Livia Benedetta would practice every second of every day, from dawn to dusk, if it meant turning herself from Janus Woman into Actress Upon The Stage.

And a real pleasure to help such a woman to her right calling.

Longhella be damned.

Wenzel scrubbed at his face, getting rid of the last traces of make-up, Heraldo nearby twittering on about some lark mirrors Helmut Knibb had put him onto.

'They're like spindles,' Heraldo was saying, 'with spiralling cross-pieces that look like seagulls in flight, sort of curved at their ends, studded with shiny bits of glass and polished metal. No one knows why they're so successful but they've been used for hundreds of years. Stick one in the ground and the larks come down, and not only larks but loads of other birds, and start settling nearby. Helmut reckons we could make a fortune netting them in. Well maybe not a fortune,' he qualified, 'but it would make them real easy to catch. And even if we didn't sell them they'd keep us going in winter time. And then there's the Little Owls. Apparently they've been trained for centuries to hunt larks. Not that I think we should train owls. That might be a bit too much. But the lark mirrors! There's an opportunity...'

Heraldo's words washing over Wenzel. His son's enthusiasm for new things, new ideas, infectious, but Wenzel was tired and Heraldo saw it and departed. Left Wenzel to take off his boots and socks, ease his feet, stick them into a bucket of water. Something Grandmother Pfiffmakler had done every night, if they'd water to spare. One tradition he didn't mean to let slip, and Oh Lord, how good it felt! She'd been right on that score at least. And right on so many others. But Grandmother was gone from them and Wenzel needed to get the troops in order, form a coherent plan.

It had always been in his head that once they'd hit Ravenna they'd go south towards Abruzzo. No need now for the flit back over the water to Montenegro, although he still liked the idea. So many places there they'd never been to, and therefore so many people who'd never seen their shows. Just needing a bit of help with the local lingo, and maybe Livia could help there. Her impassioned acting impressive. Yet another duty needed seeing to. Making sure she joined up with them right and proper. A real asset, that woman, no matter she'd one half of her face looking like it had been pressed into a burning pan. To the contrary, something they could use, if she'd allow it. Neither Ludmilla nor Longhella ever taking to masks but Livia, well. Didn't take much to figure that out.

Thinking all this when a figure approached his tent in the darkness. Ettori clearing his throat, wanting to knock—which was difficult on canvas.

'Are you Wenzel Pfiffmakler?' he asked, Wenzel looking up to see a man in monk's habit hanging at the door flap.

Wenzel sighing.

He didn't need more conversation, some itinerant actor asking for a job.

'That's me,' he said, without enthusiasm. 'But I'd be right glad if...'

Never getting to the end of his plea for the man to come back in the morning.

'The Lord be praised!' the monk exclaimed. 'I need to speak to you. It's most urgent.'

Wenzel taking his feet from the tub of water, drying them on a few old rags.

'Can't it wait?'

'It cannot, sir. It absolutely cannot. I believe one of your daughters might be in terrible danger.'

Wenzel flicking his head up in concern, waving his hand briefly to allow the stranger in. Had to mean one of his nieces. Longhella was back, he'd seen Rosa giving the girl a right royal ticking off, and quite right too; but Ludmilla was still out and about advertising tomorrow's shows, probably still carrying her money bucket, had maybe been robbed. It had happened before, though danger seemed too strong a word for it. Yet still...

'Sit,' he commanded, Ettori quick to obey, plonking himself down on an upturned crate that had been graced by one of Rosa's elegantly embroidered cushions.

'It's like this,' Ettori said immediately, leaning forward, hands in a squirm upon his lap, mind in a similar state, wondering how to get it all said. 'Started back at the basilica, after I got Signora Pfiffmakler into her carriage...'

'Old Grandmother's got a carriage?' Wenzel asked, astonished.

'Well yes,' Ettori said, rubbing thumbs against fingertips and then fingertips against palms, unable to keep still. 'Archbishop ar-

221

ranged it. Taking her all the way to Nocera and the Redemptorists. But that's not the important bit just now.'

'Pretty important to me,' Wenzel put in, relieved beyond measure that Old Grandmother wouldn't be trudging the length of Italy on her own two pins, no matter how many coins she'd squirreled away over the years.

'You're completely missing the point!' Ettori raised his voice, then lowered it, not wanting to be overheard, tale coming out in a sudden splurge of words. 'After all was done I came out and found your youngest and what her older sister had done. Or rather what I think she'd done, for I've no real proof. Anyway, I thought to bring her back here but then I was set upon by ruffians...'

Wenzel holding up his hand to stop the flow. Ettori, primed in obedience, immediately ceased speaking, holding his body still, young face contorted by agitation.

'I don't know what you're telling me,' Wenzel stated. 'I have no daughters, I have nieces. Are you're saying they've had some kind of altercation? How do you know this?'

Ettori looking as confused as Wenzel felt.

'I found the youngest in a very sorry state at the basilica,' he tried to explain, 'immediately after the older one, Longhella, had just left. But that's not the point at all!'

'So you said before,' Wenzel interrupted, not surprised in the slightest that Longhella was involved in whatever tangled tale he was being told. 'So get to it. What are you saying?'

'That your youngest has been taken, sir! They tripped me up, took her right out of my arms! Told me to tell you not to follow them. That they weren't finished. That you'd be sorry if...'

Wenzel stood up so suddenly he knocked over the shallow pail in which he'd been bathing his feet, understanding coming to him quick as that thunderstorm had presented earlier.

'Rosa! he bellowed, striding out of the tent in his bared feet, Ettori fast behind him. 'Rosa! Get everyone together and get them now!'

Hulde was being shoved into an old flour sack and hauled upon the back of a man who smelled like dog shit and alcohol, who drew straps of leather about her sack and across his chest to keep her still.

Not that she tried to move or cry out as she was taken from the hippodrome and the fair and into the maze of Ravenna's streets.

Hulde registering none of it.

Hulde right back in the village on the shores of the Adriatic where the borders of two countries met; where she'd seen the sea but never gone near it; where they'd slaughtered the ox and celebrated being in their new home; where they'd all been slaughtered as surely as that ox.

Hulde losing all the words she'd learned, losing all the new memories of what had seemed like a new family.

Hulde stripped back to the bone.

Hulde hearing only one voice.

Pull down the lid, girl, and maybe you'll survive.

Hulde obeying.

Hulde dragging down that lid, dragging down that body.

Hulde making not a peep, not a sound, not a movement.

Pull down the lid, girl, and maybe you'll survive.

Again.

23

Cogs Begin to Turn

Wenzel was incandescent.

Wenzel dragging Longhella into their circle, twisting his fingers in her long hair after seeing she was about to skulk away, the entire company troubled by his ire towards his niece Nothing new, but this entirely different.

'You've been despicable!' he shouted at her. 'Absolutely despicable. Tell them what you've done!'

Longhella delivered to the company prostrate, her beautiful skirts dragged through the mud by Wenzel's vengeful hand.

'I've done nothing!' she pleaded, though plainly she'd been discovered. 'Just gave the little upstart a taste of what she deserved!'

'As judged by you?' Wenzel was finding it hard to contain his rage. 'You set your fists against a little girl and think you've done rightly?'

Yssel feeling the need to defend her progeny.

'I'm sure she had her...'

Stopping short as she saw Wenzel's face, as Peppe held her back.

'Do you have any idea, Longhella,' Wenzel spat his words at her, 'any idea at all what you've set in motion with your misguided spite?'

Longhella didn't.

Longhella began to weep as copiously as any heroine on the stage.

'Those tears cut no ice with me,' Wenzel said, vicious as ever Longhella could be. 'Because of you, and only you, Hulde has been carried off. Of no worth to her kidnappers unless, or until, she be bargained for. And you'd better pray that's the case, Longhella, because I swear to God right now that if I don't find that girl alive then you'll be off from us. Cut out, cut off. And I'll never take you back, and no more would Old Grandmother if she knew what you'd done.'

Ludmilla running onto the scene, pushing Lupercal and Jericho out of her way.

'What's going on? What's she done?'

'She gave Hulde a pummelling, is what,' Wenzel growled, 'and this man, this brother,' nodding towards Ettori, 'was bringing her back to us only to be ambushed at the last and Hulde taken.'

Ludmilla stricken, hands covering her mouth.

'But who would do such a thing?' she whispered.

'I can take a wild guess,' Wenzel said, releasing Longhella, rubbing his hands together as if ridding himself of her. 'What did these men look like?'

Fixing his eyes on Ettori, Ettori hanging at the edge, horrified by Wenzel's treatment of Longhella, no matter she deserved it.

'Um, didn't get a great look. It was dark, but there were three of them. I'm sure of that, and the stall holder who got me up said they were partisans or separatists, or something of the like.'

'We need to find Andreas Zilboorg,' Wenzel announced, to general surprise. 'Can you stay for the while…' looking at Ettori. 'I'm sorry. I don't even know your name.'

'Ettori,' Ettori supplied. 'And yes, I suppose…although the Abbott will be wondering…'

'Very well,' Wenzel cut him off. 'Then spread out, everyone. Andreas is bound to be here somewhere.'

Heraldo hopping on his feet, needing a reason, asking what no one else would.

'But why? Why do we need to find him? What's he got to do with any of this?'

Wenzel taking a deep breath, pulling a quick hand from mouth to beard.

225

'Has no one not found it odd that we've met Andreas and Valter but have never clapped eyes on the second Balatronic brother? How even when we were on Preko we only saw him in his get up, when not even his own mother would have recognised him? How he was gone the second they were done, how he never checked on Andreas up his mast on the boat?'

Everyone exchanging glances, because it had never crossed their minds.

'I've seen him,' came a lone voice in the wilderness, Livia taking a short step forward. 'Saw him a few times in Zadar.'

'Describe him,' Wenzel commanded, 'and Ettori, you take heed.'

Livia bit her lip, did as bid.

'He's the same height as his brother, couple of years older, I'd guess. And he's very dark hair. Like really black. The kind of black that sort of shines when it catches the light. And a cleft chin, like Valter,' Livia added. 'Real deep cleft, clean shaven but always sort of stubbly in the middle.'

Ettori opened his mouth in shock.

'That's him!' he exclaimed, then chided himself, not wanting to cast an innocent man as guilty. 'At least one of them looked like that. Seemed to be in charge.' Short sharp bursts of memories coming back at him. 'And another was taller, bulkier. Javarek, I think one of them said. Mentioned a Christian village. Something that had happened there.'

Wenzel nodded. Seeing some, if not all.

'Do Valter and his brother look alike?' he asked Livia. 'Apart from the colour of their hair?'

Livia sucking in a breath. Remembering Valter far too well, nodding her head.

'Yes, I suppose. Especially in profile.'

'Gaztor,' Ludmilla whispered, looking over at Heraldo, who in turn looked over to his father.

'Gaztor,' Wenzel repeated. 'And no wonder she buried that blasted clown figurine like it was the devil himself.'

Andreas Zilboorg was having a hard time of it. He'd been allowed into the fair, donned his armband, was directed to the upper end with the rest of the entertainments. He'd asked about, eventually getting the distressing news that the Pfiffmaklers, for reasons unknown, had been sited not up top but immediately behind the stalls selling food and drink and he would have to go all the way back down again. His legs giving him such gyp he'd had to take a breather. Getting a good clean eye at what his future would be, which wasn't great. Every limb aching, joints screaming that they couldn't take much more. The punishment up the mast had done him in more than he'd realised and as much as he'd chastised Valter and Jodl he really, really needed them now. Knew he'd hitched his horse to the wrong wagon but they were all he had, and without them he was bereft. Set adrift without a paddle. No one to turn to, or almost no one. Made his way to the edge of the fair's ground, sat on the damp grass, took off the pack that held all his hedgehoggery nonsense as it had so often been called, and as he knew it to be. Used it as a headrest, uncomfortable as it was. Tried to sleep. Thought of Valter and Jodl and whatever awful deeds he knew them to be capable of, of what they might be doing even now. Rested until he felt able to get up again, go on. The hippodrome dark, night fallen. Shouldered his meagre pack, began to thread his way back towards where he'd been told the Pfiffmaklers were. The hippodrome huge, several acres, but now all the fairgoers were gone and the fairs' folk sleeping his going was easier. Andreas keeping to the edges, the hedge his guide, limping onwards.

Then stopped short.

Caught a kind of hissing wheeze coming from not too far away.

Bizarre thought in his head that maybe it was hedgehogs. The exact same noise two rival males made when they got into a fight. He'd not got into hedgehoggery by accident, had found them fascinating animals when he was a boy after unwittingly uncovering one kipping the winter through in a pile of dried leaves he'd been about to throw upon a fire. His father by then, at the grand old age of thirty-three, being unable to unknit one finger from the next, held his hands like dead crabs against his chest, had to be dragged along on a dog-cart because his leg joints were so swollen he could no longer get along under his own steam. Andreas counting himself lucky he'd lasted so long without going the same way.

His father telling him to chuck the blasted animal into the embers, give them a meal however paltry. Andreas hadn't the heart. Andreas keeping it as a pet of sorts in a small wicker cage he made for the purpose, feeding it worms, snails and slugs, its winter hibernation well and truly ended by his intervention; releasing it in the spring only to find it hadn't gone far, had made a nest of grass in the same heap of leaves in their back yard and produced young: tiny and blind, with soft white spines.

Andreas enchanted.

Andreas moving towards the source of that slight noise in the dark night as if it might bring him salvation.

The Pfiffmaklers, like Andreas, had looked.

And the Pfiffmaklers, like Andreas, had not found.

Pfiffmaklers calling it a day, settled uneasy in their tents. Yssel and Peppe speaking quietly to one another as Longhella curled herself up, turned her back on them, soon asleep despite the night's happenings. Ludmilla refusing to join them, keeping vigil, desperate for Hulde's return. Ludmilla joined by Heraldo, both sitting on the carts of their makeshift stage watching the moon climb the dark sky.

'We can't really have lost her, can we?' Ludmilla asked. Heraldo hesitating, indecisive, thinking it a real possibility.

'Maybe Papa's got it wrong,' he offered. 'Maybe it's nothing to do with what happened in that village.'

Ludmilla frowned, thought about it.

'Wouldn't that be worse?' she concluded. 'If someone's just randomly snatched her up?' She shook her head. 'But that can't be right. They knew who she was. They gave Ettori a message specifically for us.'

Heraldo rolled his shoulders, stretched his neck. He was used to dealing with complicated mechanisms, taking contraptions apart and putting them back together or building them from scratch. But he couldn't fit all the pieces of this particular conundrum together in any meaningful way.

'I just don't understand it,' he admitted. 'I know Livia told us those places are wild and lawless, but surely they don't really go around wiping out entire villages for no reason? And even if they do, how did Andreas Zilboorg's lads get mixed up in it?'

'I've been wondering the same,' Ludmilla said. 'And how much of a giant coincidence it was that we met Valter and Andreas at all. I mean Zadar's a big place and yet we met two of them out of the blue on the same afternoon, less than an hour after we got there.'

'That's right!' Heraldo animated, cogs turning, levers tripping, coils being sprung. Ludmilla ahead of him.

'Valter even told me so,' she said. 'In the thunderstorm, after the Sea Organ. Said they'd heard we were in the area, wanted to hook up, but doesn't that seem strange? I mean, we were miles away. Hadn't meant to go to Zadar, so how would they know we'd even be there?'

'And yet they did.' Heraldo taking in this information. 'And were real keen to join us. Deal signed and sealed once Valter rescued Hulde.'

Ludmilla shuddered.

'You think they did it, the brothers? Hulde could have drowned.'

She was going to tear them to pieces when she found them.

'I do,' Heraldo agreed. 'And then there's the fact that Andreas said he'd always wanted his boys to see Italy. But why would he? You know fairs folk. They stick to their own routes. Why would they all of an instant want to go somewhere they've never been before?'

'Because they had a specific reason,' Ludmilla joined in. 'Maybe only wanted there because that was where we were going...or maybe were going there anyway and we just happened along...'

Heraldo shook his head.

'I don't think anyone just happened along,' he said quietly. 'I think we were followed. Maybe got seen at that village and that we had Hulde. Think about it, Ludmilla,' he went on. 'If you'd just hacked and shot a whole load of people to pieces wouldn't you be keeping track of what happened afterwards?'

Ludmilla about to reply that no, she'd have legged it for the hills and kept on running, when she put out a hand, clutched at Heraldo's arm.

'Sssh!' she whispered. 'I think I hear something...'

Heraldo straightened up, cocked his head.

'Over there,' he whispered. 'Something's moving...'

Pointing towards the neat-clipped hedges marking the hippodrome's southern boundary.

'Stay here,' he ordered, slipping silently to the ground.

Like hell I will, Ludmilla thought, immediately on Heraldo's heels, the two heading stealthily over the stubbly grass, one to the left, the other to the right, tiny moon reflections glinting on handle, hasp and blade as Ludmilla withdrew her dagger from its scabbard. Never wetted yet by human blood. But the night was young, and Ludmilla having vengeance burning through her like a wick through wax.

24

Loyal Soldiers Begin to Have Their Doubts

The cart that contained all the props of The Balatronic Ballet had been stripped to a carcass by the time Valter got back to it. Not that he'd need of it anymore. His head was thumping, eyes black and swollen from Jodl's vicious attack, sure his nose was broken. He couldn't even sniff, nostrils blocked by clotted blood, had to breathe through his mouth, making his throat real dry and scratchy. And God, it hurt. Everything about him hurt, and more so to see that some little tyke had merited his chess pieces of so little worth they'd been scattered in the street like bad corn.

He picked up one after another, stuffing them into his pockets until they could hold no more. The chess boards were in splinters, no point trying to rescue those. He wanted to cry but his eyes were too sore, too bruised over. As was he. Bruised right down to his core. He'd always thought he and Jodl would be together through thick and thin, had never seen this day coming. Had known about Jodl's obsession with what had happened way back, but how in hell had it come to this? No more Balatronic Ballet ever again, not with his brother gone off on some crusade of his own making. Valter would have shaken his head in despair if it hadn't felt as heavy and delicate as an over-ripe watermelon. Jesus. Everything was ruined, himself included. His arguments with Andreas and then with Jodl leaving him empty and alone, having problems thinking in straight lines.

What the buggeration was he going to do? No one left to look out for him and, sad fact Valter was only just getting to grips with, he needed that grounding, that certainty. Needed Andreas.

No legitimate way into the fair's ground, not with his face all busted up, and so he waited.

Waited for hours outside the hippodrome until it emptied, until it stilled, until the night was so full down that nothing was moving except the shrews and mice and the owls that had been keeping vigil in the trees for just this moment, claws sharp and at the ready. Valter ready too, figuring the best place to get in would be near the food-stall holders so he had the chance of snatching something to eat. Spending his waiting hours gauging where their stalls were, taking his measure from them shouting out their wares. Aiming for a few yards above, not wanting to intrude on them directly and risk immediate discovery.

Then through the hedge he went, hard going, on his stomach, pushing between the close-planted box trunks, feeling his way forward, grunting like an old hedgehog until at last he was out.

Jodl and his companions took the road out of Ravenna heading south, keeping themselves distinct from the many other folk filtering out the same way: the horses and carts, the carriages and donkeys, pious folk who'd come for the sainting but wanted nothing to do with any Sausage Fair. Folk who didn't have money to fritter, or needed back to work by the morning. Back to the baskets of laundry needing washing and pressing; vines and olives to be tended; plots of vegetables weeded and watered; small dusty shops they couldn't afford to keep closed for more than a day; craftsmen worrying about what their apprentices might have got up to while they were gone.

In one of those carriages was Grandmother Pfiffmakler, being taken away to her new life, alone and in luxury. Finding half a dozen bottles of good wine and more carafes of boiled water stowed beneath her seat along with a hamper of food she'd never seen the like of, let alone tasted. Provided by the Archbishop's own kitchen: a quarter portion of some kind of poultry pie studded with raisins, spiced with multi-coloured peppercorns; a hock of smoked ham glazed with honey and mace; an intricate plait of bread yellow as the crock of butter provided in a small covered pot; a sweet jam made from azarole haws, orange-coloured, tasting of apples; several varieties of fruit she hadn't the faintest idea how to tackle, fingering the hot-house pineapple, the growing of which Mellini was justly proud, with something approaching awe.

As she travelled along the dusty tracks and byways she breathed deeply the scents of pine resin and honeysuckle; closed her eyes, trying to remember when she'd been so content, so happy, so bless-ed. Realising that never was the answer to that question. First time in her life she'd been truly alone: no clamouring family nagging her to pick a husband, any bloody husband so long as she got out from under her parents' feet; said husband cooing at her for a couple of minutes before turning their life together into one long shouting match; no extended family to keep under control; no blasted Kunterbunt and all its hangers-on demanding this of her, demanding that.

Trundling along through the countryside entirely at ease.

Nobody asking anything of her, except her driver—her driver!—who stopped occasionally to make sure his revered passenger was fine, that she didn't need a break, that she was happy for them to continue to the next ostlers or inn where they could rest the night, all expenses paid, or travel on a bit way further.

'There's no hurry, Signora,' Pietro assured her. *Signora!* What a thrill to be so addressed. 'Archbishop has directed me to take you slowly. Let you see the sights. Has given me an itinerary of places you might be interested to visit and, like I said before, all expenses covered. Just wants you to have a real good journey.'

Thank you, Alphonsus, the frequent refrain whispered from her dry old lips.

It had been a long life, tumultuous and difficult, but by God it had been worth every back-breaking, heart-hardening second of it now it had led her to this.

And only more of the same to look forward to.

Breathing easy, breathing free, breathing better than she had in years.

Jodl's companions were getting tetchy. It was a hard slog and hot, particularly for Javarek who was carrying Hulde; not that the girl had moved since they'd tied her onto his back, Jodl worrying she might have suffocated until he poked a finger at her and felt her move. Still, night well down. Time to call a halt.

'All right lads,' he said, spying a falling-down barn next to a derelict cottage. 'Let's hole up.'

'About bloody time,' Javarek grumbled. 'Don't know why it's been me has to carry the blasted cargo all this way.'

'Because you're built like an ox,' Jodl stated. 'Mergim can do the donkey work tomorrow.'

Mergim frowned.

'You sure this is such a good idea, boss? The girl, I mean?'

Jodl grinding his teeth.

'Think I'd've bothered taking her if not?' he asked. 'Goddammit, what do you take me for?'

Mergim subsided, chastised. He'd enormous respect for his leader, and Jodl was his leader. Mergim looking for one for years, ever since the Serbs won autonomy from the Turks. Someone who'd do and not just say, someone fit to lead a rebellion like Black George and Milos Obrenovich had done. It had taken a few decades, but they'd got there in the end. Something real to aim for.

Back in Zadar it had been naught but talk and chat. He'd hoped for more when the young writer fellow, Ljudevit Gaj, started up the Ilirizam. Croat nationalism suddenly on everyone's lips, and he'd thought *stick with the Croats, and Albania won't be far behind.* Only nothing changed. Not until a couple of years back when Jodl came into his ken.

Jodl talking and chatting with the best of them, but Jodl different. Jodl meaning what he was saying, didn't just blaze up after a few drinks like the others and blow out the moment they'd gone home. Jodl burning at his core.

Jodl on a mission.

Jodl having a past he was on the trail of, going by some of Jodl's throwaway questions. Mergim recognising the context of those questions, Mergim offering his services.

'Seems like you're wanting information,' he'd said, when he'd followed Jodl out of the tavern. Jodl turning on Mergim, putting out a hand, shoving Mergim back against the tavern wall, never mind he was a scrapling by comparison, several years Mergim's junior and half his size.

'Dunno what you're on about, big fella,' Jodl had said, but Mergim knew Jodl's like, had met plenty back when he was a young man, and worked his angle.

'Hold up,' he'd said. 'Kinda got the feeling you're on the hunt. Maybe to do with Karageorge and Obrenovich?'

And that had done it, the two moving off a ways, falling once more to chat and talk, with a definite end in mind. Shared experiences, shared pasts, shared nationalities, shared goals. Or so it had seemed at the time.

Turned out it was Jodl's last night in Zadar, heading off on his fairs circuit with his brother and uncle the following morning. Except Jodl, like a true leader, hadn't immediately jumped ship; had more patience than Mergim thought possible. Telling Mergim what he wanted Mergim to do, the name he'd been tracking down over the years.

'You find out what you can while I'm gone,' Jodl told him. 'Keep your ear to the ground. Poke about. Ask questions. Don't be too obvious. You know who I'm looking for. Thinking he's high up in the Serbian administration by now, seeing as how well he came out of the rebellion. Someone's got to pass through here sometime knows about him.'

Mergim nodding grimly, eager to please.

'You do that for me,' Jodl promised, 'and when I'm back, and I will be back, then we'll see what's what.'

And two years later Jodl returned to Zadar, just like he'd said. Almost to the day. Mergim ready, Mergim waiting, Mergim having probed and poked folk for information in between mending people's shoes, boots and gloves; sometimes while he was mending people's shoes, boots and gloves. Jodl finally proved right mere weeks after Serbia had inaugurated its Senate right at the start of the year.

1839.

For Ravenna a saint; for Serbia a Senate.

First order of the Senate being to give their erstwhile hero, Milos Obrenovich, his marching orders. Obrenovich obstinate, still hanging onto the dregs of his power, far as Mergim knew.

Not so some of his closest cohorts.

One of them eventually landing in Zadar; the very same man Jodl had asked him to look out for, or at least a strong possibility it was so.

Information Jodl took well. Very well.

Time for Mergim's pay off. A big ask, yet Jodl nodding, taking it seriously. Jodl knowing the countryside like the back of his hand, how to appear and disappear without a trace. Mergim telling him of the folk who'd salted themselves out of the mountains, settled in a village a bit way from the shore. Outsiders taking what wasn't theirs to take. Spotted a few days previously by a shepherd lad Mergim paid to keep an eye on the abandoned border villages, because one had been his own until the Turks increased taxes and tithes to a level they couldn't possibly afford to pay. Some of the men, including Mergim's grandfather, standing up against them. Result being a vicious gun battle they couldn't win. Mergim shoulder to shoulder with his grandfather, levelling their rifles, firing and firing until their ammunition ran dry when Mergim's grandfather ordered Mergim back to join the women and children. Mergim pleading no. Mergim's grandfather placing a hand on his boy's shoulder.

'There's lines to be drawn, son, and this is mine. But it ain't yours.'

His grandfather's last words, as he and his fellows mounted bayonets and charged.

A useless gesture, you or I might have thought, but not Mergim, nor anyone who lived in that place, at that time.

Mergim's grandfather, like Mergim's father, heroes of the Serbian revolution. Both exiled at its end, thrown back into Albania. Forced to find new homes because their last no longer existed. And a new one they'd found, defended to the death. A hard and bitter lesson learned that day, Mergim soon striking off to Zadar to find his own cause, discover where his own line lay.

Albania, Croatia and Serbia plaited together like a multi-wound loaf of bread.

Multiple borders, nationalities, languages, religions and alphabets.

Some sticking to their own, some fighting for another in hope the favour would be returned.

Mergim doing both, and still wanting vengeance long overdue.

Jodl true to his word.

Jodl not caring too much about the details, for a debt was a debt.

Mergim had done his part. Jodl quick to make a plan after interrogating Mergim and Mergim had supplied the goods.

'We'll need a third man,' Jodl had said. 'Anyone you absolutely trust?'

Only one, although he was only an inch this side of insane.

'Javarek,' Mergim said, after a few moments thought. 'Plays cards like a retard, but won't flinch at a little bit of blood.'

'Gonna be more than a little,' Jodl replied easily, Mergim smiling, Mergim sure he'd found The One.

Javarek similarly certain when Mergim put the plan to him.

'About time someone brought the fuck back into the fight,' was Javarek's response. A sentence as illogical as it was affirmative, but you had to go with what you'd got.

And it had gone better than planned: herding the women and children from their cottages midway through food preparation, men already gathered on the village green to tend their ox on its spit, and an easy thing—easy for those three at least—to cut every last occupant down, fire-pit swiftly filled in and covered, bodies piled over it.

'Dead giveaway of a celebration,' no irony intended nor taken, 'and can't give anyone any reason to believe they was only newly here when they're found,' Jodl ordered. 'And someone'll find them sooner or later. Got to seem like they've been here longer.'

Protecting himself, protecting them all, an act appreciated by Mergim if not by Javarek, who rarely thought of anything at all.

All well, until the shepherd boy had told them about the Kunterbunt arriving the following morning and hoiking the girl out of the mess they'd left behind. A shock for Mergim, if not for Jodl—who took it all in his stride and found advantage in it.

'It's perfect!' Jodl had said. '

Mergim at a loss to see how that was so, but no going back now.

'Got to do a tidy up,' Jodl advised, Jodl commanded. 'Got to get rid of your shepherd boy. Can't have him knowing all our business. Can't have him blabbing.'

Mergim raising a feeble protest, for the lad had been useful, loyal, and done no harm.

'The lad's been paid,' Jodl was not to be moved. 'And folk who've been paid will always spill their story when someone lays a boot to their neck.'

Even so, Mergim couldn't do it. Left the deed to Javarek, who came back from the hills with clothes bloodied, crowing like a cockerel about how the lad had pissed himself in his fear and the sheep had all started bleating and running away, several toppling over a cliff in their distress. Jodl disgusted. Telling Javarek to shut his mouth, go wash up before anyone else saw him.

First sign to Mergim that his own call might be swaying.

He'd known that shepherd boy, had sat with him, broken bread with him, laughed at the boy who'd insisted every single member of his flock was different.

'That one there?' he'd said, when they'd sat together in the hills and Mergim had persuaded the lad to act as lookout for a few coins. 'She's only a gimmer, but produced twins on her first go. And that one? She's a regular beauty in the sheep world, tups fighting like tomcats over her. And just look!'

Pointing at an old ewe who was on the edge of a vertiginous drop.

The boy laughing.

'She always pushes it right to the limit, goes down on her knees to get the good grass none of the others dare go for. But she never goes over. And no more do her daughters…see that one? And that one?'

The fact that the lad was lying somewhere in those hills with his throat sliced open by Javarek's knife was appalling. Mergim could almost hear the flies, the chomping of their maggot progeny, the quick shuffling of beetles' wings as they landed and took their turn.

And he'd gone and thrown in his lot with his murderer.

Quit his job to follow Jodl's calling, one debt leading to another. Passing on a bit of information hardly equal to massacring an entire village on Mergim's say so. Mergim beginning to regret it.

Mergim beginning to realise its futility, that doing to others what had been done to him and his didn't make anybody feel any better and didn't right any wrongs. Fact being that those folk from the hills had never done him any harm at all.

Second wobble for Mergim being the girl.

Stroke of luck, Jodl had called it, though Mergim doubted it. Reckoned Jodl had kept a close eye on the lass specifically to find a time to snatch her up. Proved right when, just like that, it had come to pass. At least Jodl had stopped Javarek stomping that monk's head into splinters.

And now here they were in a stinking barn on Vengeance Road, as Jodl called it. Jodl hard and brittle as a brick baked too long in the kiln. The girl a pathetic heap in one corner, still in her sack, pulling it up to her face, keeping her eyes closed all the time as if by doing so, by shutting herself off from them, all would turn out well. Which may be, he told himself, it would. He'd liked to have talked to her, reassured her but, like Jodl, he'd not spoken his mother tongue for over fifteen-odd years and it was a language lost to both. Orphans ejected from one life, thrown headlong into another. Just like the girl, now he was thinking on it. A thought he quickly shoved to one side, grabbing instead at a bottle of wine and uncorking it with his teeth, taking a few generous swallows before allowing himself to speak.

'So what's the plan from here on in, boss?' he asked Jodl, who'd been a bit short on details since he'd met up with them in Ravenna, having sent Mergim and Javarek on a couple of days ahead while he'd dallied on Preko, keeping his family none the wiser.

Jodl poked at the fire, pulled out a bit of damper he'd been baking on the end of a stick. It was charcoal black, but not as black as Jodl's hair, and as dull as Jodl's eyes were bright in the firelight.

'The villages near Termoli are our best bet. Down country in Molise,' Jodl said, taking a deep and satisfied breath, blowing on the damper to cool it.

Mergim frowning.

'That's one hell of a way,' he said. His geography a bit hazy, but knowing from Albanian compatriots heading to join the Arbëreshë that it was way down south, other communities even further, including one in Sicily. 'We should have taken a ship. We've money enough.'

'Not now we've the girl,' Jodl stated flatly. 'She'd scream bloody murder the moment she got away from us. And she'd get away at some point, or someone would come asking. You know what folk are like cooped up on deck, tattling like sparrows with nothing better to do.'

'Even so,' Mergim persisted. 'Why those particular enclaves? Why not any of the others?'

Jodl looking over at Mergim as if he'd not the wit of a cockroach.

'Have you forgotten everything of our past?' Jodl fixing Mergim with an awful glare. Mergim lowering his eyes, latching them onto the fire which didn't seem quite so hot or vengeful by comparison.

'Don't know what you mean, boss.'

'*Don't know what you mean, boss,*' Jodl parroted. 'Didn't you tell me only a few weeks back that our man,' *our* man now, Mergim noted, not just Jodl's, 'went over to Ravenna a few months previously with a couple of fine white bulls? Bulls specifically of the Podolica breed? And well done on the details, by the way.'

Mergim scowling, disliking the sarcasm, unsure if he was being mocked or praised.

'I did,' he said, shrugging his shoulders, 'but where's the what with that?'

Jodl quiet for a moment, reassessing the situation. Mergim and himself coming from very different parts of Albania. Jodl from the hills, from the wild places where borders were always in dispute, where extended family clans kept to themselves, fought bitterly against one other about where this part of their land started and that part ended. Mergim from some coastal village not that far from Zadar, where the *Caressi* might be completely unheard of. Where the acquisition and transportation of a couple of fine-bred Podolica oxen might have no significance at all, which obviously they did not.

Jodl twisting out a smile.

'Because the where is the what,' he said, paraphrasing Mergim's words, 'and the why. Means we've as good as caught our man, and that this here,' he jutted his chin at Hulde, 'is our coin in.'

Mergim looked at the girl who'd curled in on herself, was lying on her side. Had sucked up the water they'd given her. Hadn't touched the bread. Couldn't for the life of him see what Jodl was getting at. All he could see was a couple of weeks of tramping along paths and places he didn't know, carrying the girl with them like some ancient sacrifice. He couldn't exactly remember her from the village, couldn't clearly remember any of the details, only that when they'd come out of Zadar they'd kept to the back ways, Jodl having scoped out their route; seen the interlopers settled in and cosy, slaughtering their one and only ox, their one and only animal. Pouring its blood into their lime-wash and industriously painting the walls of cottages not theirs to take, never mind they'd been empty for years. Caught the strains of the hymns they'd sung as they went about their work. Javarek scraping his dagger's blade again and again against his soapstone until it was sharp and vicious as it could be. Jodl loading bullets into the gun Mergim had procured for him. Mergim holding sweaty hands about his billhook that had never done anything more savage than layering a hedge.

And then the extraordinary had happened: the entire lot of the menfolk gathering on the village green digging their fire-pit, getting their recently deceased ox onto a spit and into the flame, splitting themselves off from the women and children, and oh, so much easier to attack.

Like a sign.

But signs seen from one angle are rarely the same as from another.

Mergim thinking that Vengeance Road might not be all it was cracked up to be.

That finding a leader was one thing, following him blindly quite another.

Mergim not so stupid as Jodl took him for, but not clever enough to think his way out.

25

Black Mountains, Black George, Black Memories

Andreas hobbled forward warily, making out a form squiggling its way through the bottom of the hippodrome's boundary hedge. A man struggling hard; whimpering, wheezing, pulling himself onwards by means of digging his fingernails into the grass and dragging himself forward on his stomach. The moon high and bright, which was a blessing, for all the cressets and fair stalls' fires were long extinguished, guards gone home, everyone asleep.

Oh you moon.

Enough light from it for Andreas to recognise the form finally pulling himself free from the undergrowth. Valter a desperate looking character, face swollen and bruised. Andreas's heart lurching to see it so, despite his previous decision to be done with both the blasted brothers. Andreas too slow to shout out a warning as two dark shadows flitted in from left and right and hauled Valter to his feet, Andreas seeing the unmistakeable glint of a knife held to Valter's throat.

Andreas's mind a maelstrom.

Valter had come back for him!

But Valter was hurt.

And Valter set on by these shadowy vagabonds.

Although they weren't acting exactly like vagabonds.

Andreas seeing a flash of orange in the night.

Andreas jumping from one assumption to another, hoping he was right.

'Pfiffmaklers!' he appealed. 'It's only us! It's Andreas and Valter. Please don't do us harm.'

Oh but that knife wavered at Valter's throat, drew blood, if not much, and nothing compared to the dried smears of it down Valter's cheeks and chin, the front of his shirt.

'I think you've much to tell me, Valter Poppelmann,' Ludmilla whispered loudly in his ear. 'And pray God you do, or I will personally drop you down the nearest well and rejoice as I let you go.'

The attack posse returned to the upturned carts with their captives, though a sorry looking bunch they were, Andreas seeming to have shrunk and curled in on himself, crabbed about his cane. And Valter, well...

'What happened to you?' Ludmilla demanded, wanting to rip the skin off him despite his swollen face. He could barely open his eyes for the bruises, looked as if he'd been rubbing his face in rotting medlars.

Valter feeling tears coming on. He didn't think his day could have got any worse. Felt like shit. Discovered the second he'd come through the hedge despite what he'd thought had been superhuman stealth. Held at knifepoint by a mere girl and that same girl now pitying him.

'Nothing,' he muttered sullenly, Ludmilla letting out a short, scornful laugh.

'Would hate to see it when it's something, if that's the case,' she said.

Heraldo walking quickly to his father's tent, poking his head in, calling softly.

'Papa. Wake up! There's been a development.'

Wenzel groaning but quickly awake, as was Rosa beside him.

'What is it?' Wenzel croaked, stretching out a hand to find his boots, Rosa hauling a shawl about her shoulders.

'We've got Valter Poppelmann,' Heraldo informed his parents. 'Andreas too.'

Wenzel put a hand over his mouth to stifle his usual morning coughing spree, come too early.

'You and that filthy pipe!' Rosa admonished, more from habit than concern, a small pantomime they went through every day.

'Hush, woman,' Wenzel said his part, though neither of their hearts were in it, both getting themselves standing, both partially dressed in case they'd needed up in a hurry. Proved right.

'Where've you got them?' Wenzel asked, moving softly, didn't want to raise the rest of the family. Lucky for them they were some way distant from the food-holders' stalls, isolated by their grass stage, so no cause for concern there, unless the situation got rowdy. 'Come quiet did they?' he added.

'Got them by the carts. And yes, you could say that,' Heraldo answered, leading his parents on, one grim trio joining the other grim trio centre stage.

Moon round and beneficent, despite a few clouds scudding before it every now and then.

Grass shivering with dew.

Entire hedge cocooned with glistening spider webs putting on their own silent show that would be invisible come the morning, unless the dew still clung.

Night-flying insects and spring moths on the wing, bats swooping low over hedge and grass to scoop them up.

A whole microcosmic universe of fight and flight going on around our players, each as ignorant and uncaring of the other's plight as theirs was of them.

'Andreas,' Wenzel nodded curtly. Andreas tipping his head in response, leaning up against the cart, utterly exhausted.

'And Valter,' Wenzel added, amused and a little alarmed to see Ludmilla playing with her blade, ready to slash or stab the man if he made a move. Which he did not. And no wonder. Had plainly undergone a far more vicious beating than Longhella had inflicted on Hulde, could feel Rosa by his side itching to get at Valter with her liniments and medications.

Valter didn't raise his head, was halfway to snoozing where he sat on the cart, hollowed out by the events of the day.

'Got some questions for you both,' Wenzel not put off by the pitiable remnants of The Balatronic Ballet, 'and I'm needing answers soon as.'

Andreas wasn't sure what was happening, why Ludmilla and Heraldo had seen fit to drag Valter up at knifepoint. Presumed it to do with what he suspected had happened on the ship.

'So let me tell you what I know,' Wenzel said without preamble, directing his accusations at Andreas who at least had the grace to follow what he was saying, Wenzel ticking the points off on his fingers as he went on.

'I think you knew who we were before we even arrived in Zadar. Decided to get in with us, and how easy was that was going to be? Andreas bumping so fortuitously into Heraldo, fairs people looking after fairs people and all that. Am I right?'

Andreas breathed hard, let out a long sigh.

'So I'm right,' Wenzel taking the reaction as agreement. 'And even more so when you heard we were on our way to Italy when, for some reason, your attachment to us became imperative. So just to make sure, to make doubly sure you were in with us, you took advantage of a child wandering about alone on a dark ship...'

And he'd an idea of how that had come about: Longhella leading the girl away to her great-grandmother, Old Grandmother telling Wenzel how *she joined in,* and *God forgive me, for I might have…*

'And made a quick plan to chuck her overboard,' he went on, 'effect a heroic rescue. And if it didn't work, well what the hell. Just an orphaned girl drowned, and the Kunterbunt eternally grateful you'd even tried.'

He studied his suspects. Valter still hanging his head. Not so Andreas, who had creased his brows, listening intently.

'But the real stumbling block,' Wenzel went on, 'has been the why. Why would you go to all that bother? Why did you need access to our ranks so badly? And why the interest in Italy all of a sudden, out of the blue, when it's never been part of your circuit? No,' Wenzel gave a brief shake of his head. 'There's something black at the heart of all this. It's taken me a while to figure it out, but I think I have some of it. So Valter,' Wenzel asked casually. 'When exactly was it that you and your brother fell in with the partisans?'

Valter didn't answer.

'Valter,' Andreas implored, 'you've got to tell them what you know!'

Valter pinched the end of his nose with his fingertips and sighed out his answer.

'Two years back. Last time we was in Zadar. But only Jodl. Not me.'

'Oh Valter,' Andreas's voice sad and soft. Valter always a follower. Andreas not realising the larger implications until Wenzel spelled them out for him, for them all.

'So let me guess. It was Jodl and some of his activist friends,' he was maybe putting two and two together and making six by excluding Valter, but he doubted it; he'd not seen much of Valter but recognised him to be a crower and not a fighting cock, 'who perpetrated a massacre in a village over the water. A massacre to whom the only living witness is Hulde.'

'Oh Lord no!' Andreas wheezed out, could have been the last gasp of a hurdy-gurdy dying on a street corner when its owner has seen the guards coming and legged it, leaving instrument and monkey to their sad fate.

'No!' Andreas said again. 'Valter, tell me—'

'And furthermore,' Wenzel interrupted, 'some scout of theirs was watching the place, saw us arrive, take the girl and tagged us back to Zadar, where Jodl made it his business to know our business. Needing to keep track of the girl.'

An awful sound came out of Valter: a retching, wretched blubbing; a shoulder-heaving keen as if he was a bairn again. All the years of hiding catching up with him, the memories no longer staunched, the memories bleeding out of him into the quiet night with his terrible soft lament. Wenzel momentarily thrown off guard. Andreas trying to get to his feet, scrabbling upwards, wanting to explain, excuse, defend.

'You don't know what these boys have been through,' he tried, triggering Wenzel back into action.

'I'm guessing almost exactly what Hulde did,' he announced quietly, to general surprise, to his own surprise if he was truthful. But Valter's visceral reaction to his interrogation was finally bringing sense to the entire situation, and not about to let Valter off the hook. Not yet. Wenzel shaking his head.

'I'm sorry, Andreas, but that's not the last of it.'

Andreas stumbling the yard and a half separating him from Valter, putting his hands on Valter's knees, partly to comfort the lad, the man, partly to keep himself upright.

'We've to tell them everything, Valter,' Andreas pleaded. 'For God's sake, we've got to.'

Valter snuffling, gulping, choking back tears.

'But he's gone, Uncle.'

And no side to that word *uncle*. Valter saying it like he really cared.

'Jodl's already gone,' Valter stuttered on. 'But I told him no. That I'd not go with him.'

Ludmilla and Heraldo exchanging glances, Wenzel frowning.

'Where's he going, lad?' Andreas tried. 'Can you tell us that?'

'I don't know!' Valter wailed, far too loudly for anyone's liking. 'Reckons he's on the trail of the man what did our family in! Got information that he went down Italy somewhere a few months back, like some regular Arbëreshë. Told him I wasn't going for it… told him no…told him…'

Andreas took Valter's hands in his own and squeezed them.

'I know, lad. I know. But anything you can tell us more, anything…'

The company held their breath, excepting Wenzel who had one last spear to fling. Wished Livia was here with her axe, knowing how much damage it could do in her hands, wooden as it was for, Goddammit, someone had to pay.

'He's taken Hulde,' Wenzel said. 'Jodl has taken Hulde. And if we don't find her then you know what Jodl's going to do. He's going to use her as barter. But if she proves of no use? If she outlives her purpose? Think hard, Valter, because whatever he did to you for refusing to bow down is nothing compared to what he's going to do to her.'

Valter and Andreas flinching, thinking of small toads squished into non-existence beneath Jodl's boots.

So what? What have they ever done for me?

Wenzel right about that. Jodl going over everything in his head after Mergim and Javarek were asleep, or in a drunken stupor—however you wanted to call it. Hard to get the help these days. Javarek a knucklehead, only in it for the fight. Any fight. For Javarek it made no difference. Called himself a Croatian Separatist, but really wasn't. No idea of politics apart from what he'd leeched from a few drunken conversations in Zadar taverns, most of which he couldn't remember. Couldn't have given you one name important to the cause if you'd stretched his hefty bones on a rack and snapped them one by one.

Mergim different.

Mergim understanding. No great thinker either, but he had morals, loyalties, was a man of action. Believed the Serbian model could serve for Albania too. That Jodl was the man to carry it through. Mergim's idea to slay the village, and a good idea had been Jodl's reasoning at the time. A debt for a debt. And exhilarating. Sealing the three of them together on their quest. On Jodl's quest. One that was almost at an end, however it panned out.

Except Mergim was wavering, Jodl knew it. Taken out from Zadar to unknown shores. Simpering over that shepherd boy like he'd been family.

Family, Jodl mouthed the word.

Not meaning Andreas nor Valter, who were no longer part of his world, had sloughed them off easily as a snake does its skin.

Meaning instead his real family, of which nothing was left but a pile of bones somewhere in the Shkodër mountains, and Jodl himself. Jodl not unlike Hulde on that score. Not that he considered the comparison nor, if he had, would have considered it with any empathy.

Green mountains, scabby goats scraggled up from a few high pens.

No white bulls; oxen stolen from them on the first round when the men had been killed.

Only mothers and children left.

Women of little use without their men or their men's weapons to protect them, of which there were none.

Black mountains, dank caves, cold snow and ice.

Everyone listless from lack of food.

Hugs and kisses, bland reassurances.

And then another raid, Black George's men not yet sated.

Women ravaged and dispatched. Children left to fend for themselves.

A miracle any had survived.

Excepting Jodl and Valter, the few others leaving, unable to be so pragmatic, stumbling off through thigh-high snow and never seen again.

No fire by then.

No tinder, no flint, no fuel.

No mother, no father, no guiding hand.

No tales, no bedtime stories.

No bedtime, no bed.

Nothing and no one but Jodl and Valter left at the end of that last long month in the mountains, snowed in, no way out until spring.

Jodl and Valter clawing and crawling their way down the mountain's slopes, chewing at the grass, the celandines, the unexpected primroses, as they descended beyond the snowline.

Teeth loose in their gums.

Souls far looser than their teeth.

And who could blame them for that?

Not Andreas Zilboorg, who'd picked the two up a while later as he'd skirted the edges of Croatia a bit far out of his usual zone. Andreas, who'd pitied them, who'd looked into Jodl's eyes and taken up the challenge.

Memories of that time sharp and hard in Jodl's mind.

For he who avenges blood is mindful of them;
He does not forget the cries of the afflicted.

Only Jodl remaining to walk the Road of Vengeance.

And by God, by that verse in the Psalms, he was going to get to its end.

He glanced at Hulde, who appeared to be sleeping in her sack though it was so dark she might be wide awake for all he knew.

Jodl and Hulde.

Two survivors who'd taken new names, both inexorably heading down the oldest of roads that rarely ended well, even if the end of them was all your horizons rolled into one and all you lived for and all you sought.

Jodl's mind-track interrupted by a large white-feathered barn owl swooping in through the open door space, low and majestic, blunt-faced, inscrutable, landing with impeccable grace on one of the barn's beetle-rotted eaves, coughing up a pellet of shrew bones and fur that fell like a gift at Jodl's feet; promptly tucked it's head beneath its wing and went to sleep.

Jodl prodding the pellet with his foot, looking over at Hulde in her sack.

Like a gift.

26

Valter Gives Away the Game

Valter had spilled out about as much of his guts as he could.

Valter telling Wenzel that yes, he was right about what had happened to Hulde on the ship; and yes, he was right that Valter's association with Jodl, or rather Jodl's association with Valter, was at an end. That Valter had called a halt to his stupid quest, but Jodl wouldn't have it.

But no, Valter knew nothing about the village massacre. Good God Almighty! He'd had nothing to do with that! All he knew was that Jodl was right in with the Croat and Albanian partisans, wanting to drag Valter with him, until Valter had refused.

'Why didn't you tell me any of this?' Andreas asked, Valter turning his eyes away from Andreas, Andreas's shoulders slumping, would have been glad of a bit of fight and fire, but whatever protestation had ever been in Valter was gone. Valter couldn't bring himself to apologise, and certainly wasn't going to admit how glad he was that Andreas was sitting by his side, how comforted he was by Andreas's mere presence, how it emboldened him enough to speak out about Jodl.

'Didn't think it would do any good,' Valter muttered, leaving off as Rosa tipped his head up and laved some ointment onto his nose and forehead.

'Should take the worst off the pain,' she said. 'But that nose is broken good and proper. Wenzel could pop it...'

'Wenzel,' Wenzel interrupted, 'is going to do nothing until we get to the end of this.'

Rosa brushed her hand through Valter's hair, something he'd not felt since he was a child.

'Just get it said,' she advised him, 'and then we'll see what can be done.'

Valter, softened by Rosa's ministrations, wanting nothing more. Just wanted sleep, to wake up and be back in Zadar before any of this had begun.

Shaking his head, which made it throb the more.

'He just couldn't let it go,' he mumbled, 'what happened to us. Couldn't let it lie. Wouldn't let it be. Finally found a name, don't ask me how.'

They were huddled by now in Wenzel's and Rosa's tent, needing to keep their conversation close, keep all this tidy, away from outsiders. Wenzel had completely forgotten about Ettori, whom he'd specifically asked to stick around and who, always obedient, had done exactly that. Even after the most of the Pfiffmaklers had

253

gone away to their beds Ettori had felt compelled to stay, partly because it was far too late now to go anywhere, partly because it had all been so exciting he needed to see how it played out. Awful to him that he'd been included in the first part of the drama yet might be excluded from the last. Spellbound by the events he'd witnessed so far, as if he'd been granted a walk-on part in a folktale still in the making.

And then Valter spoke a word that had meaning to him. Ettori curling and uncurling his hands, eventually moving forward from the shadows to the tent door, having the absurd urge to knock again. No need, for Heraldo heard his approach and was up on his feet, hands pulling back the canvas flap, dragging Ettori in. Everyone's hearts jumping at this sudden intervention, shifting their eyes from Valter to Ettori, who stumbled, knocked his head on the lantern hanging from a tent strut so the light jittered on the occupants, making them seem ghostly and conspiratorial, as if he'd wandered into Stribor's enchanted forest.

'Why are you still here?' Wenzel asked.

'You told me to stay,' Ettori answered simply. 'So stay I did.'

Wenzel raising his eyebrows, smiling wryly. Found it rather touching Ettori had taken his words so literally.

'Well then. You might as well come in, seeing as you already are.'

Ettori scratched at his neck where his habit always chafed.

'Wouldn't have interrupted,' he began his apologies, immediately interrupted by Ludmilla.

'Would just have stuck about outside like a bad breath earwigging what's none of your damn business?' she demanded tartly. Ettori reddening, not only because she was right, eavesdropping appearing to be a vice he was going to have to confess to and make redress for, but because she looked so like Longhella at first glance. Up close she was older by a shade, Longhella's sullen petulance transmogrified into a self-confidence he found startling, and horribly alluring. Such thoughts thankfully brought to an end by Heraldo shoving him down onto a chest from which a tiny hand protruded, one of Kaspar Larriscarri's fat children having it's wooden arm chopped off at the wrist by the chest being closed too quickly.

'Excuse my niece,' Wenzel said, not sounding particularly apologetic. 'It's been a rather fretful night.'

'I'll say,' Heraldo chimed in, as he sat himself cross-legged on the floor, the company in the tent smiling grimly for the most part, though certainly not all. Ettori taking advantage of the short hiatus.

'Um well,' he explained himself. 'I really didn't want to intrude,' Ludmilla clearing her throat ostentatiously, Ettori blushing a little deeper. 'But I heard someone mention the Arbëreshë?'

Wenzel curious, for yes, they'd been mentioned.

'And?' Wenzel prompted. Ettori itchy about his collar, not really knowing where this might go, how to handle it. Scratching his forehead, brushing at his hair.

'We've connections,' he finally decided. 'Our monastery and the Arbëreshë communities further down south. We share certain key points of liturgy, and ever since Alphonsus Liguori…'

'The man just canonised?' Wenzel broke in, scenes of his grandmother playing through his head.

'Exactly right, sir,' Ettori went on. 'He, Alphonsus, had as his central teaching that Christian folk needed to forget their differences, get out into their local communities, lead by example, expound tolerance…'

'Tolerance!' Andreas exploded unexpectedly, inferring from Ettori's words what no Pfiffmakler did. 'Do you know what happened to Valter's family? How can that be called tolerance? How can anybody be expected to live through that and know what tolerance means?'

Pfiffmaklers silenced, puzzled, leaving Valter and Ettori to fill in the blanks.

'It's all right, Uncle,' Valter said, Andreas blinking at Valter's new use of the word.

Ettori clearing his throat softly.

'Alphonsus knew all about the history of the Arbëreshë,' he explained, 'which kind of illustrated his point precisely. Because if…'

'Wait a minute,' Wenzel held up a hand. 'I'm completely lost here. The Arbëreshë are who exactly? And what have they to do with any of this?'

'Because that's where Jodl's going,' Valter said dully, Wenzel pulling at his beard in irritation.

'Yes. I mind you said that…'

'*Like a regular Arbëreshë*, Valter said,' Heraldo put in, remembering the phrase precisely. 'So what's one of them when they're at home?'

Rosa supplying the answer.

'That's what they call themselves,' she said. 'The Albanian enclaves in Italy, where we were taking Hulde.'

'They've been coming over since the fifteenth century,' Ettori added. 'Escaping persecution from other Christians, or the Turks who wanted them to convert to Islam. In fact wouldn't let them not.'

Who knew that one day all those dry history lessons would come to use.

'They were establishing an academy in San Benedetto Ullano to keep the old teachings going, went to Alphonsus for help as he'd already—'

'Oh for God's sake!' Ludmilla couldn't keep quiet any longer. 'Can someone please tell me why this is of any use? Hulde's out there somewhere and we've got to have some place to start looking for her before…before…'

She broke off, eyes filling with tears. Ettori's throat constricting. So like her sister, and yet so not. Both magnificent.

'I'm sorry,' he blustered. 'The Arbëreshë are expatriated Albanian Christians, been in Italy for generations. Stick to the old ways, are Eastern Orthodox, share many of the rites our monastery does, us being Ambrosian…'

'I don't care!' Ludmilla wailed, stood up, completely frustrated by all the words. 'I simply don't care! All I care about is where Valter's blasted brother is taking Hulde!'

Heraldo too stood up, put his hand on Ludmilla's arm.

'Ludmilla,' he said, his hand thrown peremptorily off.

'Don't you Ludmilla me,' Ludmilla said, breathing hard, tears let loose, couldn't get out another word, everyone flinching. Her agony so obvious, so raw.

Valter raising his head an inch or two, tilting his neck to look at Ludmilla through barely opened eyes, seeing her like he'd seen his own sister once long ago, distraught on a snow-bound mountain from which there'd seemed no escape.

I'll not die here, not like this.

Come on Valter.

Come on Jodl.

Jodl having another strategy for survival, a strategy no one else, and especially not their sister, had the stomach for.

Then off you go! Jodl had shouted. *Off you go, you idiots, and see how far you get!*

Valter wanting to go to with his sister, held back by his older brother. Jodl proved right. No escape for any of the others, he and Jodl finding scraps of them here and there as they scraped their way off the mountain weeks later once the snow had begun its thaw.

Valter unable to get rid of the feel, for there'd been no taste, of what he'd forced himself to eat, what Jodl had forced him to eat. Valter bound thereafter to Jodl for saving him, keeping him alive.

Until now.

When another child, another sister, was about to be lost.

'He was talking about the bulls,' Valter offered in contrition, in despair. 'Said the man we was, he was,' Valter amended, 'on the trail of was taking over to Italy a couple of fine white bulls.'

Flashes of fire and light going through him, for oh! The bull runs he remembered as a child!

White bulls, always white bulls if they could manage it, harnessed to chariots, slats of wood strung between two large wheels, men standing on their wooden boards and whipping away, shouting, shouting! The excitement, the fear, as they came galloping onwards, stampeding downs the streets.

My father! There's my father! Right up top! Right in the lead!

Valter almost trampled as one chariot came within an inch of him, Jodl pulling him back, laughing loudly.

Nearly lost you there, brother! Good job I caught you, or we'd've never lived it down!

Memories cascading through Valter's head.

'Well that narrows it down considerably,' Ettori carried on with enthusiasm, oblivious to Valter's head dropping again, cheeks wet, memories burning. 'There's only a few places still carry on the tradition. Let me think…'

'Think fast,' Wenzel urged, Ettori doing just that.

'Remote villages in the Molise region, for the most part,' scanning his brain for the particulars, envisioning the large painting hanging in the refectory, donated to the monastery by one of those same communities, of a terrifying bull race, animals thundering down a narrow street, small handwritten explication beneath…

'Portocannone,' he recited, closing his eyes, 'San Martino, Ururi, Chieuti. All tied into the feast days of their patron saints whose relics…ooh. Wait a minute…'

Trying to conjure up the dates on that painting's legend, all quite close together…the Monday after Whit Sunday, seven weeks after Easter: 30th of April, 2nd of May, 3rd of May…

Everyone waiting, though several seconds was quite long enough.

'Wait a minute what?' Ludmilla demanded, fists clutched tightly to her stomach, blood rushing through her veins like those bulls down the streets of the villages Ettori had named. Places where Hulde might be heading even now.

'They're all just around the corner,' Ettori got out. 'All going on end of April, early May…'

Pfiffmaklers and Andreas taking this information in, looking to Wenzel for direction. For no wonder Jodl had been so keen to get in with them, get The Balatronic Ballet over to Italy the quickest and most unobtrusive way he could, leaving no obvious trail. Must have been torture for Jodl to know the Pfiffmaklers had Hulde with them, counting down the days while they trundled their way with no urgency up the coast to Zadar, wondering if there was time to optimize his plan, travel undercover with them, snatch up Hulde when he could; or if he shouldn't just hightail it over to Italy anyway he could and take his chances.

They'd no idea—unlike Mergim—how patient, how calculating, Jodl could be.

For of course he'd waited, observed and planned, figured out the odds.

Figured them right down to the day.

Figured out how and when to arrive at the exact right time.

The prize worth the wait.

And he'd been waiting twenty years.

A day, a week here and there, nothing at all.

Not to a man like Jodl.

27

Rebellion and Assassination

Pfiffmaklers gathered in the braw bright morning, surrounded by the dawn chorus of the fair: folk yawning and stretching, clattering pans and cups, blowing on small fires and braziers, heading off to the latrine pits and next to the fountains, splashing water on their faces, rubbing at their teeth, filling cannisters, slurping down a quick drink and repast before setting out their stalls for another day's trading. Two more to go before the Sausage Fair shut up shop, before shifting on to the next place where all would be repeated.

Wenzel keeping his company close, spelling the situation out to them.

'We think Jodl's taking Hulde to one of the bull races near Molise, due to happen in just over two weeks, nearly two hundred and fifty miles down the way.'

Heraldo quick to calculate.

'Could do it on foot, if you're fast, strong and unencumbered, like Jodl and his companions…'

'But not with carts, like we have,' Wenzel put in. 'But we've a plan,' he said quickly, holding up his hand to allay questions. 'Brother Ettori here,' who'd gone a little pink under the scrutiny, 'belongs to the monastery…'

'The Brothers of the Blessed Virgin Mary of Mount Carmel of Ravenna,' Ettori supplied in a quick garble.

'Quite so,' Wenzel went on, 'either way, he—'

'There's trade ships going up and down the coast,' Ettori couldn't keep quiet. 'And we've connections with…'

Stopped by Wenzel.

'Let's get it cleared first. Point is this. We put on a couple of good shows today, rake in a bit of coin, buy ourselves a place on one of those trade ships…'

'I'll get the Abbott to send someone with you,' Ettori garrulous, quick to help, wanting to be the one who went with them, make a more memorable role for himself in this tale as it developed. 'Some of us speak Arbërisht, which is the ancient Tosk Albanian dialect—'

'Thank you, Ettori,' Wenzel interrupted again. Ludmilla quick on his heels, and quick to see the downside.

'How do we know they're going by foot?' Ludmilla asked. 'Surely they'll take the quickest way too. What if they get there with Hulde before we do?'

Wenzel looking at Ludmilla, how thin and drawn she seemed to have become, the life drained out of her by Hulde's disappearance. Hoping to God he wasn't wrong.

'Precisely because of Hulde,' he explained his reasoning. 'Because she's with them they've limited themselves. Folk on ship for a long journey notice who's around them. And Jodl's not going to want that.'

Ludmilla closing her eyes, imagining every wrong turn this scenario might take.

Wenzel swallowing, he and Rosa having discussed all this, and the ending not looking as bright as he was making it out. But time to get going. Time to start moving.

'So here's the plan,' he stated, wrapping things up. 'Get ourselves down to Molise long before Jodl arrives with Hulde. Agreed?'

All agreed.

How could they not?

'Andreas, a word,' Wenzel said, the rest of the Kunterbunt quickly dissipating, heading off to their duties. Heraldo making a beeline towards Helmut Knibb, a list of questions lined up in his head.

Andreas regarding Wenzel with trepidation, wondering if he and Valter were about to be told to sling their hook. Guts grumbling with hunger. Had not eaten anything since the previous morning, face sallow, his usual cherubic salesman's smile lost during the events of the night. Wenzel clearing his throat. Andreas stiffening, leaning heavily on his cane, watching it slip down into the grass, finger joints throbbing.

'I've to ask you a few things,' Wenzel said, Andreas unable to stop the loud rumble from his stomach. Wenzel taking pity, taking Andreas into his tent, presenting him with bread, cheese, olive oil and sausage, although Andreas couldn't eat, not until he knew what this was about. Wenzel seeing it. Understanding.

'I'm not going to throw you and yours to the wolves,' he reassured, the relief on Andreas's face so apparent Wenzel lifted his lips partway to a smile. 'But there's things I need to know. Like the circumstances of what happened to Valter and his brother.'

Andreas letting out a deep breath, fogging up his spectacles. Face frozen.

'Something very like what happened to Hulde?' Wenzel asked.

Andreas breathing a little quicker.

'Something like,' he got out. 'But so much worse.'

Wenzel shook his head. 'I don't need the details,' he said softly. Didn't want them, if he was truthful. Something so much worse than what had happened to Hulde's village hard to conjure up. 'I gathered from your little outburst last night about tolerance...'

Andreas came to life.

'I'm sorry about that,' he apologised quickly, took off his glasses, rubbed them clean. Genuinely upset he'd let himself go in front of practical strangers. Had not stuck to the patter, kept to the persona everyone knew him by even if they despised him for it. But those boys. If anyone had seen them like he had, if anyone had heard some of the things they'd said...

'I'm not after an apology, Andreas,' Wenzel said, surprised by the man's contrition. 'I'm after explanation. Because it seemed to me,' Wenzel only getting the implication later, when he was lying in his dark tent after all the talking had been done, 'that you were saying their folk, their tribe, their people, whatever you want to call them, were maybe set upon by their own. And I'm curious why that would be.'

He waited.

Andreas replaced his spectacles, looked at the full platter of food on offer, seemed to fix his eyes on it and then suddenly turned his head to one side and retched. Nothing coming out but rancid dribble and the bile that had been building in his throat ever since he'd seen what Jodl had done to Valter, his own brother. Imagined what he might do to the girl, if she didn't fit the bill.

Wenzel stoic, solicitous, handing Andreas a rag that Andreas gratefully took and clamped to his mouth. The change in Andreas having Wenzel completely baffled. So far from being a snake in human skin he could have been a different man. Or maybe a different snake, if not so venomous. 'Let's start again,' he said, taking out his pipe, lighting it, giving Andreas time to compose himself. Summing up what he thought he knew. 'When did it happen, to Jodl and Valter? How many years back?'

Andreas took the rag from his mouth long enough to stutter out an answer.

'Twenty, or thereabouts. But it don't seem that long to them.'

'Right then,' Wenzel said, as if he was constructing a scene for a play in his head. 'So they were what age?'

'Valter was almost seven,' Andreas answered. 'Jodl a couple of years older.'

So young.

No one that age should have seen the things they had. Done the things they'd had to do to survive.

Not that Andreas knew the worst.

Not all. Never all.

'And I'm assuming from what you said about tolerance,' Wenzel persisted, 'and because Jodl has apparently tracked the supposed perpetrator and discovered he's gone to join the Arbëreshë in Molise that he's Albanian, and so are Valter and Jodl?'

Andreas giving a quick nod of his head.

Wenzel puffing at his pipe.

'Do you know why it happened?'

Andreas's shoulders slumping, for who knew where all this began, or when it would end. Wenzel not put off by his silence.

'Do you know who Jodl's after? Does Valter?'

A puff of Wenzel's exhaled smoke floating about the tent like a genie released from its lamp.

Andreas frowning, fragments of an old folk tale popping into his head about why the wren always skulked in the undergrowth, hardly ever seen. How the birds got together to elect a leader, the eagle suggesting it should fall to the one who could fly highest; how the wren saw the trick, perpetrated its own, hid in the tail-feathers of the eagle, waited until the eagle got as high as it could go when the wren filtered out of the feathers and flew higher. Variations of the tale heard in many countries, many tongues, and how hard done by Andreas always thought the wren, plainly the wisest, thinking itself out of the strictures that were going to make the eagle the winner every time. How in every version of every tale, in every tongue, the wren was condemned for what it had done and the eagle always won.

Jodl always a bird of different feather, Andreas suspecting that where the wren had failed Jodl might succeed.

'Valter and Jodl's people lived in Albania,' Andreas began. 'Their father was of Serbian descent so his family joined the first Serbian revolt against the Janissaries, the ruling group of Turks, under Black George in 1804.'

Wenzel puffed at his pipe. Plainly Andreas was having difficulty getting his story together, but they had time. And Wenzel was intrigued. The Kunterbunt had never travelled in that neck of the woods, only there because of Grandmother Pfiffmakler's obsession with seeing the Black Madonna of Montenegro and the quickest way, as far as she'd dictated, being to go in through Albania, skirting up the border between the two countries.

Hulde's village right on the edge between the two.

'I don't suppose you've heard any of this,' Andreas said, Wenzel shrugging in agreement. Andreas pinching a piece of bread between his fingers, dipping it in the oil, putting it in his mouth and chewing slowly, glad he was not being rushed.

'Strange thing was,' he said, once he'd swallowed the bread, 'when the Serbians defeated the Janissaries the Turkish Sultan was pleased. Didn't like them Janissaries one bit. Glad they were gone. Thought they were out of control, yet wouldn't agree to any kind of Serbian nation until a few years later.' Andreas paused again, cut off a piece of sausage, more settled now he wasn't talking directly on Jodl and Valter. Painting the picture of their past. 'Russia declares war on the Turks, and the Serbs join in with the Russians who gave Serbia brief independence with Black George as First Supreme Hereditary Leader.'

'Ah,' Wenzel nodded. 'So things going well for the Serbs.'

'Not really,' Andreas rebutted, another piece of sausage, another dip in the oil, 'because next thing you know Napoleon appeared on Russia's doorstep and the Russians go home to sort him out, taking the Serbian army with them. Result being the Sultan's forces crashing back into Serbia, squashing the rebellion, putting Black George on the run.'

Wenzel discombobulated. Having trouble seeing where all this was leading. Paying close attention nonetheless, for if they did return over the Adriatic, and he was liking that idea more and more, this was a story he could use.

And what a story.

The Life of St Peter of Verona a mere shadow-play by comparison.

Here was the stuff the Kunterbunt dreamed of: rebellion of the weak against the strong, alliances made, wars fought on the strength of them. Promises made and broken, self-imposed exile of the erstwhile hero and—soon to come, in the next tranche of Andreas's narrative—more rebellion, bitter rivalry, folk swapping clan loyalties to bolster the rebellion's chances of success. Assassination of said hero followed by counter-assassination of his assassins and their entire tribe, in extreme and very bloody retaliation.

Which was where it all became a bit sticky for Wenzel. Andreas telling him that Jodl and Valter's menfolk, at first great supporters of Black George, utterly despised him for running off to save his own skin when the Turks crushed that first rebellion right and proper. Swapping their allegiance to the leader of a new insurrection, to Milos Obrenovich, a few years later. Only to have Black George turning up again, right when victory seemed imminent, and Black George beginning to split the ranks. Not looked on well by Milos nor his new die-hard supporters, Jodl's father amongst them. Who took direct action: took out Black George before he could do any real damage to the cause. Rewarded by being given leave to bring their families from Albania into Serbia, now Serbia's freedom was practically guaranteed.

Black George's loyal supporters outraged.

Patient and perspicacious as ever Jodl could be.

Returning the favour the moment Jodl's father and folk took their families into the hills for the long walk over. Jodl's tribe targeted by Black George's men as prime suspects in Black George's assassination, wiping them out. Killing the men, chasing the women and children into the hills. Men blood-high, lust-lit, daggers out to do their worst.

Message enough to Milos that his treachery had been rewarded, blood for blood.

And no better time than now for Jodl to seek his own revenge, since the Senate had been declared in Serbia this very year, in January 1839, and Obrenovich about to be ousted in favour of his son. As ousted too was Jodl's man, who'd fled the country heading for the Arbëreshë, old Albanian that he was. And traitor, as Jodl held him to be.

Jodl never a liker of heroic folktales, although maybe at the centre of a new one:

Our hero never stopping in his thirst for vengeance
Since the slaughter of his family, his tribe.
Our hero surviving the cold, dark mountains,
Tracking the traitor down the years and lanes
Of history, pursuing his glorious revenge.

Two rebellions, two leaders, Georg and Milos, who couldn't abide one another despite their common cause.

Our hero always told how Black George betrayed Serbia's soul when he left for cosy exile, coming back to take over the new rebellion when it was already under way, threatening to divide it. A few good men and true picked from the fold—hoorah for Jodl's father and his compatriots!—who had the stealth and agility of pine martens, the stout hearts of wild boar, who spilled Black George's guts before the new rebellion was strangled from the inside out.

But always two sides to the same story: the Karageorge clan creating their own folk tales, ballads of their own brave men and true who tracked Black George's killers through wild mountains and winter blow, hacking at Black George's killers until their blood pooled crimson in the snow.

Blackness at the heart of all this, Wenzel had said.

And was right.

Jodl and Valter's tribe massacred, just like Hulde's.

Jodl and Valter the only survivors.

Two boys, as Andreas told it, crawling out of the mountains on their stomachs, chewing at grass and early celandines.

Two boys who grew into men who now hated each other quite as much as Milos had hated Black George, and *vice versa*.

Not the end to the tale Wenzel had wanted.

Then again, he reminded himself, this particular tale was not yet done.

28

Making Plans

Ettori could hardly contain himself.

He'd returned to the monastery after speaking with the Pfiffmaklers, had gone straight to the Abbott with all he knew. Explained about Hulde being taken, how the Pfiffmaklers planned to get down to the Arbëreshë villages, how they would need a translator.

'And I could go!' Ettori exclaimed. 'I know the language. I'm no expert, not like some. But I've the rudimentaries. And I know what the girl looks like,' he rushed on. 'I'm sure I could help. And I feel so badly about…'

The Abbott holding up a hand to stem the flow, pursing his lips in amusement as Ettori immediately stopped. Although it didn't seem, in this particular case, that his care was misplaced. And a bit of travel and adventure would do Ettori good. Open his eyes to how the world worked outside the monastery walls that had hemmed in his life since a boy. Not so the Abbott himself, who'd been a mendicant priest of the Redemptorist order when Alphonus Liguori had been alive. And such a great day to bring that man's body into Ravenna as a saint. Such a great honour to be included in the service of his resting here. Plus the monastery hosting the theological debate after the service that, he fervently hoped, would make Alphonsus' teaching of equiprobiblism the central tenet of the Church's moral framework and faith. He'd been particularly impressed by a man come over from Zadar who'd given a very precise illustration of the Redemptorist stance by his citing of an incident that had happened to him only a few days previously: of a man and a child jumping into a puddle, of his at first perceived offence that the jumping of the man had been deliberately meant to splash him head to foot in filthy water.

'But no!' the Zadar theologian had countered. 'It was not the case at all, for the man, as I was informed a few moments later, was an imbecile, with no notion whatsoever of what was right or wrong. Key point being that, despite the outcome, despite the immediate impression, there'd clearly been no intent. Which is tantamount to telling us that as Christians, as believers in the true way, the Church needs to have tolerance at its core, just as our new saint always taught us. That our moral position must always be not to judge until we know what we are judging. Tolerance our base mark, the position from which we start and not later migrate to. That we never pass judgement, or law, or moral high ground, until we know every fact.'

Stirring stuff.

The Abbott all behind it.

Men and puddles.

You never really knew anything about them, until you asked.

Exactly as Alphonsus Liguori would have done, the Abbott holding Alphonsus in the highest regard. Quickest line to sainthood for anyone in the last few centuries, and rightly deserved, as far as the Abbott was concerned. Cardinal Archbishop Mellini and Pope Gregory himself apparently agreeing.

He knew too about Mellini's special interest in the Pfiffmakler woman, her witness statement including the recital of the little Christian girl her theatre troupe had stumbled across who had indelibly decided her on her course. An outrage for such an innocent to be snatched from the Pfiffmakler family at such a time, and being in the care of one of his own.

Time to make his pronouncement.

'Very well, Ettori. You are hereby blessed to…'

Ettori up from his seat before the Abbott had even finished.

'Are you sure? Are you absolutely sure?'

The Abbott smiling. Ettori's enthusiasm so obvious, and so obviously well meant.

'I'm sure, Ettori. But, before you go,' up went that hand again, Ettori obediently lowering his head, hovering about his seat. 'Confession first, I think.'

Ettori never one to leave out details.

Orange skirts and urges needing purged before he sent this particular young monk on his way to rescue the kidnapped and dispossessed.

Heraldo, once Wenzel had summarised what Andreas had told him, went to find Helmut Knibb. No immediate sign of him. The entire stall covered by a patchworked tarpaulin staked down strategically at its corners, looking like the giant tortoise he'd seen once that was purportedly over a hundred years old. He'd doubted it on being told, until the animal protruded its ancient legs and neck from its ancient shell, its face so wrinkled and wise-looking, its movements so torpid.

'So large, ladies and gentleman!' its owner showman had begun. 'Imagine what a feast they'd make in the South American Islands where they hail from. But don't you worry,' going on hurriedly, knowing how quickly people formed attachment to the wizened old creature. 'Our friend here isn't about to go that way. Not at all. He's as old as you, you and you,' pointing at the youngest children, 'as well as you and you,' pointing at their parents, 'put together. And will live another half century, so I'm told. I've left instructions that he carry my coffin to the graveyard when I go. It'll be a mighty slow journey,' laughing jovially at his own impending doom. 'And make my family mighty annoyed,' as it would anyone, the animal covering only a few inches in as many minutes, 'but what a sight it will be!'

Heraldo much impressed by the man's patter and his singular exhibit, begging Grandmother Pfiffmakler to let them add a small menagerie to their acts. Grandmother answering in much the same words she'd said to Longhella the previous afternoon.

'But you know, Heraldo, what happens to every animal we've ever had. Every donkey, every mule.'

Heraldo nodding, eyes filling with sad tears.

Nauseous to think of the giant tortoise, hoping his showman's promise was real, that'd he'd never slaughtered the old gentleman and basted him in his own oil, cooked him in his shell. That he'd lived long enough to carry that showman's coffin to the cemetery.

'How do?' Heraldo startled by Helmut Knibb's head appearing from his tarpaulin carapace exactly like the tortoise from his shell. Helmut crawling himself out, dragging an empty trouser leg behind that had been tied in a knot for the night. Helmut shoving his artificial leg in Heraldo's direction.

'Give us a hand, would you?' he asked, as he got himself sat, undid his trouser knot, pulled the material back to reveal the stump of his leg which ended mid-thigh. An unwieldy, thickly scarred protuberance moving up and down like a toddler's fist might do in a tantrum. Heraldo not put off, picking up the disembodied wooden leg.

'Uncle Peppe could make you a better one,' he observed, as Helmut produced a worn leather strap that attached the dead leg to the living. 'Maybe put in some kind of articulation at the knee. We could use one of your ratchet mechanisms, or what Kempelen used to make his automaton Chess Player. I mean I know the actual chess player was a dwarf hidden inside the box, but the pretend player, the automaton, was really well articulated.'

Helmut groaned as he attempted to get the buckle rightly placed about his thigh, ended up falling on his back in the plentiful mud.

'Oh for God's sake,' he muttered, swinging himself back to sitting after a couple of goes. Heraldo quick down on his knees, getting the artificial leg in place, tightening the buckles, keeping it right.

'Sorry,' Heraldo apologised. 'Shouldn't have interrupted.'

Helmut using Heraldo as a prop to get to his feet.

Letting out a breath.

'No need for apologies, son. Been doing this for years and years. But gotta tell you, it gets old with the repetition and, as it happens, already working on a new prosthetic similar to your own ideas.'

Heraldo pleased to hear it, helping Helmut unpeg the tarpaulin from his stall.

'You ever hear of someone called Black George?' Heraldo asked.

'Good Lord!' Helmut exclaimed. 'Haven't heard that name in years. He's long gone, of course, but his clansmen still thick on the ground.'

'And Milos Obrenovich?' Heraldo asked quickly, Helmut cocking his head at Heraldo, studying his bright young face.

'Indeed. Very alike, those men. Both come from peasant stock, both goat-herders at the start. Became great leaders nonetheless, and too alike for their own good. Why all the interest?'

Breaking lumps of brown sugar and compressed green tea from their blocks into a bowl, pouring on hot water.

'Got a missing girl,' Heraldo said briefly, getting a whiff of whatever Helmut was whipping up, which smelled unusual but good. 'And think it might be to do with whatever went on between those two.'

'Ah.' Helmut giving his concoction a slow stir, taking out two mugs, pouring tea, passing a mug to Heraldo.

'So you know something about it?' Heraldo asked, blowing on the hot liquid, about to take a sip when Helmut held up a finger.

'Not yet,' he admonished, taking out a lemon picked the day before, slicing it swiftly into six neat crescents. 'Give it a squeeze first.'

Heraldo obeying, Helmut doing the same, both lifting their mugs, appreciative of the new aroma.

'Rosa would love this,' Heraldo commented as he took a taste, for it was truly delicious.

'Don't know who Rosa is,' Helmut countered, 'but know about the feud between the Karageorge and Obrenovich clans. Here,' he added, levering himself up from the crate he'd been sitting on, ferreting about his stall for a moment, returning with a book, flicking through its contents, handing it to Heraldo.

'Pages 56 to 57,' Helmut said, sitting down again, laying his bad leg straight out before him like a compass dial, staring at it with venom as he detected the slight clicking of beetle larvae deep within its wood. 'Language is a little purple, but you'll get the gist.'

Heraldo reading the frontispiece: *The Adventures and Discoveries of a Geologist in the Mountains of Albania and Montenegro* by Johann von Hahn. Opening the book out flat on his knees, finding the pages indicated, the relevant paragraphs, reading out loud as he moved his fingers from one line to another.

I arrived in the region of the Shkodër *mountains, also called the Prokletije Range—that traverse the borders of both Albania and Montenegro—with some trepidation, for they are called locally Accursed. And they are that, indeed. Terribly hard places. Black pinnacles rising up like dragon's teeth from the valleys beneath them that are always cast in shadow and never see the true light or warmth of the sun, excepting on a few summer days when the sun is at its highest. Several of these wicked peaks are over 8,000 feet in height. They display the characteristics of tectonic crash, so common in this region. But what we—what I and my guide—found was not at all what we expected. What we found was most appalling, and yet most indicative of why these mountains are called Accursed. For we found the remnants of a massacre.*

Heraldo stopped, flipped to the beginning of the book, looked at the date of its publication: 1822. A few years after the killing of

Black George and, presumably, of Valter and Jodl's people in its wake. He carried on reading where he'd left off, silently, Helmut intent on frying up sausages for his breakfast.

We found the butchered remains of upwards of twenty bodies scattered, as one might expect, by animal activity, in the region of several caves where one must assume these people had been living, or at least seeking shelter. On closer inspection of the caves we found a few paltry belongings: one comb, a few wooden utensils, several pans, indications of a fire-pit. As we gathered the remains for burial it became apparent that all the bodies were of like size and, most disturbingly, remnants of hair, clothing and jewellery—including crosses on broken chains on several of the victims—led us to deduce that all were most likely women of various ages. It also became apparent, from the marks on many of the bones, that they had been hacked limb from limb in the most vicious way imaginable. But yet more disturbing were the scrape marks on some of the bones, presumably made by wild animals...

Heraldo paused, remembering the sound coming out of Valter at the mention of a massacre, and Andreas's anguished words.

You don't know what those boys have been through!

He swallowed. Carried on reading.

I could not begin to comprehend how such slaughter had come to pass, but when my guide questioned the natives of the region we had brought with us, to see to the mules and the baggage, they informed us—quite without surprise or regret—that such events were not so uncommon in the recent history of these regions. Indeed they cited several examples, mostly to do with the exchange of peoples between Serbia and the Ottoman Provinces of Albania with whom they share one of their shaky borders. One young man became very excitable and proceeded to tell us that he believed we were witnessing the aftermath of a feud initiated by the assassination of a certain Karageorge, a Serbian freedom fighter, who had been murdered on the very eve of that nation's successful bid for independence. He was

*convinced of this, he told us, because he himself—an Albanian who
had joined the fight—had been forced to flee Serbia accused of this
very crime, Karageorge's men knowing it to have been committed by
several of his countrymen.*

*'Do you know my boy's name?' he asked us, which of course I did
not. 'He is called Mergim,' the man went on. 'I named him Exile,
because from that moment on we Albanians who fought for the Serbs
have found ourselves in exile. Unable to return home to the coast in
case of retribution, that what happened here would happen to my
family because of my return.'*

Heraldo left off reading, left the book open on his lap. He'd
wanted to know about Black George and Obrenovich and now he
had an answer of sorts. No specifics, no dates, no quotable refer-
ences. And if Jodl and Valter had been witness, been involved in
something similar to what he'd read—as Andreas believed they
had—then no wonder that twenty years down the line they'd cur-
dled into men unfathomable. And all the more worry for Hulde
who'd be neither here nor there for Jodl, not if he truly believed he
was on his right track.

Strangest thing being that Heraldo found no blame in Jodl's
initial course of action, more blame on Valter for refusing to go
along with him, because if someone had done the same to him
and his then Heraldo would have done exactly as Jodl had. And
twenty years would have been as nothing. He'd have tracked down
his family's murderers until he drew his last breath. And if there
was life after death he'd have gone on tracking and looking and
would not have rested until they were found and made to pay for
what they'd done.

'Find what you were looking for?' Helmut asked Heraldo, shoving a sausage in his direction.

Heraldo closed the book.

'Mind if I take this?' he asked. 'I'll bring it back later.'

Helmut shrugged.

'Have away,' he said easily.

'Might be a while,' Heraldo added as he stood to go.

'Take all the time you need,' Helmut said. 'But tell me, what do you plan to do? About the girl, I mean.'

Helmut sensing something in the offing. A missing girl. Harkings back to the old days of Serbian independence when ethics got chucked out of the window.

'We're doing a couple of last performances,' Heraldo told him, guileless as ever, 'then Papa's arranging for us to join a ship going down to Termoli. Thinks we'll find her nearby with the Arbëreshë.'

Helmut raised his eyebrows.

The Arbëreshë.

He'd not heard that moniker in a while. About as long as he hadn't heard of Black George.

'Well good luck, lad. But one last thing. Come back and tell me how it all works out. I've a small bookshop on the Via Alighieri, and a workshop you'd be very interested in.'

Heraldo smiled with all the ease of a lad who has no idea how badly things can go.

'Of course,' he agreed, thanking Helmut for his time.

'And being me back that damned book!' Helmut called as Heraldo departed.

Helmut sanguine, Helmut old and having a gippy leg. Helmut having once played a blinding game of chess in Zadar on the steps of the Sea Organ with a young blow-by playing five games at the same time. The blow-by beating the other four with ease. Helmut holding him off, forcing the lad into a stalemate.

'See you soon, old man,' the blow-by had said as he'd taken the money owed him from the others.

Helmut chilled by the look in that lad's eyes, like a serpent ready to strike; had watched his back for several weeks after his return to Ravenna, although nothing had come of that idle threat.

Felt the same chill now as he watched Heraldo walking away, the same threat waiting in the wings, and worried for the boy. He'd been meaning to speak to Heraldo's father, offer Heraldo an apprenticeship. Selling books a pleasurable by-line, main work being the mechanicals in which he was skilled and sent all over Europe. Fond of telling his passing bookshop visitors, on the way to visiting Dante's tomb just down the road, that after Dante had been exiled from Florence—accused, falsely, of barratry—that he'd wandered all over Italy yet spent his last years here in Ravenna, finally finishing his masterwork, *The Divine Comedy,* days before his death in 1321. *And now his sepulchre—and here comes the irony,* he'd say, in case his visitors had lost the thread—*is lit by a perpetual lamp fed on oil donated by the city of Florence.*

A small revenge, perhaps, but Helmut sure the great Italian master would appreciate it.

And it was of Dante he thought as he watched Heraldo go, specifically a line from *The Inferno:*

Non ragioniam di lor, ma guarda, e passa.

Let us not speak of them but look, and pass on.

Virgil talking of the great mass of The Futile, who'd done neither good nor bad during their lifetimes but neither had paid any regard to others' troubles, nor to God. Needless to say, their stories hadn't ended well.

Helmut troubled, in case he himself was the same: looking, and passing on.

Or, more specifically, that he was looking and choosing to stay exactly where he was.

29

Playing the Game

Javarek yawned loudly, went outside the barn and relieved himself noisily, to Jodl's evident disgust. Mergim poking up the fire's embers, got a kettle going to boil up rice for breakfast before they set off again. He'd been thinking hard since he'd woken a couple of hours before the others, staring up into the barn's decrepit eaves, watching the owl that had settled there during the night, white feathers glimmering in the soft light of dawn filtering through holes in the barn's roof.

He was having serious doubts about why he was here. And more so about the girl. It was going to be a long slog to get where they were going, would take a couple of weeks, averaging twenty miles a day. The distance and walking would be no hardship for any of them, all used to tramping. Jodl having spent practically his whole life doing exactly that; Mergim equally hardened, going on long expeditions with his father, when he'd been alive, trekking up into the mountains for weeks on end, toting Grand Tour tourists wanting a taste of the Real Albania. A habit he'd never lost. Spending his free time up there in the hills whenever he got the chance.

Javarek just Javarek, who could probably walk to the moon and back, if anyone ever built a road there.

No.

The going wasn't the problem.

The problem was what might happen when they got there, and he needed to get it straight. Needed to tackle Jodl while Javarek wasn't here. He cleared his throat. Jodl took no notice.

'Got to ask you something, boss,' Mergim began, Jodl not bothering to look over at him, carried on packing his gear.

'It's about the girl,' Mergim tried again.

'What about her?' Jodl terse, obviously didn't want to talk.

The girl herself was still in her sack, though looked to be asleep. Mergim having a new worry about how and when she was going to be allowed to pee. But not his primary concern, which was why they'd taken her in the first place.

'I just don't get it,' Mergim went on. 'Why we're taking her down there. Surely first thing she's going to do is blurt out that we…what we did to her family.'

First pause in Jodl, who left off his packing for a moment but didn't look up.

'No need to bother yourself about that,' Jodl finally replied.

But bothered Mergim was. Bothered enough to argue. They'd done terrible things together; a lifetime of anger making Mergim do what he'd never dreamed he was capable of once Jodl made it a reality. Mergim regretting it, as neither Jodl nor Javarek did. Beginning to understand that whatever Jodl did he did for a purpose. Mergim and Javarek bound to him because of what they'd done. Hobbled hand and foot. He needed to understand.

'How not?' he asked. 'I just don't see how she can get us closer to your man.'

Jodl sighed, looked directly at Mergim.

'I've spent the last twenty years planning for this moment,' Jodl stated, 'and it was your idea to massacre that village.'

Mergim scratched at his collar.

'I know that,' he said, frowning as he heard Javarek outside straining at his stools. 'But how are you so sure she'll not denounce us the moment she can speak to someone who knows her own language?'

Jodl smiling. Mergim finding such a hardness to that smile he turned away, went back to the kettle, poured its contents into the pan of rice and set to stirring.

'Well she may or she mayn't,' Jodl stated. 'Either way we'll be long gone. I know that, Mergim, because I've a brain that can play five games of chess at the same time and win them all.'

Thinking back to one of the few times that hadn't happened, when the man with the wooden leg had forced him into a stalemate. How he'd meant to go back and challenge him to a replay, or maybe steal his wooden leg. He'd been young, and hadn't decided which. Andreas, of course, had insisted no. Their regular time in Zadar done. Time to move on.

'Do you know what that means?' Jodl asked Mergim. Mergim having no idea, Mergim carrying on stirring his rice, unable to meet Jodl's eyes.

Jodl supplying his own answer.

'It means I think ahead. That I plan. Look for loopholes. Study what might happen and account for every eventuality. That I intend to use the girl to bargain with the Arbëreshë to give me the man I want. And who do you think they'll value most? A man I can prove perpetrated a massacre on his own people—on their own people— or a girl who's undergone a massacre of her own?'

Mergim couldn't answer. His throat gone dry. Awful realisation that he'd been played, that he'd been a part of Jodl's long game, that he'd done exactly as Jodl had intended him to do ever since that first talk outside the tavern. That he'd provided Jodl his path. A memory then of when they'd entered the first cottage in the girl's village and how the woman at the cooker had turned and smiled, possibly as she would have at any visitor but, now Mergim was thinking back, she'd smiled directly at Jodl. Not at him. At Jodl. As if she recognised him, as if she was about to invite him to sit, eat, drink. Jodl swiftly stepping to one side, allowing Mergim to come forward brandishing his billhook, and the look on that woman's face had been…frightened, certainly, but something more in the way she'd closed her eyes and crossed herself.

Mergim suddenly realising in a rush how this might all have come about: that Jodl had climbed those wild hills and found those people, told them about an abandoned village, a place they could start over. And how grateful they would have been! Maybe Jodl leading them partway there, giving them their last directions.

And then there was the shepherd lad, and how fortuitous it was that he had seen those people winding down the track, seen them arrive, got the message to Mergim so quickly. And the words he'd used fit to press every button in Mergim's head, maybe primed by Jodl to say them exactly so:

Taking over someone else's village? It's not right. Especially with them being Christians. And didn't you say you and yours lived in that village, or somewhere nearby? No, he'd said, *it's just not right.*

And it wasn't right. Not right at all, for a few days later Jodl had miraculously reappeared, Mergim steaming with the injustice of it, fuming, getting angrier and angrier, passing to Jodl the information he'd gleaned and Jodl acknowledging it, thanking Mergrim, asking what he could to in return. A debt for a debt.

And oh God, Mergim saw it clearly now.

Manipulated from the start.

Jodl knowing all about the village and how to get to it, how he'd planned the timing of the attack; thinking now that maybe Jodl had deliberately spared the girl, buried her under her folk, must have known all along the Kunterbunt were coming, were only a day away, that the girl would be found.

That Jodl had counted on it.

That Jodl needed her to be found.

That Jodl was already thinking five or more moves ahead of any of them, including the Kunterbunt.

Mergim looking for an exit strategy.

Mergim looking at the girl.

Jodl's way in, he'd said.

But maybe Mergim's way out.

30

Villains and Heroes

The Kunterbunt alighted at Termoli, first view being the massive stone tower of the castle and the tall walls hemming the entire promontory, keeping the town tight within its fist. A few hours of light left, so they trundled along below the walls, Wenzel asking for the first name on Ettori's list.

'Portocannone,' Ettori informed him, with some excitement. 'The first Arbëreshë community in Italy, came here in the late fourteen hundreds after Skanderberg, the great Albanian hero, had died, because he had—'

'How far?' Wenzel interrupted. 'Can we get there before nightfall?'

'Oh I should think so,' Ettori said brightly, though in truth he'd no idea. 'Just a minute. Let me get out my map.'

He delved into his knapsack and retrieved the piece of paper he'd been given containing the combined knowledge of several rather elderly brothers from his monastery who'd actually been this way, instead of merely communicating by correspondence.

'Seems to be a bit way down the coast, but sort of in the hills too…'

'Which is it?' Wenzel demanded. 'Coast or hills?'

'Um,' Ettori bit his bottom lip, Ludmilla coming up beside him, snatching the paper from his hands, studying it for a few moments before letting out an exasperated tut.

'What kind of map is this?' she demanded. 'This is just a load of scribblings with a few landmarks and names drawn in. What the blasted hell are we to take from this?'

Slapping the paper against her thigh in frustration.

Ettori embarrassed, not knowing how to answer. Heraldo releasing himself from his harness and coming up beside Ludmilla, taking his own look, scratching at his ear.

'It isn't very detailed,' he admitted, which was an understatement, 'but I can kind of see what's been drawn. This here,' he pointed, 'is obviously Termoli, and this has got to be Portocannone,' a little heap of hatching someway down the coast and some way in the hills with the name scratched out beside it. 'But Ludmilla's right. It's not exactly giving us tracks and traces, definitive directions.'

Ettori coloured, took his map back from Heraldo, pointed out several key features.

'Maybe not to you,' he argued weakly, 'but all these little crosses? They mean churches, places we can go for refuge, where people can tell us where to go from there.'

Wenzel had had enough. The sea journey hadn't been good, their passage cheap and no wonder: the ship taking longer than anticipated, calling in everywhere and anywhere the whole way down the coast, taking an age to unload and reload at every stop. Wenzel beginning to worry they'd not enough time. Four villages to scope, a day's travelling between each of them, maybe more. And now Ettori not seeming so reliable a guide as he'd first presented himself. Only reason he was with them being he could take them directly to the Albanian enclaves, speak their language. But surely if the Arbëreshë had been in Italy all this time, for centuries, apparently, they could speak Italian. Which made Ettori's presence moot.

'We'll stop and regroup,' Wenzel decided. 'We'll go up this track by the river until we find a good spot, set up camp for the night…'

'But Uncle!' Ludmilla protested, Wenzel holding up his hand, carrying on where he'd left off.

'And from there we'll send out several scouting parties while we've light left, get someone to Portocannone, everyone to ask about the other villages too. Agreed?'

Ludmilla placated, agreeing, as did everyone else.

Finding a perfect place not half an hour's walk away: a swathe of spring-green grass leading down to the river's edge where it shifted into shingle, giving easy access to a wide dark pool into which water rushed from between large boulders forming stepping stones from one side to the other.

'Hey, look at that!' Lupercal called, several dragonflies skimming up about them, thick-bodied, scarlet, almost furry; others slim and agile, brightly metallic in their blue jackets, others seemingly sprinkled with silver dust.

'Oh my!' Heraldo shrugged off his harness, ran with Lupercal and Jericho to the water's edge where more could be seen clinging to a stand of rushes, nymphs emerging, getting ready for flight.

Wenzel eying the copse of mulberry and pistachio trees growing on the opposite bank, the taller walnut and chestnut trees towering up beyond them, the vague tumbles of stones to his left that must have once been walls. Only wonder being why its inhabitants had abandoned the place. Vague thought back to Hulde's village, and to Hulde apparently telling Heraldo and Ludmilla how her folk had come there straight from the mountains on a direct, if difficult, path. Like maybe they'd known precisely where they were going. Or maybe Hulde just a child who thought in straight lines and drew the simplest route from past to present with no notion of all the decision-making behind it. Another question racked up to ask the girl.

If they found her.

'Everything all right, my dear?'

Rosa appearing at Wenzel's side.

'Fine,' he said. Though plainly all was not. Couldn't quite put his finger on it; brought to their present situation by seemingly unrelated components, needing to figure what those components were, where they'd come from, where they were supposed to lead. Had the feeling he was missing the glaringly obvious.

Easiest moves first, scouting parties organised: Heraldo and Ludmilla off one way, Longhella and Ettori, a mismatched pair if ever there was one, going another; Lupercal and Jericho sent across the boulder bridge, sure-footed as the goats they could see in the lower branches of the trees. Goats good at climbing, which not everyone knew. Lupercal quick to unwind the rope about his waist, loop a noose about one animal's neck, dragging it back to camp while its companions snarked, leapt and scattered.

'Oh well done, boys!' Rosa exclaimed, Peppe leading their dinner away to be gralloched and butchered for the fire. The boys setting off on their scouting mission.

Rosa and Yssel fetching water, Livia heading off with Peppe who was keen to show the woman how to fish. Always keen to show anyone, and this one a complete newcomer so he'd much to tell her. Off to the boulders they went, a perfect point from where to throw in their baited lines once they'd dug up a few worms. Livia not squeamish as Peppe showed her how to shove a hook into a worm's belly and right up through its throat. Livia proving to be the better fisherman, snagging the first catch and the second and the third.

'Seems like you've done this before,' Peppe said, a little miffed.

'A lot, when I was a girl,' Livia replied. 'In the sea, perched on the highest boulders just like this.'

Livia standing astride, never minding her skirts. Livia not giving a fig about how she appeared to others now she was part of the Pfiffmaklers. Now she had Peppe, Rosa and Wenzel fighting her corner. Would never have to be that woman again at the back of Valter Poppelmann's tent.

And how blessed was that release.

So much so that when Lupercal and Jericho returned from their wanderings and, after a quick chatter with Wenzel, stripped themselves off and leapt into the pool, she passed her line over to Peppe, took off her boots and socks, divested herself of her outer

285

dress and leapt from the boulder with a wild cry of *watch out boys!* And down she went into the clear water, surfacing moments later with hair plastered to her skull, quick and certain in the water as an otter. Lupercal and Jericho enthralled, immediately climbing out and heading for the nearest high boulder.

'Wait!' she yelled, but too late, Jericho already at the top.

'Here I come!' he shouted, curling himself into a ball, chucking himself off willy nilly, going so far down into the pool Livia had to dive to retrieve him before he drowned.

'And me!' Lupercal not slow to follow, doing the same, though not from so great a height, requiring no rescue, coming up gurgling, burbling water from his nose.

'You two!' Livia chided. 'You can't just fling yourself off like that. You've to understand breathing before you do such things!'

Fishing ruined.

Peppe bringing in his empty lines but no matter, Livia having caught enough for them both. Peppe needing to speak to Wenzel, a thought occurring: *You've to understand breathing before you do such things.*

Wenzel sucking at his pipe, regarding the fish slithering in Peppe's net awaiting their time to die as Peppe approached.

'Anyone tell you anything useful?' Peppe asked, taking out Judas stick and knife, dispassionately dispatching each fish.

'Good and bad. The boys came back with nothing,' Wenzel replied. 'Heraldo and Ludmilla got near to Portocannone, found their bull run is done. Got vague directions to San Martino and Ururi which are on a straight line up country from there.'

'And the bad news?' Peppe asked, unzipping one of the fish from its bones.

Wenzel puffed.

'Chieuti's a fair way further, and their festival happened yesterday.'

'Ah,' Peppe replied. 'Anything else?'

Wenzel took out his pipe, dottled it, stuffed in a bit more tobacco, got it tamped and lit, Peppe carrying on the preparation of Livia's fish.

'Could be good, could be bad,' Wenzel said. 'Chieuti's the furthest away, but Ururi hardest to reach.'

'So maybe the most likely settlement Jodl's man's headed to,' Peppe offered.

Splitting another fish belly, pulling out its guts. Wenzel scratching at his beard.

'It's what I'd do, if I was on the run, which is what Andreas believes. Serbia agrees its constitution. Milos whatever-his-name-is gets ousted along with his greatest supporters. Politics,' he sighed. 'You know how it goes, Peppe.'

Peppe nodding grimly.

'Guessing a few secrets got leaked in the aftermath,' he said, 'like maybe who carried out the revenge killing of Black George's executioners and how bad that went.'

Remembering the passage Heraldo had read from the book he'd got from Helmut Knibb, though only Peppe, Heraldo and Wenzel knew about it at the moment. Agreeing to keep it private for the while and certainly from Valter, for who knew how closely it resembled his own experience. Or maybe was precisely his own experience.

Wenzel puffing smoke about his head to stop the insects biting.

'Seems those Serbs and Albanians have long memories.'

Thinking, as Heraldo had done previously, that twenty years wasn't long at all, given what had been perpetrated on Jodl and Valter's folk.

'Had a thought,' Peppe said, cleaning his knife. 'That Valter really knew how to swim, so where did he learn? And how? Didn't he tell Ludmilla he and water didn't get along?'

Part of the conversation she'd had with him on Preko, handed over after Valter's apparently heroic rescue of Hulde.

'She did, and therefore he lied,' Wenzel stated, wondering why. Wondering what else Valter might be lying about. Realising he'd not pushed Valter into coughing up the name of the man Jodl was supposed to be after, because having a name would be key. One of the missing pieces he'd been worrying about, and a bloody big piece it was too.

Ururi their most likely destination, though couldn't be sure. Needed to check, find out all they could. Scouting parties back, except for the last.

Ettori and Longhella following the track going up beside the river, Longhella stomping, angry at everything. Ettori trailing her, shy and embarrassed, taking little pleasure in the tumbling waters, the scents of pine resin in the warm afternoon, the honey buzzards wheeling and keening above them, the profusion of bees and hoverflies droning and buzzing in the chequered flowers of fritillary and red-petalled heads of marsh cinquefoil growing in pretty mats by the river's side.

They'd been walking for more than an hour, the path becoming steeper and more indistinct, it apparent to both that sometime soon it was going to peter out completely. Which it did, at the head of a chasm from which fell an extraordinarily straight line of waterfall from the rocks above, after which the pine trees became too thick to navigate.

'Oh, for pity's sake!' Longhella cried out, as her skirts caught in a runner of bramble going straight across what little was left of their path.

'Let me,' Ettori said, going down on his knees to free her, Longhella allowing him to do so before throwing up her arms in despair.

'This is completely useless!' she said loudly, suddenly turning and sitting down on a rock, Ettori horrified to see her pretty young face puffy and tear-streaked, her eyes swollen and red.

'You've been crying,' he said unnecessarily.

'Of course I've bloody well been crying!' Longhella lashed out, looking so young, so vulnerable, that Ettori no longer saw her as anything other than a child in need, inappropriate urges gone for good; this the engendering moment that gave Ettori his true calling, that he wasn't fitted to the monastery, instead wanted to become a parish priest, be involved with people, be a part of their stories.

'But why?' he asked, choosing to sit on the grass beside her so she would be above him, not able to look at his face, not be stopped from saying what she needed.

'Because I started all this,' she whispered, holding hands to cheeks, weeping quietly, getting words out in stutters and hiccups. 'Everything with Hulde, with…Grandmother…with us having to come here…'

Ettori's heart beating faster, needing to react rightly, not get it wrong.

'How can it be your fault?' he asked, wanting to sound hopeful, pragmatic. 'If anything the fault is mine. I allowed the child to be taken, not you.'

'But it is my fault!' Longhella greeted. 'If I hadn't taken her to Grandmother on the ship, if I hadn't…if I hadn't…roughed her up a little…but honestly I didn't do much…I just…she just…it was like she just folded in on herself…and I was so angry… I left her there…a little girl…I just…'

More weeping. Ettori remembering Grandmother Pfiffmakler's words in the basilica about Longhella's histrionics. This not seeming manufactured. This feeling like true remorse confessed to a stranger as she couldn't do to her own. He caught the soft scent of thyme and wild rosemary, saw a dipper dodging behind the cascading waterfall and coming out the other side.

'You're not to blame for any of this,' he said, Longhella snuffling into her sleeve. 'I know because bad things have been done to good people the whole world over, in every time and every place. And because good people do bad things when bad things have been done to them. And I believe Valter's brother is one those people.'

Taking a breath, a leap of logic and faith. Taking in all the history of the Arbëreshë as it had been told to him, history lessons coming alive, having consequence.

'What I'm trying to say, Longhella,' shifting himself in the grass, coming to sit before her, looking into her troubled face, 'is that I don't think it would have made any difference what you did or didn't do. Valter's brother is a man on a mission. He merely took advantage of circumstance, of yours, of mine. If he wanted to take Hulde he was going to do it, no matter what.'

Longhella brushed her hand across her eyes.

'Do you really believe that?' she asked, looking at Ettori as if he were her last hope.

'I do.'

Longhella blew her nose, waterworks slowly ceasing.

'So it's not my fault? Everything that's happened? To Hulde, I mean?'

'It isn't,' Ettori stated.

Longhella letting out a long sigh.

'I wish the rest of the family believed it. I don't think any of them like me any more. Not at all.'

A few more tears dripping from those long lashes. Ettori not fooled, nor swayed, nor about to be manipulated.

He cleared his throat, stood up, brought Longhella with him.

'Come on, young lady,' he said, a great family priest in the making. 'Let's get you back and see what they say.'

'And you'll take my side?' Longhella pushing it as always, brushing back her hair, squeezing Ettori's hand in her own, Ettori immune now he'd seen the girl bare her soul. No more yearnings for orange skirts. All brushed away and done.

'Back to camp for us,' he said brusquely. 'And yes, I'll state your case, and yes I'll state mine too, because we're neither of us blameless but nor are we entirely to blame. What's done is done. Only path now is to move forward.'

If only his Abbot had been there at that moment it would have made Ettori's later breaking away from the monastery so much more understandable. There'd been a bit of spit and fight when Ettori got back and declared his intentions.

'A parish priest?' the Abbott asked with incredulity. 'Do you have the slightest idea what you're getting into?'

'I do,' Ettori had answered. 'And I'm quite certain.'

As much as the Abbott ever learned, and a parish priest he had become. The very best of them.

Wenzel put a wet cloth across his eyes to ease them.

Decisions to be made.

He'd followed up on forcing a name out of Valter, who'd concentrated hard and, after several long minutes finally dredged it up.

'Jovan Kastrioti? I think that's what he told me in Zadar. One of the northern highland clans, like we were. Means he's Albanian. Maybe has Serbian blood in him, just like us.'

No idea how Jodl had found out the name, nor how he'd followed it.

Wenzel puzzling, uncertain how to throw the die, make the huge decisions dictated by their random fall.

Wenzel sitting by the river, night long fallen, everyone filled to bursting with sizzling slices of fish and roasted goat. Rosa joining him, everyone else gone to sleep awaiting his counsel in the morning. Longhella and Ettori the last people he'd dealt with, during which encounter Ettori had forced him to forgive Longhella and urged the rest of the Pfiffmaklers to do the same. Longhella's contrition still evident on her tear-streaked face which even Wenzel had found convincing.

'You'll get there,' Rosa said, no need for him to say what was troubling him, Rosa tucking her head in against his shoulder. 'And if we've to stay here all night then that's what we'll do.'

A mystery, this woman, a godsend. How he'd managed before she'd come along Wenzel had no idea. She completed him, slotted into him, made him more than he knew he was capable of. Adding herself to him like blue paint to yellow makes another colour you know is just right. No criticism, no demands, and such certainty in her words Wenzel had no choice but to believe her. Wenzel putting his arm about Rosa's shoulders. Wenzel waiting, looking at the dark pool of water beyond glinting in the moonlight. No fishing lines, no Peppe, no Livia, no children: all long removed from his ken.

Not so Jodl and Valter, nor what Heraldo had discovered in his book.

Wenzel recalling the words Heraldo had read out to him and Peppe.

There were scrapemarks on the bones we couldn't account for. We're thinking wild animals…

Wondering what that meant, if it meant anything.

A large fish breaking the surface of the pool, rising up, plashing back again, sending out sparkling silver droplets. Wenzel thinking of the folk who must have lived here way back when the cottage still had walls and doors, a roof of reed thatch. How it must have been to open that door every morning and look down on the water; had maybe set a basket or line from side to side overnight and saw it taut and quivering with caught fish; looked over to their goats nudging amongst the bole-twisted mulberries and rough-barked pistachios, the blackness of the walnut trees and twisted bark of sweet chestnuts looming beyond. A place a man and his wife—some other Wenzel and Rosa—could have lived out their days in quietude, everything they needed to survive right on their doorstep. He didn't doubt that if he looked a little harder he'd find a few ancient olives nearby to provide them with oil, cleared land in which to grow staple crops: wheat, most likely, and maybe peas. Something with which to make their bread through good seasons and bad.

A perfect place, he thought and, as he did so, the plan he'd been seeking came fully formed into his mind. As did something else. His eyes coming to rest on the covered pan Rosa had set over the embers in which the goat bones would slowly stew the night through, provide a tasty broth come the morning.

You don't know what those boys have been through.

Wenzel having a sudden skin-shivering intimation of what extremes two young boys bound in by a winter they couldn't escape might have been pushed to, especially if those two boys had seen the rest of their family butchered. Two boys who'd remained alive when no one else had.

No goats skipping gaily through copses of life-giving fruits.

No option of throwing lines or baskets into well-stocked streams.

Nothing but cold, snow and ice, and those vast black mountains going up behind them holding back the light. And no way forward either. No option but to stay put until winter released them to other options.

Wenzel having an awful thought.

A terrible, terrible thought.

One that might explain a lot.

Rosa feeling her husband stir as he took his pipe from his mouth and knocked out its dead ashes.

'All decided?' she asked, yawning, not yet shifting. Meant what she'd said about remaining the whole night through if it was what her husband needed, nuzzling back into Wenzel's shoulder, watching the glow worms blinking in the wet grass about their feet, Wenzel pulling the blanket closer about both their shoulders.

'Do you ever think,' Wenzel asked, voice a mere whisper above the water falling into the pool beyond them, 'about how far you'd go to survive in extreme circumstance?'

Rosa yawning again, trying to stifle it.

'I don't know what you mean,' she spoke softly back. 'I mean I guess it would depend. Didn't like slaughtering that mule we had years back. But sometimes you've got to go with what you've got.'

She felt Wenzel shiver slightly against her.

'And if it wasn't a mule?' Wenzel asked into the darkness. 'If you had to rely on... something else?'

Rosa frowned. No idea what her husband was getting at.

'I mean,' Wenzel said. 'What if you had to do the absolute worst, Rosa? The absolute worst. What if...'

He couldn't bring himself to say what that might be. Not to Rosa. For he understood, in this dark night, that Rosa was incapable of contemplating what he believed Jodl and Valter might have done; actions so completely incomprehensible to Rosa, to most people, he daren't even spell them out.

But he thought them.

And, God forgive him, he understood.

Had to wonder how'd he'd have fared in their place.

Whether he'd have done as he feared Jodl and Valter had done.

Whether he'd have had such a need to stay alive he'd have done just about anything to keep himself going.

Morality fine when you've food and drink on the table. But what if you've not? What if you're all alone and can't count on anything?

He'd heard it happened to sailors set adrift on the open sea. And how were the mountains any different? Water all around you, liquid blue or frozen white, it made no difference. No one coming for you, no direction to go, nothing but yourself—or maybe your brother—to rely on to get you through the next day and the next and the next.

He shook his head.

Too much to think about. More practical goals to concentrate on.

Namely Hulde.

Hulde the centre of this circle rippling out and about them all, beyond his and certainly her control and possibly beyond Jodl's too, for all he knew.

And so, my friends, our hero makes his decision, although the direction of the story is no longer clear; for who the true hero is and who the villain remains to be seen.

31

Real Natures, Real Names

Everyone gathered on the green by the river, Rosa and Yssel doling out broth and flatbreads cooked on the hot stones of the fire they'd chivvied back into life, a fire that would remain lit—like the candles about Saint Alphonsus Liguori—until the action was done. Until the story found its end.

Wenzel emerging from his tent a few minutes later, tired but animated, the leader of the Kunterbunt striding towards them with the unmistakeable gait of a man who is in charge and will brook no argument. Rosa offering him a cup of broth that he refused with an almost imperceptible flinch and an upheld hand.

'No thank you, my dear,' he said, coming to the edge of the gathered circle and beginning his spiel, as if introducing his latest show. 'Apologies for keeping you all waiting,' he began, 'but there's had to be some hard thinking done. But done it has been, and here is my decision. Myself, Peppe and Ettori will head off to find Hulde. The rest of you will stay here.'

Met by immediate opposition, Ludmilla quickest to her feet.

'You're not going anywhere without me,' she stated defiantly.

'Nor me,' Heraldo up by her side. 'And anyway, why aren't we all going?'

Wenzel cleared his throat.

'We're not all going because firstly the going would be too slow with the carts and, more importantly, the last thing we want is for Jodl to get wind we're anywhere near, that we might be on his tail.'

'That's good thinking,' Peppe said. 'Wouldn't take long for people to tattle about a fair going on in these parts. And far as Jodl knows we've stopped back in Ravenna.'

'That's exactly my point,' Wenzel agreed. 'What's needed is speed and stealth. We've two possible villages left, both reached by the same direction. Get in, get out—if it's the wrong one—and move on.'

'And how are we to know if it's the wrong one?' Ettori asked, not quite up to speed, filled to the brim with his new revelation about how he wished to live his life, casting a glance at Longhella, a little dismayed to see her apparently so disinterested in the proceedings, now he'd absolved her of her guilt, she was plucking up daisies, beheading them, casting their petals into small piles about her feet.

Not so Wenzel, who was so intent on his own plan he'd no time for niceties.

'We're looking for a man named Jovan Kastrioti. He is Jodl's goal, and Hulde is his play.'

Andreas, who'd been silent for a long while, silent since they'd been on board the ship that brought them to Termoli, silent since they'd come to this place by the river apart from a thank you here and there, quick to see the flaw in this otherwise admirable plan.

'There's something you need to know about Jodl,' he said, hesitating before he went on. 'He's not an ordinary man,' he tried to explain, Wenzel too fired up to take any notice.

'From what we previously knew and from what we've gathered from our scouting parties, we think Jovan Kastrioti's most likely in Ururi,' Wenzel went on, 'the most remote and hardest to reach of the Arbëreshë villages in this region and whose bull race has yet to be run. So I think we have to assume that's where he's most likely chosen to hole himself up.'

Andreas took in a breath, almost choked on that same breath when Valter chose to take the stand as he'd been about to speak.

'Uncle's right. You don't know Jodl,' Valter stated. 'But I do. And if any of you are going anywhere then I want in. And what's more,' Valter coughing briefly before carrying on, 'I can tell you right now that he's already thought on you interfering. That he's made provisions for it. 'Cos that's just him. That's what he does. Thinks everything out, plans for every possibility.'

Wenzel put off guard. Wenzel reappraising, reordering.

'All right then,' he decided. 'This is what we'll do. Peppe stays behind, takes charge of the home camp. Folk who are going with me are Heraldo, Ludmilla, Ettori and Valter.'

'And me too,' everyone astonished when Livia got to her feet, looking strong and determined, a completely different woman to the one who'd offered her shaky services on the ship going over to Ravenna.

'Why?' Wenzel asked. 'We've no need of your Albanian, now we have Ettori.'

She shook her head.

'It's not that,' not caring to admit her ineptitude on that front, 'but like I said before, some of my former troupe were Croat and Albanian nationalists and we went to Serbia specifically because of it. Because they...'

'We've no time for this, Livia,' Wenzel warned, wanting to snap things up, get going now the plan was made. Livia newly emboldened.

'I might have seen him, back in thirty-five when the first constitution...only a glimpse, but you never know...'

'Well hallelujah!' Wenzel exclaimed, almost laughing, for surely no matter how perspicacious Jodl was he couldn't have foreseen this. Clapping his hands together twice in loud succession. 'So Livia comes with us too. Let's get moving, people!'

The pieces shifting again, like the remnants of Valter's chess sets jumbling in his pockets. Clowns, soldiers, fallen women, getting themselves into motion. Heraldo and Ludmilla quickly to their tents to snatch up a bag of necessaries; Rosa and Yssel packing food for the journey; Wenzel making sure he'd enough tobacco to last him a few days—no harm being prepared. Livia off to do who knew what, seeing as she had no possessions and nothing to pack.

Only Valter left, standing immobile by the river, and Andreas making his way towards him.

'All right, son?' he asked, the familial slipping out without conscious thought. Valter breathing deeply, looking down at the water, at how easily it flowed between its banks, how it must have started high up in the mountains, found its way to this place of comparative peace, moving on with barely a murmur to the next place and the next.

'I am,' he said, taking a deep breath.

'You don't have to go,' Andreas replied, putting a hand on Valter's arm. Valter unexpectedly smiling despite the bruising still evident, though much alleviated by Rosa's ministrations and time past.

'I think I do,' Valter answered. Another deep breath. Another look at the incomprehensible water flowing implacably between its banks. Just like people did. Normal people, anyway. People who lived within the boundaries they'd been given and kept to their whole lives through. People always flowing in the same direction: getting born into family, working within the family, growing up, getting married, having children, dying. Always within their bounds. Unlike him and Jodl, who'd started as water and been turned into ice and stone.

'For why?' Andreas asked, Andreas implored. 'Wenzel's got this all in hand. And you're all I've got, lad. All I've got.'

Andreas never feeling so helpless.

'Let's sit down,' Valter said, and was so gentle with Andreas, getting him settled on a nearby boulder, that Andreas was close to tears.

'Never really told you stuff,' Valter said, sitting down beside Andreas in the dew-wet grass. Andreas's throat closing up, fearing what he would hear.

'Never been one for talking,' Valter went on, 'and never ever said how glad we was you came by. Took us in. You don't even know our real names, nor why Jodl picked the ones he did.'

Andreas didn't react. He'd thought about this often, and was anxious so close to revelation.

'Jodl means nothing,' Valter told him. 'No one knows where the name comes from. But my name? My name,' he laughed shortly, 'means *powerful ruler*. Can you imagine it? Jodl giving me that name? Me!'

Andreas finding no humour in it, just another of Jodl's vicious jibes coupled with that oddly generous streak he could be capable of, for who knew which was which when he'd given his brother his new name. That Jodl had chosen to hide behind one that had no meaning didn't surprise him at all.

'And your real names?' Andreas asked, Valter shaking his head in apparent disbelief.

'Georg and Milos,' he answered quietly, the irony given the circumstances not lost on either. 'Jodl, Georg, born when our family were fighting the last gasp of Black George's rebellion. By the time I came along they knew it wasn't going anywhere. Found Milos Obrenovich, who seemed ready to take on the world.'

As if Valter and Jodl's lives weren't complicated enough. No wonder they'd changed their names first chance they got. No one needing history like that hanging around their necks for the rest of their lives.

'My dear boy,' Andreas whispered, placing his hand on Valter's shoulder, Valter heaving a great sigh, leaning in, resting his bruised head against Andreas.

'Just promise me you'll come back safe,' Andreas said.

Valter unable to promise, no knowing how things would go where Jodl was concerned. But dammit he would try, just to feel this peace again, this hand upon his shoulder, see the river soodling between its banks unaware of the ill men do to others, even when its waters ran red with their blood.

32

Grand Plans, and Grandmother's too

They were off, our disparate troupe, heading for Ururi. On and up into hard hills, following rough tracks through unpopulated terrain. Ettori's map proving of worth when it brought them to an outlying church where they got more detailed directions from a young curate charged with looking after the place, although who his congregation could be they'd no idea.

The balladeers might have been waiting in the wings, singing out their songs:

Here come our party, on the trail of Jovan Kastrioti
Who is fleeing his crimes in these uncertain times.
Who massacred the murderers of Georg
Not knowing that Jodl is on his tail
And is not to be diverted,
All the powers of his mind exerted,
Moving his pieces on the board,
Sharpening his vengeful sword.

The tramp down Italy's backbone had been hard going, Jodl's not so merry band of men footsore and weary by the end of it. Rations meagre, purchased here and there from villages they passed through, using up the last of Mergim's money so assiduously saved before he'd quit his job. Veered down to the coast once they were near Termoli, Jodl spending long hours sitting on a high knoll giving him a perfect view of that garrisoned town and its harbour, eyeglass held to his face. Anyone else would've got cramp, but not him. And eventually he slammed shut the eyeglass, stowed it in his pack.

'They're coming,' he said.

'Who's coming, boss?' Mergim asked.

'Never you mind,' came the terse reply, Jodl getting to his feet. 'Time to get going. Enemies to track down and all that.'

Sounding jovial, Mergim not feeling the same. He and Javarek sharing the duty of carrying the girl, who seemed to be getting skinnier, lighter and sadder by the day. Until he'd woken in the night a week back, bivouacked inside an old cow shed, and heard Jodl talking softly to her. He'd assumed that Jodl, like Mergim himself, had no Albanian left to him. Obviously wrong on this count as on so many others. Why Jodl had chosen to keep this fact hidden he'd no idea; nor how many times previously he'd spoken to the girl unbeknownst to him and Javarek. As far as Mergim could make out in the darkness the girl made no reply to whatever Jodl was telling her, yet clearly was speaking Albanian, and clearly the girl understood. Mergim might not remember the meanings of the words yet recognised the sounds and cadences of his childhood language.

Whatever Jodl had been telling the girl seemed to work, keeping her calm and passive. And a few days before reaching Termoli Jodl dictated she be let out of her sack, allowed to walk on her own two legs. Weak legs at first, Jodl making sure she got the best of the last of what they'd got, and she was stalwart, plodding on with them, had never run or attempted escape.

Which made Mergim's counter-plan to Jodl's a little shaky. He'd been thinking to extricate himself by grabbing the girl and legging it, getting to the first Arbëreshë community he could find, handing her over like he was a hero and not a perpetrator, explaining how he'd been coerced, in anticipation of what she might tell them under her own steam, and look! Here he was, a guilty and contrite penitent releasing the last survivor to their care. Thinking now his explanations in whatever language would not suffice, especially given he'd no idea what Jodl had said to her, that maybe he was giving her an alternative view of events, maybe convincing her he hadn't been there at all. Maybe telling her that Mergim and Javarek were all to blame. She'd seen the three of them, albeit with slipping scarves about their faces and only for moments, but she was young and malleable and some folk—folk like Jodl—could convince anyone that black was white, if he put his mind to it.

Mergim out-thought and out-maneuvred, worried by how the girl kept to Jodl's side as if sewn there, as if Mergim and Javarek were the monsters and Jodl her road to salvation. Mergim looking for opportunity these last few nights. Thwarted at every turn. The girl choosing, or maybe made to choose, to bed down right by Jodl, only an arm's length away. Mergim beginning to think Jodl could read his mind. And not only his, for the day after Jodl's looking down on Termoli he'd directed them up alongside a river until they'd reached a particularly spectacular waterfall.

'Can't stop out in the open,' Jodl advised when they first got there. 'Place like this? Pretty as it is? Bound to be local folk come visiting.'

Shuffling themselves away further up into the fir trees, found a small glade where the only inhabitants were coal tits and pine martens who soon made themselves scarce. Jodl right, because the very next day after they'd ensconced themselves they heard a couple of interlopers forging their way up the hill, getting as far as the waterfall, sitting themselves down, having some kind of altercation and then appeasement before taking themselves off again.

'What did I say?' Jodl asked of Mergim, as they glimpsed through the tree stands the partial movements of a girl and, rather oddly, someone in religious garb, going back down the valley. Mergim too far away to recognise an Ettori glimpsed only partially one dark night two weeks previously. Mergim by then convinced Jodl could divine what others couldn't see.

'We're almost there, friends.' Jodl confided. 'If anything goes wrong this will be our meeting place. It's perfect. Well hidden, good views, close proximity to Termoli, and a only a short hop over the water to Zadar.'

Mergim about to demand: *well, if that was the case, why the hell hadn't they come directly here in the first place? Saved all that bloody boot leather?* Words dying on his lips as Jodl looked directly at him.

'I know you think this whole journey's been a big waste of time, Mergim. But believe me, I had my reasons. And believe me too when I tell you that when we turn up in Serbia with Jovan Kastrioti clapped in irons we'll all be heroes. Heroes, dammit!'

Mergim unable to keep up with Jodl's complex plans and stratagems.

Mergim desperate to believe this would all be worthwhile in the end.

Mergim seeing street parties and medals in the offing.

Mergim realising he was bound to Jodl, come what may.

A crack of light had opened up in Hulde's dark world since the man had talked to her.

He only spoke to her at night when the others were sleeping, the biggest of them always snoring gently like a happy kitten— so at odds with his daytime appearance she would have found it peculiar, if she'd thought of it all. Which she did not. What she thought about was what the man had said to her: that her family were bad, bad people, who'd taken over other people's homes that did not belong to them.

'Do you remember when I visited you in the mountains?' he'd asked, Hulde nodding slowly, the man's voice soft and sad. 'I told them then they shouldn't do it. That my friends wouldn't like it one bit. And you have to stick with your friends, don't you?'

Hulde nodding again, supposing it was so.

'So you see, when I came to your village later and all the bad things happened, I only did it because my friends wanted me to do it. You do understand, don't you?'

Hulde biting her lip, not wanting to remember; but since she'd been with these men day after day she couldn't stop the memories leaking back, filling up her dreams with wild black maelstroms, disembodied screams skirling with the wind high up in nameless winter mountains. She'd never known anything but those mountains, her family always on the move, shifting from cave to cave, always keeping to the topmost crags so they could see if anyone was approaching from down below. She'd never understood it until now.

'Because they were bad people,' Jodl explained, 'trying to keep one step ahead of all the folk they'd done wrong to. But not you, my little one,' he put out his hand and chucked her beneath the chin. 'You're not bad. I knew that straightaway I saw you. And that's why I spared you. That's why of everyone I allowed you to live. You remember that, don't you?'

Hulde frowning, for it hadn't seemed that way. At least she thought it hadn't, but everything about that time had splintered into fragments: big men coming into their new home, her mother dragging a pot off the stove so it wouldn't burn, them running outside with all the others. Getting to the green, herded up like sheep in a pen...

'I knew it straightaway I saw you,' the man repeated. 'You were like a bright star amongst all the badness. And so I saved you. Left you alive when I didn't need to. And I was going to come back for you, but those other people found you first.'

'Were they bad people too?' Hulde's first words to him, sensing this was what he wanted to hear, needing to please, needing to get something right, because he was being so kind.

Jodl nodding.

'They were. I know they might have seemed good at first, but they were only keeping you as a kind of pet. Have you ever had a pet?'

Hulde hesitating, not really sure about the word. Living in the mountains not engendering the keeping of pets as a natural adjunct to their way of life.

'Gomar Nikolla?' she asked.

'Well, yes,' Jodl agreed. 'Gomar Nikolla might be one such instance. And what happened to Gomar Nikolla?'

Oh so sly, our Georg-Jodl, for he knew perfectly well what had happened to Gomar Nikolla. His mission to the mountains yielding all sorts of useful information. Like how desperate Hulde's people were to be settled, how they'd been dispossessed of their own lands several years previously when the local Pasha had seen fit to declare all Christians, Orthodox or otherwise, unfit to occupy even an inch of their bailiwick, backed up by the Ottoman incursions demanding taxes so high they couldn't possibly be met. How in consequence they'd been forced into a nomadic existence merely to survive, necessarily killing off their animals one by one. For what was the point of pack animals when you'd no pasture? And what was the point of one old donkey when you and yours were on the brink of starvation?

It had taken Jodl two years to find his perfect mark. Plans always in his head for the precise moment, for the time when he would discover who had been the murderer of his family, of his tribe, and how to exact his perfect revenge. Hulde an integral part of his plan, which had nonetheless been evolving ever since. Kunterbunt finding Hulde exactly as he'd desired; Kunterbunt taking Hulde in; Kunterbunt, given their connections to the Italian Albanian communities almost inevitably choosing to take her there. Jodl correct in his thinking, for they'd done precisely as he'd predicted.

'What happened to Gomar Nikolla is what happens to all pets when they're no longer useful,' he assured Hulde. 'And how long do you think you'd have been useful to the Kunterbunt?'

Hulde unable to reply.

Hulde seeing herself as the rest of her family had ended up: butchered, left to rot in the sun. Although apparently her own fate was to be worse. Apparently she'd been about to be served up on a plate to Ludmilla and Heraldo and all the others.

It didn't seem possible, yet the man's logic was impeccable to a child too young to have learned the rudiments of reasoning. She'd become a pet. And she knew what happened to pets, no matter how well loved.

'And so you see why I had to snatch you up?' Jodl went on, Hulde agreeing. 'I'm only here to look after you,' he assured. 'I saved you once, and I saved you twice because you're special. Because you're my bright star.'

And oh, how Hulde wanted to be special, be that bright star and oh how much she didn't want to be that pet who'd outlived its usefulness.

But now she had Jodl looking out for her, so everything would be all right.

'I'm on your side,' he'd said that night in the stinking cowshed. 'And I'm going to make sure the others get what they deserve. And I'm going to make them let you go. Keep you out of your sack. But before I do, before I do any of that? I have to know you absolutely trust me.'

Hulde desperate to do so.

Hulde desperate to be out of her sack.

Hulde believing him.

'I'm your salvation,' he whispered to her a couple of mornings later—after a couple more nights of him skewing her belief systems, tutoring her responses as he wished them to be—as he undid the knots, picked her up, set her on the ground, her legs wavering like a new-born fawn's, but soon set and ready on their way.

'I'm your way out,' he whispered, 'so remember all I've told you. Don't let me down.'

Jodl a man, as Mergim had supposed, capable of convincing someone that nothing is as it seems: that black is white, that swans fly south in the winter, that birds sing because of merriment and not as a declaration of their domain.

Hulde young and malleable.

Swallowing down every word.

Grandmother Pfiffmakler having the time of her life, thanks to Archbishop Mellini.

'Take her to see the sights,' he'd instructed his coachman, writing out a hurried itinerary. 'Nothing too tiring. Tiberius's Bridge in Rimini would be good, and the Mole Vanvitelliana in Ancona. And the castle at Ortona.'

They were away from the coast now, having skirted the hills of the Marches, heading beyond Abruzzo into the region of Molise where a handy gap in the mountains would take them over to the other coast, to Nocera, to Grandmother's final destination. Her personalised Grand Tour almost done, one last place on the Archbishop's itinerary to be seen.

She'd brought very little with her, no need of possessions where she was going, but had made one purchase on her way: a small battered Bible she read from every night, preferring one previously used to one brand new. One already leafed through and loved; one that had underlinings, notations in the margins, where earlier owners had found messages of good cheer, or dire warnings, or verses to be read out in church.

She'd flicked through the pages at random, looking for those places others had found so meaningful. One in particular standing out, a page she'd left the violet ribbon marker in because she found the verse so significant, and vaguely uncomfortable.

Isaiah 11:6.

Where the wolf lay down with the lamb, the leopard with the kid, the lion with the fatling calf. Where wild beasts and tame were no longer distinguishable, led on by a little child into the holy mountains, where the earth would be as filled with the knowledge of the Lord as the sea is with water.

Except wild animals, she knew—whatever the scriptures said— could never change their nature, no matter who was leading them on. Sharp memory of that Tipu's Tiger contraption Heraldo had rigged up which, once cranked, produced the sound of a man screaming beneath the tiger's claws.

The Lord will show us who is holy.

Words she'd said to Wenzel, as Alphonsus had said to her half a century ago.

Grandmother worried, because something was bubbling up in her. A memory, an idea, and not a good one.

Wolves and lambs.

A specific wolf, a specific lamb.

She may not have thrown Hulde over the side of that ship on the way to Ravenna although, God forgive her, she'd thought on it. But if she hadn't done it then someone else had and it was only now, shuggling down the spine of Italy in a luxurious coach, she'd time to think about the entire situation. About what really might have happened, and why.

Jodl not the only one able to think around corners.

Grandmother Pfiffmakler doing the same her whole life.

She'd never played chess, didn't need to. Had negotiated fairs and passes, tariffs and taxes, towns and bishops—and now an Archbishop too—since she'd been a young woman.

And knew one thing for certain: wolves never lay down with lambs, nor leopards with kids, and certainly not lions with suckling calves.

She didn't know exactly where Wenzel was taking Hulde though knew enough: heading for Molise where they'd picked up the Cordellina side of the family: Peppe and Rosa. Picked them up like seashells from a shore, so eager to be taken away from their dull lives they'd practically jumped into the Pfiffmaklers' carts, Rosa marrying Wenzel, Peppe marrying Yssel.

And now she was thinking on it she was remembering, looking out over the landscape realising she'd seen all this before. Seen that hump of a hill, that turn in the track. Recognised every stone, every tree, every boundary boulder. She'd a prodigious memory for place markers. Had not been this far south for years, not since Matthys and Lotte had chosen to quit, Grandmother Pfiffmakler spitting at their feet, brushing their dust from her hands, vowing never to come back to these lands again.

Thinking of her miracle son Matthys because she was seeing those strange walled structures in which the bergamots grew best, where the stones held the sun's warmth and kept out the wind. Structures that could be roofed over in winter to keep the trees safe from snow and frost.

Coming to the conclusion there was one last thing needed doing before she entered her own spiritual bergamot garden, walled herself in, drew the protective roof of the church over her head. One last sight to see, one more place to go. Telling it to her driver.

'Already on our itinerary,' said he.

Pushing their carriage on.

33

Goings-On in Ururi

'Where is everyone?' Heraldo asked, as Wenzel led them into the small town on a small hill filled with square buildings, high arches, wide streets. It was late morning, two days since they'd been travelling, yet the entire place seemed eerily empty. Heraldo feeling the hairs going up on the back of his neck, as if walking into Hulde's village again. Wenzel more pragmatic.

'If Ettori's calendar is right,' about which no one could be sure, 'it might well be their festival day. Maybe they're all indoors preparing food, or out seeing to their bulls.'

'Or at the church,' Ettori put in. 'Santa Marie della Grazie. That's where the relics are kept.'

'More bloody religion,' Wenzel muttered. Ettori not put off.

'That's the whole point of the festival,' he informed them enthusiastically. 'The Holy Wood of the Cross. The family that wins the race has the great honour of carrying the relics through the town.'

'I hear something,' Ludmilla said, cocking her head. 'Singing, I think.'

Taking them off down a side street, emerging into a large square at the top of which was a three-tiered church edged with elegantly curved stonework so the whole tapered upwards towards its God. Motley and colourful wagons apparently abandoned in the square, but no people. Not a one. Until the bell sounded in the tower of Santa Marie, when the townsfolk emerged, pouring onto its steps, chattering and laughing, heading for their wagons. Priest following on their heels.

'May the best team win!' he called out, like the showman he was allowed to be on this one day, and this one day only. 'Whether it be Giovanis or Giovanottis, our usual sparring partners, or maybe our new contender descended from one of Albania's greatest leaders: Jovan Kastrioti, who is running with original Podolica bulls!'

The crowd went wild.

Clapping and cheering.

The festival always special, but since Jovan Kastrioti had turned up a few months earlier with real white bulls from Albania the entire contest had moved up a notch. Everyone curious, everyone eager to check out this new team, the usual betting schemes going seriously awry. Jovan Kastrioti himself hardly keeping a low profile, instead shouting out his credentials as if his life depended on it. Which it did. Nothing but shame and penury, and probable imprisonment, left for him back in Serbia. But here, in Ururi, he meant to re-establish himself, set up a Podolica bull stud, keep up the oft-vaunted, if somewhat dubious, family connection to Gjergj Kastrioti—or Giorgio Castriota, Iskender bey, or Skanderberg, as he was variously known in the annals of Albanian history. What wasn't in doubt was the importance of that name here in Italy. He'd some difficulty being understood when he'd first arrived, but his name alone—coupled with the white bulls he had in tow—sufficient for Ururi to enthusiastically adopt him as one of their own. Yet still, if his ultimate plan was to succeed, his bulls needed to prove themselves, as did he.

And today was the day.

All riding on the race.

And the race almost upon them.

Jodl and Hulde moved away from the crowds. Jodl attending the church with the specific intention of scoping out the main players of the town, studying each in turn as they came up to the lectern and gave their readings to celebrate the Festival of the Holy Wood. Because of it he had his mark, was on his tail. La Caresse wouldn't start for a few hours yet. All the bulls, horses, jockeys and riders gathering three miles out of town at Pontoni Masseria.

'Are you ready, little one?' he asked Hulde, giving her small hand a quick squeeze. Hulde blinking spasmodically, overwhelmed and confused. Everyone speaking sort of like she understood them, but also sort of not. A bit like the woman on the ship with the bad face who'd told Hulde that yes, it hurt sometimes, *when too dry is the weather or it's big damp*. Like they knew all the words but put them together in a different order and with a different syntax. Jodl impatient, trying to hide it.

'It's now or never,' he warned her. 'Do you want me to hand you over to those false friends who made you a pet? Let them finish what they started?'

Hulde shivering, for no. She didn't want that at all.

Jodl felt that shiver, capitalised on it, went down on one knee.

'Just remember all I told you,' he cajoled. 'I know they talk a bit differently from what you're used to, but you can speak to me and I'll speak for you. They're like birds who've been marooned on an island for years and years and have developed their own kind of song. Does that make sense?'

Making some sort of sense to Hulde, and so she nodded.

'Good girl,' Jodl encouraged. 'There's nothing to be fearful of. Remember why I brought you here?'

Hulde hesitant, searching through her prepared speeches to find the right one.

'To find me a new home?' Hulde suggested.

Another quick squeeze of her hand.

'That's exactly right,' Jodl said. 'Because you're such a good girl. A shining star that needs to find its right place in its right constellation. And I showed you those, didn't I? Those bright stars in the sky?'

Hulde nodding again because yes, Jodl had done exactly that when they'd been in the wood glade by the waterfall, when the other big men had been asleep again, when he'd sat beside her and pointed up into the night.

'I don't want you to worry about your family,' he'd said, 'because they're right there, looking down on you. Can't you see them all up there twinkling and smiling?'

And Hulde supposed she had.

'And they'd want you to do the right thing, wouldn't they?' Jodl had prompted. 'They might have been bad, but you're not. You're my shining star. See that?'

Oh and yes, Hulde had! A bright streak across the sky! And another, and another and another. No notion that Jodl had witnessed the Lyriad meteor showers year on year end of April start of May, and knew to the day when they would come.

'That's them telling you you're on the right track,' Jodl confided. 'That you're on the right track with me.'

Ilo Urosh left the church wanting nothing more than a light breakfast: a cup of strong coffee, a couple of small *burek* with their pastry warm and flaky, the cheese still soft, the herbs piquant. Nothing worse than a *burek* left to go cold and stodgy, when all you could taste was grease. He shook the bag holding the *burek*, buying his usual four though had sworn he would only eat two, save himself for the feast that would come after the race when the whole village gathered in the square and everyone brought food for the tables.

He loved this celebration above all others, in awe of the fact they had in Ururi a sliver of Christ's actual cross with that pinprick dark spot on it that had to be Christ's own blood. He'd always worked hard at his little reading in the church, unlike some of the other Elders who merely read out a couple of Bible verses and sat back down, quick as they could. Not him. Not bothered by some of the audience yawning behind their hands as he got up to give his piece every year. This a day needing to be celebrated not for the bull race, but the great honour lying at its core. He'd raced a little in his youth, though only as a horse rider, after he'd arrived here from Serbia. Had forgotten how up close and vicious the races went until he'd got his leg trapped between his horse and the next, smashed his knee cap into splinters. It was still the size of a bloated grapefruit forty years later, hard and knobbly as a pinecone with all the internal scar tissue, and had about as much bend in it as an iron bar, making his gait slow and ungainly. Worst of it being he couldn't kneel down in church like everyone else, though always bowed his head low as he could to make up for it.

On the verge of entering his home when he heard someone calling.

'Excuse me, sir! Excuse me!'

Turning to see a dark haired man coming up the street behind him, a small girl clinging to his hand, running to keep up with his fast stride.

'I'm so sorry to disturb you,' the man said, as he closed on Ilo Urosh, 'but we've urgent need to speak to the Town Elders and...'

Jodl paused, as if getting his breath back before hurrying on, apparently afraid Ilo would turn his back on them and go indoors.

'We heard you in the church and I thought, well, if any man can help us it would be you.'

Ilo raised his eyebrows, flattered someone had been listening to all he'd had to say about the Holy Wood of the Cross and what it should mean to every single one of them. *We're unaccountably blessed to have such a relic in our midst, have such a forcible reminder that Christ lived and died for the salvation of our souls…*

'How can I help you?' he asked, leaning uncomfortably on his stick. Standing for any length of time always making his knee throb. The stranger apparently noticing his discomfort.

'Oh but please, don't let us hold you up if it's…not convenient.'

A quick embarrassed glance at Ilo's knee where it bulged against the cotton of his loose trousers in the slight spring breeze. Ilo warming to the man for his care and consideration.

'Come in, why don't you,' Ilo leading the way. 'We can discuss your concerns over a cup of coffee. And I've a few *burek* here,' he added, shaking the little bag from the bakers. 'I always buy more than I need.'

'If it's no trouble,' Jodl said, quick upon Ilo's heels, Hulde's hand tight within his own. 'It's rather a sad tale, I'm afraid.'

'The best tales always are. That's what myths are made of,' Ilo agreed stoically, as he led his visitors on. 'But if I can help, on this day of all days, then of course, I'll be glad to do so.'

After the flooding out of people from the church there was pandemonium in the square, all the wagons off to the graveyard on the edge of town where they'd be individually blessed, and from there to the farm where the bulls and their teams were gathering. The entire populace in colourful costume representing whichever team they were backing, horses' and oxen's bridles and harnesses ringing with bells, fluttering with ribbons; the wagons clanking, everyone shouting and laughing, pushing them on.

'This is madness!' Ludmilla exclaimed, having trailed up the street behind the wagons, spending another half hour at the churchyard while more blessings took their course. 'How are we ever to find Hulde in all this crowd?'

'We're not,' Wenzel decided. 'We're not going to throw ourselves in without more information. Look,' he said, pointing to Father Stephanus finally edging out of the crowd and heading back to his church, enraptured and a little hoarse after all the blessings, his chasuble caked in dust and a few splatters of animal excrement. He was smiling broadly, eager to get on with his day, get a prime spot to witness the racing of the bulls.

'Ettori, you speak to him first,' Wenzel directed. 'Stick to their tongue, gain his confidence. Ask our questions for us.'

Ettori delighted, hurrying after Father Stephanus and introducing himself.

'You're who, did you say?' Stephanus asked distractedly. 'From the Ravenna monastery?'

'That's right,' Ettori agreed.

'You've none of you been here for years,' Stephanus was taken aback, 'although I have been corresponding regularly with a Brother Frances—'

Ettori interrupting.

'He's the one told us we should come here and talk to you.'

Stephanus confused. He'd studied at the seminary the disciplines of philosophical logic, metaphysics and ethics, which was why he was in correspondence with Brother Frances. The two very recently exchanging heated arguments about the various merits of Probabilism, Probabiliorism and Equiprobabilism and which way the church should go. Deep stuff, and important, yet couldn't see why Brother Frances would send someone to him here because of it. Suddenly deeply suspicious.

'Is this to do with my paper? The one Brother Frances was to deliver for me at the conference? Has the Cardinal taken some offence at it?'

Ettori's turn to be bewildered, having completely forgotten about the conference and all those worthy ethics masters droning on about the minutiae of the church's moral canon. Never mind that it would have worldwide implications trickling down the centuries.

'No,' he said shortly. 'Not that.'

Ettori bouncing excitedly on his heels in a manner that had Stephanus irritated, not least because the paper he'd worked on so long and arduously had been so summarily dismissed.

'No,' Ettori explained, possibly with a little too much glee. 'We're here because we're on the trail of a missing person. A young Albanian girl. Her family massacred over the water. The only survivor, but she's been kidnapped by the man who perpetrated that massacre. And we believe they're here, in Ururi.'

Father Stephanus stopped his progress for this was news indeed, although you didn't have to be trained logician to see there were holes in this story big enough to sail a boat through.

Like why on earth would the man who'd perpetrated the massacre go to the trouble of kidnapping the single survivor?

And how would he know there was a survivor in the first place?

And who had he kidnapped her from?

Even given that the first two premises were true—which seemed unlikely—then how did they lead to the third? Namely that he would feel enough guilt to bring the girl to her people, yet why here, of all places? Why not dump her outside the first Albanian village near where she'd been living?

Something wrong.

Stephanus knew it.

And so he took his time answering, spent that time regarding Ettori's companions now they'd come to a standstill in the otherwise deserted street: the young woman who was staring at him in a really unnerving way, a young man who might have been her brother protective at her shoulder, another woman standing tall despite her blatant disfigurement, a man who had obvious—if healing—bruises on his face and kept scratching at his cheeks, and the older man who had the look of someone in charge, if perhaps not in charge of the language.

This had the feel of something deeper, something going on beneath the surface.

'I think,' he said, 'that perhaps you need to explain a little more, and if—and only if—I am convinced, then I will arrange a meeting with the Town Elders, although maybe not..—'

'Anything you need,' Ettori interrupting, Stephanus irritated again, Stephanus looking over at Wenzel.

'Can I take it you're in charge?' Stephanus asked the older man, who seemed to understand, nodded his head.

'He is,' Ettori supplied eagerly. 'This is Wenzel Pfiffmakler, and it is from him and his family the girl was kidnapped.'

Another detail that for Stephanus didn't ring true, for how had they come across the girl?

What was she to them and they to her?

And what did any of this have to do Ururi?

Of all the blasted days this could have happened…

'Come on then,' he sighed, heading off again, uncomfortable to be leading such a disparate crew up the steps to his church, catching snippets of conversation in an odd mixture of German and Italian that raised his suspicions all over again.

'But it's been too long…'

That had to be the girl, her voice strained and impassioned, possibly referring to the time he'd taken to bless the wagons, which always took a while, and quite rightly too. All part of the pageant.

'It's been hours!'

Hearing the click and snap of a pocket watch. Another voice, the older man, he guessed.

'We've still plenty of time…they might not even…'

'We should have gone after the bulls…' another man speaking, another lot of oddly accented words.

'We should. I might be able to…'

The older woman, speech slightly slurred from her scars.

Stephanus shook his head, put his tongue to the corners of his mouth. Needed to get to the bottom of this. No way he was going to call up the Town Elders until he had their story straight. Even if he could find them, which wasn't certain. Most likely already on their way to their viewing platforms, the Elders being the most influential men of Ururi, those with the deepest pockets, and deep pockets what you needed to see a bull race through. Those animals needing a lot of investment, one way or another.

'In here,' he commanded, taking them to his private chambers where he prepared his sermons, changed his garb, wrote his letters to Brother Frances. Glancing at the books lined upon the shelves, thinking on those moral tenets again: the one that dictated tolerance and liberty if the legality or illegality of the action in question was in doubt, which seemed the possible case here; the other that said one should advocate tolerance and liberty if, and only if, the action in question most likely fell inside legality, which had to be moot; and Alphonsus Liguori's wise midway course steering between the two: liberty and tolerance being the first benchmark, unless or until it could be established that the action in question fell inside or outside the law, or pursued a course the law had never accounted for. And that last had to be applicable here, given what these people had been telling him about massacres, survivors, kidnap, guilt, repatriation.

Tolerance and liberty had to be where he started from with this story, Liguori—as so often—giving the most level-headed advice. And mighty glad he'd been so recently immersed in such moralistic nit-picking, because it seemed he was about to put all his theorizing to the test.

319

Ilo Urosh had heard enough, his kind old heart beating to the tune of Jodl's drum.

'She's such a young thing to have been through so much,' he sighed, 'and you, young man, should be very proud of yourself for bringing her here.'

Jodl hanging his head, abashed.

'It's only because I went through very similar myself,' he too sighed, shaking his head. 'My own family—the Serbian side—fought in the revolutionary wars for that country. Got caught up in the horrible clash between Obrenovich and Black George. I don't suppose you know about them.'

Ilo Urosh leaned forward, swallowed the bait. Didn't even feel the hook sliding down his throat.

'Oh but of course I do! You must have missed that part of my little talk in the church or maybe,' he scratched at his beard, 'I should have made it clearer.'

'I don't understand,' Jodl said, apparently perplexed. 'I listened very carefully. Everything you said was…so…so…well, I'm not sure. But it seemed so heartfelt. So holy. Not like the others. More like you were speaking to me directly.'

Ilo cleared his throat, immensely moved.

'It was an aside, really,' he apologised. 'It was when I talked about how the bull races here are a direct link back to the old days over the water. About how the old traditions represent more than is on the surface. I was referring to our constant fight against the Ottomans, about how the races represented that fight, our battle for independence. But of course, you weren't to know that.'

'Oh but yes!' Jodl declared. 'That makes so much sense, now you explain it!' So much sense he'd seen it straightaway. Not that he was going to mention it. 'So you were there? In the early days of the Serbian revolutions?'

Jodl sounding surprised, excited. Because of course Ilo Urosh had been there. Jodl picking that up almost the moment Ilo had begun his tedious speech. A couple of words popping up here and there that only came from an Albanian who has mixed with Serbians. Indistinguishable, unless you'd been looking for them, as Jodl had.

'I was,' Ilo admitted proudly. 'As were many hereabouts. It wasn't only native Albanians got the call. We rallied around the Serbians because we knew that if they got their independence then Albania might be next, and although our families have been here for hundreds of years there's still some hankering for the homeland. For getting back to where we truly belong.'

'If only that had happened,' Jodl replied sadly. Ilo agreeing, pouring out coffee, the girl forgotten despite her being the primary reason for his meeting with this bright and considerate young fellow.

'Can I ask what happened to your family?' Ilo treading carefully, not wanting to jeopardize this new and extraordinary friendship.

Jodl saying nothing.

White mountains, dark caves, fathers already murdered, mothers being violated before their children's eyes. Children scattering and hiding. But children, or at least Georg-Jodl, watching intently from his hiding place, making note of every face, every feature of every man, especially the one in charge.

'It was brutal,' Jodl squeezed out. 'A revenge killing for the murder of Black George.'

Jodl stopping, unable to speak—as Ilo saw it—Ilo holding his breath, realising he was on some kind of redemptive curve here with history, his history and his visitor's, feeling the creep of two worlds colliding, his unfinished business from twenty-odd years ago might yet having a way to be tied up and done. Jodl always so good at reading people, so good he could play five chess games at a time and still come out the winner in every one, or almost every one.

The one-legged man in Zadar still rankling.

Jodl too on the brink, about to play his wild card, the one he'd kept to himself, had never told Valter about and certainly not

Mergim or Javarek. Keeping it close, keeping it for the one and only time it might prove to be decisive. And this was the time. Twenty-one years later. Right here, right now.

'All I have of those men…those…murderers,' he faltered, producing from his pocket a small medallion, 'is this. I found it in the snow when I was…when I was burying my…mother…I'd seen it fall. Thought it might tell me something…but it never did.'

'Oh you poor boy,' Ilo said softly, knowing all about that sorry episode in Serbian history, as would anyone who'd been there at the time, as he had been. The turning point of the revolution. The joining of two forces to make a stronger one, until Black George's reappearance threatened to split them down the middle. The assassination of Black George the only reason they'd had the numbers to fight and win, Black George's men joining in with Obrenovich's. Including the few who'd returned after their hunt, *tracking Black George's killers through wild mountains and winter blow, hacking at Black George's killers until their blood pooled crimson in the snow.* And here was the result of that hunting: this young man before him, possibly the only survivor of that old fight who'd seen the worst things imaginable and yet had chosen to rescue another innocent from another butchered family and brought her here to him. To Ilo Urosh.

'Can I see that?' Ilo asked, as Jodl flipped the small medallion between his trembling fingers. And they were trembling, Ilo could see that clearly. Jodl apparently wavering. Jodl, the man who'd engineered the massacre of an entire village precisely so he could reach this moment seeming to hesitate, and then his shoulders slumped.

'I don't suppose it will do any good,' he murmured. 'It's been so long. I've never been able to find out anything about it.'

Jodl watching intently between lowered lashes as Ilo Urosh took the small silver medallion from Jodl's fingers. Studied it. Turned it this way and that, his facial expression shifting from puzzlement to bewilderment. He got out his eyeglasses, put them on, looked at it again.

'But…this can't be,' Ilo stuttered.

Except that of course it could, exactly as Jodl knew it would.

Ilo turning the little medallion again and again in his fingertips, shaking his head, feeling himself on the brink of history about to be remade.

'We have to get you the Town Elders,' Ilo said. 'Can I hold onto this for the moment?'

Holding up the bright flash of silver, Jodl looking confused, partially holding out his hand before letting it drop.

'Well, I suppose. But why? Does it mean something to you?'

Which of course it did. It was Jovan Kastrioti's family's coat of arms, artfully adapted from that of the original Gjergj Kastrioti. Pedalled for years to give them history and grandeur. Same coat of arms painted on the side of wagons pulled by the white bulls.

Jovan Kastrioti a swaggerer to the last.

Where are those balladeers when you need them?

Where those people who stand outside and look in, compose their songs after having seen both sides of an event?

Apparently not in Ururi, where events were moving so fast you'd need an army of them to keep up.

Ilo Urosh not so slow. He knew the Town Elders would soon be dissipating to their chosen places to see the end result of the race. Sent messengers here and there and soon had the raggle-taggle of Elders gathered at his house, all of them bar two. But ten of the twelve, himself included, would suffice. They might all be querulous, annoyed to be so summoned, but Ilo had a great wrong to put to rights.

And Ilo had the proof of it: he had Jodl, the girl and the medallion.

'Arrest them!'

Father Stephanus was as surprised as anyone when he led his visitors from the church and found the two man militia of Ururi on the steps, along with several members of the Elder Council.

'Who are you arresting?'

Although that was obvious enough. Wenzel not understanding the words and therefore too slow to react, finding his hands swiftly bound, as were Ettori's, Valter's and Heraldo's, amidst a swift uproar of objections.

'What does this mean?' Wenzel asked, Valter supplying the answer.

'Means Jodl's already here.'

Ludmilla and Livia exchanging quick glances, the two left unbound, being women and there not being enough rope.

'What are you doing? And by what right?' Stephanus shouted, as the convicts were hauled down the street towards the town gaol. 'They've done nothing wrong! They're just here to…'

'To do what?' Ilo Urosh demanded. 'To aid and abet the kidnapping of a young girl and put her to their own pecuniary advantage? To wilfully mask the murderers of that young girl's family, and the far more heinous murderer of another family—an entire tribe— before hers? No, Stephanus. They've no rights. No rights at all.'

Stephanus couldn't understand it, not after all he'd heard for that hadn't been the tale at all. He could hear Ettori babbling out to his captors.

'But you've got it all wrong! These are good people! You don't know…'

Ettori ceasing his speaking as he was clubbed across the face, so stressed he'd been speaking in his native Italian and not in Tosk, so nobody listening to him anyway.

'What's going on?' Stephanus asked. 'Elder Urosh, wait a minute,' grabbing importunately at Ilo's arm, Ilo shaking him off.

'I don't know what these people have been telling you, Stephanus, but it's all lies. All of it. These...fairs people...' he spoke the last two words with disgust, 'have been holding a child captive, and I know that because I've spoken to that child and she's confirmed it.'

'I don't understand,' Stephanus repeated, 'but...Brother Ettori isn't one of them,' clutching at straws, 'at least have him released. I can vouch for...'

'You can vouch for nothing,' Ilo informed him bleakly, Stephanus blinking impotently, knowing Ilo was right on that score. Stephanus an incomer from Naples, foisted on this congregation by joint agreement of Rome and the Lungro Eparchy, who administered the affairs of the Albanian Orthodox church in Italy. A politically expedient effort to bring the two Communions and communities closer together. Everyone riled up by the wars between the Greeks and the Turks throughout the 1820s that had supposedly been concluded with the London Conference in 1830, which had served only to bring England and Russia into the mix. And no one wanted that, not the Italians, nor the Arbëreshë. Wars going on ever since, the Turks getting increasingly aggressive, the latest news—only a couple of weeks before—being that they'd invaded Syria.

Everyone knowing themselves to be vulnerable—Italians and Arbëreshë alike—when all that divided them from Africa to the south, and the Turks from the east, was the thin strip of the Mediterranean Sea.

Everyone closing ranks.

Stephanus realising that was what the Arbëreshë of Ururi were doing now. Closing ranks. Shutting him out.

Stephanus fearing for Ettori and the others because he knew how swiftly the Arbëreshë could mete out their justice, and how summary and cruel it could be.

None of the niceties of Catholic Canon Law for them, caring nothing for it, no matter their attachment to Alphonsus Liguori.

Oh my God, Alphonsus Liguori!

The thought sudden in his head, a way he might be able to turn things around.

'Elder Urosh!' he called. Ilo Urosh already a few yards away, turning to Stephanus with evident irritation.

'What now?' Ilo asked, a tolerant man, even to outsiders.

'These people you've arrested,' Stephanus got out. 'Can I be allowed to speak for them?'

Ilo seeing Stephanus before him, appreciating what Stephanus was trying to do which was what any good priest should: fighting for those who had no means to fight for themselves. Stephanus always a good priest, no matter he wasn't one of their own.

'Of course,' Ilo assured him. 'And you've time to get your case together. Nothing will happen until tomorrow, until the bull race is done.'

Ilo away then, narrowly avoiding a carriage sweeping up the avenue towards the church, Ilo having to lurch on his cane to avoid being clipped by one of the horses. Visions of that old injury coming back to his mind, but mind already moving on. La Caresse first, everything else put on hold. Turning down a side street towards home, completely missing the commotion further up the street as Ludmilla and Livia broke away from the group, dashing down a ginnel, the two militia men calling after them to no avail. They were short-handed as it was, everyone off to their chosen points along length of the race, and neither about to miss their own by running after a couple of wayward prisoners.

'Let them be,' one said. 'They're only women. What the hell are they going to do? Storm the gaol and free the captives?'

The other laughing, finding the idea as ludicrous as his companion, missing the swift smiles on Wenzel and Heraldo's faces, because yes. That was precisely what they might try to do, and might well succeed.

34

Whirring Cogs, Moving Pieces

Stephanus stepped back, mind in a maelstrom.

He was certain the Pfiffmaklers and Ettori had been telling him the truth.

Certain they'd rescued the girl and looked after her, Ludmilla and her cousin absolutely convincing on that front. All those details about tinkle-boxes, lines in the sand, about spending time with her.

He needed to get his act together, gather their statements, get their case ready for tomorrow morning. Put the teachings of Alphonsus Liguori into action.

So wrapped up in his thoughts he hardly registered the carriage pulling to a stop before him, the strong black steeds pluffing and snorting, the driver leaping from his platform and assailing Stephanus.

'Excuse me, Father, but we've come to witness La Caresse. Could you advise us the best place to view it from?'

Stephanus creasing his brows. Not unusual for folk from around the district to come to Ururi on race day, but rarely in so grand a carriage, looking at the gold-painted emblem on its side…heart lurching with recognition. The arms of the Archbishop of Ravenna. He couldn't fail to recognise it, what with all the broohaha about Liguori's canonisation and resting place and the fact the Archbishop had attended the race here a few years back.

'Is it really…' he murmured.

'It really isn't,' came a querulous voice from inside the carriage, 'but I'm as stiff as a stoker's iron in here.'

The driver smiling, having warmed to his passenger on the journey. She was old and cranky, amusing him by how sly and obstinate she could be when bartering for their provisions on market stalls, which she'd insisted on doing. Far better than he could have done.

'It's all right, Signora Pfiffmakler,' he called out. 'I'll beat ourselves a way if I have to!'

Some of Old Grandmother's ways rubbing off on him.

Stephanus blinking rapidly. He couldn't have heard right.

'Pfiffmakler?' he asked loudly. 'You didn't say Pfiffmakler?'

'That would be Signora Pfiffmakler to you,' the driver corrected him. 'The very honoured guest of the Archbishop of Ravenna, witness to the miracles of Saint Alphonsus Liguori, on her way to join the Redemptorist nuns at Nocera.'

Pietro loved saying this, felt her honour as his own, straightening his shoulders, puffing out his chest. Only to be met on this occasion by rather manic laughter.

'But aha! Aha!' Stephanus bouncing on his toes in the same manner Ettori had done that he'd found so annoying. 'Signora Pfiffmakler! Can it really be *the* Signora Pfiffmakler? Grandmother of Wenzel?'

Her part of the story not left out by Wenzel, who'd supplied as many details as possible, and Ettori's finding of Hulde at the basilica an integral part.

Grandmother Pfiffmakler sticking her cane out of the window and poking Stephanus in the chest.

'Don't know what it is to you, but yes. Wenzel is my grandson, and I reckon you could say I'm *the* Signora Pfiffmakler. Don't think we're particularly thick on the ground.'

'But this is extraordinary!' Stephanus stuttered, tripping on his words. 'You must come with me, you must!'

Heading off up the street, waving his arm to bid them follow.

'Signora?' the driver asked, unnerved by this odd turn of events.

'Oh just do it,' Grandmother commanded. 'Might be as mad as a mongoose, but might be fun. And can't have too much of that before you go where I'm going.'

Pietro smiling, leaping back onto his platform, settling down, turning the horses, following the rapid pace set by Father Stephanus as he strode, maybe even skipped a little, up the cobbled street.

'What now?' Livia asked, once they were sure they weren't being followed, Livia giddy with excitement. They'd just escaped arrest, for God's sake! And not in a play but in real life. Her scars throbbing as her blood pumped fast with adrenalin, breathing hard, fingers tingling, felt bright and alive like a spring breaking ground, no idea where she was heading.

'Got to get them out,' Ludmilla stated, the two leaning their backs against the stonework of a deserted butcher's shop, the meat inside left on their platters, this narrow alley always in the shade, carefully chosen so its wares wouldn't spoil too soon. 'Either that or we head off for wherever the race is due to start in…well. I don't know how long.'

'The Father said three o'clock,' Livia supplied, 'and it's what? I'm guessing not far off.'

Her guess confirmed a few moments later by the bell of Santa Marie pealing out two of the hour. No rest for the campanologist who kept time for the town, especially on the day of La Caresse.

'Do we have a plan?' Livia asked Ludmilla, Ludmilla replying by whipping out her knife.

'Not as such,' Ludmilla admitted. 'But we do have this.'

Livia regarding the vicious-looking blade with awe, wishing she'd kept one with her all her long years since she'd left her home. Could have saved herself from a lot of humiliation, pain and grief if she'd a blade exactly like it. On the other hand, would probably have landed herself on the gallows first time she'd cause to use it, or on any one of those times since. Thinking on Valter, of how she'd have liked to thrust such a blade right up through his ribs and into his heart.

But she'd not known anything about Valter then, nor been privy to how he'd come to be the way he was. Had only recently heard Valter trying to tell Father Stephanus what his brother Jodl was capable of, none of it coming easy, squeezed out of Valter word by word, line by line. The terrible admission of their childhood experiences being so uncomfortable, so beyond normal human parameters, they seemed impossible. Until Heraldo had taken out a book and read to them of some similar incident, although incident seemed too light a word, when a thin keening came out of Valter's throat like his soul was being ripped apart at the seams. She'd never heard anything like it, nor wished to hear it again.

But there were the facts all the same.

Marks on bones unexplained, the implications clear to all given Valter's visceral response.

Livia's thoughts interrupted as Ludmilla made her decision.

'Did you manage to hear from all the garble in the churchyard where the race was to start from?' she asked Livia.

'I did,' Livia responded, mildly surprised her limited Albanian had come into use.

'Then that's our priority. That's where we must go. You've seen Jodl before and we know the man he's after is in charge of the white bulls, so we have the advantage.'

'Elder Urosh! Elder Urosh!'

Urosh about to re-enter his house when he heard Father Stephanus's urgent calls and the clattering of hooves on cobbles.

'Give me strength,' Ilo murmured, turning to see Stephanus running up the street towards him, the grand carriage that had almost run him down keeping pace at his back.

'There's nothing more to say, Stephanus. The council will meet in the morning to—'

'Just wait,' Stephanus interrupted, out of breath, fighting a stitch in his side from the running. Ilo Urosh waiting, shocked to see the emblem on the side of the coach as it drew near, clearing his throat in case it really was the Archbishop back in Ururi, given how supportive he was of their community, of their Orthodox beliefs and his diplomatic connections to the Eparchy. Relieved to see it was not the Archbishop but a small black merle of a woman being helped out by her driver.

'Someone had better explain pretty fast what's going on here,' Grandmother Pfiffmakler demanded as she got to her feet, taking in the scene: the agitated Father, the irritated man he was accosting who had a silver-topped cane she immediately coveted, despite her new calling.

'They've got your family incarcerated in the town gaol,' Stephanus informed her, 'by this man's order.'

'By the council's order,' Ilo Urosh protested.

'But on your say so,' Stephanus argued.

Grandmother tapping her own cane decisively on the ground.

'Let me take a wild guess,' she said, and it was a wild guess, if not an illogical one. Time not wasted on her travels, Grandma thinking on all that had happened since the Kunterbunt had stumbled over Hulde and all that gone on since. Taken aback when she'd mentioned to her driver she wanted to visit one of the Arbëreshë communities before they left the area and he'd said it was already on their itinerary. Absolutely not surprised when Stephanus told her that her family had been incarcerated, which should have been the most surprising fact of all except, as her driver had already discovered, Grandma Pfiffmakler was quick witted and sly despite her age, and had been mulling over the salient facts for quite a while.

'Let me take a wild guess,' she therefore said to Ilo Urosh. 'A man you don't know has turned up out of nowhere and is claiming that my family—the Pfiffmaklers, the Kunterbunt—has kidnapped a child.'

Ilo Urosh startled.

'Well yes, but how…'

'And I suspect,' Grandmother Pfiffmakler went on, 'that the same man told you how suspiciously fortuitous it was we turned up the morning after her village had been put down like rabid dogs, and possibly that we were so negligent in our care of her that she went overboard and had to be rescued by this same man's brother.'

Ilo Urosh's wiry white eyebrows grew closer together,.

'He did say something…'

'And did he also suggest that he would be able to deliver up the murderers of the girl's family once he'd bargained her over to you? And he has offered her as a bargain, has he not?'

'Well not exactly,' Ilo beginning to falter, no chess player he.

'I think, sir, you've been taken advantage of,' she commented. 'Did the child actually speak to you? Or did she merely confirm what he was telling you?'

A bit of a gamble on her part, for she'd no idea which brother—or maybe both—might be involved, but she knew a long con when saw one, and the joining of Andreas Zilboorg and his two putative relatives to the Kunterbunt had set alarm bells ringing the moment she'd clapped eyes on them. Not that she'd mentioned it to anyone, still bitter as an unripe almond when that had happened. Wenzel not alone to notice the second brother had been mentioned but never met, only seen when he'd been so buttered over in Balatronic Ballet makeup he couldn't have been recognised by his own mother. Although it seemed likely to Grandma Pfiffmakler he hadn't had a mother for a very long time.

Ilo Urosh let out a long breath.

'It's as you say,' he admitted, feeling weak, needing to sit down. 'Perhaps we should go inside and discuss this.'

'The man and child are still in your home?' Grandmother asked, glancing up at the windows, Ilo straightening, getting a little strength back to his voice.

'Well yes, as it happens. He said he'd wait while I went to… apprehend the…your family.'

Grandmother raised her eyebrows.

'Are you sure about that?' she asked. 'How long have you been gone?'

'Maybe half an hour,' Ilo admitted, going up the steps with his limited gait, opening the door, going inside. Finding the house empty, a note on his writing desk:

Gone to take the child to see the bull race. Please, please, Ilo, find my man if you can. You know how much it means to me. Georg Schwarz.

Ilo handing the note over to his interrogator, Grandmother Pfiffmakler twisting her mouth as she read it.

'Georg Schwarz. Very amusing. Couldn't even be bothered to add her name,' she observed. 'So what does that tell you?'

Ilo wincing, because it told him a lot.

'It's Hulde,' Grandmother Pfiffmakler said. 'And do you know what that means in our language?'

Ilo stumped. Albanian and Italian as free on his lips as fast flowing streams, but no other.

'Beloved,' Stephanus finally finding his voice. 'In German, I think?'

'Well let's all bow down to the clergy,' was Grandmother's acerbic reply. 'But you're right. And be in no doubt, Mr Urosh whoever you are, beloved is precisely what that girl is. Beloved by certain members of my family, including me.'

333

'I can't stand this!' Heraldo exclaimed, young muscles and body protesting against confinement. And they were confined, rather bizarrely in the hollowed-out heart of an ancient oak blocked by a stout iron grille. Heraldo having grasped and shaken it several times, to no avail.

'Have patience,' Wenzel advised. 'Ludmilla's out there. She won't let us rot. And it seems to me Father Stephanus is on our side.'

Heraldo knew this to be true, was still jittery.

'We have to get out of here,' he said. 'We have to explain.'

Wenzel sucking in his cheeks.

'All this means, like Valter said, is that Jodl got here before us. Best course of action is to keep calm. Tell the town council all we know come the morning.'

'But it'll be too late!' Heraldo shouted. 'Jodl will have swapped Hulde for his man and...'

'Exactly so,' Wenzel intervened. 'And how will that matter to us? Hulde safe, Jodl finding the man who killed his family. All good, far as we're concerned.'

'Unless they convict us of kidnapping Hulde,' Valter whispered, 'which I suspect was the point. To punish me for going up against him, punish you for getting in his way.'

Heraldo leaning forward.

'Except we weren't in his way, were we, Valter?' Quick timeframe of events flicking through his mind. 'He knew we were on our way to that village. Knew we'd find her, which means he knew she was alive. Which means he was there just before...which means...'

'He played every last one of us,' Wenzel said. 'Us, Valter, and Andreas. Though I don't see how he knew we'd head for Zadar and not go on, or make the choice to go over to Italy.'

Valter hanging his head, unaware of precisely how long Jodl's strategies had been in place but knew how Jodl worked, how Jodl— ever since the day they'd crawled off that snow-clad mountain—had been in charge, been on his mission, would never stop until he reached its end.

'He'll have been watching,' Valter said, voice dull, without inflection. 'Twenty-one years he's been at it. He'll have met you somewhere and studied you, logged it all up in his head. He'll have had a whole load of other folk logged up there too but, come the day, he chose you. Must've known you were coming, had us hanging around in Zadar for weeks.'

Wenzel getting it, all of a sudden. *He'll have been watching…*

For years and years and years.

'And would have forced our hand into going over the water, if we hadn't already decided on it,' Wenzel said, remembering Rosa's sudden longing for her homeland, wondering who she had spoken to, who had put that thought in her head. Someone who'd learned all about them, shifted them around like Valter's blasted chess pieces. Wenzel scanning back through the years, wondering where Jodl had intersected them. As pointless as looking for one speck of dust in a straw-filled barn. Not a comfortable thought to have been watched and marked out for later use if and when it took Jodl's fancy. To have had their behavior so accurately predicted. To realise that their traipsing down country towards Montenegro had very likely been the catalyst for Jodl's entire plan, including what had happened to Hulde's village for which they were therefore indirectly responsible.

Wenzel having another shocking thought.

'When did Grandmother first mention the Black Madonna?' he asked Heraldo. 'Can you remember?'

Heraldo sucked at his lips.

'I think we were at that winter festival on the River Drava, just over the Hungarian border. The one that had all those men on stilts and the masked procession.'

'That's right,' Wenzel agreed. 'Shrove Tuesday celebrations.'

Valter sniffing in recognition.

'It's called the *fašnik*,' he put in quietly. 'Culmination of the Croatian Christmas season in Osijek. We go there every year.'

Seeing it clearly now, how Jodl had engineered all from first to last. Remembering when they'd first seen the sea, years back, how Jodl had taken Valter clambering over rocks, pointing at the rockpools, leaping over one and then another.

'Makes you feel like a giant!' Jodl had exclaimed. 'Like these are mountains and those pools are oceans!'

Jumping down and running around a sandy inlet before the waves came flooding in behind him.

'Not even the sea can stop me!' Jodl laughing, leaping onto the rocks to escape the incoming tide, striding from mountain to mountain, surveying his kingdom. Which was what everyone outside Jodl was to Jodl, Valter now understood. Moveable parts of his world to be arranged as he pleased. Including Valter.

Wenzel got out his pipe, got it lit. Sorted the situation in his mind.

Their involvement in this mess all mere serendipity.

Valter and Jodl might go to Osijek every year but it was the first time the Kunterbunt had been to the place, following in the footsteps of fairs folk already on their way there who'd said it was not a mark to miss. Slight shiver passing through Wenzel to understand that Jodl must have seen them there, had already known about them, their ties to Italy, selected them from amongst the many, chosen to bring them into play.

'I think Jodl met with Grandmother there,' Wenzel said, her religiosity no secret. Wenzel gazing out of the grille towards the bright blue sky. 'I think he was the one put the idea into her head.'

No mention of other ideas he might have put into Rosa's head.

'Convinced her the shrine of the Black Madonna was a place she must visit.' If it even existed. 'And I suspect he told her the best way to go, how close she was. I always wondered how she was so certain.'

'*From Osijek to Brod to Zenica, Sarajevo and Dubrovnik,*' Heraldo quoted the litany of their journey as she'd directed them, his memory as prodigious as hers. '*Turn left when we hit the coast, keep going and we'll not go wrong. And don't ask me how I know, I just do. And plenty good places to provide our entertainment on the way.*'

Don't ask me how I know, I just do. Because Jodl had told her.

And no wonder therefore that Jodl had kept himself hidden from the Kunterbunt.

Wenzel had assumed it had been Hulde he'd been hiding from, and presumably he was, though it now seemed likely he'd also been keeping out of view of Grandmother and of Rosa too, for their recognition of him would have unravelled his entire plan.

And oh Lord, what a plan it was.

Wenzel could see it now, just as Valter did.

One that had been years in the making.

The Kunterbunt landing in Osijek only weeks after the Serbs had proclaimed their independence, declared their Senate, sent a great many of their previous reigning members running for the hills, or for the Arbëreshë in one particular case. A man with two white bulls whom Jodl had—at some point—clocked moving from Zadar over the water into Italy.

Jodl not content to simply follow the man, seek him out, confront him, cut him down—like any ordinary man would have done.

Jodl no ordinary man.

Jodl needing to orchestrate an elaborate scenario involving everyone around him, dissipate the blame, make everyone complicit with his plan of vengeance. Jodl in charge of every detail, every movement. All of them whirring cogs in Jodl's master plan. Jodl not unlike Heraldo in that respect, with Heraldo's need to understand how a clock worked, how to resurrect long-defunct musical instruments, or automatons.

Heraldo wanting to make things better, put them back to useful life.

With Jodl it was all about control.

The control he'd lost when, as a boy, he'd seen his father and all the menfolk of his clan butchered.

The boy having to run to the hills with the survivors, tracked down like the quarry they were. Forced to witness his mother, and the other women he'd known all his life, brutalised before being dispatched.

Him and his brother, and presumably other children too, abandoned in the snow-frozen mountains with no place to go, no one to look after them, no way up, no way down, not until winter was done. Fine for strong men with strong horses and supplies. Not for children who'd escaped with nothing but the clothes they could barely stand up in.

Jodl most likely the one who'd taken charge, given what they knew of him.

Jodl making the decision to eat the only provisions available to them, vile as the prospect was. Must have done, because they'd survived—or at least Jodl and his brother had.

Wenzel watched the bluish haze of smoke from his pipe going up into the air, out through the grille, dissipating, disappearing.

Just like he suspected Jodl would do, if no one stopped him.

35

The Race Begins

The estate farm of Pontoni Masseria was a heaving seething throng of colourful noisy humanity piled into a large field cleared for the purpose. Ludmilla following up a track clarted with animal ordure, fallen ribbons, scattered groups of villagers camped out here and there waiting for the action to begin. Families settling themselves atop bails of straw sited strategically to provide good viewpoints, insure against injury should one of the bulls or horses go off course and run amok.

Everyone shouting at the tops of their voices: folk giving tallies and pedigree histories, how teams had fared in previous years; others jostling to place their bets, young men fighting over who was to be riding the horses that would set the pace and flank the oxen, keep them in a straight line right back to town; others gathering at the edges with mules and ponies ready to scream on their favoured parties at their backs. Unfortunately for Ludmilla it seemed the largest conglomeration of action was taking place around the team with the two white bulls. The beasts magnificent. Strong wide shoulders, sharp-tipped horns, pelts washed, brushed and oiled, being slotted into their harnesses, hitched up to their chariots whose two cartwheels were almost as tall as the oxen themselves.

'This is hopeless,' Ludmilla cried out. 'Do you see them? Do you see Jodl or…oh God! I've forgotten his name!'

'Jovan Kastrioti,' Livia said, 'and no, I don't see either of them. But then it's really hard to make out anyone in this crowd.'

Ludmilla crying with frustration. She'd made a bad plan. Should have stayed in Ururi, got everyone out of that prison by whatever means necessary. She was no Wenzel, and certainly no Grandma Pfiffmakler. She'd come here to find Jovan and Jodl, secure Hulde. Hulde presumably some kind of bargaining chip the one for the other. No notion how hard it was going to be, how many people would be here. Jodl about to give Hulde away or dispatch her if she proved of no use. Ludmilla never going to see her again. The Arbëreshë might take her in, cosset her, care for her. Far more likely she'd be farmed out to some childless couple who needed the labour. Hulde sold to the highest bidder. Orphans not much favoured in places as remote as this unless they could prove their worth. Ludmilla had seen it a hundred times.

'We've got to go back,' she said, Livia patting Ludmilla's arm, hating the younger woman's distress, that she hadn't been able to deliver Jodl to Ludmilla's unsparing knife.

'I think you're right,' she comforted, 'but we'll need to move fast. Race is due to start in about half an hour from what I can gather, and once they're on the move…well.'

No need so spell it out.

Whole track overtaken by rampaging horses, ox chariots, hordes of people running helter skelter on their heels.

The Archbishop's carriage swept through the empty lanes, drew up by the old lightning-hollowed oak. Father Stephanus spilling from the door before they'd come to a proper stop, ripping his chasuble as it caught in the back wheel.

'Good news!' he yelled, spying Heraldo's young face pressed against the bars, the others getting up from the benches at his back. 'You're to be freed!' Stephanus continued. 'And we've to hurry. There's not much time.'

Ilo Ulosh alighting, jangling his keys, finding the right one, opening the grille, releasing the prisoners.

'Grandmother!' Wenzel dropped his pipe in surprise as he saw the driver helping her out of the carriage. 'What on earth…'

Shaking his head, smiling broadly as he strode towards her, gave her the biggest hug. Grandmother tutting as he held her by her shoulders and looked fondly on her.

'You look so well,' he said. 'You look positively blooming!'

'And you look like the same young scrap who could never get himself out of trouble,' Grandmother Pfiffmakler shot back. 'Not without someone else's help.'

'And if it had to be anyone, I'm glad it's you.' Wenzel feeling overwhelmed, as was Heraldo who pushed away his father's arms and gave Grandmother a short bow.

'We're indebted,' he said formally, 'and I'm very pleased to see you, Grandmother, but we've got to get going.'

Wenzel's earlier counsel of patience completely lost on him.

'We've to find Ludmilla. Something must've happened, else she'd have come back for us herself.'

'Well thank you too,' Grandmother Pfiffmakler said tartly, 'but before you all go careering off willy nilly, I think you'd better hear what we have to say.'

Jodl had written in his note that he was off to take Hulde to see the race, which was not where he'd gone at all. Instead he'd slipped his way back out of Ururi to the meeting place he'd set up with Mergim and Javarek. A small dip beyond the trees hemming in the town where snowy egrets covered the marshes like cotton grass, bobbing and strutting as they fed, or flew up to their nests in the surrounding copse.

'At last!' Mergim said, sweat gathering in his armpits, not a man who liked sitting still doing nothing, especially in times of crisis. Unlike Javarek, who'd parked himself on a handy rock and was busy chewing the juicy base-stems of new grown grass, picking pellets of sweet-gum from reeds broken by the egrets' frantic nest building.

'Thought I wasn't coming back?' Jodl asked, Mergim sweating all the more at the sneer imbued in those few words.

'No, boss,' he said. 'I mean no, I didn't think it, I mean...'

'Oh cut the snivelling,' Jodl fixing Mergim with a stare that had Mergim shrivelling from the inside out. 'Of course I came back. When I make a plan I don't deviate from it. You should know that by now.'

Mergim feeling a tic starting in his left eyelid and scratched at his stubbled cheek to try to stop it. Javarek levering himself to his feet by Mergim's side.

'All set then?' Javarek asked, oblivious to Mergim's discomfort.

'All set,' Jodl said. 'You know what to do.'

'Hang onto the girl until you comes for her,' Javarek agreed, pulling the bad old sack out of his backpack and grabbing hold of Hulde's arm, Hulde resisting, clinging to Jodl.

'It's all right,' Jodl said to the girl. 'It's only for a short while. And it's only to keep you safe, until I can get you to your new home.'

Peeling Hulde's fingers from his wrist, handing her over to Javarek.

'Does she really have to go back in the sack?' Mergim asked on her behalf. 'No one knows we're here. Surely we can just…'

Stopping as Jodl narrowed his eyes.

'A plan is a plan, Mergim. And we're going to stick to it. Agreed?'

'Agreed,' Javarek quick to respond, shoving the sack over Hulde's head, drawing it down to her feet, securing the drawstrings, heaving her onto his shoulder, taking her off into the trees. Not a peep of protest from Hulde, who didn't understand what was going on. She'd believed herself saved, done all that had been asked of her by Jodl, closed her eyes as she bumped along on Javarek's shoulders, finding the world too cruel and unpredictable a place to respond to. Breathing deeply, chest heaving, tears leaking down her cheeks, thinking on Gomar Nikolla and what must come.

'We're too late!' Ludmilla skirled out her protest.

She and Livia running fast as they could back towards Ururi.

The race faster.

Starting gun fired when they were still a good distance from town.

Bulls tearing towards them at twenty-five miles an hour, many times quicker than they could run.

Hearing the stampede coming, the yelling of team drivers and followers, the jangling of bells, the shouts of people to left and right of them as they held their hands up to shade their eyes. And too soon Livia and Ludmilla could smell the sweat of all those beasts bearing down upon them, the soil beneath their running boots reverberating with the hammering of galloping hooves.

'We've to pull off the track!' Livia shouted urgently, grabbing hold of Ludmilla, dragging her out of the way in the nick of time, the space they'd emptied immediately filled by slathered horses being whipped on by their riders, hooves driving up the dust. On their heels a thundering as of a waterfall in spate as the bulls came into view, the charioteers standing high on their planks, teetering this way and that as they lashed their animals with long whips. A brown pair first, coloured ribbons flying high, folk on the straw bales yelling and screaming as a white pair caught up and the two chariots chivvied and swerved away from each other as they drew broadside; sounds of scraping wood, of loud and godforsaken curses; another lot of bulls, two more chariots, a sweating mass of horses at their flanks urging their favoured chariot team on; a straggle of mules and ponies following, blankets slipping about their backs, boys gripping on with bony knees, hands clutched to manes or thrown around their paltry steeds' necks; chokes of dust left behind by the stampede, as were Ludmilla and Livia, lying panting on their backs, covered head to foot with detritus. Getting to their feet, gazing distractedly after the morass, defeated. Joining in with the several bands of people who were running towards the town, the motley procession of wagon floats appearing in the distance, swaying like many-flagged ships on stormy seas, forging onwards.

'They're coming,' Grandmother Pfiffmakler's driver said, unnecessarily, for they'd all heard the starting pistol and the several loud gunshots following that signalled the start of the race, and just under half an hour later the bulls were almost on the town. The rag-tags of the Kunterbunt clustered at the top of two small towers bordering the town's gates on the invite of Ilo Urosh, giving them a grand view. All that could be seen being a huge plume of dust seeming to rush of its own accord down the track like a red sirocco, until the leading horses began to materialise, and then the chariots—and the men astride them—and next the bulls themselves: heads and shoulders bowed low as they strained towards their goal under the merciless lash of whips to keep them straight and true, legs churning, blurring in the dust, ribbons flying; a sudden influx of people flooding through the gates yelling wildly, flinging themselves to one side or another as the leading chariots came bolting for the gates, hue and cry going up as pair of brown bulls galloped between the towers, swiftly followed by the white team, when the crowd went wild.

'Come on! Come on!'

'Giovanotti's in the lead!'

'Kastrioti's going to lose the prize!'

'But they've still to get to the church!'

The two leading bull teams racing side by side down the wide street, the noise deafening, the braver menfolk of Ururi charging after them even as the next team came lunging through the gates on their tail, Heraldo about to leap down the steps and after them, caught up in the moment. Wenzel holding his son forcibly back, looking over at Stephanus.

'Two minutes,' Stephanus advised, and right to do so because in came the last chariot, veering wildly from side to side, its driver having toppled off a hundred yards back in his wild excitement, pummelled and crushed beneath the hooves of all the following horses, ponies and carts, bones splintered from top to toe. He'd be

344

a hero of La Caresse in following days, but not now. Now there was an in-rushing of people surging through the gates, slow-stepping mules snorting and braying, taking umbrage as their riders kicked them furiously to bring them on.

'Who's winning? Can anyone see?'

'Get on! Get on, you useless pile of meat! You'll be glue by the time I get to the end of this.'

'Look ahead! White bulls are overtaking!'

'He might do it! Kastrioti might really do it!'

'Bloody hope so. Put my bloody shirt on him.'

'Oh Christ! That's them both round the corner…can't see who… come on! Come on! We've got to go!'

36

White Bulls, Brown Bulls

The church of Santa Marie well placed to be the end of the bull race—wide square, loads of stopping room—first chariot reaching its steps to take the prize.

Jodl there with the crowds, waiting for the outcome.

Not that the outcome mattered to him, only the man who was financing one of the teams. He was hoping there'd be recognition, always telling Valter he remembered the man's face, though in truth it had been too long and he'd been too young, so he wasn't going to count on it. Recognition, though, of the bull race itself, his heart thumping as he heard the first of the them rampaging into town, remembering how it had been back at home, when they'd had a home.

Heard the bulls running.

The shouts of encouragement and regret.

Smelt the dust and sweat, the heat of anticipation rising through him as the first of the chariots came hurtling down the street from the town gates, white bulls and brown bulls neck and neck, chariots screeching side by side as they clattered against one other and then parted, the men atop them flicking out their whips, the folk on the steps beside him yelling, jumping up and down as if they'd their own sticks in their hands.

'Kastrioti! Kastrioti! Kastrioti!'

'Giovanotti! Giovanotti! Giovanotti!'

And, despite himself, Jodl shouted too, found himself shouting for his country, for his enemy.

'Kastrioti! Kastrioti! Kastrioti!'

'Time to move,' Wenzel commanded, waving over to Valter and Ettori in the other tower. 'Coming, Grandmother?'

Grandmother's cheeks bright with excitement, heart beating a little too quickly.

'You go, we'll follow,' quick nod at her driver who nodded back, eager to be in at the end, his trip south with his revered witness having become something completely other than expected: a child to be rescued, murderers to apprehend.

'I'll take care of her,' he said.

'Make sure you do,' Wenzel counselled, then he and Heraldo were off, met at the tower's base by Valter, Ettori, Father Stephanus and Ilo Urosh.

'All ready?' he asked them.

'All ready,' Father Stephanus answered for them all, Ilo shaking his head.

'I'm not at all sure about this,' he quavered. 'I don't know how the council will—'

'Just stick to what we decided,' Wenzel cut him off impatiently. 'We've got to move fast.'

Everyone doing just that. Ettori, Heraldo and Stephanus peeling off one way, Wenzel and Valter going another, the two groups moving towards the square in a pincer movement in the hope that one or other could spot Jodl before he spotted them. Ilo Urosh hobbling off on his own, tasked with seeking out Kastrioti and sticking by him under pretext of congratulation or sympathetic regret, depending on how the last gasp of the race panned out. And it seemed there might be some doubt about it as they all closed on the square, met by a tumult of angry men, voices and colour high, everyone loudly bickering like rooks in the tops of their trees, all shouting together as they surrounded the returned chariots, the men atop them shouting as loud as everyone else, waving their caps in the air as all the riders dismounted without grace and joined in the argument.

'It can't be a draw! There's never been a draw!'

'It wasn't! Are you lot blind? Kastrioti won it fair and square.'

'Fair and square my arse. Giovanotti's lot were a neck ahead. Any idiot could see that!'

Fisticuffs breaking out amongst men who'd gambled far more than they ought, furious their winnings might be halved or, far worse, completely lost. More pandemonium as other bull teams came sweating and panting into the square.

'Do you see Jodl?' Wenzel asked Valter urgently as they came in from the east, although it seemed impossible Valter might, the crowd too volatile, too many moving parts, too much pushing and shoving.

'I don't,' Valter said. 'But we should get our way through to Kastrioti's bulls, he's bound to—'

'And Kastrioti? Do you see him?' Wenzel interrupted, Valter shaking his head.

'I told you. I don't know what he looks...'

Valter stopping abruptly mid-sentence as a scrum of men were jostled to the top steps of the church, his stomach lurching, throat suddenly dry as tinder, because there he was. Recognition sudden and immediate as a knife in his side. He'd never believed he'd remembered the man, had never had his face in his head as Jodl always claimed to have. But by Christ, there he was. Valter knew it. Valter's hands went cold. He stumbled, almost fell, Wenzel gripping him hard by the elbow to keep him upright, misinterpreting.

'You see him?' Wenzel asked. 'You see Jodl?'

'No,' Valter squeezed the word from his throat.

'Then who do you see?' Wenzel urged.

Valter shut his eyes and opened them again.

Had to be sure.

And he was.

'It's Kastrioti,' two words coming out thin as a sheet from a mangle. Words he never imagined he would say, nor what he was thinking—which was that Jodl had been right all along. Jodl really had tracked down the man who'd butchered their family, ruined what they might have become.

'Which one? Are you certain?' Wenzel urged, eyes scanning the crowd, not seeing what Valter was seeing—which was a dark narrow tunnel leading straight down to his past. To frozen mountains. Terrible choices. A life hollowed out at its core. A couple of brothers who'd had no bedtime stories. Had no stories at all, except the one growing through them, bitter roots spreading unseen through body and soul to make them what they were: despicable men, regarding other people as worthless as they were themselves.

'Which one?' Wenzel took hold of Valter and shook him. Valter holding up a hand and vaguely waving.

'The man in the green jerkin,' he answered, 'up top the steps.'

The same green jerkin.

Or not the same but a new one, one of many successive versions.

Same green Valter had seen flashing through dark woods, white tracks, blood-boltered snow.

Same silver-embroidered emblem that declaimed Kastrioti to be linked to the hero of Albania in their fight against the Turks, exactly like Jodl had said.

And if you're not my friend, Valter, then you have become my enemy. And you know what I do to them.

And oh yes, Valter knew.

Regretting now he'd not stuck to Jodl, that he'd not believed in him as Jodl neared the end of their tale. They might be despicable men, and there was no doubt they were, and no doubting that everything Jodl had done to get to this point was worse than despicable and so complicated Valter would never understand it. But they were brothers, bound together by a shared past they'd never talked about with each other, let alone anyone else.

Wenzel left him on a run and Valter, abandoned, felt so unutterably alone, so utterly useless, that he put back his head and howled.

Nobody noticing. Just another noise lost amongst the rest.

Livia and Ludmilla came through the gates on a run, swept their way by the oak gaol and found it empty, carried on for Santa Marie, pushed one way and another by the swirling throng, clasping hands so they would not be put asunder.

'I see Jodl!' Livia said, feeling Ludmilla's hand tightening about her own.

'Where? Where is he?'

'There… no wait,' Livia lost him as the crowd moved again, tossed about like unanchored kelp on a stormy sea. 'He was right there! Come on, this way.'

Dragging Ludmilla around the edges of the square, scanning desperately for another sighting, finally getting one as the strong sun of early May glanced down on his unclad head, dark hair iridescent with it, shining like peat-oil in a pool. Closing in, nodding the direction with her head, Ludmilla allowing Livia to lead her on, Ludmilla unclasping the knife-sheath with her thumb, drawing out her weapon, narrowing her eyes, looking for someone who looked vaguely like Valter, suddenly catching a glimpse of that profile, that cleft chin, that shiny black hair.

'There he is,' she whispered, Livia concurring, letting go each other's hand by tacit consent and moving towards him. He was shielded by a thicket of angry men, but they weren't concerned, had him in their sights.

And then Livia was taken hold of, caught in the grip of strong hands.

'Ludmilla!' Livia shouted, struggling against her captor, Ludmilla turning to see Livia caught about the waist, arms pinioned, Valter's strong hands laying hold. Valter shaking his head, tears trickling down his face, and that face—God knew what was going on inside it. Anguish, misery, desperation. Ludmilla couldn't tell, nor did she care.

'I can't let you do it,' Valter croaked as Ludmilla approached, as Valter dragged Livia away from the crowds, as Ludmilla swiftly hid her sharp knife behind her back, following them with measured steps, waiting for her chance.

Grandmother was sat up beside her driver. It had taken a bit of doing but she was adamant.

'I need to see what's going on,' she said. 'And being up with you will give me a better view.'

Pietro smiling, complying, setting off the carriage at an easy pace for fear of toppling her.

'Seems your family have got themselves into a bit of a pickle,' he commented.

Grandmother snorted.

'Got that right.'

Though not of their own making, she was thinking. *That was down to me.*

She couldn't grasp the entirety of all the connecting parts, but knew very well the start point: her very own Pontoni Masseria, the first domino sending the rest to fall. That man telling her, oh so casually, about the Black Madonna of Montenegro. How wondrous a shrine it was, not to be missed, a holy of holies, and not so far away, even for an old woman like her, and how easy to reach.

Hair as black and shiny as the Madonna's ebony wood had been made by the thousands of pilgrims visiting her over hundreds of years, caressing her, kissing her, as they prayed for their miracles.

And she, of all people, had fallen for it.

Old Grandmother Pfiffmakler, who'd been most of her life on the circuit, duped.

Old Grandmother Pfiffmakler, who'd already been in receipt of two miracles so greedy for more she'd swallowed it hook, line and sinker.

And look what had occurred because of it.

Never had Grandmother Pfiffmakler felt so shamed and indignant, and so blasted outraged. Conned by a man with a silver tongue, and a heart that had to be far blacker than his hair.

A heart she swore to herself she would cut out and heave to the dogs.

Ettori and Heraldo stopped short as they came into the square, Stephanus a few yards behind them. Too much going on. No chance to make out any individual from the rest, until Heraldo caught a swift orange flash.

'Ludmilla's here,' he said, sounding certain, Ettori following his charge. 'And I think I see Valter! Over there, to the left of the square.'

'Isn't it the other brother we're going for?' Ettori panted, making long strides to keep up with Heraldo.

'It's Valter!' Heraldo cried. 'He's gotten hold of Livia! Come on, come on!'

Ettori went.

Stephanus did not.

Stephanus had done too much running for one day, looked after the youthful forms of Ettori and Heraldo leaping about the edges of what was apparently a very angry crowd, and decided his particular skills, such as they were, might be better utilised elsewhere. Such as with the town council who were all atop his church's steps, appeared to be about to rip out each other's throats.

'God forgive me if I take the easy path,' Father Stephanus whispered under his breath as he made his oblique way up the steps towards the Town Elders. No easy path apparent once he'd reached his goal.

'What the hell do you think you're doing?' Kastrioti said querulously, as Wenzel gripped him from one side, Ilo Urosh from the other. 'Elder Urosh. Explain!'

Ilo at a loss to explain anything, the whole town seeming to have erupted. Wenzel filling in the gaps.

'We think your life is in danger,' he said. 'Someone out there in the crowd who wishes you ill.'

'Nonsense!' Kastrioti argued. 'I'm just a bull runner from Albania. Why on earth would anyone...'

'Ever been to the Shkodër mountains?' Wenzel put in. 'Ring any bells?'

Kastrioti hesitated.

'Well of course I've heard of them. Like I said I'm...'

'A bull runner from Albania,' Wenzel said. 'Yes, we know about that. But we both know that's not entirely true. That you came from Serbia a few months back.'

'I don't know what you're talking about,' Kastrioti blustered. 'All I've done is reintroduce to the Arbëreshë their true heritage. White bulls running, as was always the case back in the day.'

'There's certain questions, Jovan,' Ilo put in, 'that need answering. But please, please, come with me so we can get them sorted.'

Jovan Kastrioti throwing off the hand Ilo Urosh had placed gently on his arm.

'I'm not going anywhere! This is my livelihood we're talking about.'

Taking a stance up top the steps. Wenzel right beside him, not about to let him go further than he could grab him, though Kastrioti seemed in no hurry to depart despite Wenzel's warnings and veiled accusations.

'This is such a mess,' said a member of the town council, several more on his heels, approaching the knot on the top steps. 'Did anyone actually see who got here first?'

'White bulls,' said some without hesitation, possibly swayed by the fact they were the first proper Albanian bulls to have raced in living memory.

'Absolutely not!' Others took umbrage, those in Giovanotti's camp. 'Browns got in by a whisker.'

Unwilling to let an outsider take the glory, or their money.

'For God's sake!' an Elder complained. 'We've to make a decision. There's people fighting over it down there!'

'Well,' another added equably, 'we all saw them coming into the square...'

'But what's our actual finish point? It's never been this close.'

'Ilo must decide. And oh, thank the Lord, here he is, with Father Stephanus! The only two who have no bias. So we go either by first entrance into the square, or the team who first reached the steps. Ilo? Stephanus?'

Father Stephanus still getting back his breath, gazing out over the raucous scene playing out below them. The scuffles of men vociferously defending their favourites, some already swinging their fists; the bulls slathered with sweat and foam being unhitched from their chariots, shoulders sagging, sides heaving, crowds too dense for them to be led away; the wild mêlée of all the rest, wild-eyed, hearts pumping, both men and beasts.

Something had to be done.

'I'm a relative newcomer here,' Stephanus eager to push the decision over, Ilo recognising it, taking the fall.

'Rules are rules,' he adjudicated. 'First one into the square, if there's only one. Otherwise its first one to the steps.'

Elders agreeing, sensible men shaking hands, quick count of their votes from how they'd seen it.

One of them nominated to disseminate the news.

'White bulls have won!' he yelled. 'Decision's in! Elders have decided Kastrioti has won! Kastrioti has won!'

Kastrioti beamed, held up his arms in victory as if he were a druid welcoming the sun.

'Albania has triumphed!' he called out to the crowds. 'Which means we've all triumphed! Every single one of us! Hoorah for the Podolica bulls! Hoorah for the Old Country! Hoorah for the Motherland!'

The best thing he could have said, the previously warring factions joining in the shout.

'Hoorah for the Old Country! Hoorah for the Motherland!'

Hustle and bustle about the square as the wagon floats belatedly tottered in, dragged by their exhausted steeds, the children atop the wagons, clad in garish costumes, waving their arms. The folk who'd watched the race from the safety of their straw bales coming in behind them. A gaggle of women materialising from side streets, setting up trestle tables, piling them with food. The bells in the campanile beginning their celebratory peels. The square a tumult of humanity, bookies setting themselves up ready to settle their debts and count their winnings, and there would be winnings. Bookies always making sure of that.

And from a ginnel beside the church came Javarek, staying in the broad shadows of the afternoon. Javarek slotting a bolt into the portable crossbow Jodl had procured for him designed by Jodl himself, with a little help from a man he'd been corresponding with for a few years. Their combined efforts producing the spring-jointed crossbow that could be collapsed and stowed with ease into an ordinary backpack, and just as quickly taken out again and sprung into use. An invention requiring expertise and discretion, the finished article collected by Mergim in Ravenna on Jodl's say so from the dusty old wife of a dusty old book shop, its actual owner nowhere to be seen. Helmut Knibb away setting up his stall for the Sausage Fair.

Helmut Knibb proud of his input to the invention, how parts of it could be put to use to produce for him a grand and articulated new leg. And particularly pleased when his correspondent granted him in writing all patents to it, if he chose to pursue them.

Helmut Knibb blessing to the end of his days Georg Schwarz for doing him such a favour.

Helmut Knibb and his wife living the high life, once the Sausage Fair was over and he'd time to pursue his patents.

Helmut Knibb raking it in.

Helmut Knibb never knowing how crucial a piece he'd been in someone else's game.

Hold your breaths, Ladies and Gents, for our finale is just around
the corner!
Time to find out who will be the victors and who the mourners.
All our characters set upon their stage
Getting ready to turn the final page.
None of them knowing how the action will turn out;
The ends of every one of them in doubt.
Will it go well for them, or will it go badly?
Will it turn out for the good, or turn out sadly?
As yet, we can't be certain.
But be assured we won't bring down the curtain
Until we've got to our end.

37

Into the Church

Wenzel took a step closer to Kastrioti, fearing he'd launch himself
into the exuberant crowd and disappear. He didn't care much what
Jodl might do to him, needed only to make sure Hulde was safe
before that happened. Having Kastrioti captive his only advantage.
Stephanus seeing what Wenzel was doing and moving in from the
other side to flank their common goal.

Valter dragging Livia into a side street, telling her not to worry,
that he meant her no harm, just needed to stop her and Ludmilla
catching up with Jodl before Jodl caught up with his man. With
their man.

Heraldo and Ettori closing on Ludmilla as Ludmilla closed on Valter.

Heraldo catching the glint of Ludmilla's knife at her back, fearing this time around she really might stick it straight into Valter's guts.

Thinking on the oak tree gaol, and how much he didn't want to see Ludmilla locked up inside it.

Mergim fidgeting in the copse, watching the egrets going about their business, wondering how life could be going on so serenely all about him when he'd the awful duty of guarding a girl who'd been imprisoned inside a sack. Kept running through his options. He could leg it and leave the girl in her sack; he could leg it and take her with him, dump her in her sack on the nearest doorstep; he could untie the sack and tell her to scram, and then he could leg it. But at the end of each scenario all he could see was Jodl, and that Jodl would never let him go. Most likely find some way to deliver Mergim up as the murderer of Hulde's village. Set the Arbëreshë on his tail. And he'd stick out like a loose nail on a shoe in these parts. No. The only way was to go along with Jodl, stick to the plan. He wasn't sure he could actually kill the girl if he was asked to, but neither Jodl nor Javarek would have such qualms. Best way to keep them both alive was to do as he'd been told. Pity enough for the girl to keep whispering to her, telling her it would all turn out fine. He knew she couldn't understand him, but hoped he was somehow giving her comfort.

He was not.
Hulde in fear.

Hulde in darkness.

The gruff mumblings coming from outside her sack she interpreted as baying wolves, sharpening knives, boiling pots, clattering plates. Hulde wishing she'd never moved from beneath her mother's body, wishing she'd died with kith and kin. Wishing she'd never been given the light again only to have it snatched away. Wishing back the kind man who'd spoken to her in her own language, told her it would all turn out for the best, that there was only a little way left to go. Not that she believed him any more, but still. But still. And still was all she knew how to be.

Hulde's kind man, Jodl, was fighting down the fever of Kastrioti's victory, the shouts for the Old Country and the Motherland. Jodl slipping to the edge of the crowd, not quite in it and not quite out. Jodl raising an arm above his head like so many others were doing, though didn't wave his wildly, kept his arm straight, kept it vertical for five seconds, ten, glancing over to his left, dipping his chin once, turning his head back to the church, and let drop his arm.

Javarek in his ginnel catching that drop.

Javarek not thinking for one second of the consequences of what he was about to do.

Javarek a soldier in Jodl's army, doing as he'd been told. And that was all right with him.

Javarek raising his crossbow, getting his target in his eyepiece, waiting for the optimum moment.

Letting go the bolt.

Wenzel didn't understand what was happening. Found himself falling backwards, heard his head cracking on the stone, had a terrible pain in his shoulder, saw the end of the bolt that had been driven into the bone wavering as he fought for breath. Wenzel feeling cold and sick as the warmth of his blood pooled about the back of his neck.

'My God!' Stephanus the first to react, pulling Kastrioti back with him, an arm forcible about his waist, Kastrioti stumbling as Stephanus went down on his knees.

'What the hell do you think…?' Kastrioti began, angry to be removed so peremptorily from his victory, until he saw the blood gurgling about Wenzel's head and shoulders, the bolt sticking up from his shoulder.

'Keep down!' Stephanus warned. 'That was very likely meant for you.'

'For me?' Kastrioti seemed confused. 'But why? For what reason?'

Keeping his head low nonetheless.

Stephanus in no mood for tolerance, equiprobabilism not at the forefront of his mind as he got Wenzel Pfiffmakler's head upon his knees, saw the blank look in Wenzel's eyes, felt the warm blood seeping from the wound in Wenzel's shoulder.

'Because it's all about you!' Stephanus barked at Kastrioti. He took a breath, put a hand to Wenzel's forehead, felt it cold. Ripping away the last of his chasuble, scrunching it up, placing it against Wenzel's shoulder to staunch the blood that didn't seem like it was going to stop. 'And because of you, a good man might be about to die.'

Ilo Urosh and the other Elders rushing onto the scene, aghast, beginning to twitter like old women.

Ilo taking charge.

'Get Kastrioti away into the church! And get this poor man lifted in there too. Come on! Come on!'

Several Elders moving in, taking Kastrioti by the arms, pushing him forward. Several more taking Wenzel up and carrying him in afterwards. The sudden commotion noticed by a few men down below who came stamping up the steps.

'What's going on?'

'Where are you taking Kastrioti?'

'What's happened to that man?'

Ilo standing fast, holding out arms and cane to bar their way.

'This man has been wounded by someone's attempt to assassinate Kastrioti, and so Kastrioti is taking sanctuary in the church.'

'Sanctuary? Why does he need sanctuary?'

'Who's trying to murder who?'

Ilo didn't answer. Ilo got to the church doors and disappeared inside, bolting the doors behind him.

'You can't stop him! You mustn't stop him!' Valter shouted at Ludmilla as she advanced, Ettori and Heraldo appearing at her heels.

'Why not, Valter?' Ludmilla asked softly. 'You've got to explain. Maybe I can help you.'

Valter faltering. Finding it difficult to see through all the tears, kept blinking them back but they kept on coming. And he was shaking badly. Couldn't seem to get a grip on anything, except Livia who'd stopped fighting him, was laying her head back on his shoulder looking up at him with the good half of her face.

'You can stop this whenever you want to,' Livia whispered. 'Look at me, Valter. I understand. I really do. That man? That Kastrioti? He's your enemy, not us. All we want is Hulde. Do you know where she is?'

Valter stiffened, pulled his arms harder about Livia's waist.

'Don't you pity me!' he wailed at Livia. 'Don't you dare pity me! You, of all people!'

'But I do,' she said simply. 'And do you know why?'

Valter couldn't answer.

'Because everything going on here is to do with your brother. You know it. I know it. Your whole life has always been about him, never about you. I don't know why you can't see that.'

'Enough,' Ludmilla said, advancing. 'Let her go, Valter. Let her go now.'

'I can't!' he cried out. 'I don't know what to do! God help me, I don't know what to do!'

Ludmilla taking her chance; Ludmilla lunging forward, whipping out her knife and jamming it hard into Valter's thigh, the jet of blood as bright as it was spectacular, splattering all three of them as Valter crumpled to the ground taking Livia with him. Valter writhing like Laocoon with his snakes, grunting with the pain and the immediate and voluminous loss of blood.

'You've clipped the femoral artery!' Ettori on them in a moment, Ludmilla standing back, horrified.

'I didn't mean to!' she cried frantically, trying to wipe Valter's blood from her face.

'It's all right, it's all right,' Heraldo came up beside her.

'It really won't be if we don't get a tourniquet on him,' Ettori shouted, Livia coming to the fore, pulling the knife from Valter's leg, releasing another bright rainbow of Valter's blood. Livia slicing the knife through her dress, handing Ettori a good long strip of it. Ettori's heart pumping wildly as he wrapped it quickly about the top of Valter's thigh and pulled it tight. Livia handing him the knife, Ettori taking it, using the handle to twist the material tighter and tighter until the bleeding slowed and ceased.

'You've done this before,' Ettori breathed out his relief, smiling quickly up at Livia.

'Saw it done,' she corrected, not so calm as she'd liked to have been.

'Something's going on in the square,' Heraldo interrupted. 'I don't see Kastrioti, and I don't see father.'

Heraldo away, Ludmilla hovering, looking towards Livia for direction.

'Go,' Livia commanded. 'We'll take care of Valter.'

Enough for Ludmilla, who ran off after her cousin.

'I...don't know...why you're bothering...'

Words stuttering from Valter's blue lips.

'Every human life is valuable,' Ettori intoned, as behoved his calling. Livia cutting him off.

'You men are such arses,' she stated, standing up, unburdening a lifetime of bitterness in so few words. 'You always think everything revolves around you. You stamp about the world causing mayhem and Lord knows how many unnecessary wars. And what's become of it? What's become of Valter here for listening to the insane plans of his ridiculous brother?'

She shook her head. She was on a roll.

'Let me tell you. You make people like me feel worthless. We're not pretty, so we're worthless. We're scarred, so we're worthless. We're just here to make you feel more worthy than you really are. But no more.'

'Livia,' Ettori looked up imploringly as Livia looked down upon the pitiful pietá.

'I'll go fetch help,' she sighed. 'Which is more than Valter deserves.'

Jodl smiled as he edged himself away and joined Javarek in the ginnel, the two slinking back into the shadows.

'Well done,' he commended his soldier.

'Got it right, boss?' Javarek asked.

'You did,' Jodl put a comradely hand on Javarek's shoulder.

'Great piece of kit, boss. Real easy to assemble and real accurate.'

He'd practised with it before, but there was a distinct difference between firing at hay bales and the odd hare and a real moving unpredictable human in a shifting crowd. It had been very satisfying.

'Glad to hear it,' Jodl answered, watching Javarek swiftly removing the catches from the spring-loaded joints, folding the contraption flat and compact. 'Ready for the next part?'

Javarek nodding.

'Sure thing boss. But you know negotiating ain't my thing. Mightn't you rather send in Mergim?'

Jodl shook his head.

'Not entirely certain I can trust him,' Jodl said, 'not like I trust you. In fact I'd best be away, make sure he hasn't taken it upon himself to release that blasted girl and ruin everything.'

Javarek scowled.

'Always over-thinking, is Mergim,' he agreed. 'So hand it over. Let's get at it.'

Jodl taking out a letter, passing it to Javarek.

'Don't let them goad you,' he warned, 'and don't say more than what I've told you to say.'

Javarek lifted a lip in what passed for a smile.

'No worries, boss. Tight-lipped as a cockle I'll be.'

'Ever seen one? A cockle, I mean?' Jodl asked, remembering hauling handfuls of them out of the sand while Valter had been away at the oysters. Putting them in the hot ashes at the edge of a fire when they'd popped open up within seconds. No interrogation needed.

Javarek thought, hard work for him.

'Can't say as I have, `cept in a bit of sauce with some linguine.'

Jodl raising his eyebrows. A surprise Javarek had any knowledge of pasta.

'Time to go,' he concluded their conversation.

Javarek lumbering away, Jodl watching him for a few seconds, having a vision in his head of Javarek in some high-end café dithering over whether to have the penne or the pappardelle. It was too ridiculous. Jodl turned and went on his way, shuffling the last pieces of his plan in his head. So close now. It might still go wrong, though he couldn't see how. And if it did. Well, all part of the thrill. He had his exit strategies. Ever since he and Valter had crawled down from the Shkodër mountains he'd been compelled to juggle and mess with other people's lives like his own had been juggled and messed with. Getting better at it, honing his talents, chess making him more strategic, forcing him to think fifteen, twenty, God, the whole game ahead. Today the end of all that planning, all that juggling, all that control.

Years until he'd figured out his man was Jovan Kastrioti.

More years to figure where he'd ended up.

More years still until Mergim finally had a lead on his present whereabouts after he'd been cast out of the Senate, just as Jodl had been closing in.

Lines aligning.

Kunterbunt brought into play.

Jodl placing his bets.

And, given all his planning, it had to go in his favour.

Heraldo and Ludmilla got to the square.

All was celebration, food, and the settling of the bets made on the bull race.

A knot of men at the top of the church steps arguing loudly about what they should do.

'We should demand entrance. We need to know what's going on.'

'And what is going on?' Heraldo asked, taking two steps with every stride, breaking into their company.

'They've got Kastrioti inside, at the very time he should be out here,' one said, scratching at the back of his neck, having previously arranged with Kastrioti that if his bulls won he'd be more than happy to farm them out to stud.

'And someone injured, don't forget that,' another added.

'Only because he was standing next to Kastrioti,' the first man said.

Heraldo didn't care.

Heraldo started hammering on the doors.

'Let us in! It's the Pfiffmaklers! It's Heraldo and Ludmilla. Let us in!'

Ludmilla causing a mild stir as she leapt up the steps beside her cousin, for a pretty lass she was and no mistake, and what a pretty lass was doing in this mix no one was entirely sure.

Sound of bolts being drawn back, the door opening, Heraldo and Ludmilla flitting inside, along with a couple of Ururi men quick enough to take their chance, getting their boots in and then their bodies.

Doors closing immediately behind them.

Heraldo and Ludmilla charging down the nave towards Wenzel, who was laid out before the altar like a man already dead. Ilo Urosh standing adrift, wiping his forehead, wondering what would happen next. Which was Javarek barging up the church steps from the square, pushing people aside. Ilo Urosh hearing his bellowing from the other side of the wood.

'I've come from Georg Schwarz. I've come to speak with Ilo Urosh. Open the door!'

And no sooner had Ilo opened it when there was another commotion, a group of men lifting Valter up the steps, Ettori bleating at his side.

'Keep him still! We've to keep the tourniquet tight...'

In they came, and behind them another rush of Ururi men eager to find out what was going on, the church filling up as if a river had overrun its banks.

38

Just Before the Curtain Drops

Centre stage: two bleeding men, surrounded by clergy and family.

Left of stage: Jovan Kastrioti, Ilo Urosh and several Elders.

Coming onto stage: Javarek, striding with dramatic emphasis down the nave.

Their audience: the menfolk of Ururi who had, in local parlance, smelled fish in the air and come to see what was making it stink.

Ilo Urosh recognising it was up to him to orchestrate the finale, stepping forward, holding up his arms to quell what might very quickly turn into a riot.

'Gentlemen!' he therefore asked. 'Please, keep your distance. Sit down. Take a pew. There's a lot going on here you don't know about.'

'And you do?' someone queried, though did as asked and sat.

'I do,' Ilo assured. 'It's a little… complicated. I will explain all in due time. This is a situation that requires calm and good judgement.'

'I can concur with that.' Father Stephanus taking a place at Ilo's side, for which Ilo was immensely grateful. 'It seems our community has become the focus of an incident that entwines the history of your motherland with that of Serbia's independence.'

The audience murmuring, shifting in their seats, trying to figure out what that meant.

'I was approached this very morning,' Ilo began, 'by someone claiming his clan had been wiped out in the Shkodër mountains. Killed by soldiers in revenge for the assassination of Black George during the wars for independence…'

The audience getting agitated, remembering old songs, old allegiances, old fights. They may have been born here, which hadn't stopped many of them from travelling and joining the cause.

'Brutalised the women, left the children to freeze to death, so I heard,' one man called out.

'Poor little bastards,' another weighed in.

'Wait, wait!' Ilo tried to halt them. 'You have to listen, because there's a lot more at stake…'

Javarek didn't know what the Arbëreshë were babbling about, nor did he care. Italian their common language here. They might consider his Zadar-Venetian dialect coarse but they'd have to put up with that.

'I'm here on behalf of Georg Schwarz,' he announced loudly, shutting everyone up, Jodl's adopted moniker hitting home. 'He's given me a letter to give to the council.'

Complete silence as Javarek took centre stage, took out Jodl's letter and waved it at the priest and the man with the cane. Stephanus taking it, opening it, scanning its contents. Showing it to Ilo who went a little pale, the audience becoming restive, holding back not being the Arbëreshë way.

'What the hell does it say?'

'Come on, come on! Read it out!'

Several men standing up to get a better view.

Stephanus holding out his hands, waving the letter in the air and, at a nod from Ilo, got it read, despite several interruptions from the crowd.

Dear Pfiffmaklers. Sorry it has to end this way. It's been a pleasure dealing with you.

'Who are the Pfiffmaklers? And what the beggeration's this got to do with them?'

To the Town Council of Ururi, Stephanus persisted. *Apologies, and particularly to Ilo, evidently a kind man and true. But being kind is not in my remit.*

We were Albanians, crossing over to Serbia to re-join the wars of independence. Struck down in the mountains. Butchered. And I've spent my life tracking down the perpetrator, and I have achieved my goal. His name is Jovan Kastrioti...

'It can't be!'

'How can he know that?'

'Is this why he's taken sanctuary?'

Everyone looking at Kastrioti, who seemed ready to shift himself off stage. Was going nowhere, Ludmilla and Heraldo seeing to that.

'It's all lies!' Kastrioti shouted, the blow-in from a few months back not necessarily taken at his word. The audience waiting. Stephanus carrying on.

His name is Jovan Kastrioti, he repeated, *and Ilo Urosh has the proof.*

Small eruption in the crowd.

'Proof? What proof?'

'We need to see it!'

Ilo closed his eyes, a hand going to his pocket, fingering the small medallion Jodl had given him, taking it out, holding it aloft. Not that anyone could see it clearly.

'What the hell's bells is it?'

'Some kind of button?'

Ilo cleared his throat.

'It's a medallion,' he explained, 'found at the scene of the crime in the Shkodër mountains by one of the two survivors.'

'So there were survivors!'

'But how does that prove anything?'

'Because,' Ilo said, 'it bears the same coat of arms our Kastrioti here has embroidered on his waistcoat and emblazoned on his carts...'

'It proves nothing!' Kastrioti protested. 'He could have picked it up anywhere. He's setting me up! I'm just a bull runner from Albania.'

'No, no you're not.'

The voice so weak hardly anyone heard it. Stephanus holding up his hand, the audience taking a communal breath as the Father turned and looked behind him.

'Wenzel, are you sure? Are you absolutely sure?'

Wenzel sighed through his pain, feeling stronger, had been following all that had been going on since Javarek's loud voice broke through the cobwebs, got his mind focused. And Lord, there was a lot to focus on: where he was, what was happening, why it might have happened, why Jodl had caused it to play out the way it had. Beginning to understand. Jodl needing to be the fulcrum of the wheel of his world as it turned about him, spreading out his message through spoke and rim and every inch of earth his wheel touched as it rolled on through the years. Not enough that he'd tracked down his man. Needing his tale, once the end had been decided on, to be disseminated to as many people as would listen. As the menfolk of Ururi were listening now.

He pushed himself up, got himself to sitting. The pain in his shoulder excruciating, though knew now it would heal. Inflicted precisely so he could bear witness.

'Valter knew Kastrioti the moment he saw him,' Wenzel declared. 'And he knew him, Stephanus. He really did.'

Enough for Stephanus, who turned back to his congregation.

'We have another eye witness, another survivor from the Shkodër mountains, and one who is right here with us!'

Even Javarek surprised. Couldn't see through the men in front of him, but it had to be Valter; and yet Jodl had always said his brother remembered nothing of Kastrioti.

'Who is he?' shouts coming up from the crowd.

'He's got to speak!'

'He can't bloody speak!' Kastrioti yelled. 'He's right there, bleeding to death on the floor of your church!'

A surging forward then of men no longer willing to be contained by mere pews of wood.

'Christ, he looks badly,' said one, as he spotted the man Kastrioti had pointed to.

'He's gonna lose that leg if he ain't careful,' commented another.

'Let me through!' shouted the town doctor, one of the last to make it into the church on the tail-end of the crowd.

Ilo turning to Kastrioti.

'And how, sir, did you know that was him?'

Kastrioti baulking, backing away, right onto the point of Ludmilla's knife.

'Don't think you're going anywhere,' Heraldo said, standing close, standing right next to Kastrioti, bringing Kastrioti's hands up behind his back by his wrists.

'This is nonsense!' Kastrioti barked. 'This is absolute nonsense!'

'So how did you know him?' Ilo persisted. 'It's been twenty years, and yet you know the man from the boy? How is that possible?'

Because Kastrioti had seen those two boys in the snow.

Because Kastrioti had never seen that particular bright orange mop before nor since.

Because Kastrioti remembered it like it was yesterday.

How they'd stared at him, how the older boy with the jet black hair had fixed on him and followed him without a flinch as his men defiled and then dispatched the women, one of whom must have been his mother, and how that boy had watched as the horses skirled up the snow before departing. How Kastrioti had met the boy's eyes for a few seconds, how he'd taken the medallion from his pocket and spun it with his fingers before throwing it in the boy's direction because he knew he'd been challenged.

By a mere boy and his cowering carrot-headed brother who'd screwed up his eyes.

Their pale white faces fixed in his memory ever since.

A mistake to leave them to the snow and the cold, never mind his orders.

Should have realised that a boy who could look at him like that would find some way to survive and bring his snivelling brother out the other side with him

Should have butchered the both of them, and all the other children too, when he'd had the chance.

White mountains.

Cold snow.

Red blood.

But give the children a bit of mercy.

And like an idiot he'd done as he was told.

Nothing left to him now but bluster.

'Well of course I don't. How could anyone?'

'And yet,' Ilo stated, 'it appears you did. Read out the last of the letter, will you, Stephanus?'

Stephanus obliging.

I want him. I want Jovan Kastrioti. I will take him back to Serbia where he will answer for his crimes. I will swap him for the girl the Pfiffmaklers are so fond of.

This is my only demand.

'I claim sanctuary!' Kastrioti roared. 'I claim the protection of the church!'

'He can't do that!' Ludmilla cried out. 'What about Hulde?'

'Who's Hulde?' someone asked, as the doctor pushed roughly past to see what was what; a strutting man who thought himself better than the rest on account of his extensive education.

'Let me through, let me through,' he grumbled, viewing the man with the bright red hair, his pallid damp skin made all the paler by blood loss. The doctor realising at once what he would be called on to do, and could not do it here. 'We've to get this man to my surgery,' he began, immediately over-shouted by Ururi men who wanted details and would not be content until they had them.

Stephanus caught on the hop now sanctuary had officially been called.

Ilo dithering at his side for the same reason.

Wenzel trying to think, a process not aided by the shouted arguments going on about him. One thought sticking like wool to a carding comb.

Jodl wouldn't miss all this.

Jodl had to be nearby.

And surely that meant Hulde was nearby too.

'Get me to the square,' Grandmother commanded once she'd got herself aloft. No simple task, the square filled up by now with bulls, wagon floats, trestle tables, bustling women, shouting children, though strangely divested of men. You or I might not have noticed it, but Grandmother was no fool. You or I, even if we'd noticed, might have concluded that all was lost, no way through except on foot and nothing to be done when we got there. But neither you nor I are Pfiffmaklers, nor brought up in the Pfiffmakler way, and the Pfiffmakler way was never to give up, despite the odds. Grandmother Pfiffmakler thinking through hoops. Grandmother Pfiffmakler seeing the last few men atop the steps of the church, clustered about its doors like pheasants at a feeding station. Grandmother Pfiffmakler realising the end was nigh, that whatever Jodl's plan was it was playing itself out right now inside those doors. And if she had been Jodl she'd have been looking at the long game, trapping all the relevant players into one place whose entries and exits were easily observable. Like a church that rose up above the crowds by reason of its steps. A church hard to get to because the biggest festival of the year was in full swing. And if she'd been Jodl she'd need to be here to witness the final denouement of the plan two decades in the making.

All thought through.

All deviations and scenarios accounted for.

Except possibly for Grandmother Pfiffmakler.

Inside the church: absolute pandemonium. Folk shouting out their views about sanctuary, others demanding Kastrioti be immediately handed over to answer for his crimes, yet more yelling that it was all long done, that whatever had been carried out for the independence of Serbia had also been done for the Mother Country, never mind their own independence had never come about.

'What ever happened to forgive and forget?'

'You can forget it if you like, but I can't. My uncle was one of those murdered by Kastrioti.'

'Only if it's him. And what proof is a button?'

'It's not a button, it's a medallion, you idiot. And what? Do you think he gives them out by the boat load?'

'We can't give into this!'

'It's blatant blackmail!'

'He's claimed sanctuary, and we can't discount that.'

'And yet he knows the survivor, the other brother. We all saw that.'

'And what's the what about this girl? Are we to let her to be murdered like all her folk?'

'And who were they?'

'Albanians from the mountains, that's what Stephanus said.'

'And the man who's holding her killed all her people, so we've got to bargain.'

'But sanctuary! That's got to be worth something. And Kastrioti won the bull race. And we could do with good bulls.'

'We can keep the bulls if Kastrioti's dragged away to Serbia, so where's the loss?'

Javarek losing patience, Javarek taking the course Jodl had told him to, Javarek taking a few steps forward, grabbing Ilo Urosh about the throat in the crook of his arm, dragging Ilo off his heels, Ilo's cane clattering to the flagstones.

'I'll snap his bloody neck if you don't all quieten,' he growled, pulling Ilo with him, separating him from the rest. 'Bargain's simple. Kastrioti for the girl. No arguments, no deviation. And if I ain't the first person out of this church with Kastrioti then the first person out there is going to get a crossbow through the heart. And if I ain't out there within ten minutes you'll find the girl's dead body in a sack at the town's gates. And it won't be a pretty body, I can tell you that.'

Jodl was feeling fine. Jodl was feeling dandy. Jodl had the crossbow folded inside his jacket, making his way on foot through the square, weaving through the loud participants, snatching up a couple of warm rolls fresh from the town's ovens because he was absolutely ravenous. Jodl going up the steps outside the church and asking the men there what was going on.

'Whole bloody town's gone mad,' said one.

'Right stramash going on inside,' informed another, who had his ear to the door. 'Sounds like they're at each other's throats.'

'They've a couple of wounded in there and Kastrioti, and all the council,' said the first.

'And some outsiders called the Piffel something or other.'

'Is that so?' Jodl asked. 'And what's going to happen to the celebrations? That's all I came for.'

'You and the rest, brother,' said another man. 'Be a right damn shame if someone puts a spoke in it...'

'Shssh!' hissed the man with his ear to the door. 'Something's happening. It's gone all quiet...'

His fellows leaning forward in expectation.

Jodl leaving them to it.

Jodl knowing precisely what was going on.

Time he was gone.

Hush in the church, though no one was at prayer, save possibly Ilo Urosh.

'Make your decision,' Javarek barked, 'and make it quick else this man here'll be the first to die and he won't be the last.'

The townsfolk could have rushed the stage, except by that time Ilo Urosh would be dead. Not a one of them doubted it. They may have deemed him a fussy old man but he'd always been good and true, as Jodl had divined.

'We've to agree to the bargain,' Stephanus said quietly, looking towards the Elders who'd drawn themselves together in a huddle. 'We agree to it,' Stephanus went on. 'We get the girl, and then we'll decide what's to be done.'

We'll track that bastard Jodl down and string him up, Stephanus was thinking, as were a great many of the men of Ururi, not that they knew Jodl's name.

The Elders shuffling, swapping glances then nodded one by one.

'Thank you,' Wenzel murmured

'Don't let it take all day,' the doctor snarked. 'Got a life to save here.'

As if he was the only one with that gift to give, as if the same wasn't being enacted all about him.

Ururi men backing down, returning to the body of the church, clearing a gangway to the doors.

Ettori loosening the rope from about his waist, allowing his habit to hang free, handing it to Ludmilla and Heraldo who got their prisoner tied by the wrists and led him on.

'Not that way,' Javarek commanded, pulling Ilo with him. 'We're going out the back, and don't you lot think on storming the front and catching us 'cos I'm taking this man with me.'

'My cane,' Ilo croaked, Javarek's arm hard about his neck.

Stephanus picking it up, about to take it to Ilo. Javarek stalling him.

'I don't think so, my fine Father. Not about to be coshed about the head with the likes of that. Give it to the girl.'

Never mind the girl already had a knife, secreted now Kastrioti was secured.

Stephanus obliging.

Ludmilla accepting.

'Fifteen minutes before a one of you follows,' Javarek warned, 'then send one of your lot to the town gates.'

Wenzel getting his pocket watch out with difficulty, with shaking hands.

'It will be so,' Stephanus said for him, watching the small tableau making their way through the transept chapel, Javarek walking backwards, knowing the way and where was the door choir and clergy used at its farthest end. Ilo feeling the steady thump of Javarek's heart at his back, as if he did this every day. No deviation to its beat, no speeding up to indicate panic or worry. Unlike Ilo's, which was pattering inside his chest like a shot bird. Ludmilla and Heraldo leading Kastrioti on, Heraldo dipping his chin at his father as he passed him by.

'Go careful, son,' Wenzel said. 'Get Hulde. That's all you need to do.'

Meaning: *No heroics. These are dangerous men. And keep your cousin in check while you're at it.*

Heraldo nodding briefly, understanding.

Heraldo shaking inside like a leaf in a storm.

Jodl went around back of the church and set himself up, hiding in a doorway, crossbow at the ready. Only fly in the ointment of his plan being a drunk lurching down the lane towards him.

'Oh God,' the man was mumbling. 'Why don't I ever learn?'

Bracing his hands against the wall as he retched and heaved, staggered on a bit way before fumbling at his trousers, letting go a stream of urine. Retched again, spat a couple of times, passing right by Jodl without seeing him. Jodl hearing his wretched mumblings as he went.

'Every year. Every year. Can't never do this again.'

Slumping briefly against the wall to Jodl's right before getting back to his feet and staggering on.

The door at the back of the church slamming open and out came Javarek, right on cue, his arm about Ilo's neck and, on their heels, Heraldo pulling Kastrioti by his rope, Ludmilla at Kastrioti's back.

'Oh what a pretty sight,' Jodl murmured, though didn't let his guard down, nor his crossbow, nor did he move from his spot. Javarek had this covered. Javarek doing exactly as he was supposed to do. Javarek motioning his small party down the lane and into a skinny vennel hung side to side up top with washing. Javarek motioning Ludmilla, Heraldo and their captive on, taking up the rear.

Jodl careful, Jodl checking the street to left and right and the door to the church. The door now closed. No sound coming from within. Everyone quiet inside. Everyone waiting out their minutes.

He could imagine them there, the Ururi men sweating in their oxters to be so emasculated on the day of their Great Race. The Elders bleating. Wenzel bleeding and Valter too. A plus he'd not anticipated, though wasn't saddened by. Valter had turned against him and Valter had been warned. If someone else hadn't already done it then Jodl would have sought Valter out somewhere down the line and done it himself. As Valter must have known.

If you aren't with me then you're agin.

No truer words from Matthew, nor from the Christ he was quoting.

No mercy there.

No city or house divided against itself will stand.

If only the Albanians and Serbs had understood that simple premise at the start of their Wars of Independence.

If only the two leaders—Black George and Milos Obrenovich—had been able to find common ground two decades back then none of this would have been necessary.

No massacres tit for tat; no murders in the mountains, nor murders by the sea, no girls in sacks, no threats nor plans.

But where would have been the fun in that?

Jodl, hiding in his doorway, could not regret the way all had gone.

It had been his lifeblood, throbbing through his veins for years.

It was what kept him alive.

If wars didn't already happen, Andreas had once thought, *then they'd have had to be invented for the likes of Jodl.*

Andreas right.

Jodl thriving on the injustice of his early beginnings that had made him what he was, and Jodl glad for it.

Kastrioti right about the boy watching in the snow, the boy watching the women defiled and butchered without batting an eyelid.

Kastrioti giving that boy the excuse to be the way he'd always been.

But that was then, and this was now.

Javarek had done his turn.

Time for Jodl to bring all to its end.

The wren become the eagle, about to bring home his prize.

Jodl turning into the vennel after Javarek, could see Javarek twenty yards up shifting to the left as planned, heading to the town gates where Mergim would be waiting with the girl. And Mergim would be waiting. Mergim would have been wavering and havering for the last while—had been wavering and havering ever since they'd got to Italy—but Jodl knew folk and how they moved and went, how they thought and acted. Had Mergim pegged the first time he'd met him. How Mergim would think on ideals but never act on them unless directed, would always save his own skin when push came to shove, would always take the easy path.

The folk in the church were biding their time, as given by Wenzel's pocket watch that was now in Stephanus' hands.

'Three minutes…four…' he intoned.

The ticking of the watch was torture.

'Five…six…'

'Hey mister, mister…gi's us a hand.'

Jodl frowned, turning to see the drunkard limping up the lane behind him.

'Think I went an' busted me ankle when I went down earlier. Jeez! Feel like I'm dragging a millstone here.'

Jodl hissed between his teeth, would've sent a bolt straight through the man's heart except he couldn't risk being seen, the vennel otherwise deserted but someone was about because he could hear singing.

'Only got a coupla doorways to go,' the man said, falling heavily against the nearest wall.

Well bloody well crawl there, Jodl was thinking.

'Only take a minute of your day,' the man pleaded. Jodl grimacing, collapsing the crossbow with swift fingers, tucking it inside his jacket.

He strode towards the man, roughly shoved his hands beneath the man's armpits and hauled him up.

'Which one?' he demanded, baulking at the stink of piss and alcohol.

'The one below that yellow sheet...me mam's gonna kill...aargh!' he cried out in pain as Jodl dragged him without care or compassion the two yards to his mother's doorstep, about to dump him like the garbage he was when came a wild clattering of hooves reverberating up the alley and the drunkard pitched and swung and suddenly brought himself up against Jodl with such force Jodl hadn't time to react, found himself shoved against the wall, the man pinning him there with his body.

'Escaped bull!' the drunkard yelled, the words reverberating in Jodl's ears as he fought to press himself further into the wall, stretched out his arms, tried to make himself as skinny as he could be. Nothing more dangerous than an escaped bull, as he well knew. Held up his head, seeing the yellow sheet fluttering above him, the blue sky beyond.

This scenario not in any of his wildest plans.

An escaped bull, for God's sake!

How on earth was he supposed to have thought of that?

Getting ready to chuck the piss-head who was shielding him beneath the wild hooves, if it would save him.

Seven minutes...eight...

Everyone in the church trying to rein themselves in.

It wasn't easy.

It wasn't fair.

Hated being held hostage.

But a girl's life depended on it.

Not exactly one of their own, but near enough.

Nine minutes…

And then the oddest sound coming into their self-imposed silence.

The back door of the transept not entirely closed, just ajar, pulled open again by the slightest of breezes, the muted celebrations in the square that were apparently going on whether the men of Ururi were there or not.

'Trust the bloody women,' one tutted, immediately quietened by another.

'Wait. Listen. That's not ordinary.'

They cocked their heads, heard the loud clattering of hooves in an enclosed space, the battering of those hooves on cobbles bouncing from wall to wall.

And all bar Stephanus and the Pfiffmaklers had heard it before. Not often, but enough to know what it was.

'Escaped bull!' several shouted at once.

'And no wonder, because we're in here and not out there taking check of them!'

No stopping the men of Ururi.

Every one of them piling for the main door, lifting the bolts, pushing past the few men who'd been blocked out, spilling onto the steps, shouting at the tops of their voices.

'Escaped bull! Get yourselves under! Take cover!'

Lots of screaming.

Trestle tables overturned and made into barricades.

Food and drink flying everywhere.

People terrified because they knew what this meant.

A panicked bull on the run could kill just about anyone in its path. No one knowing which bull it was or where its path would lead, and a panicked bull, if it didn't find the gates, could be back any moment.

And in the alley, Jodl trying to get his head up and out to see exactly what the danger was, take evasive action, but the drunk man was hard against him, keeping him tight against the wall, and the thundering of hooves was getting closer and closer, Jodl's heart hammering hard, until the beast was upon them.

'All right, Grandmother?' he heard the drunkard yell, as the dark form swept by with a whisper to spare.

'All well, my lad! See you at the gates,' came the reply. Jodl suddenly seeing the ruse, the bull no bull at all but a large black horse. Jodl pushing, punching and hollering, trying to get the crossbow out, but by God that drunkard was no drunkard at all and was quick and mighty strong, had Jodl's arms up behind his back in a blink as the horse galloped off and a great gang of Ururi men came crowding around the corner, whips and sticks in hand, ready to head the bull off towards the town gate, flying past the two men scuffling in a doorway, men no one recognised and gave no mind to.

Mergim was at the gate, shuffling his feet. He'd carried his captive with him and had, as directed, secreted her a short way off in a thicket of willows growing up by a bubbling spring, wiping his eyes as he did so because it all seemed so wrong.

'If you're up in the mountains and short on water,' his father had told him, 'always look out for alders or willows. Especially willows. They're bound to water like babes to milk. Their seeds needs a lot of moisture to grow, though oddly not the older trees. But those older trees can shed a few branches in a storm and those branches will root again hundreds of yards, hundreds of miles, downstream.'

Mergim one of them. A branch blown off during the storm of the wars for independence and borne downstream to Zadar where he'd eventually met Jodl, who'd provided the soil into which he could root himself, be part of a new patriotism, bring a war criminal back to Serbia with himself, Javarek and Jodl the delivering heroes. Except they weren't heroes. They were criminals, murderers, and no getting around it.

Still time to let the girl go, he was thinking, as he scuffed his boots in the dust.

Still time to...

And then there was no time, because out of a small lane came Javarek lumbering towards him with his arm crooked about an old man's neck, dragging the old man so his heels left a trail in the dust, and close behind a boy dragging another who had to be Kastrioti, followed by a girl.

'Boss'll be here in minutes!' Javarek shouted out to Mergim. 'Get ready to...' Javarek's words stuttering to a stop as a huge black horse came swerving out of the lane behind them, closing the last hundred yards between them with unnerving speed, its rider bent forward, skirt-clad legs clutched to its flanks, twig-thin arms clutched about its unbridled neck.

'Now, Ludmilla, now! If you're going to do anything then do it now!'

Ludmilla needing no explication, Ludmilla answering the call, Ludmilla giving Javarek a god almighty thwack to the head with Ilo's cane, closing in, not wanting to use her knife, not wanting to repeat what she'd done earlier to Valter. Heraldo quick on her heels, letting go the rope that bound him to Kastrioti and piling himself on top of the collapsed Javarek, Javarek roaring, Javarek fighting, Ludmilla's blow to his head having him confused, and moments later came the Ururi men yelling and waving their sticks, wrong-footed by the scene they were running headlong into.

'Get him! Keep him!' Heraldo shouted and they obeyed, several of them falling on Javarek's back, and no way was Javarek getting up again without their say so. Javarek getting punched and beaten with their sticks for the indignities he'd thrust upon them in the church. Several more helping Ilo to his feet, dusting him off, Ilo cupping his hands about his bruised throat, gasping for air. Thankful not to have had his head torn from his neck by the force with which Javarek had been dragging him.

Kastrioti running, Kastrioti trying for escape despite his hands being tied, despite the rope that was trailing from them, Kastrioti thinking he might just make it, heading for a copse of tangled willows, until Mergim's boot came down upon the rope and Kastrioti was jerked from his feet.

'I don't think so,' Mergim said, grabbing up the rope, getting down on one knee to study the face of the man who'd set all this in motion: long cheeks, long nose, both scribbled with thin red veins; dark brows, eyes and beard; lips chalky, sullen, bereft of victory.

'We're done for, you and I,' Mergim said quietly. 'It's at its end.'

'Where's Hulde?' Ludmilla cried out, and Mergim nodded her in the direction of the trees, thinking how odd it was that her skirts were the same colour as crack willow bark in the autumn, and how fitting.

Fear. Dark. Aloneness.

Weight of silence whumping in Hulde's ears like swans flying low.

Panic in Hulde's chest as she hears running feet.

Sacking about her face limp with the moisture of her quick breathing.

Sacking about her legs warm and damp with urine.

Pulling herself inward.

Keeping herself still.

Hulde's eyes wide and wet.

For this was the moment.

This the now, and this the end.

Ludmilla beating back the branches with her hands, boots wet with the bubbling of the spring; Ludmilla calling out Hulde's name as she scanned about the glade; Ludmilla spying movement, a slight shift in a child-sized sack; Ludmilla down on her knees, pulling at the ropes that kept its mouth in silence.

'Come on, my love,' Ludmilla whispered, peeling off the sack from feet to head, lifting Hulde out.

Same words Ludmilla had spoken over the water.

Hulde safe again.

Hulde wrapping her arms about Ludmilla's neck, Ludmilla lifting the small body out and kissing the top of Hulde's head. Hulde never really believing Ludmilla would eat her favourite pet.

39

Wrapping It Up

Peace and calm returned to Ururi, if by peace and calm you meant a fully-fledged carnival, with no escaped bulls running loose and no mad incomers upsetting the norm. Trestle tables returned to standing, as much food as possible rescued, no one minding a little dust and grit. Wine and gossip free-flowing as a mountain stream, and by God there was a lot to gossip about.

Most exciting thing that had ever happened in Ururi, bull races included.

Folk taking periodic visits to the oak tree jail to gander at the prisoners. Javarek still alive after his pummelling, but only just. Not that the doctor was going to waste his time on scum like that. He had an important operation to perform and had garnered several midwife-nurses to aid him in slicing open Valter's thigh, sew the artery back together if possible. Off with the leg if it was not. First scenario proving optimal, to the doctor's chagrin who'd been looking forward to trying out his new bone saw.

Mergim, entirely against his expectations, called to give first account of the affair to the Council of Elders, alongside Stephanus and Wenzel Pfiffmakler. Which took a few hours. Next came Jodl, proud of all he'd done, meticulous in every detail, leaving out not a jot.

Songs will be sung, he knew, composing them in his head.

Ilo reading out the Elders' judgement from the top of the church steps, fires flickering in the cressets set up about the square, folk lazing in the warmth of the evening, everyone eager to hear what had been decided, bar those men who, unlike Jodl's drunkard, had already passed out and were snoring gently.

'Javarek and Jodl will hang,' Ilo announced flatly, after a swift summing up of the plot for those who weren't already cognisant, to general murmurs of approval. 'They will be given one week in gaol to set out any measures they need to put their affairs in order.'

Time for Javarek to mend enough to stand for the gibbet.

Time for Jodl to write his songs.

'Mergim, who stopped the escape of Kastrioti and has fully confessed to his part in all this, will be taken back with Kastrioti to Serbia along with several of our men to ensure they reach their goal. They will carry with them Jodl's sworn deposition. Valter, Jodl's brother, is cleared of all wrongdoing in this matter, and has agreed to travel with them as the only surviving witness to Kastrioti's crimes.'

'What about Kastrioti's bulls?' someone shouted, Ilo holding up his arms as if welcoming the question.

'All Jovan Kastrioti's possessions are forfeit. They are now the communal assets of Ururi.'

'Hoorah!' went up the cry.

'Sure they're both accounted for?' put in some wit. 'Not running amok up and down the streets?'

Boisterous laughter then, though some a little shamed they'd been caught out so easily.

'And the girl?'

Ah indeed. What of Hulde?

You or I might have left her with her own, now the drama was concluded.

But you and I are not Pfiffmaklers. You or I would probably never have got involved in the first place. You or I would most likely have hightailed it out of that village on the border of Montenegro and Albania and dumped her the first chance we'd got, if we'd bothered to find her at all.

But that was not the Pfiffmakler way.

They followed their own counsel, made their own decisions, took their leave once Ururi was done with them, piled themselves into Grandmother's carriage, Pietro, her driver, having swapped out the horse she'd galloped on through the town and replaced with another.

He didn't think Mellini would mind, given the circumstances.

In the glade by the river the rest of the Pfiffmaklers were calm, if anxious. Nothing they could do but wait. Lupercal and Jericho joining their uncle in the fishing, bored within the hour when they'd not got a bite and went into the woods to see if they couldn't get themselves another goat.

'You're no Livia Benedetta!' Peppe called sarcastically at their backs, though was glad to be left alone. Their incessant chattering enough to scare off every fish for half a mile.

Rosa and Yssel occupying themselves with all their usual tasks. Washing clothes, wringing them out by hand, hanging them on lines to dry; darning socks, smocks and shirts; touching up a couple of puppet heads and backdrops with paint, leaving them to dry in the sun; preparing bread dough, deciding to use the last of the lump of yeast they'd purchased in Ravenna to make several different kinds of leavened bread the family didn't often have the pleasure of.

Lupercal and Jericho returning several hours later, clothes muddy and ripped, no goat snared within their ropes.

No one knowing whether they should be preparing for a feast or a funeral. No one knowing if all, or only some or, God forbid, none were coming back, though that bleakest thought was at the back of all their minds.

Andreas the most mindful.

Setting himself as lookout in the days following the departure of Valter and the other Pfiffmaklers. Stumping up and down the track, holding his hand over his eyes against the sun to see if anyone was coming. And now the evening was upon them he'd settled upon a rock a little further up from the glade towards the waterfall. Didn't want to speak to anyone. Could hardly bear the thoughts going on in his head. Looked down upon the clear blue waters of the Adriatic, at the great walled town of Termoli, the tracks leading away from it to east and west. Finding it calming to watch the sea, the various boats and ships plying up and down its waters. A large rocky outcrop white with cormorant excreta, the black huddle of the birds up top opening their wings like dark angels.

And then he leaned forward, saw a pale horse coupled with a black pulling a carriage up the track towards them.

Heart thumping in panic, until he made out several people's heads jutting from the windows, someone flinging open a door and two bodies jumping out, running on before the carriage and then he was levering himself up on his cane, calling out to the Pfiffmaklers fifty yards below.

'They're coming! They're coming! I see them! They're coming!'

The Pfiffmaklers hearing his faint calls, craning their necks. Andreas still calling out as Ludmilla and Heraldo ran into view, the carriage lumbering and labouring up the hill behind them.

So be still, my friends.

Here are our returning heroes, gathering about the fire in the falling night.

No funeral but a feast, for which all are glad.

The story told in every detail, and several times, for here was a play in the making and one of their own.

'Grandmother was magnificent!' Ludmilla said for them all, hugging Hulde to her side.

'As was Pietro,' Grandmother put in, nodding at her driver. 'Couldn't have done any of it without him.'

Pietro beaming.

'My absolute pleasure. First time on the stage, as it were, and it was the most exciting thing I've ever done!'

'Isn't it just!' Livia put in, catching his eye, Pietro smiling all the more because he found the Janus Woman quite as fascinating as he'd found Grandmother Pfiffmakler. This adventure expanding his world tenfold.

'Think I might quit the coach driving once I get your lady to the Redemptorists,' Pietro added. 'Become an actor. What do you think of that?'

Grandmother snorting, but tapped his shoulder in encouragement.

'Very good as a drunkard, but you'll need to expand your repertoire. Maybe get Livia here to give you a few lessons on how to slaughter innocents. I hear she was very good at it.'

Pietro frowned, though not when he saw Livia smile.

'My first time too,' Livia said, immediately beguiling him. Grandmother rolling her eyes, never one for young love. Or slightly older love, which was what this would be if these two ever got together.

The carriage driver and the Janus Woman.

Not even Jodl could have predicted that.

'And are you still going, Grandmother?' Wenzel asked, sucking at his pipe, his shoulder more comfortable since Rosa had ripped away the doctor's bandages and performed her own small miracle of healing. 'Hasn't all this fired you up again for the road?'

Grandmother cackled.

'Christ, son! If you could feel my arthritis and rheumatism you wouldn't even be asking the question. Feels like I've been shook up and set back down all wrong. No. Quiet life's for me, and no mistaking. But gotta say, one last wild ride on a horse was entirely welcome. Just like the old days. The real old days.'

'Hulde wants to say something,' Ludmilla put in, Hulde shy at her side, leaning against Ludmilla, Ludmilla nodding at Ettori who leaned in close, cupped his ear.

'She says to thank you,' he said simply. 'Asks if Grandmother could sing the hymn they sang together on the boat.'

Everyone looking at Grandmother, Grandmother's throat closing up.

Grandmother dottling out her pipe.

Grandmother needing some time.

Grandmother knowing that when she was inducted into the Redemptorists, which would be soon, this was the song she would choose to mark her calling.

Grandmother starting a little croakily, everyone soon joining in. Ettori adding the mournful descant so typical of the Ambrosian Rite.

Jesus Saviour, on thy breast I would lay me down to rest.
Forgive my wayward heart, teach me to be my best.

And when the day of my life is past and the twilight comes at last,
When my eyes finally close and I take my last repose,
May your angels vigil keep
As I lay me down for welcome sleep.

And safe we are this night, we who are reading this. Maybe huddled in our beds or chairs on a dark winter's night, our eiderdowns and blankets wrapped about our shoulders to keep out draughts; or perhaps sitting in the sun, maybe shaded by a fine black walnut tree from whose green nuts the Albanians make the Gliko paste we have yet to taste. Maybe you can hear the sea breaking over seaweed-shrouded rocks as I can, or lapping its way up white coral sands.

Either way, we are safe.

Safe as Hulde, the start of whose story we have hereby partaken in.

Safe enough and long enough, we hope, to one day learn its end.

Historical notes

A great many of the details in this novel are facts, including everything about Alphonsus Liguori—barring that he was not laid to rest in Ravenna after his canonisation in 1839. He gained his degree in law at the age of 16, practised for eight years before disillusionment at worldly greed and vanity led him to the church, first as a travelling preacher around Naples. Ordained in1726, founding the first house of Redemptorists in 1731. His teachings influential right up to the late nineteenth century, rehabilitating Probabilism after a short period of the church adhering to the stricter regime of Probabiliorism, and latterly expounding his own theory of canon law, namely Equiprobabilism, which took a midway course between the two. He died in 1787, aged 91, and was beautified a remarkably short time afterwards in 1816, canonised in 1839 when the crowds were so great one Franciscan really was crushed to death. The traditional Rite of Canonisation is as described, including the seven caged singing birds.

The lives of Archbishop Mellini and Pope Gregory are likewise true to history (see below.)

The intertwining histories of Serbia, Croatia and Albania and their various fights for independence are easily as complicated as presented, if not more so (see below) including the feud between Black George and Milos Obrenovich and the latter's assassination of the former. It is hard, in the context of a novel, to give such complexity the simplicity it needs to be understood, so I hope any mistakes will be forgiven.

Likewise for the background of the Albanian conclaves in Italy, who still exist.

As do their bull races.

As for the Black Madonna of Montenegro: I could have sworn I'd dragged this up from some ancient memory, but can't find any supporting evidence. If anyone knows anything to the contrary I'd be glad to know of it.

The mention of the Sea Organ at Zadar is a massive anachronism: constructed in 2005, designed by local architect Nikola Bašić, but too good a feature to miss out.

We've included a version of *The Banks of the Nile,* as sung and interpreted by the hugely talented Sandy Denny who died well before her time.

The Adventures and Discoveries of a Geologist in the Mountains of Albania and Montenegro by Johann von Hahn: this is a fiction, though there is a real Johann Georg von Hahn who later wrote down the tale of the Kastrioti family following what he'd been told by a priest in the district of the Shkodër mountains.

Gliko paste: heard about it, never tasted it yet.

Historical Characters

Cardinal Mellini: Chiarissimo Falconieri Mellini, Archbishop of Ravenna.

Pope Gregory XVI: formally known as Bartolomeo Alberto Cappellari.

Giorgio Castriota, also known as Iskender bey, or Skanderberg. Albanian hero who fought against Ottoman incursion for a quarter of a century. In the 1400s: forges the first connections between Albania to Italy, allying himself with the Napolese Court. Fights for the Pope, successfully joining with the Venetians to see off the Ottomans, and is tipped to lead a Crusade from Albania and Italy. Singlehandedly established the area around Abruzzo and Termoli in Italy as a safe haven for Orthodox Albanian Christians (the Arbëreshë) fleeing persecution, who settled there immediately after his death in 1468, and continued to do so in the following centuries.

Histories of the areas involved

The series of Pfiffmakler books, beginning with *Out of Albania,* are underpinned by the intertwining back-stories of Albania, Serbia and Croatia. In order not to overburden the text, here are their summaries which can be referred to, or ignored.

Albania

15th century	Part of the Ottoman Empire.
1744–1822	Under the military dictatorship of Ottoman Ali Pasha, which caused bitterness and a rise in nationalism.
1831	Nationalist rebellion crushed, Turkish rule continues despite continued unrest.
1804–1817	Many Albanians join the fight for Serbian independence, believing their own independence would come in its wake.
1877–78	A National League created during the Russo-Turkish Wars, Albania not gaining true independence until 1912.

Serbia

12th century	Serbia established as an independent state.
1300	Serbia a vassal state of the Ottomans.
1331–55	Serbia under the reign of Stephan Dushan, which saw the annexation of Macedonia, Albania and parts of Greece under rule of a codified law.
1371	Disastrous defeats by the Ottomans brings this union to an end.
1389	The Battle of Kosovo (Serbs v Turks) St Vitus' Day, June 28th. The single defining moment of Serbian history. Seen as a heroic defeat from which later rebellions constantly drew inspiration.
1389–1804	Serbia held in a stranglehold by the Ottomans.
1804–1812	**Black George (Kara George)** leads an insurrection, main support base being the Eastern Orthodox population. Attaining the briefest of independence status, soon crushed.
1813	Black George goes into exile.
1815–1817	**Milos Obrenovich** leads his own insurrection.
1817	Black George returns to join the fight, threatening to split the rebels down the middle because of their differing bases of support.

1817	Black George assassinated, on the order of Milos Obrenovich.
	Serbia gains some autonomy under suzerainty of the Ottoman Sultan. Milos Obrenovich recognised by the Sultan as Prince of Serbia.
1829	This confirmed by the Treaty of Adrianople.
1830	August 28th The Turks grant Serbia official autonomy. Hereditary status granted to Milos Obrenovich as Prince of Serbia.
1833	More of Eastern Serbia is ceded to Milos Obrenovich by the Turks.
1835	Milos Obrenovich is accused of being too autocratic, forced to present the First Constitution of Serbia.
1838	Milos Obrenovich forced to repeal his constitution, both Russians and Turks deeming it too liberal. The Turkish Sultan putting another in place in December.
1839	January: in accordance with this second constitution, Milos Obrenovich appoints a council of seventeen senators who immediately demand his abdication.
1839	June 13th Milos is forced by the Senate to abdicate. Retires to his estates in Walachia, his son Milan taking over.
	Milan dies four weeks later, a sufferer for many years from tuberculosis. Princedom passing to Milos's younger son Michael/Mihailo, only seventeen years old. Born in Kragujevac.
1339–1842	Constant political bickering between Michael and the Karageorgevich faction, who now called themselves *The Defenders of the Constitution*.
1842	Michael forced to flee. Alexander Karageorgevich elected by the Skupshtina in his place.
1872	Karageorgevichs defeated. Prince Milan Obrenovich, descendant of the first, takes the rule.
1877	Serbs ally themselves with the Pan-Slav movement.
1878	Congress of Berlin: Serbia gains sovereign nationhood under Prince Milan Obrenovich.

1882	Prince Milan Obrenovich (the fourth descendant of the original) is declared king.
1882–1908	Constant battle of power bases shifting from the Milan Obrenovich camp to that of the Karageorgevichs.
1914	Austrian archduke Francis Ferdinand assassinated by a supposed Serbian nationalist, thereby precipitating World War I. Arguments ongoing about Serbian involvement in that assassination ever since.

Croatia and Slovenia

First Croatian state formed after the collapse of the Carolingian Empire.

Struggles between Hungary, Venice and the Byzantine Empire result in rule by the Hungarian crown.

1242	Overrun by the Tatars, kept at bay by King Bela IV patrolling the Adriatic strongholds. Under Hungarian control until the Venetians begin to erode that control. Remains under Venetian rule for the next 350 years.
1300	Ottomans make Serbia a vassal state.
1301	House of Anjou takes control.
1381	Civil war for many years.
1493	Turks smash the Hungaro-Croatian forces at Krbavsko Polje, just south of Plitvice.
1526	Battle of Mohacs: most of Croatia brought under the control of the Ottomans, the remainder to the Habsburgs.
1540s	Turks now in control of the whole of Slavonia almost to Zagreb, which Croatia still hangs onto in a thin strip; Venetians holding Istria and the rest. Huge numbers of Christian refugees flood into both Serbia and Croatia, which are still nominally Christian. These are the Vlachs, a mixture of Catholic and Orthodox Christians. Hungarians giving them lands along Croatia's borders in return for military service: this is known as the Military Frontier (Vojna Krajina) ruled directly from both Graz and Vienna, remaining

	in existence until the mid-nineteenth century, by which time Ottoman influence had long receded.
1809–1813	Croatia becomes part of Napoleon's Illyrian province, provoking a rise in nationalism.
1848	Revolution reasserts Croatian Independence.
1848	March 23rd Ban Josip Jelačić becomes the first leader of the semi-autonomous Croatian state.
1848	September: Jelačić declares war on Hungary, as the Habsburgs had hoped; Hungarians push them back to Vienna; Jelačić teams up with Prince Windischgrätz—whose wife had been shot dead by revolutionaries in Prague. They bombard Vienna, executing all the radical leaders. Which leads to the abdication of the Emperor Ferdinand who'd appointed Jelačić in the first place. Hungarian leaders defect to the Turks once the Russians get involved.
1849	August 9th Battle of Temesvar crushes the Hungarian rebellion once and for all. Nine generals are hung, a further four shot. Jelačić's power-base eroded as the Viennese court re-establishes itself. Croatia proclaimed an Austrian crownland.
1868	Creation of Austro-Hungarian Empire; Croatia becomes the autonomous Hungarian crownland of Croatia-Slovenia (apart from the coastline of Dalmatia which remains an Austrian province).
	Only in 1918 did Croatia once again become an independent state.

A few Albanian words:

Bosh: meaning empty

Said: Meaning *Then*.

Acknowledgements

My huge thanks must go to everyone at Sparsile Books who took me on when not many others would. They have been an inspiration and a home. Especial hand-claps go to Lesley Affrossman for the wonderful cover—someone who actual gets me!—and to Stephen Cashmore for reading so assiduously through the proofs.

And to Sheelagh, one of my most faithful readers, I need to tell you this.
I know Sean, your brother, could behave like a toddler in a tantrum at times, but at heart he was a kind and very generous man and there are a great many people in this village, in Balintore, who are going to miss him.
And one of them will be me.